W9-BEZ-539

CHANGE
IN PLAN

DANA PETERS

Happy reading!
Dana Peters

Copyright © 2018 Dana Peters
All rights reserved
First Edition

PAGE PUBLISHING, INC.
New York, NY

First originally published by Page Publishing, Inc. 2018

ISBN 978-1-64138-897-9 (Paperback)
ISBN 978-1-64138-898-6 (Digital)

Printed in the United States of America

For Jackie.

Sadly, you left us before the end of the chapter.

Until we meet again, keep the coffee fresh and hot.

CHAPTER 1

DESCENDING GRACEFULLY FROM the private Cessna aircraft, she stepped lightly onto the tarmac. Pausing as she adjusted to being on solid ground again, she took in the seemingly quiet surroundings with great appreciation and curiosity. Directly ahead of her stood the building she knew to be the airport, and—she smiled—evidently it also housed the local country store, post office, and barber shop, if the signs on the building were anything to go by. To the left and right, she spotted various houses mixed in with what she assumed were other businesses. Her eyes rose, her smile growing, and all this was neatly nestled in the lap of the majestic snow-covered mountain ranges surrounding them. Her long legs steady now, she headed toward the airport.

"Ms. Hailey?" A male voice behind her stopped her.

Turning, she waited, watching a tall man striding toward her, his eyes hidden behind his aviator sunglasses.

"Ms. Hailey?" he asked again, stopping beside her.

"That would be me," she said hesitantly.

Was this the man sent to meet her? She hoped so. She was anxious to be on her way.

"Hi. Jack Lance, your pilot," he introduced himself, offering his hand. "Nice to meet you."

"Nice to meet you too, Mr. Lance," she smiled, shaking his hand.

"Jack, please. My father was Mr. Lance."

"I'm Madison."

Pleasantries out of the way, Madison glanced past Jack. She'd been under the assumption she was continuing her trip in another type of plane but didn't see one waiting. Were they taking the Cessna? Not that it mattered, as long as she got where she needed to be.

"My luggage is still on the plane, if you'll give me a minute," she angled her head toward the airport. "I'll be back out and ready to fly again in just a few minutes." She started toward the airport.

"Sorry?"

Pausing, Madison turned back to Jack.

"We're not flying anywhere."

"I beg your pardon?" Madison stared at the man, wishing she could see behind the glasses. "I was under the impression we were flying out this afternoon." She glanced at her watch "Did I arrive too late? I thought we landed early actually."

"No, ma'am," Jack began slowly, suddenly realizing that Madison wasn't aware of the situation. "You didn't arrive too late." He paused. "It's just that there's a storm coming in and all flights have been grounded until further notice."

No way! Shielding her eyes, she studied the bright blue sky for a moment.

"Seriously? To coin a phrase, there isn't a cloud in the sky!"

Jack smiled; this wasn't the first time he'd been questioned when it came to the weather. And he knew it wouldn't be the last. He pointed skyward.

"See those wispy clouds?"

She followed his finger, nodding.

Okay, so the sky wasn't completely cloudless, but they certainly didn't look like storm clouds to her!

"Those are weather makers."

Letting his words sink in, he watched Madison frown. Didn't matter that she wasn't in the mood for a lesson about the weather, she was getting one anyway.

"If a storm's predicted, trust me, we'll get a storm. And they mean business when they ground flights. We go up and it's not an emergency, I lose my license." He paused dramatically. "That is, if we don't die first."

Her eyes widened. He didn't like being so blunt, but he needed her to understand the severity of the situation. Too many others hadn't heeded the warnings, got other pilots to fly them out. Some made it. Most didn't.

Madison wasn't stupid. Listening to Jack, she knew they weren't going anywhere, and she wasn't about to try. He knew this country; she didn't. If he said they weren't going anywhere, well—she thought, gazing back toward the airport—she might as well settle in till they could go. A sense of nervousness slid through her. She wasn't keen on the idea of hanging out in the airport alone, but what other choice did she have? She couldn't chance missing her flight out when it did finally go. It just would have been nice if someone had let her know ahead of time! Someone had to have known about this pending storm, didn't they? Feeling her temper stir, she pushed it down.

"What about the team I was meeting up with? They'll be expecting me. Are they safe? Will they be caught in the storm?"

She glanced toward the airport again. There was supposed to be a packet waiting for her inside. In it would be a SAT phone as well as other information needed for her journey into the mountains.

"I was notified that the team had already been alerted to the pending storm earlier today. They've been picked up and taken to a small town about 150 miles from the campsite. They'll be safe there for the duration," he readily assured her.

"Safe, good," Madison said, scanning the sky again. "How bad is this storm supposed to be?" *And how long am I going to be sitting here?*

She swallowed her groan. It wasn't Jack's fault that she was stuck here. She needed to remember that.

No sense in downplaying it, Jack thought, his eyes turning skyward briefly. Storms like the one predicted, until it was over, no one could be sure how bad it might be or how long it might last. He

7

might as well give her the worst-case scenario now and hope later he was proven wrong. But knowing the weather as he did, he was fairly certain this storm was going to be a game changer.

"Honestly, it's supposed to be pretty bad. You'd call it a blizzard," he smiled at Madison. "We just call it a nasty snowstorm."

Her eyes widened.

"You're talking feet then, not a few inches."

"Yes."

"Care to tell me how many feet?"

"Can't exactly," Jack answered. "It's easier to wait it out and measure later."

"You make this sound like a common occurrence," Madison commented dryly, swallowing her nervousness. Blizzard? Feet of snow? Shit!

"Well, up here, at this time of the year, yeah, it more or less is," Jack replied lightly.

He really wasn't trying to alarm the woman, but judging by her suddenly pale face, clearly he wasn't doing a very good job. Crap. He had to give her credit, though; she was handling the news a whole lot better than he'd expected. Some women he'd dealt with in the past had thrown major fits when they'd found out their plans had changed, not understanding why or how the weather could affect them so much. Thankfully, Madison wasn't acting like that—so far, anyway. He studied her from behind the reflective lens of his sunglasses. No, already it was obvious to him that she was different from any woman he'd ever flown up here before. If anything, in fact, she seemed more curious than upset at the change of plans.

With her studying the clouds, Jack had a moment to really study Madison. Her hand shielding her eyes from the sunlight, Jack knew her eyes were sapphire blue; he'd noticed them first thing. Any man who had the pleasure of seeing those eyes sparkling would be one lucky bastard. Her chocolate-brown hair hung in a loose braid all the way down her back, the tip of her braid resting at the waist of her loose-fitting jeans. Her red fleece jacket, while not clingy in any way, suggested a curvy body underneath. His eyes rose. She wore no makeup, the sun and breeze giving her all the natural color she needed. Refreshing. He wasn't fond of women who wore lots of makeup. Made him nervous, like they were trying to hide something. He was a natural kind of guy and liked his women the same. And that voice! The low, husky timbre of it! Oh yeah, that voice alone could easily bring a man to his knees!

Shielding her eyes against the bright sun, Madison studied the wispy clouds, knowing Jack was studying her. Didn't matter that his Ray Bans hide his eyes; she knew. She could feel it. She was used to it. But Jack's casual open and friendly demeanor dismissed any concerns she might have had. Her never-failing internal threat radar wasn't pinging. No, he was of no threat to her, in any way. She turned a dazzling smile on him, happy she wouldn't have to kill him.

Curious and surprised at her smile, Jack paused. It was like she knew something he didn't. Shaking it off, he returned her smile with his own easy one before turning toward the airport.

"When I found out about the storm, I took the liberty of booking you a room at our hotel. I hope you don't mind," he glanced at her as she fell into step beside him. "It's clean, comfortable, and a good place to weather the storm."

Touched by his thoughtfulness, she was relieved to know she wouldn't have to hang around the airport—especially as it sounded like she could be stuck here for a while. She glanced back at the airplane in time to see her luggage coming off.

Good, she thought, turning back to the airport.

Now she just needed to pick up the packet waiting inside for her. She was anxious to get the SAT phone.

"Thank you, Jack," Madison smiled as he held open the door for her, following her inside.

Pausing as her eyes adjusted to the dimly lit area, she gazed around the small terminal. Terminal? More like just a large room. If it weren't for the lockers lining the far wall, a counter sporting a large "Check In" sign, and an oversized luggage cart—she never would have known it was the airport terminal. She glanced around; there wasn't even a security scanner for departing passengers!

"Yeah, it's not much, but they're building us a new airport next year," Jack quickly explained, seeing the surprise on Madison's face.

He'd seen that look on many faces and would be happy when they finally had an "official" airport.

"But don't let all this fool you," he said with a wave of his hand. "We're more high-tech than we look. And our security is top-notch."

"Sure it is," Madison mumbled, searching but not seeing anything that even whispered that they were protected in any way.

"Trust me," Jack laughed. "Just because you can't see it doesn't mean it isn't so."

She tossed him a knowing glance.

True enough, she thought, *true enough*.

"Come on, we'll get your luggage."

Following Jack out to the parking lot, Madison tossed her two duffel bags into the back of his pickup, opting to hang on to her backpack. Holding the door open as she climbed in, he waited as she got settled before closing the door, walking around to climb into the driver's seat. Expecting to carry her stuff, he'd been pleasantly surprised and more than a little impressed when she picked it up herself without a second thought. He'd offered to take it—her "No, thanks, I've got it" just ramping up his respect for the woman that much more. So far he was finding her to be a welcome breath of fresh air. He wondered if the team she was meeting up with had any idea what they were in for; she was a most pleasant surprise. In many ways.

Pulling off his gloves as he started the truck, sun bouncing off his gold wedding band as he gripped the steering wheel, Jack was glad he was happily married. While he couldn't put his finger on exactly why, he knew that Madison was a dangerous woman. And it wasn't just because of her looks. He glanced sideways at her. No, there was something more to her, something lurking underneath. He wondered if he'd ever find out what that was. He smiled, not sure he really wanted to know.

"Ready?" he asked, buckling his seatbelt.

Nodding, Madison sat back as Jack steered the truck out of the "airport," turning on to Main Street.

Looking around, Madison quickly realized that the town had been built up around the airport; it literally sat right in the middle of the small town!

How unusual, she thought. Most airports she flew into were well away from any town of city.

"The town built itself around the airport," Jack said, confirming her thoughts as they drove slowly along the road running parallel to the airport. "It was originally just a refueling station, then a few settlers thought it might be nice to live up here. For convenience and safety, given the weather and the terrain around here, building the town around the airport seemed the smartest thing to do at the time."

"At the time?"

"Yeah," Jack smiled. "There are times when we've got quite a few planes going in and out. The noise gets a bit much sometimes."

Watching a small plane land neatly on the runway, Madison found herself fascinated. The only thing that separated the airport from the neighboring houses was a tall, sturdy chain-link fence. Probably more for keeping people and animals out than for the protection of the airport.

"But they're just small planes," she noted as the small plane, having landed smoothly, turned toward the terminal. "I guess you don't get the big 747s and the other jumbo jets coming in."

No, she thought. Clearly the runway wasn't long enough for anything big to land. She filed away that information in the back of her mind.

"Actually, we had a DC-10 make an emergency landing here once."

Madison turned to him with wide eyes.

"Yeah, you can imagine the excitement that caused!"

"What happened??" She looked back at the runway, trying to visualize a big plane landing on that little, itty-bitty landing strip. That couldn't have been good!

"It came in during a snowstorm in January, some years back. Fortunately, we had plenty of snow, and when the plane ran out of runway, it just plowed into the huge snowbank at the end."

"Holy shit!"

Seeing another plane drop out of the sky, Madison watched as it executed a perfect landing before taxiing to the airport, stopping beside the other plane.

"They make it look so easy," she said in awe. "I hope no one was hurt when the DC-10 landed?"

"Thankfully, no, but it was a bit difficult to understand them when they came off the plane, so who really knows."

"Oh?'

"It was a Russian plane, the passengers only spoke Russian."

"Oh my god!"

Trying to visualize where exactly they were in regards to Russia, Madison gawked at Jack, remembering her geography. She was in the Yukon Territory now, Alaska being right "next door." Closing her eyes, envisioning the map, she blinked. Not only was Russia close by, they weren't that far from Japan either! Holy shit!

"They were friendly people," Jack continued, "more than happy to have landed safely, that's for sure. At least that's what they told us once we found someone to translate!" He paused, chuckling. "As you can imagine, not a lot of people spoke Russian around here. We fixed that, though, it's one of the required languages in our schools now!"

"That's very neighborly of you," Madison chuckled.

"Yeah, we thought so too. Now if any of them feel like dropping in, we'll be able to welcome them better."

Jack glanced quickly at the last stretch of runway that they were passing before turning his eyes back to the road.

"Not that we're hoping for another DC-10 or anything close to that size. Yeah, no, thanks! That was definitely too close for comfort. Watching that thing slam into the snowbank, not something I want to see again anytime soon, thanks. It was definitely a testament to how well the plane was constructed, though. Amazingly enough, there was no severe structural damage, the plane stayed intact. And the pilots, they were incredible, putting that plane down safely and managing to slow enough that the nose didn't crumple when they hit. And not a single person was hurt! Incredible."

"I'm sure," Madison said thoughtfully. "How long were they stranded for?"

"Believe it or not, only two days. The DC-10 was able to take off the next day, but none of the passengers were in any hurry to board that plane again. I can't imagine why," he tossed her a smile. "Anyway, they went out on various other smaller planes that were made available for them."

"They flew to Russia in small planes?"

That couldn't have been comfortable! She'd had a hard-enough time coming up from Edmonton in the Cessna, and her plane had made three stops before arriving here!

"Oh, no," Jack quickly assured her, "there's another much larger airport about three hours away. They flew there before getting on a larger plane for the rest of the ride. So while they were a bit delayed, everyone finally got home safely. And isn't that the name of the game?"

"It is," Madison agreed with a smile. "That's quite a story."

"Yeah, well, even our small town has its share of excitement."

And pulling into a parking lot, Jack stopped the truck in front of a well-worn log cabin. Okay, it wasn't really a cabin but a huge house.

Strike that, she thought, spotting the "Inn" sign swinging above the entrance.

Evidently, they'd arrived. Had it even been a ten-minute ride? She didn't think so. Good to know, in case she needed to walk back to the airport. Or run.

"Welcome to your home away from home," Jack said, throwing the truck into park and shutting off the engine. "Don't worry," he patted her leg lightly, "it's got running water and cable TV, all the amenities of home!"

She smiled at him, wondering what he'd think if she told him that this place most likely had more amenities than her own home!

"I'm sure it'll be fine," she said instead, climbing from the truck. "Outside entrances only?"

Jake shook his head at what he thought was an odd question.

Good, Madison thought, unconsciously sizing up the rustic building.

Three floors high with, if she judged right, fifteen rooms per side, each room offering a sliding glass door that opened up to the deck lining each floor. What looked to be a sturdy birch railing of standard height completed the picture. The hotel looked to be nothing more than a huge log cabin. She smiled. She couldn't wait to see the inside, guessing it would be comfortable and welcoming. Having just come from one of the most sterile of hotels in Los Angeles, what with its shining stainless steel fixtures and sharp square tables and beds, the room had had absolutely no character. And really hadn't even been that comfortable!

No, Madison smiled as she grabbed her duffel bags, this place was going to be heaven! And the fact that if necessary, she could jump that railing with no trouble, yeah, another plus.

CHAPTER 2

"AFTERNOON, ETHEL!" JACK greeted the matronly gray-haired woman as she beamed up at him from behind the front desk.

"Hi, Jack, I've been waiting on you!" Ethel's sharp, bright eyes moved past him, landing squarely on Madison. "And I see you've brought our girl along."

Jack nodded, stepping aside, giving Ethel a better view of Madison.

"Don't be shy there, girl, step right up, let's have a look at you!"

Our girl? Madison nearly laughed. When was the last time she'd been referred to as a girl? She couldn't help it and found herself smiling.

"Hello," Madison said quietly, unzipping her jacket in the warm lobby.

Knowing Ethel was giving her the "once-over"—and thoroughly so—Madison stood quietly, tolerating it as best she could. She was well aware that her looks made it nearly impossible for her to go unnoticed, but that didn't stop her from attempting to keep a low profile whenever possible. Clearly, however, that was not going to happen here! No, Ethel was studying her as if she was specimen under the microscope! Madison suddenly found herself fighting down the almost-uncontrollable urge to fidget. Jesus Christ, she'd stared down the barrel of a gun and hadn't felt this nervous!

When Ethel twirled her hand in the air, signaling for Madison to turn around, she wisely swallowed the retort that sprang to mind. The feeling of being inspected rankled; Madison detested it! It was one thing to be noticed; it was another to be studied. Especially in her world. It was dangerous and too often led to trouble. The dead kind of trouble.

Taking a deep breath, Madison reminded herself that Ethel was harmless and in no way a threat to her. And given that this was a small town, this kind of scrutiny was to be expected. She was the new kid in town, and evidently, to pass GO and collect her two hundred dollars, she needed to pass inspection first. She hoped Ethel would finish her inspection soon, though! Jesus, all this for just one night! What happened to those who stayed longer?

Standing by helplessly, Jack waited patiently. One did not rush Ethel in these things, and he suffered silently with Madison, knowing there wasn't anything he could do to help her. This was Ethel's domain; Madison was on her own here. And if Ethel decided she didn't like Madison, for whatever reason—well, Jack thought—he just hoped Nancy wouldn't mind him bringing a guest home with him. Thinking back, Jack could only remember one time that Ethel had turned away a potential guest. And she'd been right to do so; the guy had moved on to the next town where he'd proceeded to kill a bank teller who dared look him in the eye when he'd demanded money from her. Jack gazed proudly at Ethel as she studied Madison thoroughly; the woman did have an uncanny ability to read people. Watching Ethel's eyes narrow, Jack paused. Uh-oh . . . He reached in his pocket for his cell phone, prepared to call his wife. She'd want the heads-up about a possible guest.

"You're a refreshing one, you are," Ethel suddenly announced with a grin, approval ringing in her voice.

Relaxing, Jack smiled at Madison, wondering if she realized she'd just been given Ethel's personal stamp of approval.

"I beg your pardon?" Madison asked cautiously.

Had she just passed GO? She thought so, but her eyes met and held Ethel's; the jury seemed to still be out. The woman had certainly given her a thorough once-over! Only when Ethel's eyes had narrowed had Madison felt a twinge of concern.

"You're obviously not some foolish, skinny city girl," Ethel stated with a grin. "You know how to dress sensibly, and you've got meat on your bones." She turned to Jack. "Nothing I hate more than skinny, frail, and bony-looking women!"

Ethel turned back to Madison, eyeing the younger woman's casual bulky sweater, turtleneck, jeans, and comfortable, well-worn hiking boots with approval.

"You're not covered in makeup either," Ethel glanced at Jack again, "something else I detest—women thinking they need to cover up their beautiful, natural-looking faces!"

Well, the woman certainly wasn't afraid to voice her opinion, Madison thought—admittedly happy she'd forgone her usual light makeup that morning. Only because she'd been running a little behind schedule had she decided to pass on it, opting for just moisturizer. Tossing a silent thanks to God for giving her naturally healthy and clear skin, Madison paused. Since when did she care what someone else thought of her? Yet here she was, pleased that Ethel approved of her. The mountain air must be getting to her!

"Thank you," Madison smiled, glancing sheepishly at Jack, slightly embarrassed to have been complimented in front of him.

"You're welcome," Ethel said, not caring that she'd embarrassed the girl.

Besides, Ethel thought, Madison could take it. Reaching out, Ethel's fingers slid down Madison's braid. She'd had hair that beautiful once, Ethel remembered. And it'd driven men crazy! Smiling at the memory, Ethel dropped the braid and, taking a step back, nodded.

"Yes," she declared, "I like the looks of you."

Pausing, her eyes narrowed again as she studied Madison.

"You're a tough one too," Ethel murmured, "strong and determined. Lots of spunk."

Well, shit! Madison hadn't expected Ethel to delve into her psyche and wasn't sure how she felt about the brief yet disgustingly accurate analysis. She'd just have to watch herself around the older woman, especially as she'd just made it abundantly clear that not much got past her!

Deciding the best course of action was to just remain silent, Madison nodded slightly, her smile tentative.

Oh, yeah—the older woman thought, turning back to Jack—the girl standing in front of her was not all that she appeared to be. Oh, no, there was much more to her. But despite all that, Ethel found herself immediately liking the girl. Trusting her gut, Ethel smiled at Jack.

"Don't worry, Jack, I'll take good care of our girl," Ethel announced, stepping back around behind the front desk.

There it was again, Madison thought, *"our girl."* What was that all about? And all this for just one night? But secretly pleased she'd passed "the test," Madison stepped up to sign her registration form.

"Thanks, Ethel," Jack smiled before turning to Madison. "I've gotta get going, but I'll check back in with you later. Don't worry, I'll be keeping a close eye on the weather. Anything changes, and I'll let you know right away."

Knowing Madison still expected to go out in the morning, Jack considered telling her how wrong she was. But he thought better of it. Mother Nature could still fool him; she'd done it before. He knew he wasn't wrong, but just in case. No sense in worrying Madison. Let her get settled in and rested up, there'd be plenty of time to talk about the weather later.

Understanding that the man had other things to do besides babysitting her, Madison nodded. She had work to do herself, and the sooner she got to it, the better. She resisted the urge to pat her backpack where the SAT phone was now securely nestled.

"Thanks for everything, Jack," Madison smiled. "I really appreciate you taking the time to help me out like this."

She glanced out the window, noticing that in the short time since they'd arrived that it'd turned gray outside.

"I hope the storm isn't as bad as predicted, but," she turned back to Ethel, her smile growing, "I'm glad I've got a warm place to stay."

"You certainly do!" Ethel gushed happily.

"You're in good hands," Jack said, heading for the door. "Talk to you later!"

And with that he was gone.

Turning back to Ethel, Madison found the woman studying her again. Okay, enough was enough!

"What?" Madison demanded, careful to keep her tone even.

"Why are you here?"

Madison's eyes widened briefly. Okay, so while the question was harmless enough, it was the woman's suspicious tone that had Madison considering her answer very carefully.

"You mean, you don't already know?" Madison laughed, surprising Ethel. "Come on, admit it, you knew everything about me before I even set foot off the plane."

Her blunt statement had Ethel pausing.

Oh, yeah, the older woman thought, *there's more to this girl than meets the eye*. She just wasn't sure what it was. And she suddenly wasn't sure if she wanted to know either.

Guessing not many stood up to the older woman, Madison softened her tone. Despite the earlier scrutiny, Madison found herself liking Ethel. And she didn't like many people.

"I'm here doing research," Madison continued easily, confident her cover would stand up. "But you already knew that."

I might like you, Madison thought wryly, *but that doesn't mean I'm going to let you keep grilling me*.

The two women stared at each other for a moment. Then with a burst of laughter, Ethel broke away.

"You are a breath of fresh air, to be sure!" she declared, handing Madison her room key.

Not about to admit that Madison had been right, Ethel gave her directions to her room and, with a "get settled and then we'll talk some more," sent Madison on her way.

Stepping into her room, Madison gasped in wonder. A wooden four-poster king-sized bed dominating the large room blended comfortably with lush, deep-blue carpeting. An old yet clearly sturdy wooden desk with its matching chair offered her efficient work space while the brightly overstuffed chair in the corner with its matching ottoman beckoned her, inviting her to relax and put her feet up while watching the TV nestled in the armoire opposite the bed. A gas fireplace burning brightly completed the picture. Too bad she was only here for one night.

Dropping her bags, Madison pushed open the drapes covering the sliding door, allowing what little light there was to come streaming in. Her view of the nearby mountains was nothing short of breathtaking, and Madison gazed in awe as the clouds bounced across the mountaintops. If she didn't know better, she'd swear she could almost smell the snow coming! She smiled, turning back into the room. Eyeing the four large pillows on her bed, her smile turned wistful. Oh, to have the time to just lie back and relax! When was the last time she'd done that? She couldn't remember.

Poking her head into the equally large bathroom, she nearly laughed, remembering Jack's promise that there'd be hot water. There was no doubt about that, especially given the size of the Jacuzzi tub! Again she cursed her luck at having to leave the next day. Pouring herself a glass of water from the tap, she did finally laugh. The hotel she'd just left in LA had provided bottled water for their guests. For a price, of course. Drinking down the refreshing water, Madison sighed happily. Bottled water didn't have a thing on glacier-fed water.

Wandering back into the room, Madison turned in a slow circle. From the Keurig coffeemaker sitting on the counter over the mini fridge to the lamp on the desk that would also allow her to plug in and get the Internet, the room had everything she required. Too bad, she thought again, that she'd only be here for one night!

Glancing at her watch, figuring the time difference, Madison turned on the coffeemaker before going to her backpack and pulling out the SAT phone. Moments later, coffee and phone in hand, she dropped into the overstuffed chair, propping her feet on the ottoman. Sipping her coffee with a happy sigh, Madison dialed the phone.

Eight hours away in Kassel, Germany, Sarah checked her caller ID before answering her phone. At least, Madison wasn't calling in the middle of the night, as she was often prone to do!

"How was your flight?" Sarah asked, dropping onto her couch and propping her feet up on the glass-topped coffee table.

"No problems," Madison said, "except that I'm currently in stand-by mode."

"Oh?"

"Evidently, I've been sidelined by an incoming snowstorm."

"Incoming?"

"It's not here yet, but I'm told it'll get here soon enough. Until then, all flights are grounded."

"Hmm," Sarah said, her mind churning. "Any idea how long you'll be stuck there?"

Hopefully for days, Madison thought, snuggling further into her chair.

"I didn't see anything on the weather satellite about any possible storms."

"I'm in the far reaches of Canada, and it's winter," Madison stated. "Evidently, the weather plays by its own rules up this way."

The women chuckled. The weather wasn't the only thing that played by its own rules.

"So for now I'm just hunkering down, good time to catch up on some paperwork." Like expense reports that she kept forgetting to send in. "The team at the campsite have already been evacuated because of the storm, so there's no need to change that plan. Just the timetable, a little bit. Unfortunately, I don't have a specific departure time yet." She paused. "My pilot's a by-the-book guy, and there's no pushing him."

Turning to glance out the window, Madison's eyes widened. Snow was falling heavily.

"Looks like he knows his stuff, though," she murmured, relaying the weather back to Sarah.

"Let me know when you're flying out," Sarah said, pushing herself up off her couch and glancing at the clock.

Her brother would be calling soon. From where she had no idea. At least she knew where Madison was. She should; she sent her there!

"In the meantime, stay safe."

"Will do," Madison said and, concluding with the usual pleasantries, ended the call.

CHAPTER 3

HUNGER PAINS FINALLY drove Madison out of her cozy room. Having unpacked a few things and taking a quick power nap followed by a refreshing shower, she now needed sustenance.

And more coffee, she decided, pausing just outside the lobby.

Staying just out of sight, Madison watched and listened to Ethel checking in a group of guests. Judging by the conversation, it appeared these folks were waylaid because of the storm as well. Ethel's cheerfulness had the desired effect, she noticed, watching the guests visibly begin to relax.

Understanding their frustration and worry at being stuck for an unknown amount of time, Madison paused, one of the men in the group catching her attention. Something about him had her eyes narrowing. Did she know him?

Seriously? she berated herself. *Like you're going to run into someone you know up here? In the middle of nowhere?*

She turned away, only to turn back when the man spoke, his distinct Brooklyn accent making his low voice laced with ice that much harder to ignore. Her eyes drifted over the group; had any of them picked up on his tone? It didn't appear so. She couldn't see Ethel, wondering if she would have noticed. Probably not though, Madison thought, especially as there wasn't a reason for her to notice. But Madison did, and it bothered her, especially since she couldn't put her finger on why. His back still to her, she noticed that his height and hair color were nothing more than average. Well, that didn't help her any! Just under six feet tall, his short, light-brown hair brushed the collar of his turtle neck that was peeking out from under his navy-blue down jacket. The jacket hid a lot and Madison could only assume he was of average build. Worn denim jeans and sturdy, well-worn winter boots completed the picture. Nothing about this man stood out; everything screamed average. And that's precisely what worried her. But at the same time, her internal "bad guy" radar, as she liked to call it, wasn't going off. So who was this guy then?

Christ, she thought wryly, *he's probably just some guy I passed in the airport or some such place!*

Staying out of sight, her hunger momentarily forgotten, she focused on the man, wishing he'd turn around, knowing for sure that she'd recognize him then. Her photogenic memory made it nearly impossible for her to forget a face, disguised or otherwise. If she'd seen this guy somewhere, she'd know it.

Turn around! her mind cried out. *Let me get a look at you!* Just one quick look—that's all she needed!

But it wasn't to be. Giving the group their individual keys and directions to their rooms, Ethel sent them on their way. Well, that was a plus, at least—Madison thought—overhearing one of the guests mention what floor the group was on: they weren't staying on her floor. If she did know this guy, it was better for the both of them to be as far apart as possible. Her stomach growling in hunger, Madison counted to 100 before approaching the desk. No sense in chancing running into the group.

Glancing up from her paperwork, Ethel smiled at Madison, noting her relaxed and refreshed appearance.

"How's everything with your room, dear?" Madison nearly laughed.

Dear?

"It's wonderful," Madison gushed, remembering the comfortable bed and the invigorating shower. "I'm sorry I'm only here for one night."

Glancing over Madison's shoulder, out the front window of the Inn, Ethel smirked but stayed silent.

One night? The girl was in for a big surprise if she was still thinking that way. The snow was steadily falling now. Oh, no, the girl wouldn't be leaving anytime soon.

"I'm glad you like it," Ethel said instead with a knowing smile. "If you need anything, please let me know."

"Well, now that you mention it, I am in need of a good dinner." Ethel's smile grew.

"Preferably a good steak dinner?"

Nodding, Ethel came around the desk and, taking Madison's arm gently, steered her toward the entrance.

Glad the girl had thought to put on her jacket, Ethel gave Madison quick and precise directions to the local steakhouse, assuring the girl that it was the best in town.

Probably the only one in town, Madison thought as she listened to the directions, nodding.

"I'll call them and let them know you're on your way," Ethel said, gently pushing Madison toward the door. "You're going to love their food!"

And with a wave, Ethel sent Madison on her way before hurrying back to the desk to call the restaurant. She couldn't wait to tell Ruth who was coming to dinner!

Stepping outside, she immediately picked up the mouthwatering scent of grilling steaks.

Follow Ethel's directions or follow her nose, she thought, lifting her nose and sniffing; either way, she knew where she was going! Zipping up her jacket and shoving her hands into her pockets, Madison stepped off the porch into the falling snow and simply followed her nose.

Minutes later, Madison came to the source of the heavenly smell: Sam's Steakhouse. The large, rustic building boasting an equally large and clearly hand crafted sign, proclaimed that the best steaks in the province were served here. Judging by the number of vehicles parked in front, as well as the juicy smells coming from inside, Madison knew she'd hit the hotspot of the town. Lengthening her stride and bounding up the front steps, she idly noted that there were no cars out front, only trucks. Interesting. Pulling open the heavy door, she stepped inside, praying she wouldn't have to wait long for a table.

Waiting patiently while the hostess seated the couple in front of her, Madison brushed the snow off her jacket, remembering Jack's prediction for a snowfall amounting to more than a foot. A nasty snowstorm he'd called it. While she didn't doubt he knew his weather, she wasn't giving up on the hope that she'd be able to fly out in the morning either. Her timetable wasn't set in stone, but the sooner she could finish the job, the sooner she'd be able to move on. Although the idea of staying longer in her comfy room at the Inn was definitely appealing.

I wonder . . .

"Welcome! How many?"

Pulling her thoughts back to the present, Madison smiled at the hostess before realizing that someone else was calling her name. Forcing herself to remain calm, Madison turned toward the direction of the voice. Who the hell knew she was here? Her eyes scanning the crowd, relief swept through her when she spotted Jack waving at her from across the room. Motioning for her to join him, Madison nodded to the hostess before weaving her way through the crowded restaurant, pausing only slightly when she spotted the pretty blond woman sitting next to Jack.

"Join us," Jack insisted as he rose, pulling out the empty chair for her.

"Thank you," Madison said quietly, glancing at the woman. "I don't want to intrude."

"You're not intruding at all," the blond woman assured her with a genuine smile as Madison dropped into the chair. "I'm Nancy, Jack's wife," the blond continued. "Nice to meet you! Welcome to our little corner of the world!"

"Thank you," Madison smiled, giving the woman sitting across from her a quick yet thorough glance.

Blond hair hanging in a bob to her chin, her glistening green eyes were filled with warmth as she studied Madison with her own unabashed curiosity.

"And thanks for letting me join you."

Turning a quick glance at her husband, Nancy turned back to Madison.

"We're happy to have you join us! It's your first night in town, nothing worse than having to eat alone."

Nancy's infectious smile wound its way through Madison's normal defenses, and she found herself relaxing and smiling back. To top it off, Nancy was right. While eating alone was more than a common occurrence for Madison, that still didn't mean she enjoyed it.

Jack hadn't been kidding when he'd described the "new girl in town" to her earlier, Nancy thought, eyeing with envy Madison's long, dark hair. Pulled back into a smooth ponytail, it only made her brilliant sapphire-blue eyes stand out that much more. Wearing no makeup, not that she needed it, her clear complexion made it nearly impossible to judge the woman's age. No, Jack had been right. In a simple, elegant way, Madison was stunning. Turning her smiling eyes on her husband, Nancy unconsciously ran her hand over her stomach, basking in the knowledge that Jack truly loved her and only her.

Following the movement of Nancy's hand, Madison's smile grew. The woman was very pregnant.

"Congratulations!" Madison said happily. "When are you due?"

Jack, all but forgotten as the conversation turned to the pending birth, sat back in his chair, happy the women were getting along. He'd been a little worried; one never knew how an outsider was going to be accepted. Especially one that looked like Madison. She'd turned more than a few heads when she'd walked in, although he was fairly certain she hadn't realized it. Or if she had, she certainly hadn't paid it any attention. That in itself was refreshing. No, Jack pondered, Madison clearly was not like any tourist he'd ever brought up here. She was altogether different. He paused, not entirely sure if that was a good thing or a bad thing. Nancy's face crinkling in pain pulled his attention back to her, and he leaned forward to soothe her.

"You feeling okay?" he asked worriedly, his hand resting gently on her belly.

Nancy nodded, smiling through the discomfort as she turned back to Madison.

"I'm due in ten days," she said, unconsciously rubbing her belly. "That is, if he can wait that long!" She smiled at her husband. "I'm fine, he's just being an active boy tonight, that's all."

"You know it's a boy?" Madison asked. "Is this your first?"

Nancy shook her head, smiling.

"Oh, no, that's the kicker of the whole thing," she laughed, "this one's our third! Although you'd never know that looking at Mr. Nervous Dad here!"

Patting Jack's hand on her belly, Nancy's smile grew larger.

"Don't let his concern fool you, he really does have this all down to a science."

Madison laughed at Jack's sheepish grin, either ignoring or not noticing the heads turning at the sound of her husky laugh.

"But no, I'm not sure it's a boy. But the girls didn't move this much, so that's why I'm thinking it might be a boy."

"The girls are four years old," Jack added, laughing at Madison's wide-eyed expression. "Yeah, twins."

"Are you sure there's only one in there now?" Madison couldn't help asking, suddenly realizing that Nancy had probably been asked that same question a million times already. "I'm sorry, I'm sure you've heard that more than enough."

"It's okay," Nancy nodded, "and the doctor assured us there's only one this time."

Shifting in her chair to get more comfortable, she grimaced.

"So help me God, though, if he's wrong I'm gonna kill him!"

She ground out, shifting again.

"You don't know any good hit men, do you?" Nancy laughed, finally finding a comfortable position.

Madison paused. Of course, the woman had been only kidding! But still . . .

"I might know one or two."

"Well, give me their numbers," Nancy laughed, "just in case!"

Enjoying the easy laughter, Madison sat back in her chair as the waitress appeared, taking their drink order and leaving them with menus.

Oh, if they only knew, Madison thought, studying the menu, her stomach growling again.

"I'm starving," she confessed. "What do you recommend?"

Catching Jack and Nancy smiling at her, Madison put down her menu.

"What?"

"I was just remembering the first time I arrived here," Nancy said wistfully. "All those years ago. My first night's dinner was here too."

"You're not from here?" Madison asked, curious, suddenly wondering if anyone was originally for the area or if they'd all just "arrived" one day.

"Oh, no," Nancy shook her head. "I flew in just like you. And my trip was rerouted because of weather, just like yours. Ethel took me in and then sent me here for dinner."

She tossed a loving glance at Jack, knowing he was remembering too.

"And just like you, I was starving. I came in, nervous as hell because I was alone and, well," she paused, glancing around happily, "the rest is history."

"You met Jack here." Stating the obvious, Madison smiled at the couple.

"Right here," Nancy nodded, rubbing her belly again. "And looked what happened!"

"Yeah, you're suffering," Jack laughed.

"I am, you bastard!" Slapping her husband playfully, Nancy dove into the basket of rolls as the waitress placed them on the table. "You've made me fat!"

"And happy!"

"More fat than happy right now."

Laughing at the couple's banter, Madison snatched a roll, breaking it apart and buttering it lightly before popping it in her mouth.

Oh my god, she thought, closing her eyes. They were homemade! She thought she'd cry. When was the last time she'd had anything homemade?

"Are any people originally from here?" Madison said in between bites.

"A few, but most, like myself, started coming here because of the fishing and the hunting. It's unbelievable! Anyway, eventually people stopped coming and going and just settled here. The town sorta grew up around them, I guess."

Smiling, Jack's gaze drifted around the room. There wasn't a face in the crowd that he didn't recognize tonight. He knew the same couldn't be said for Madison. And he knew he'd be getting the third degree about her later. He couldn't remember the last time a pretty face had arrived in town. Alone anyway. Suddenly feeling very protective of their out-of-town guest, Jack sat up a little bit straighter.

"Did you ever finish your original trip, Nancy?" Madison asked, biting into another roll.

Nancy nodded, reaching for another roll herself.

"But as soon as I could, I came back," she said, taking Jack's hand. "Of course, I had something to come back to."

"And you, Jack? How long before you settled here?"

"Only took me three trips. I was flying fishermen and hunters up on a regular basis. Got stuck in a storm on the third trip in, and with time to kill, I had a chance to check things out. Before the weather cleared, I knew I wouldn't be leaving."

Signaling to the waitress, Jack turned back to Madison.

"That was nearly twenty years ago. I was a youngster, of course, back then." He chuckled before continuing, "I've never once regretted my decision."

The pride in his voice made Madison smile.

"Who knows, Madison," Nancy winked, "you might end up staying too."

Shaking her head, Madison clearly knew otherwise. While visiting longer might be nice, moving here permanently? Not likely. Someone in her line of work didn't settle anywhere. It was too dangerous. Instantly liking Nancy and Jack, the idea that trouble could land on their doorstep because of her—no, that was something she'd never allow. She'd stay only long enough to do her job. Then she'd be moving on. But maybe she could come back for a visit . . .

"I don't think so, Nancy, but thanks for the thought," Madison said quietly, happy when the waitress came to take their order.

Guessing Nancy could be very persuasive, Madison ordered her dinner before steering the conversation away from herself.

"So if you're not from here," she asked them, "where are you from?"

"I'm from Calgary, Alberta," Jack answered.

"I'm originally from Edmonton," Nancy said. "But I was living in San Francisco when I first came here. I went back there just long enough to pack up and come here."

She squeezed Jack's hand lovingly, her smile wide as she leaned toward Madison, whispering loudly, "Don't tell the big lug, it'll only go to his head, but moving here was the best decision I've ever made in my life."

Squeezing her hand gently in return, Jack just smiled. She hadn't said anything he didn't already know.

Returning with their drinks, the waitress smiled, quietly telling Nancy how long it'd be before their dinner came out. Nodding and assuring the waitress that it would be fine, Nancy leaned back in her chair, rubbing her belly again. Raising her glass to the couple, Madison toasted their happiness before sitting back, sipping her Bailey's Irish Cream. As expected, Nancy had a soda; Jack, a very tall beer.

Her eyes drifting around the crowded room, Madison marveled at how relaxed she was. While she normally shied away from large crowds, she found herself totally at ease sitting with Jack and Nancy amidst a crowd of complete strangers. Glancing over her shoulder, she wasn't surprised to catch the people at the next table eyeing her curiously. It was to be expected. She didn't like it, but she wasn't about to have anyone think she was an unsociable and rude bitch either! Besides, she reminded herself, no one knew her here. Smiling and nodding at the people, Madison turned back to her table.

"See anyone you know?" Jack asked playfully, watching Madison gazing around the room.

"Amazingly enough, no!" Madison laughed. "And in this crowd, you'd think there'd be someone I'd know!"

Laughing easily, her nose picked up the scent of freshly grilled beef and, glancing around, watched the waitress approaching with their dinners. Her mouth watered as her plate was placed in front of her.

"What did your family think when you told them you were moving to whereabouts unknown?" Madison asked with a smile, pushing her clean plate away with a happy sigh.

Her steak had been superb! She'd eaten in restaurants around the world and couldn't remember having ever enjoyed her steak more! No doubt, she quickly decided, it was largely in part to there being no fancy garnish and no special seasonings. Just an excellent cut of beef grilled exactly how she liked it. A little salt and pepper was all the seasoning she'd needed. Her baked potato drowned in sour cream had been huge and perfect. Green beans completing the meal, Madison looked forward to getting her hands on the dessert menu. If dinner had been great, she could just imagine how great dessert was going to be! She smiled happily, resisting the urge to snatch the dessert menu out of the waitress's hand before she took Madison's plate.

"Well, my mom wasn't all that excited," Jack said, leaning back as the waitress took away his plate. "Okay, she was in a panic," he admitted with a chuckle, remembering his mother's shocked face when he'd announced he was moving up to the Yukon Territories.

People had gone up there only to never be seen again! His mother had argued fruitlessly.

"But she finally accepted your decision?" Madison asked hopefully.

Her own parents had never come to terms with their only daughter's decision to become a world traveler. Of course, they'd never known her true profession either; they just assumed she worked for a major conglomerate out of Los Angeles, thus the reason for her traveling so much. On one hand, Madison wished they'd asked more questions, wished they'd shown more interest in her and her life. But at the same time, by ignoring her, the distance they kept allowed Madison the freedom she needed to do her job without ever having to really lie to them. Sarah had told her once that it was because of her parents' indifference toward her that helped make Madison the cold, calculating assassin that she was today. Even more ironic—it was Madison who later killed the man who'd taken her parents' lives when he'd invaded their home, killing them needlessly. She didn't bat an eye when she pulled the trigger, killing him with one shot to the head. Parents, guess you just never know how they're going to influence your life.

"Oh, yeah," Jack nodded. "Mom not only accepted it, she followed me."

Madison's eyes widened.

"She's standing behind the bar as we speak."

"That's your mom?"

Madison sat up a little straighter as she spotted the tall, stately woman standing proudly behind the bar. Their eyes met for a split second before the woman turned her attention back to the men sitting at the bar.

"She works here?"

"That's her," Nancy smiled, rubbing her belly again. "She only works occasionally now, she turned sixty this year and decided she was going to slow down some." Nancy laughed, as if working in the restaurant five nights instead of seven was slowing down!

"Incredible," Madison murmured, catching the woman's eyes again.

Smiling and nodding, Madison knew she'd be getting an introduction shortly and readied herself.

"What's even more incredible is that she moved here and fell in love herself!"

Nancy's infectious smile warmed Madison.

"The man standing behind her . . ."

Madison watched as a big man stepped up behind Jack's mother, wrapping his arms around her.

"He's not copping a feel, that's Sam, her husband." Nancy laughed. "He owns this place. They own the place," she quickly corrected herself.

"My dad died a couple of years before I moved up here," Jack explained, "and I guess she figured the easiest way to keep an eye on me was to follow me up here."

Glancing around at the woman smiling at the man holding her, Jack smiled softly.

"For the longest time she denied having feelings for Sam, denying that he cared for her too. You can see how far that got them," Jack laughed, turning back around.

Her heart melting just a bit, Madison smiled wistfully.

"I don't care what you say," she said, swallowing the unexpected emotion, "you, your mom, both your stories are so romantic!"

Squeezing his wife's hand gently, the couple exchanged a look so full of love that Madison had to look away. What would it be like to have someone look at her like that? No sense in wondering, though; relationships weren't her specialty, Madison quickly reminded herself. And it had nothing to do with her chosen profession. Well, okay, maybe that did have a little something to do with it.

"So, what do you do for a living?" "I kill people. And you? What do you do?" Madison nearly laughed at the absurdity of it all.

CHAPTER 4

HUNGER PANGS NAGGING at him, Jeremy headed toward the steak house. Knowing it'd be busy, he hoped he might be able to at least snag a place at the bar. A good meal, a beer, a chat with his mum, and his day would be complete. Later he'd fall into bed and hopefully not wake up until after the storm had completely blown through. Not that he'd ever be that lucky, though, he thought, brushing off the snow that had settled on his jacket since just climbing out of his truck as he pushed open the door to the steak house.

"Hi, sweetie," Jeremy greeted the hostess with his usual friendly grin. "Got room for me at the bar?"

"Always, Jeremy, always. Just go push yourself in," the hostess laughed. "You know, like you always do."

Nodding his thanks, he made a beeline for the bar, patting a few shoulders in greeting as he weaved his way through the crowded room. The place was always busy, but a snowstorm was guaranteed to pack the place, and tonight was no exception.

Catching sight of his brother, Jeremy paused. Who was the woman sitting with them? Changing direction, he headed toward their table and the empty chair next to the woman—the chair that just happened to have his name on it.

"Hey, big brother!" Pulling out the chair, Jeremy dropped into it, leaning over to kiss Nancy's cheek before shaking his brother's hand. "How's junior doing tonight?"

Glowing, Nancy smiled happily.

"Junior's quiet right this very second, so don't be offended if I don't move to hug you," she laughed, her hand resting protectively on her belly.

"No offense taken," Jeremy smiled, swinging around to face the woman he'd only seen from behind.

His eyes widened briefly as her natural beauty struck him squarely between the eyes. His chest constricted for a split second before he pulled himself together. Sapphire-blue eyes met his dark-green eyes in a challenging and slightly curious look.

"I'm Jeremy, Jack's brother," he smiled, offering his hand.

Despite engulfing her small hand in his, Jeremy was pleased her handshake was firm and confident. And soft. He held her hand longer than necessary, watching as she leaned toward him.

"Madison," she said close to his ear. "And may I have my hand back please?"

"Sorry," Jeremy smiled, releasing her and sitting back in his chair, ignoring his brother's knowing smile. "Nice to meet you."

Madison just nodded, also leaning back in her chair. The man had blown in like a whirlwind, and approaching from behind her, he'd sat down before she could really gauge his height. Her hand had nearly disappeared in his, a telling sign that he was a big man. But it'd been his green eyes that had caught her attention. Emeralds came to mind; his eyes sparkled so much. She guessed they'd glitter with passion.

Where the hell had that thought come from?

"I was supposed to fly Madison up north today, but," Jack said with a wave of his hand, "the weather screwed that up big time, as you can see."

Jeremy nodded in understanding. His own plans had changed as well because of the storm. But used to it, he just rolled with it. Really, there wasn't much else he could do about it. No sense in getting all bent out of shape over something he had no control over. But he knew how it could affect others, especially if they weren't prepared.

"What brings you up our way?" Jeremy asked, waving down the waitress.

"Research," Madison answered simply. Her cover was full proof—but still, the less said, the better.

"Climate?" Jeremy asked, turning back to her, giving her his full attention.

Resisting the urge to squirm under his potent gaze, Madison just nodded.

"Among other things," she said carefully, thankful when the waitress appeared.

Noticing it wasn't their original waitress, Madison studied the younger girl over her coffee mug.

"Hi, Jeremy," the waitress all but gushed—her eyes bright, her smile brighter—as she placed a beer in front of him. "Your mom sent this over with instructions that you're to see her before you leave."

Nodding, Jeremy returned her smile, his thoughts on the woman sitting next to him and miles from the waitress standing in front of him.

"Will do, Mary," Jeremy said absently before giving her his dinner order.

Pulling herself together long enough to write it down, Mary lingered a moment longer before turning away. Watching her disappear into the kitchen, Jeremy sighed. He was well aware of her feelings—that she'd had a crush on him for as long as he could remember, although he'd never done anything to garner her attention. Always friendly to her, Jeremy knew he'd never have feelings for the much-younger Mary. But until she met someone new, he knew her attention and hopes were pinned on him. Talk about having to tread lightly.

Jeremy's eyes danced around the restaurant before landing on his mother. Their eyes met and locked—hers, knowing; his, sheepish. Making a mental note to talk to his mom about Mary later, Jeremy raised his beer in a silent toast to the woman. She'd know what to do; she always did. Acknowledging Jeremy with a nod and a smile of her own, his mother turned back to the customers sitting at the bar. Oh, yeah, they'd be talking later, for sure.

"Good crowd tonight," Jeremy commented, bringing his attention back to their table. "Guess I was lucky to get my chair tonight!"

"Guess you were," Jack laughed, Nancy and Jeremy joining in.

Not following the joke, Madison sat quietly, enjoying her coffee. While she might not be included in the joke, she found herself enjoying the company nonetheless.

"I'm sorry, Madison!" Nancy angled slightly to include their guest. "We didn't meant to be rude and leave you out. Jeremy and his chair, well, it's sort'a an inside joke."

"This chair has my name on it, is all," Jeremy went on to explain with a cocky grin.

Not sure what to say, Madison cocked an eyebrow but remained silent.

"No, really!" Jeremy went on, standing up quickly, spinning the chair around. "My name really is on this chair!"

Following where he pointed, Madison couldn't help it and she chuckled. Carved neatly into the wooden chair, the words, "**Jeremy Was Here**" stood out clearly. So much for clichés, she thought; his name really was on the chair!

"See," Jeremy's grin grew, the dimples always so popular with the girls hidden under his full beard, "I told ya."

"So you did," Madison laughed easily, enjoying the feeling of belonging. If only for a little while.

"Evening, all of you."

Eager to meet the dark-haired beauty already captivating her middle son, Ruth joined the group, resting her hand on Jack's shoulder as her gaze drifted around the table.

"Mom," the boys greeted her in unison.

"Hi, Ruth," Nancy smiled up at her mother-in-law.

"Is he behaving himself tonight?" Ruth asked with a broad smile.

Nancy returned her smile with one as broad.

"All the boys are behaving tonight," she laughed, her eyes dancing around the table. "But I must admit, this one's getting a bit fidgety."

Shifting in her chair and rubbing her belly, Nancy sought a comfortable position, failing miserably. Her eyes following Nancy's hand, Madison paused, detecting movement. Had the baby just moved? Her eyes widened in wonder. Following Madison's eyes, Nancy nodded.

"Yes, he just moved," she said, immediately guessing that Madison did not have any children of her own.

For some reason, she'd already suspected it, but watching Madison stare at her belly only confirmed her suspicion. The baby picked that moment to make his presence clearly known, causing Nancy to grimace as she shifted again in her chair. Jack was on his feet immediately, followed closely by Jeremy.

"Time to take you home, sweetheart," Jack announced, helping his wife up from the chair.

Is it time? Madison wondered.

"I'm fine, really," Nancy quickly assured the table. "I think dinner woke him up, is all."

But the idea of lying down in their big feather bed—oh, yeah, she was all for that!

"But I think I would like to go home."

Noticing the room had suddenly quieted, Ruth glanced around the crowded restaurant. Concerned faces watched as the very pregnant woman moved slowly toward the door. Around the room, men rose from their chairs, ready to help if necessary. Like most nights, there wasn't a single person in there who didn't know Nancy and her family. The benefits of a small town.

"Everything's fine, fellas," Ruth assured them, her voice carrying easily as she followed Jack and Nancy to the door.

Sitting back down, it was only a moment before conversations resumed around the room.

"Call me when you get home," Ruth instructed Jack as she helped Nancy with her coat.

Nodding as he pulled his own coat on, Jack wrapped a protective arm around Nancy as the two left the restaurant.

Watching the family scene play out in front of her, Madison nursed her coffee. Their love and concern for each other was strong and clear, and she wondered for a moment what it would be like to have family like that. Spending as much time alone as she did, watching this family together was an experience, to be sure. Her eyes drifted around the room. In fact, when was the last time she'd even been in such a crowded place? No, she brought a whole new meaning to being a loner, dealing one-on-one being more to her liking. And even then, a sniper rifle usually separated them.

She didn't know her targets; she didn't establish relationships with them. She took a job, executed it, and moved on. Never did she stop to consider that the target might have a family, let alone friends. In her line of work, thinking about those things only got you killed. And she had no intention of letting that happen to her.

Just the same, she sipped her coffee thoughtfully; she was happy no one here was her target.

"Well, that about covers it for our excitement around here," Jeremy laughed, sitting back down.

Pleased Madison didn't appear to be in any hurry to leave now that Jack and Nancy had left, he took Jack's vacated seat so he'd have a better view of this new girl in town. Relieved to have her space back, Madison matched Jeremy's curious stare with her own. While his gaze was undeniably direct, it didn't bother her, and she took no offense. For a moment, they played a silent game of "who could stare who down first," breaking it off only when Mary returned with Jeremy's dinner. With a losing smile for Madison and an offhanded thanks to Mary, Jeremy attacked his steak dinner with a vengeance.

Not wanting to leave but not having a reason to linger, Mary pulled her lovesick gaze from Jeremy to glance at Madison.

"Can I get you something else?" Mary asked, her tone flat and dull, clearly not caring if Madison wanted anything or not.

The girl did a horrible job at hiding her feelings, Madison thought, annoyed. Wishing she could say something to Mary about her less-than-enthusiastic attitude toward her other customers, Madison kept silent; it wasn't her place. Literally.

You're only here for a night, she reminded herself. *Leave it alone.*

"I'd love a coffee to go please," Madison said, wondering if Mary had even heard her since she'd turned her gaze back to Jeremy.

Did he even know this girl was mooning over him? He had to! Especially as Mary wasn't doing anything to hide the fact!

"Sure," Mary finally said when Jeremy still didn't glance her way, concentrating instead on his dinner.

And with a heavy sigh, Mary turned back toward the kitchen.

"The girl's got a serious crush on you," Madison couldn't help pointing out.

Jeremy just nodded, popping another piece of steak into his mouth. At first glance, Madison had pegged Mary as being at least ten—maybe fifteen—years younger than Jeremy, so it wasn't likely that they'd been an item before and she was mooning over their breakup.

"Why?"

Madison's blunt question had Jeremy putting down his knife and fork as he considered her question. Actually, he was considering Madison in general. He'd known right away that she was different, and so far she wasn't disappointing him. Her direct approach was refreshing, if not slightly unnerving. Most women he'd met danced around direct subjects, such as Mary's infatuation. But not this woman—she attacked it head-on. He sat back, his eyes again meeting and holding hers. Not backing down, Madison held his gaze again.

"You certainly are a breath of fresh air," Jeremy finally said before picking up his silverware again.

Madison sat quietly.

"But to answer your question, I really have no idea why Mary's so taken with me. It's not like I'm the only single guy around here," he continued, his eyes drifting around the room before coming back to Madison. "And there are definitely more guys who're much younger than me too."

Popping another mouthful of food into his mouth, he watched her as he chewed. His mother had been serious when she'd raised her boys to not talk with their mouths full, and right about now, he was thankful for that. It gave him the perfect excuse just to look at Madison. Swallowing, he reached for his beer, washing down his food.

"I've never been anything other than nice to her," he felt compelled to add, taking another swig of his beer. "I've never led her on."

And he'd just told her that because why? Because, he blinked, something in her stare made him. Okay, that was just plain weird. He looked away. The woman hadn't said anything else, yet he felt like he had to confess everything to her! No, he quickly corrected himself; he wanted to tell her everything. Oh, yeah, this was definitely weird.

Accepting his answer, Madison just nodded, not wanting to question why his answer was so important to her.

Jesus, she thought, leaning back in her chair. What the hell was happening to her?

It's gotta be the mountain air, she told herself, *it's messing with my mind. As soon as I get back to work, everything will be fine.*

And her mind turning to the reason for her being there in the first place coming back to her, Madison reached into her coat pocket for her wallet.

Time to get back to it, she decided, glancing around in search of Mary.

Clearly she was not going to get her coffee here, so she might as well head back to the hotel; at least she knew there'd be coffee there.

Finishing his dinner, Jeremy sat back, happily full. Glancing around, he smiled as his mother returned to their table. Being called back to the bar after Jack and Nancy had left to deal with some potentially unruly patrons, Ruth had handled the matter quickly and efficiently before slipping away again. Dropping into the empty chair next to Madison, she instantly spotted Madison's wallet.

"Your money's not welcome here," Ruth announced with a smile.

"I beg your pardon?"

Surprised, Madison quickly shut her mouth, which she was sure was hanging open. Just one more thing she wasn't used to . . . someone paying for her.

"Thank you, but that's really not necessary . . ." Madison began, surprised into silence when Ruth laid a soft yet worn hand over hers.

"I know, but you're our guest. Your money's not welcome here," Ruth repeated softly yet firmly.

Having instantly recognized Madison as being a fiercely independent woman, Ruth wasn't surprised by her reaction—and was actually secretly pleased by it.

"Thank you," Madison said softly, returning Ruth's smile with one of her own. "Thank you very much."

Where the hell had the lump in her throat come from for God's sake? And why had this simple gesture touched her so? Because . . . when was the last time she'd actually been around complete strangers who were just plain nice? It'd been a long time; that was for damn sure! Gazing around the crowded room again, catching a few people looking curiously her way, Madison came back to Ruth. Without questioning it, Madison instinctively knew that there was no hidden agenda here—that Ruth's offer to pay for her dinner was nothing more than a friendly gesture to a waylaid traveler. She smiled. It was a nice feeling.

Finally returning with Madison's coffee, Mary placed the Styrofoam cup in front of her, along with two creamers.

Better late than never, Madison thought idly before thanking Mary.

"You're welcome," Mary murmured, practically ignoring Madison as her eyes devoured Jeremy yet again.

Biting her tongue, Madison turned to Jeremy, who again appeared oblivious what was going on around him.

"Thank you again for dinner," Madison smiled sweetly, ignoring Mary as she rose gracefully from her chair. "I guess I'll head back to the hotel. I need to get some stuff done before flying out tomorrow."

"Flying out tomorrow?" Mary's ears perked up, and seeing the opportunity to impress Jeremy fall into her lap, she turned squarely to Madison, "Heavens! The chances of you flying out tomorrow are next to nil!"

Madison's eyes widened briefly. Ruth glared at Mary, standing up quickly when the girl ignored her.

"This storm is going to drop a boatload of snow, you won't be going anywhere for days!"

"Days?" Madison blurted before she could catch herself. She turned to Jeremy, "Days? Seriously?"

She'd been prepared for delays, but Jack hadn't said anything about her being stuck here for days! Her mind kicked into high gear. If this was, indeed, the case, Madison needed to call Sarah immediately. Timetables were going to have to be altered, plans adjusted. Mentally calculating the time difference, Madison frowned; it was the middle of the night there now. Damn!

"Wait a second," Jeremy said firmly, glaring at Mary, "we don't know anything for sure yet!"

"But the storm, it's grounded . . ." Mary stammered, shocked by the angry look Jeremy aimed at her. *What the hell?* "You're always the first person to warn people about the storms here," she rushed on, pointing a painted finger at Madison, "why are you coddling her?"

Coddling me? Anger surged through Madison as she turned on Mary.

Only because the younger girl didn't know whom she'd just insulted did Madison resist the urge to slap the girl. Coddling her? Never in her life had she been coddled! Never would she be either!

"I beg your pardon," Madison growled, her eyes bright with anger.

Clearly, Mary needed to learn some manners and respect.

"Coddle me? Do you even know me?"

Mary just shrugged her shoulders, still focused only on Jeremy. Her nonchalant action had both Madison and Jeremy wanting to throttle the girl.

"Watch what you say there, girl," Jeremy warned softly, "you're insulting our guest."

Blinking in surprise, Mary paused; he'd never used that tone with her before. Throwing caution to the wind, Mary rushed on unknowingly into dangerous territory.

"Guest? She's only here because the flights were grounded! If the weather hadn't changed, Jack would have flown her up north, and she wouldn't even be here now and you never would have met her!"

And therein lay the problem. On a roll, Mary finally turned to face Madison only to immediately find herself shut down by the iciest of looks from the coldest, brightest, angriest sapphire-blue eyes Mary had ever seen. Her mouth open, no words emerged as Mary found herself frozen in place. In all her years of waiting tables and dealing with angry, difficult customers, never had anyone looked at her like this! And never had anyone made her suddenly fear for her very life!

Mary blinked. *Oh my god, who is this lady?*

"I'm sorry!" Mary blurted before whirling around and dashing toward the kitchen.

Only when she was safely on the other side of the kitchen door did Mary stop and take a deep breath, praying her heart would stop racing.

Pushing away from the door, Mary made her way through the kitchen, steadfastly ignoring the curious stares from her coworkers. Snatching up her coat and purse, she disappeared out the back entrance without so much as a backward glance or an explanation. What could she say anyway? It didn't take a genius to know she'd just buried herself, losing both the man she believed she loved as well as the job she knew she loved.

Her head down in the falling snow, Mary slowly made her way home. She needed to get out of town, either by plane or by truck. Flipping open her phone and dialing a number, Mary disappeared into the snow.

CHAPTER 5

"OH, MADISON, I'M so sorry about Mary's outburst," Ruth exclaimed sadly, watching Mary disappear into the kitchen.

What had possessed the girl to go off on Madison that way? Ruth wondered, immediately answering her own question as her eyes fell on her son.

She knew Jeremy had never done anything to lead the young girl on, but that didn't matter. Young girls' hearts were very easily broken, and no doubt Mary's was shattered.

"Yeah, me too," Jeremy chimed in before quickly coming to the girl's defense. "She's really a good kid, I don't know what got into her."

Madison just stared at Jeremy. Of course, he knew; he was just being nice. She smiled knowingly.

"It's okay," Madison said, pushing away her anger, "I understand. These things happen."

Not really, but she thought it sounded good. Picking up her coffee and realizing it was cold, Madison put it back down with a sigh. Figures!

"Whatever the weather, though, I do need to get back and get some work done."

She reached for her coat, only to find Jeremy there holding it out for her. Sliding her arms in and tossing him a thankful smile, she zipped up the coat. Besides needing to call Sarah, Madison just plain wanted out of the restaurant. While she'd felt many curious eyes on her since walking in, Mary's little scene now had everyone's eyes on her. And that was something Madison was seriously not comfortable with. Especially as she hadn't yet been able to identify the man from the Inn. Was he in the restaurant? She'd scoured the place, but if he was there, she hadn't seen him—a fact that bothered her more than she cared to let on.

No, she thought idly, *It's time to get moving.*

"I'll walk you back," Jeremy announced, grabbing his coat.

Wanting to protest, Madison remained silent, especially when Ruth agreed with his idea.

"I know you can find your way," Jeremy rushed on, "but the weather being what it is, I'd feel better making sure you got back okay."

Touched by his thoughtfulness and appreciating him realizing that she was, indeed, capable, Madison smiled, turning back to Ruth, thanking her again for everything.

Having liked Madison immediately, Ruth pulled the surprised woman into her arms, hugging her tightly. Later, when things quieted down and the restaurant was closed, would Ruth let herself consider the cold, calculating look that Madison had given Mary before the girl had fled. Oh, yes, there was much more to Madison than met the eye—of that Ruth was sure. Ethel had been right when she'd called Ruth earlier. This new girl was something else!

The sound of breaking glass interrupting their farewell, both women turned sharply at the sound. Two men sitting at the bar were beginning what promised to be a nasty argument if the shot glass flying across the bar was any indication. Setting Madison away, Ruth smiled ruefully, already moving away.

"Work calls," Ruth said with a sigh.

"Can I help?" the question was out before Madison could stop herself.

The look of surprise on Ruth's face had her instantly regretting it—more so when the look on Jeremy's face mirrored that of his mother's. Shit.

"No, thank you, dear," Ruth smiled, adding this new tidbit to the things she'd think about later when she had the time. "I've got it covered," she assured Madison, and with a wave of her hand, Ruth wound her way through the crowd toward the big, burly men.

Laying a strong hand on each man's shoulder, whatever it was she said quickly had the men calming down. Madison was seriously impressed. Ruth hadn't hesitated to approach the angry men, instead going at them with a fierce determination. She could relate.

"Your mom's one tough lady," Madison said, turning to Jeremy.

"That she is," he said proudly.

Taking Madison gently by the arm, he steered her easily toward the door, stopping momentarily to talk to friends who greeted him in passing before moving on. He and Madison would be the subject of every conversation before they were even out the door, especially if the look of envy on his friends' faces were any indication. Pausing at the entrance, Jeremy steeled himself for the burst of cold air he knew was about to hit them before quickly turning to be sure Madison was securely zipped up as well.

"Ready?"

When she nodded, Jeremy reached around her, pushing open the big door.

The cold rushing in had Madison struggling not to take an instinctive step backward. Christ, it was cold! But it was the snow that had her gawking. Despite darkness having fallen, she quickly realized that easily three inches of snow had already fallen! From their vantage point on the deck, Madison watched the snow falling in the white light thrown off by the nearby street lamp. It was unbelievably beautiful!

"How long was I in there for?" Madison exclaimed, nearly bounding off the deck into the falling snow.

Turning in graceful circles, her arms stretched out, she was quickly blanketed with snow. Frozen in place, Jeremy could only watch Madison—her head thrown back, her smile wide, as the snow fell around her. Feeling like he'd been sucker punched, he just stood there, watching her turn in circles. Did she have any idea how lovely she was? Jesus! What was he thinking? She was passing through, for

Christ's sake! Now was not the time or the place to think romantic thoughts! But God, she really was beautiful.

Coming to a stop, Madison paused. Why was Jeremy just staring? Glancing around but finding no one near them, she turned back to him, her head tilting to the side.

"Hello? Earth to Jeremy? What are you staring at?"

If he didn't say something soon, she was going to smack him!

Realizing she was talking to him, Jeremy snapped out of his daze, blinking.

"Sorry," he rushed on, stepping off the porch and into the falling snow with her.

Turning her around and looping her arm through his, he led her down the snow-covered street.

"I got lost in the view, I guess," he said quietly, tossing her what he hoped was an easy smile.

He'd examine his feelings later when he was alone.

"And to answer your question, you weren't in there long."

He tilted his head back, enjoying the feel of the snow on his face.

"This is how it snows here. No light flurries for us! It's all or nothing up here!"

"So I'm seeing," Madison laughed, using Jeremy's big, solid body as a blockade as much as she could against the cold.

Squeezing her arm against him, Jeremy enjoyed having her close as they trudged through the snow in companionable silence. Coming to the corner, Madison found herself pulling Jeremy to a stop.

Gazing down at her in the dim light, Jeremy had the incredible urge to just turn her into his arms and kiss her. He shook his head, chasing away the enticing idea.

"Let's walk for a bit," Madison surprised them both by saying. "Unless, of course, I'm keeping you from something?" *Or someone.*

Why hadn't it occurred to her that he might have other plans for the evening? What the hell was happening to her? It had to be the mountain air. She had work to do, plans to be double-checked. And she needed to check in with Sarah. Yet all that was quickly pushed aside, the idea of taking a leisurely walk through the beautiful falling snow too much to resist. Especially when it was on the arm of handsome mountain man!

Admit it, she told herself, *you aren't ready to let him go yet.*

She found herself holding her breath as she waited for his reply.

"No, no, I don't have any place I need to be," Jeremy quickly assured her.

And even if he had, he thought wryly, he would have changed those plans in a heartbeat!

Madison would be leaving when the snow stopped; he knew that. But until that time came, he thought, gazing down at her again, he was going to spend as much time with her as possible. God, how he hoped it'd snow for a few days!

"Sure you're warm enough to stay out for a while?" he quickly asked, not wanting her to get too cold. Although the thought of having to warm her up didn't hurt his feelings!

"I'm fine."

Thank God, she'd put on her long underwear! Tossing him a mischievous smile, she tugged him forward.

"It's just too beautiful to go inside just yet. But trust me, if it gets too cold for me, I'll be the first to let you know!" Although she knew the likelihood of that happening was close to nil.

In the course of her career, she'd spent countless hours outside and in much-colder settings. No, she loved this weather! Tilting her head back, the falling snow coating her long, dark lashes, Madison sighed happily. Maybe getting snowed in for a day or two wouldn't be so bad, especially if she could spend the time in the company of the burly man next to her. She could use a little downtime, a break from work. And her target certainly wasn't going anyplace.

Strolling leisurely along the snow-covered sidewalk, Madison found herself surprised to see so many people out and about. Thinking the snowstorm would have driven them inside, she quickly learned otherwise. Snow or no snow, Jeremy had readily explained, people still had to live their lives. Dealing with the weather was part of the charm—or the challenge—of living in the far outreaches of Canada, he went on to further explain.

That certainly makes sense, Madison thought as they continued on in companionable silence.

Noticing a large pickup approaching them, Jeremy scooped up some snow, quickly making a solid snowball. Throwing it easily at the truck, his aim was dead-on, the snowball hitting the windshield squarely in the center. Jeremy laughed **as** the driver gave **him** the finger in grand fashion before driving off .

"I take it you knew him?" she asked with a smile.

"A friend," Jeremy laughed, glancing over his shoulder.

"Should I be worried he's going to turn around?" Madison asked, also glancing over her shoulder.

"Nah. He'll get me later, when I least expect it."

Of course, Madison thought. That'd be what she would do.

Continuing on, she found herself glancing back from time to time. Just in case.

"I told you, he won't be back," Jeremy said, catching her looking over her shoulder.

"Sorry, old habits," Madison replied automatically. Crap!

Tossing him a sheepish grin, she kept walking.

"Ah huh."

Strolling along in easy silence, Jeremy glanced at Madison out of the corner of his eye. He found himself seriously intrigued. Since leaving the restaurant, he'd waved and talked to at least half a dozen people, and not once had she asked him who they were or question why he hadn't introduced her. She'd been content to just stand back and watch—no, he corrected himself—observe. In fact, if he didn't know better, he'd swear that she'd *studied* everyone he talked to. He had the distinct feeling that if asked, she'd probably be able to describe every single person he'd talked to. And probably waved at too. Okay, that definitely wasn't a trait he found in many women. Or people in general, for that matter. Time to dig a little deeper into the mysterious woman walking beside him.

"You know," Jeremy began tentatively, "you offering to help my mom with those guys back at the bar, that was cool." In for a penny, in for a pound. "A surprise, but cool just the same. Would you really have taken on those guys?"

Wondering when he was going to say something about that, Madison concentrated on watching where she was walking. She knew she never should have offered her assistance. But she'd reacted out of habit.

"I spent some time working in a bar," she lied easily. "Old habits, I guess. It just popped out of me." Well, that was true enough, anyway. "I'm just glad your mother didn't take me up on it!"

Relieved was more like it, she thought, *because if you thought me just being there caused a scene, seeing what I could have done to those guys would really have blown your mind!*

There it was again: "old habits." Tilting his head, Jeremy let the snow fall over his face. God, he hoped it kept snowing; he wanted to find out what made this woman tick! More importantly, he wanted to know what those "old habits" really were. And where had they come from. One thing was for damn sure, though: those guys back at the bar had no idea how lucky they were to not have come up against Madison. If there was one thing Jeremy was positive about, it was that there wasn't a helpless bone in Madison's body!

Feeling his eyes on her, Madison searched for something to say. Idle conversation wasn't her strong point.

"Is it just you and Jack?"

Oh, God, she nearly groaned. Did that sound as lame to him as it did to her?

Recognizing idle conversation when he heard it, Jeremy paused. She didn't seem the type to ask mundane questions. Deciding to see where it would go, he played along.

"Nope, there's five of us." Jeremy nearly laughed when Madison stopped, her mouth hanging open. It was nice knowing he could surprise her, at least a little. "Three boys and two girls, actually."

"Are they all here?"

Gazing up at Jeremy, snow beginning to cover his beard, Madison tried imagining five kids as big as him—at least the boys anyway—and failed miserably. An only child, larger families had always fascinated her. Would she be in the profession she was in if she'd had a brother or sister? Or five of them? Most likely, she decided, thinking of Sarah and her twin brother. Yeah, it most likely wouldn't have mattered if she'd had siblings. She'd probably still kill people for a living. She blinked, chasing away a rare feeling of loneliness.

In the dim light, Jeremy recognized the flash of loneliness in Madison's dark eyes. It didn't matter that he was part of a large family; he still knew the feeling. And wondered why she did.

For a moment they stood still, their eyes locked together. Madison had the sudden urge to lift her hand to his snow-covered face. How would his lips feel against hers? Judging by the way his eyes were glittering in the snow-lit darkness, she sensed their thoughts were running along the same lines. She blinked, looking away hastily.

You're here to do a job, she reminded herself harshly even as her eyes drifted unintentionally back to Jeremy's.

What was it about this man? She'd met lots of men in the course of her career, a few she'd even been briefly involved with. So what if she couldn't remember any of their names, or even their faces, at this very minute? She blinked again. What was it with this guy that had her thoughts going in a million different directions? Whatever it was, she'd have to watch herself carefully; she couldn't afford to make any mistakes, have any more slipups! People died for lesser mistakes; she wasn't about to be one of them. And she wasn't about to jeopardize this man and his family!

Jeremy could all but hear the wheels turning in Madison's mind as he brushed an errant snowflake from his eye. Standing there in the falling snow, at that very moment, with no one around them, he felt like they were the only two on earth.

He nearly gagged. When the hell had he gone soft? And talk about cliché! He nearly laughed, pulling his gaze away from Madison, chasing away the sentimental thoughts. God! Sure, he was the first to admire a pretty face, but he felt like he was being pulled into something deeper—stronger—when he looked at her! What the hell?

The sound of a truck approaching had Jeremy turning, thankful for the interruption. Taking Madison's arm gently, they continued their walk as the truck rolled past them, honking in greeting.

"I guess you know everyone here," Madison commented. She, too, was thankful for the truck's interruption.

"At this time of the year, yeah," Jeremy replied. "As to your question about my family," he smiled easily, comfortable being back on familiar ground, "Jack and I are the only two here year round. The others come during the summer and fall. But they make sure they're long gone before the weather turns."

"So they're not here for long," Madison smiled, knowing the seasons were incredibly short in this part of the world.

"You got that right," Jeremy laughed. "They wouldn't be caught dead up here come the first snow."

His gaze drifted to the mountains just beyond the town limits, still able to see their outline through the falling snow.

"The twins, Lizzy and Sara, are in Vancouver, they're bankers."

Boring job, if there ever was one, but they seemed to like it—a fact that never ceased to amaze Jeremy. The idea of being cooped up in an office all day, he shuddered at the thought.

"They've done well for themselves and seem happy." Pausing, Jeremy sighed. "Then there's Jarod."

Sensing Jeremy needed a little extra time talking about this particular brother, Madison remained silent.

"Jarod's the youngest and definitely the smartest of all of us." He smiled. "He was born blind—a fluke, the doctor said."

Inhaling the winter air deeply, he let it out just as slowly.

"He's never seen any of us, but he knows who's who without even having to touch us. Of course, his other senses are highly developed, like many sight-impaired people. And he's put those senses to good use. He's definitely the best one of us."

Madison smiled, the pride Jeremy felt for his youngest sibling clear and strong in his voice.

"Where's Jarod now?"

"Well," Jeremy began, looping Madison's arm through his again, pulling her close, "let me think. Last I heard, our boy was snorkeling off the Great Barrier Reef in Australia."

He laughed out loud, picturing his brother swimming among the different types of fish, sharks, and stingrays. And no doubt loving every minute of it. Jarod might be blind, but Jeremy knew his brother saw things clearer than anyone else ever would.

"Jarod's a professor of history at University in Sydney, when he's not playing around."

"You've certainly got quite the family!" A twinge of envy snaked through Madison.

"Yeah."

Suddenly missing them, Jeremy made a mental note to call all of them later.

"They're all a pain in the ass, but we love each other." He glanced down at Madison. "What about you? Family anywhere?" A husband? A boyfriend?

Knowing the question was coming, Madison was ready. Normally shying away from talking about herself, she knew she couldn't here. Jeremy was already curious, even slightly suspicious; he'd know she was hiding something if she dodged his question now.

"Nope," she answered easily, "it's just me. I lost my parents years ago."

At least she could be truthful about that. But that didn't mean she was going to go into detail either, though. Besides, telling someone your parents were murdered wasn't the best first-date conversation!

First date? First anything! she quickly corrected herself.

"I'm sorry," Jeremy said quietly.

Squeezing his arm, Madison just nodded.

The cold slowly seeping through her warm clothes, Madison's thoughts turned back to her cozy room at the Inn. The snow was still falling steadily, and suddenly, the idea of being snowed in for maybe a couple of days wasn't so daunting. Especially if it allowed her the chance to use that glorious Jacuzzi tub! She glanced up at Jeremy. When was the last time she'd actually taken a real walk, enjoying herself and relaxed? She couldn't remember. But work beckoned. After she used that tub, of course!

A bloodcurdling scream followed by the sound of trash cans being knocked over filled the air, chasing away all thoughts of Jacuzzi tubs and warm rooms.

CHAPTER 6

SPRINTING OFF IN the direction of the screams, Jeremy prayed it was nothing more than a wild animal wandering through town. Hadn't a cougar been spotted just the other day? Without losing a step, Jeremy pulled the revolver from his waistband. It wasn't enough to kill a cougar, but it might scare it off.

Two steps behind him, Madison's eyes widened at the sudden appearance of the revolver in his hand. Not that she was completely unarmed herself—a knife tucked into its sheath strapped to her lower leg. Confident she could reach it if necessary, she kept pace with Jeremy as they rounded the corner leading into the alley between the buildings. A few steps further, Madison nearly collided with Jeremy as he came to a sliding stop in the snow—his eyes wide, his hand steady, his revolver poised and ready to fire. His free hand snaked out, catching Madison before she could come alongside him.

"No," he whispered, relieved when she stopped.

The last thing he needed was for Madison to barge into the middle of . . . whatever this was. Seconds later Jeremy was shocked to see Mary emerging from the alley.

"Jeremy!" Mary sobbed, stumbling toward him, her bloody hands reaching out for him.

Without a second thought, Jeremy tossed Madison his revolver as he lunged forward, grabbing Mary by the shoulders, catching her before she could collapse in the snow. Holding her at arm's length, he searched for injuries, for the source of the blood, finding neither.

"What happened, Mary? Where are you hurt?" Jeremy demanded quietly.

When Mary didn't immediately answer, he looked past her, frantically searching the dimly lit alley.

"Who else is here?" he asked louder, his hard voice laced with ice.

Focusing on Mary, Jeremy pushed away the realization that he'd just been every kind of stupid, tossing Madison his revolver. If there was trouble, she wouldn't know what to do! What the hell had he been thinking? He'd acted purely on instinct—instinct that was rarely wrong. He prayed he wouldn't regret his actions.

Unable to speak, Mary sagged under Jeremy's strong grip. Wishing he could pull the girl into his arms, he knew he couldn't. They needed to preserve the evidence on her hands as best they could. He shook her gently, trying to get her to focus on him. Her hair, wet from the falling snow, was plastered around her face. Damn it, he couldn't tell if she was hurt or not! He growled in frustration. He needed to get her out of there, to get her where he could better examine her; but not wanting to turn his back to the alley, he hesitated. Beyond the knocked-over trash cans, it didn't look like anything else was disturbed, but he knew that didn't mean someone or something wasn't hiding back there. Standing completely still, he strained to hear anything out of the ordinary. A truck in the distance and the sound of the falling snow was all he heard. His heart sank. Mary's hands were covered in blood; she was in a dark alley; and there didn't appear to be anyone or anything else around. Someone or something was dead. He was sure of it. And he was willing to bet that—even worse—it was a someone, not a something. Damn!

"Take her," Jeremy said, thinking to push Mary into Madison's arms, only to find Madison creeping forward, the revolver steady in her outstretched hands. What the . . . ? She was holding the gun like a pro! And moving like . . . like someone who clearly knew what she was doing! A million questions flooded his mind, but he kept silent, his eyes glued to Madison as she moved silently into the alley.

Knowing she was doing the worst possible thing by getting involved, Madison crept silently into the alley, the gun poised and ready. Jeremy had his hands full and rather than take Mary from him, as he'd wanted, Madison reacted as only she could: taking control while assessing the situation. There was just enough light, and as she came upon the overturned trash cans, she stopped—part of her was surprised; part of her, not. Clearly jaded from years of being a professional assassin, the sight of the bloodied body sprawled in the snow didn't faze her in the least.

Quickly accessing the beaten and bloody body, she tucked the gun into her back waistband; she wouldn't be needing it. There was no one else around. She turned slowly back to Jeremy.

"He's dead," Madison announced quietly.

Not questioning why she'd put the gun away, Jeremy glanced at Mary before wrapping an arm around the sobbing girl, slowly guiding her out of the alley. Pulling his cell phone from his jacket pocket, he punched a number, speaking quietly.

Moments later, blue lights could be seen bouncing off the snowbanks as headlights cut through the still-falling snow. His arm still wrapped around Mary, Jeremy waved down the two police SUVs as they approached, an ambulance right behind them. Staying out of the way, Madison remained silent while Jeremy spoke quietly with the policemen. EMTs jumped from the ambulance, quickly assessing Mary before ushering her up into the ambulance. Moments after the rear door slammed shut, the ambulance drove off, its lights flashing.

Odd, Madison thought, *they didn't use the siren.*

"Madison," Jeremy called, "don't move for a minute."

Of course, she wasn't going to move, she thought. She knew the police needed to separate her footprints in the snow from Mary's and those of the victim's. Did Jeremy think she was stupid? She paused. Of course not. But he also didn't know what she did for a living. And he had no way of knowing that this most definitely was not the first crime scene she'd ever been involved with. While she would have preferred to keep that information to herself a while longer, given what had just happened, she knew she'd be answering questions soon enough.

"No worries," she quickly assured him, standing perfectly still as the policeman approached her.

Jeremy's revolver warm against her back, she hoped she wouldn't need to produce it. It was going to be tough enough explaining to Jeremy why she was so adept at handling the revolver; she didn't need the police asking her questions. To her relief, the officer only nodded at her before turning his attention to the body. Shining his flashlight around, Madison remained where she was until the officer was able to determine which footprints were hers. Clearly a different size from Mary and the victim, he waved her off, and Madison hurried back to Jeremy.

Wrapping his arm around her waist, Jeremy felt the outline of his gun against her back. He'd get it back from her later; now was definitely not the time or the place! When he retrieved his gun from her, they were going to be alone and in a very warm place. Especially as he definitely had a few questions for this woman who was fast becoming more mysterious than the crime scene they'd stumbled upon!

Remaining silent, aware that Jeremy's hand was resting against his gun, Madison stood quietly beside him. She knew he had questions, and rightly so. Half listening to him talking to the policeman, ideas as to how she'd explain herself ran through her mind. Her cover didn't include any background regarding firearms; she'd have to be very careful. If she could talk to Sarah before answering his questions, she might be able to have her cover altered to include that now-very-important fact.

"If you need me or Madison," Jeremy said to the officer, his arm tightening around her, "you can reach us at the Inn. Madison's a guest there."

So much for having a chance to call Sarah. Clearly, Jeremy planned to stick close to her for the time being. Crap. But Madison admitted wryly: she'd have done the same thing. Finishing up with the officer and smoothly turning Madison, they headed back to the Inn.

Thankful to find the lobby empty, Madison started toward the coffee machine, the idea of a hot chocolate suddenly very appealing. And she hoped doing something normal might ease Jeremy's mind a bit. Wrong. She hadn't taken a step when Jeremy caught her by the wrist and with a shake of his head steered her toward the stairs. Knowing arguing would be futile, Madison allowed him to lead her upstairs to her room—where, handing over her key to Jeremy, she was briskly ushered into her nice, warm room. Glad she'd left the fireplace on, Madison welcomed the warmth of the room as she turned to face Jeremy. They stared at each other for a moment, neither one ready to break the silence.

"Mind handing me my gun, please."

Jeremy's eyes bore into hers, his body tense, his voice deadly quiet. Maybe he should have done this in the lobby—at least there she'd be less likely to do something dangerous. Jesus! What was wrong with him? What happened to his calm and rational thinking? Evidently, it had gone right out the window where Madison was concerned!

"Nice and easy, if you don't mind."

Only when Madison smoothly handed him the gun, grip first, did Jeremy relax. Unloading it quickly, his actions smooth and practiced, he slid the empty gun into his waistband.

"Exactly what kind of research are you up here doing again?" Jeremy asked quietly, silently berating himself for not asking more questions earlier.

He never should have just assumed. Climate research didn't usually require knowledge in handling firearms. And if he wasn't mistaken, she clearly was an expert in handling a gun. Shit.

Her mind whirling, Madison forced herself to relax, knowing Jeremy would pick up on it if she didn't. Taking a deep breath, her eyes drifted around the room, a smile dashing across her face. Funny how earlier she'd thought the room was spacious. Now, with Jeremy standing a few feet away, the room suddenly felt very small. What the hell?

Catching her smile, Jeremy remained silent while readily admitting to himself that with each passing second, the woman before him was becoming more and more intriguing to him. He wasn't sure if that was good or bad.

"I'm up here doing research on the polar bears," Madison finally said, her eyes coming back to him.

Would he accept that explanation? Or would he want more information? She decided to wait and see, no sense in volunteering any more information if it wasn't absolutely necessary. The simpler, the better—for right now, anyway.

"You handled yourself pretty good back there too," she added quickly, hoping to deflect the attention away from herself, at least for the moment.

Recognizing what she was trying to do, Jeremy just nodded and wondered if his silence would make her squirm at all. He doubted it, but it was worth a try. Their eyes locked together, they mentally challenged the other to back down. Moments passed before Jeremy looked away with a wry smile.

"You're one cool customer lady, I'll give you that," he admitted. "What say we sit down and hash this out?"

Madison's answer was a raised eyebrow.

"I'll show you mine if you show me yours? What do you say?"

Jeremy was relieved when Madison laughed, while at the same time choosing to ignore how her low, husky laugh washed over him.

"Well, since you put it that way," Madison's eyes glittered, and Jeremy forced his gut to unclench. "Where?"

"What?" Caught off guard, Jeremy stared.

"Where do you want to talk?"

Waving her arm, she pulled Jeremy's attention away from her and to the size of the room. And to the king-size bed taking up much of the room. Yeah, they couldn't talk here. He'd never be able to concentrate! He smiled sheepishly.

"How about my place?"

At least there he had a living room. And a bedroom. On another floor. *Pull your mind out of the gutter, man!*

Shaking his head, pushing the image of Madison sprawled in his own king-size bed as far away as possible, Jeremy cleared his throat.

"My place sound okay?"

Because while the idea of getting her in bed was appealing, he still found her background more so.

Yeah, and you keep telling yourself that, old man! He nearly laughed, glad that Madison couldn't read his mind!

His place? She glanced around her room. Okay, so she really didn't want to talk to him here, but did she dare go to his place? She instinctively knew she could trust him; that wasn't the problem. No, she admitted, the problem was her. And her hands that were itching to touch him. She nearly groaned.

Well, it was either here or his place, what other options did they have? The lobby wouldn't be safe or wise. Too many prying eyes and ears. The restaurant? Too crowded and noisy. And she'd attract too much attention there being the visitor from out of town that by now everyone knew about. She glanced at the window at the still-falling snow.

"How far away is your place?" she asked hesitantly, and he smiled.

"Literally up the street. It won't take long, we can walk there."

Ominous silence filled the room as they remembered their earlier walk. All thoughts of sex and romance vanished as the imprint of his gun against his back reminded Jeremy of why he was there.

"I guess it's your place then," Madison conceded, reaching for her jacket. "But I'm getting a hot chocolate for the walk."

The last house on the street, the log cabin sat nestled among gigantic fir trees draped in a soft coat of freshly fallen snow. Trudging through the ever-deepening snow, as promised, their walk didn't take long; and brushing off the snow from their coats, Jeremy ushered Madison into his house. Heat emanating from a wood-burning stove somewhere close by, *comfortable* and *welcoming* were the first thoughts that popped into Madison's head. Shrugging off her coat and following Jeremy's lead of hanging it on the peg by the back door, she tugged off her boots, smiling her thanks when he handed her a pair of slippers. The man was prepared—that was for damn sure, she thought, even more surprised when she found that the slippers fit pretty well. Were they from a previous inhabitant of the house? She chased away the thought. Seriously? Now was not the time to be thinking about that!

Following Jeremy into the kitchen, she climbed onto a stool at the breakfast bar situated in the middle of the spacious room as he made a beeline for the coffeemaker on the counter beside the sink. Finishing her hot chocolate that she'd made before leaving the Inn, she nodded when he offered her a refill. Grabbing a hot chocolate K-cup, he flipped on the machine before turning, leaning against the counter to stare at her silently. For a moment, the only sound was that of the water heating up in the machine.

Ignoring him for the moment, Madison gazed around the kitchen. New and shiny appliances blended in smoothly with the rustic woodwork surrounding them, reinforcing her earlier feeling of being welcome and comfortable. It was very relaxing. She suspected that'd been his intention.

"I like your place," she said approvingly.

Jeremy smiled and nodded his thanks but remained silent.

"My apartment's about as boring as you can get," she added, wondering what made her say that.

"And where would that be?"

Turning back around and pulling a mug from the cabinet, Jeremy popped the K-cup into the machine, hitting the brew button. Feeling Madison's eyes boring into his back, Jeremy fought the urge to turn around, concentrating instead on the hot chocolate pouring into the cup. Grabbing another mug and K-cup for himself, he set her mug aside before making his own hot chocolate, wishing it was something stronger. Turning back around, the steaming mugs in his hand, he placed hers in front of her. She still hadn't answered his question.

Cradling the hot mug between her hands, Madison welcomed the heat and the distraction. She knew she had some explaining to do; there was no getting around that. But how much should she tell him? How much could she really tell him? And could she trust him? The answer came immediately. Yes. There was something about the man; she'd known immediately—and probably more importantly, instinctively—that he was a man to be trusted. The number of people she felt that way about was few; in fact, she could count them on one hand. How sad was that? Blowing on her hot chocolate, she took a small sip, the hot liquid instantly warming her. Wondering at the urge to just tell him everything, Madison glanced up, not surprised to find him staring intently at her. He'd asked her a simple question, and she needed to answer it as simply as possible.

"Chicago," she said finally, taking another sip of her hot chocolate.

"Chicago," he echoed, "then this weather shouldn't bother you!"

She shook her head. "Nope, it doesn't bother me in the least," she chuckled easily. "That and I actually love the cold."

His eyes widened briefly. Not many women admitted that! Guessing his thoughts, she smiled.

"I know, I'm a freak of nature. I'll take this weather over the hot and humid stuff any day, anywhere!"

Jeremy laughed, surprising her.

"I'm right there with you."

His declaration pleased her, and she found herself warming up to him a fraction more.

"If I had a choice between the islands and here . . ." his gaze drifted around the room before coming back to her. "Well, I guess you know the answer to that one."

"I do! No one in their right mind would be up here if they didn't love it," Madison declared.

"Are you implying that I'm not in my right mind?" Jeremy exclaimed, the horrified look on his face making Madison laugh out loud.

"If the shoe, or rather the snow boot, fits! . . . What are you doing?" she stammered, watching Jeremy lean around the edge of the breakfast bar. "What are you looking at?"

"The slippers you've got on and the fact that you're sitting here, basically in the middle of nowhere, in the middle of a raging snowstorm. Tell me again, who's not in their right mind?"

He had her there, and giving it up, Madison burst out laughing. Joining in, Jeremy delighted in watching Madison's eyes sparkle as she laughed freely. Sensing she didn't laugh often, he let the sound of her husky, happy laugh roll over him, knowing he'd never forget the sound of it.

"You're an unusual guy, Jeremy," Madison said minutes later.

When was the last time she'd laughed so much and so easily? And with a complete stranger? What was happening to her? Was she so lonely that she was becoming vulnerable?

No, she quickly discounted the thought. No, it was something else. There was something about this man; she sensed he understood her better than anyone had before. Was that possible?

"Oh?" Drinking his hot chocolate, he hid his surprise at her comment.

"Yeah," she said, choosing not to elaborate, knowing full well her silence would irritate him.

But it couldn't be helped, not yet anyway. Until she had a better idea of what was going on and why she was feeling this way—the less she said about her own personal feelings, the better. She concentrated on her hot chocolate.

Knowing he wasn't going to get any more out of her, Jeremy squashed his irritation. Deciding the best course of action would be to change the subject, he moved on; he'd come back to this later.

"So you're from Chicago, and you're up here doing research on polar bears."

And we're back to that, Madison sighed.

"You're pretty far from the coast, we don't have polar bears around here."

She fought the urge to tense up, focusing on keeping her expression neutral.

"I was flying there when the weather grounded me," she reminded him.

The urge to pat herself on the back at her quick retort almost made her smile. Oh, yeah, she was going to have to stay on her toes with this man! This man didn't miss much!

Nodding, Jeremy didn't comment, instead deciding he'd talk to Jack in the morning about his passenger and her destination. Jack

65

was a stickler for the rules; he would have filed a flight plan. And Jack, being the professional he was, he'd never deviate from that plan. Doing something like that up here was nothing short of suicidal, anyway. Jack knew that better than anyone, having led more than a few search-and-rescue missions into the mountains after some idiot pilot went missing after deciding to change course without notifying anyone. More than a few inexperienced pilots had thought that just because they were in the middle of nowhere that a flight plan wasn't as important as it would be if they were flying in a more populated area. Boy, were those guys wrong! Too bad more than a few had died before truly realizing the error of their ways.

"Where'd you learn to handle a gun so well?"

Watching her intently, Jeremy admired Madison's ability to stay so cool.

Oh, yeah, she was a professional, all right. But just what kind of professional? She wasn't with law enforcement—of that he was certain. Special Forces? His eyes skimmed over her. Despite the bulky navy-blue sweater over the red turtleneck, athletic came to mind.

Athletic with some really nice curves, he thought, approvingly.

When Madison didn't immediately answer, he repeated the question before settling back against the counter, ready to wait her out. He hoped he wouldn't have to wait long; her silence wasn't necessarily a good thing.

Knowing he was expecting an answer, Madison stared at Jeremy for a moment before her eyes danced away, immediately reminding Jeremy of a kid in school who was stalling for time before having to answer the teacher. Was she trying to come up with a lie, or was she stalling before telling him the truth? He honestly had no idea what to expect.

She wanted to tell him the truth, but what could she say? That she was up there to kill a guy? Yeah, probably not the best thing to blurt out. But she'd already given more than enough away about herself. Jeremy wasn't going to settle for just any answer. He was a smart man; he'd see right through any cock and bull story she might try to give him. So how much could she tell him? Damn, she wished she'd had time to talk to Sarah; that would have made all this so much easier!

"I've been handling guns since I was a kid," Madison finally answered, her eyes coming back to him.

CHAPTER 7

IRONICALLY, IT WAS the truth. At the tender age of twelve, her father had taken Madison to his gun club for the very first time; she'd been captivated by firearms ever since. Along with bonding with her father, it was evident early on that she was a natural, quickly developing the reputation for being a crack shot. Too bad that outside of the gun club, her father practically ignored her. Sadly, she later learned the reason he showered her with attention at the gun club was because he didn't want to be outdone by the other parents whose kids were also there. The fact that his daughter could outshoot practically every boy at the club didn't play into it; he just didn't want anyone knowing that while he loved his daughter in his own way, that he'd secretly always wanted a son. In her father's narrow-minded world, girls were the weaker sex and not good for much—except maybe being eye candy on the arm of a powerful man. Her own mother backed up his opinion, her impeccable bloodlines along with her beauty pageant looks making her the ideal wife and mother. It didn't matter that the woman also had an astounding mind, holding various PhDs in different fields of medicine.

Madison had never understood why her mother allowed her father to treat her like a mindless woman, but she did. Evidently, love made people do crazy things. Her father had always treated her mother well, lavishing her with whatever she wanted, whenever she wanted it—his only expectation that she remain silent unless spoken to when they were out in public. When Madison asked her mother why she allowed her father to control her in such a way, her mother simply pulled Madison behind closed doors, quietly explaining that while she was well aware that she was much more intelligent than her husband, it was also simpler to just not rock the boat. And when Madison met and fell in love with someone someday, that she'd understand that. Rolling her eyes at her mother's explanation, Madison knew she'd never feel the same way her mother did. When she met someone and fell in love, it was going to be on equal ground. Or as much as possible anyway.

Knowing her parents loved her in their own way, Madison also knew they were deeply disappointed when she announced she was not the settling-down type, nor did she have any interest in raising a family. Instead, leaving home as soon as possible, Madison quickly began honing her skills with firearms; and using the photogenic memory that she was sure she'd inherited from her mother, Madison quietly began making a name for herself. Handling some sensitive jobs for secretive people, it wasn't long before she hit Sarah's radar, prompting the woman to seek Madison out for a meeting. Recognizing Madison's talent as well as her desire to belong, Sarah immediately took Madison under her wing, molding and shaping her into the world-renowned assassin she was today.

It was Sarah who told Madison that her parents had been needlessly murdered, comforting Madison as no one else could. It was Sarah who quickly became her sister, her best friend, her confidant, and—Madison smiled to herself—occasionally her partner in crime. Remembering the various jobs they'd worked together, as well as some of the wild fun they'd had, Madison considered Sarah and her twin brother to be her true family.

If only I could call Sarah now! Madison thought frantically, *she'd know what to do, how to handle this particular sticky situation!*

Among other things, Sarah had much better people skills than she did! Madison nearly laughed, wondering what Jeremy would think if she asked, "Do you mind if I use a lifeline?"

Watching her calmly, Jeremy knew without a doubt that there was much more to Madison's story. The simple explanation she'd tried to pawn off on him was nearly laughable! Content to let her squirm for the moment, he pondered his next move. He couldn't very well force her to tell him; she'd only lie. Badly, but she'd lie nonetheless. What else could he do? Pin her up against the wall and threaten her? The image of them fighting had his body hardening.

Okay, you're just warped! He blinked, pushing that particular thought out of his mind.

But if it did get physical, he thought, remembering how solid she'd felt when he'd had his arm around her earlier, she'd undoubtedly give him a run for his money. No, if he decided to try and take her on, she'd be a force to be reckoned with. He gave up and smiled. But it still might be fun.

And what was he smiling about now? Madison wondered, and should she be concerned? Absolutely! Shit.

Watching her over his mug, Jeremy resisted the urge to laugh at her worried expression. He had her, and she knew it. Now it was just a matter of seeing what she did about it. His eyes darted to the clock on the wall. His plans for the next day were in limbo now because of the snowstorm, so he was in no hurry. And if by some miracle, Jack was able to fly her out tomorrow, it wouldn't be until mid to late afternoon anyway. No, they had plenty of time to get this hashed out. Whatever "this" was.

Her time running out, Madison took another sip of her hot chocolate. She had to give Jeremy credit; he was a whole lot more patient than she'd be. She would have demanded answers, and gotten them long before now. Had she ever been this patient? Nope. Not her style. She cleared her throat, wondering if she should just dive in or test the water first.

"Seriously," her smile sincere, "I have been using guns since I was a kid."

"Uh-uh."

"What?" Unable to stop herself, Madison laughed. "You don't believe me?"

Now it was his turn to laugh. "I never said that."

"Then what?"

Did she know her eyes sparkled when she laughed? He swallowed hard.

"I'm just wondering if you'd like to elaborate on that?"

"Sure," she said with a slow smile.

Jeremy's eyes widened briefly, surprised she was giving in so easily.

"But I'm not going to."

He laughed, of course not!

Sobering, Madison's eyes held his. "Let's just say that the less you know, the better. Okay?"

"No, it's not okay," Jeremy said, "but I guess there's not much I can do about that right now."

She nodded.

"But you realize that the police are going to want to talk to us about the body in the alley. You have to admit. The more we're together on the story, the better it'll be. For everyone involved."

He had her there. Shit.

"Especially with you being from out of town. You think you can avoid the attention you're going to get now after being connected to this mess?"

Again he had her.

"The police know me, but you . . ."

"Okay, enough! I get it!"

Sliding off the bar stool, Madison skirted around Jeremy, putting her mug in the sink. Gripping the edge of the sink, she glanced out the window, seeing only her reflection in the darkness before sidestepping away.

"There's no one out there," Jeremy said quietly, recognizing her cautious movement.

"Sorry," she mumbled, leaning a hip against the counter as she turned toward him. "Habit."

And there was that word again! What the hell?

"Okay," he said, putting his own mug in the sink before turning to face her. "Enough already. Habit? You keep saying that. You need to talk to me, Madison."

Wanting to close the distance between them, Jeremy forced himself not to move.

"Why is Jack flying you up north? Why are you really here? And don't give me any bullshit about being here to study the polar bears."

"But I am . . ."

"I told you, cut the bullshit! I know you're not here for that!"

"And how do you know that?"

Had her cover been blown? And if so, when and by whom? Oh, man, Sarah was not going to be happy about that!

"Because," Jeremy said, his voice smug, "the guy who's really here to do that was sitting at the bar tonight. He's an old friend of mine."

Crap!

Hoping to avoid showing his hand this soon, Jeremy was rewarded with the look of shock and surprise that flashed across her face before she caught herself.

"Surprise."

Anger flashed in her eyes.

"Care to try again?"

Madison longed to slap the smug look off his face, barely resisting the urge.

"And is Jack in danger by flying you up north?"

"No!" Her outburst spoke volumes.

"Then what, damn it!"

It was all he could do not to reach out and shake Madison, his anger and frustration nearly getting the better of him. He'd thought he could wait her out, but now the idea that his brother could be flying into trouble, Jeremy wasn't about to let that happen! Patience be damned!

"You've got a choice, Madison," his icy words froze her in place. "You either tell me, or you tell the police. But either way, you're going to be telling someone." He paused, his words sinking in. "Personally,

I think you're better off telling me." He shrugged his shoulders, "But what do I know?"

"Goddamn you!" Madison growled, spinning away to pace around the kitchen, her mind whirling.

She never should have taken Jeremy's gun, and she definitely shouldn't have gone into that alley! Stupid idiot! Had she compromised everything? No, there was no way her target could know she was coming for him. And while Jeremy might know the guy who was actually studying the polar bears, she was sure he didn't know her target. She paused, glancing at Jeremy as he stood silently, watching her. No, she started pacing again. He couldn't know her target. Unless her target had come through the same airport. It was possible. Unlikely but possible. Shit!

"Glad I replaced the old floor in here last year," Jeremy said casually.

He chuckled when Madison stopped in mid step, glancing down at the floor before tossing him a questioning glance.

"Because the way you're pacing, you would have worn right through the old floor."

"Fuck you."

Jeremy just laughed.

I've killed people for saying less. Bet that would wipe that smug look off his face if she told him that! Instead, she took a deep breath before climbing back onto the bar stool.

"Happy now?" He just smiled at her, causing her to blurt out, "You know, it's all I can do not to slap you!"

"I dare you."

And while he tensed up in anticipation, she only growled at him.

"I'm not your enemy here, Madison. The sooner you realize that, the easier this will be."

"I know you're not the enemy," she growled. "I just don't want to involve you in anything you don't need to be involved in, that's all." She paused. "And I promise you, Jack is not in any danger. I would never do that to him."

73

For some reason, Jeremy believed her. Maybe it was because he'd seen how Madison had been with Jack and Nancy. And his mom. No, it wasn't just that. It was the way she'd stepped up, offering to help his mom with the guys causing trouble at the bar. And the way she'd rushed headlong into the alley. She might not be afraid, but she sure as hell was going to protect those who were.

When was the last time he'd sensed that about someone? Not since he'd left the RCMP. Fifteen years traveling around Canada, working behind the scenes with the RCMP, he'd crossed paths many times with some very colorful and interesting people. Possessing his own unique set of skills combined with being an accomplished bush pilot, Jeremy's skills had taken him to some of the most remote parts of Canada as well as into the middle of the biggest cities. He'd met and mingled with Canadian royalty in Montreal and fought off an angry grizzly bear in the Northwest Territories. And all in the same week, he remembered ruefully.

While he'd worked primarily alone, he'd been part of a close-knit team of men and women he'd trusted with his life on more than one occasion. Never doubting their loyalty, he always knew they had his back. Whether it was from some remote base in the mountains or their home office in Toronto, they protected their own no matter what.

He'd left the team a year ago, heading into the mountains to hook up with Jack before figuring out his next move. Taking some of the flight load off his brother so Jack could spend time with Nancy and the kids, it didn't take Jeremy long to realize he wasn't going to be leaving anytime soon. Enjoying the slow and easy pace of the small town nestled in the valley between the mountains, Jeremy found himself entertaining the idea of settling down once and for all. God knew his mom would be happy about that idea. She'd always worried about him, where he was and what he was doing. And not being able to tell her what he was doing made it that much more difficult. So when he'd sauntered into his mom's kitchen one morning, announcing his intention to stay, the woman had been beyond ecstatic. His mother had been through enough herself, and being able to make her so happy so easily, well, he'd never once regretted his decision.

Quietly and peacefully beginning the next chapter of his life, Jeremy put his life with the RCMP behind him.

That is, until Madison flew into town. Suddenly feeling like he'd just been thrust back into his old life, Jeremy studied Madison and wondered why.

Because, he immediately answered himself, *her actions, the skills she'd exhibited, whether intentionally or not, she had professional written all over her.*

The question was, professional what?

"What are you?" Jeremy murmured.

"What do you mean what am I?"

Not realizing that he'd spoken aloud, Jeremy blinked. Madison repeated her question. Not having a direction to retreat to, she needed to know what Jeremy was thinking, what he thought he knew about her. Or her reason for being there. Once she knew that, well, at least she'd have a direction to go in.

Caught, Jeremy pondered his next move carefully. He knew she was waiting and that she'd work off of whatever he said. And most likely dish out a plateful of lies again. Frustration rippled through him as he realized he was caught between a rock and a hard place.

Yeah, he thought ruefully, *I've been out of it too long, I fell right into this. Damn!*

Could he backtrack? Sure, but would she let him? Did he care? One thing he knew for sure—he couldn't let on what he was think-ing about her. At least not yet. She needed to give him something, anything, so long as it was the truth! Or at least enough of the truth that he could gauge his next move. His eyes skipped to the cabinet over his refrigerator.

Following his eyes, Madison studied the cabinet. Too high to store a gun. And she suddenly knew exactly what was in the cabinet.

"I could go for something a little stronger than hot chocolate too," she said with a knowing smile.

"Busted," Jeremy smiled, grabbing two glasses from the dish drying rack beside the sink before moving to the cabinet.

Barely needing to stretch, he opened it, revealing a variety of bottles.

"Anything interest you?"

Madison smiled at the selection. While she normally avoided alcohol, she caught sight of a welcoming label.

"A glass of Bailey's would be great," Madison said.

Nodding, Jeremy pulled down the bottle, and pouring them each a glass, they clinked glasses in a silent toast. The silky, smooth drink slid easily down her throat, and Madison nodded her thanks. Wishing he could suggest that they move into the den, Jeremy knew getting too comfortable with her now wouldn't be the smartest move on his part. Whether he wanted to or not, for now he needed to get her to talk to him. There would be time enough later to get comfortable. He hoped, anyway.

Focused on Madison, Jeremy jumped when his cell phone rang. Tossing a sheepish grin at her, he snatched the phone, answering it briskly, his eyes never leaving Madison. Moments later, with an apologetic nod, he turned and disappeared into the living room.

While tempted to follow him, Madison erred on the side of caution this one time and stayed where she was. Jeremy was already on edge where she was concerned; he'd be royally pissed if he caught her eavesdropping. She took a sip of her Bailey's, considering her next move. So far, Jeremy's patience had impressed her. She knew she was being difficult, but she couldn't help that right now. Again she wished she'd had time to talk to Sarah!

Move on, she told herself firmly, *you can't, and that's all there is to it. You're just going to have to think on your feet.*

It wasn't like this was the first time she'd ever had to do that!

What was she? Had Jeremy really asked her that?

Well, I'm not an alien if that's what you're thinking! She'd so badly wanted to blurt that out!

Unable to stop herself, Madison chuckled, sure that Jeremy would have laughed at that answer too.

"What's so funny?"

Surprised, Madison whirled around as Jeremy came back into the kitchen. How had he snuck up on her like that? Pocketing his phone and reaching for his glass, Jeremy took a long pull off his drink.

"I didn't mean to surprise you," he said quietly.

"You didn't surprise me."

"Bullshit, but okay." He was really getting tired of her denying everything. "I promise I won't tell anyone I caught you off guard, how's that?"

Knowing she was pissing him off again, Madison nodded. If she was ever going to trust this guy, she had to stop being so defensive! Easier said than done!

"Okay, yes, you surprised me," she grudgingly admitted and was rewarded with a bright smile from Jeremy.

"Bet that killed you, having to admit that."

Madison nodded, not daring to speak because she knew she'd just swear at him again.

"Trust me, it gets easier."

Biting her tongue, she just growled at him.

"So what were you finding so funny?"

"You asking me what I am," Madison admitted.

If she was going to take a chance with him, it was now or never; she quickly decided.

"You made it sound like I was an alien or something."

"Are you?"

She couldn't help it, smiling at his quick response as she shook her head vigorously.

"Are you sure? Because I'm pretty sure I've never met anyone quite like you before . . ."

His words ended on a whisper, and he cleared his throat. Choosing to ignore how his words warmed her, Madison sipped her drink.

"I'm from Chicago, not outer space. There's a difference."

"True. Better food in Chicago, I'm thinking."

"You got that right! Although the traffic in the city is ridiculous! What I'd give for a flying saucer or even a flying car!"

And giving up, Madison just laughed, the tension she'd been feeling slowly washing away. How had she landed in such a place?

Literally! She'd come here to do a job, get in and get out. But thanks to Mother Nature, her entire plan had been changed.

Hell, why deny it—her whole fucking life had seemingly changed in a matter of a few short hours! She was stuck in the middle of nowhere—in a blizzard—with people she'd literally just met yet who'd somehow managed to worm their way into her heart within a matter of minutes! She was involved with a murder she had absolutely nothing to do with, and now she was sitting across from a man whose bright-green eyes were making her burn up with desire! What else could she do but laugh about it? Never in her life had this happened to her! And yet here she was now, wondering what it'd feel like to have Jeremy's hands on her, his mouth covering hers. She couldn't stop laughing at the absurdity of it all.

CHAPTER 8

LEANING AGAINST THE counter, Jeremy's broad smile split his face as Madison laughed until the tears were nearly rolling down her cheeks. Here was the changing point he'd been waiting for, and he wasn't about to rush it. Her laughter filled the room, throaty and strong with a hint of hysteria mixed in. Rubbing the tears from her eyes with the heels of her hands, her shoulders shook as her laughter slowly quieted.

Minutes passed before Madison's laughter subsided, and she sat quietly, a silly smile on her face.

"Feel better?" Jeremy chuckled. He certainly did!

"Yes," she sighed.

Swallowing one last chuckle, her eyes rose to his, and Jeremy found himself startled by the openness of her gaze. Gone was the veil concealing her thoughts and emotions. Staring into bright-blue eyes glistening from laughter, he had the sensation of being pulled into the depths of her soul. His breath caught.

"I haven't laughed like that in . . ." she paused, "I can't remember when!" She chuckled again. "It feels good."

"Nothing better than a good laugh," Jeremy agreed.

Rubbing her eyes again, Madison nodded.

"Jesus, what a day it's been, though!" she exclaimed, surprising Jeremy yet again.

"You got that right," he smiled, concentrating now on controlling the reaction her smile and laughter was having on his body.

If she kept staring at him, her eyes bright and inviting—well, he wasn't going to be responsible for his actions! He turned away, busily rinsing his glass in the sink.

Oh, she felt so much better, having had a good laugh! Between everything that had happened, and in such a short period of time, it was a wonder she hadn't lost it much sooner! Her life was normally more organized, well planned. While in her line of work, changes happened more often than not, she still preferred to try and live by the strict rules she set for herself: leaving little to chance. So much for that idea now! Since the moment she'd stepped off the plane this afternoon, nothing had gone as planned! Absolutely nothing! She gazed at Jeremy's strong back, her fingers itching to find out if it felt as strong as it looked. Jesus, she needed to pull herself together! She paused. She also needed to offer an olive branch to the man. She needed to trust someone in this foreign land, and she found herself wanting that someone to be Jeremy. Only one way to find out . . .

"I'm sorry for earlier, for being so difficult," she offered hesitantly.

Turning slowly back around to face Madison, Jeremy just nodded, not trusting himself to speak just yet.

"I'm feeling a bit like Dorothy in the Wizard of Oz. I'm definitely not in Kansas anymore!" She blinked. "Nothing has gone as planned or has been what it seems."

"That's putting it mildly," Jeremy smiled, slowly beginning to relax as well. "I know how it is to have your plans suddenly changed, to be thrown off balance. It takes some time getting used to. And you definitely haven't had much time, especially since every time you've turned around, something else has happened."

Madison nodded, relieved and pleased that he understood.

"But I will say this, at the same time, you definitely keep up," he added, remembering how she'd acted in the alley.

Her movements had been calculating, smooth, and professional. There'd been no hesitation; she'd jumped in feet first. She'd caught his gun as smoothly as if they'd been throwing a football around. She might not like her plans changing, but she reacted better than she gave herself credit for. And he told her so.

"Thank you," she smiled, her eyes dropping for a moment in embarrassment and secret appreciation. "Well, at least you know I'm not some weak-minded female."

"You are definitely not that! Not in the least!" Chucking, he remembered his earlier thought about actually fighting her. Oh, yeah, she'd give him a run for his money—if she didn't beat him outright!

"And now what are you laughing at?"

"I was just thinking that if it came down to it, that I'm not sure you wouldn't kick my ass in a fair fight."

Madison's dazzling smile nearly had his knees buckling.

"I said in a fair fight."

"I fight fair!"

"No, you most certainly do not!"

And pushing away, he came around the counter and, grabbing her by the shoulders, kissed her hard and fast, setting her away just as quickly.

"But neither do I!"

Her eyes wide, her lips tingling from the fleeting kiss, Madison found herself totally at a loss for words. When had that ever happened to her? Her eyes followed him as he disappeared into the other room, and without thinking, she rose to follow him. Finding him in the den, dropping a log into the wood-burning stove, Madison paused while he finished the task. Then tugging on his shirt, she forced him to turn around. Grabbing the front of his shirt, she pulled him to her, kissing him equally as fast and hard before shoving him away. Her eyes bright, her lips still tingling, her face flushed, and her chest heaving—she stood before him proudly.

Who the hell was this woman? The thought raced through his mind as he reached for her again, pulling her back to him. His mouth captured hers as he wrapped his arms around her, holding her tightly, his tongue diving into her mouth to tangle with hers. Her arms snaked around him, and molding herself against him, her head tilted, her eyes closed, and her lips softened under his as she lost herself to the kiss. Jeremy's body hardened as hers softened, and gently walking her backward, he pressed her against the wall as his hands slid up and down her back, kneading and caressing her gently. Arching into him, Madison reached up, cupping his face gently as she kissed him deeply, feeling it all the way down to her toes. With a stop in between at the juncture of her legs, heat flowed through her as she grew warm and wet at the same time.

Fighting the urge to let his hands wander over her body, he released her. Bracing his hands against the wall, his body pressed against hers as he pinned her up against the wall. Grinding his hips against her, she felt his hardness while his mouth wreaked havoc on hers.

Pulling her mouth from his, her head fell back against the wall with a thud.

"Ouch!" she groaned, her voice husky, making his body harder as his lips moved down her cheek to her chin before her turtleneck detoured him.

Not wanting to move, liking the feel of her body against his, Jeremy dropped his head down to her shoulder as he struggled to slow his breathing. Sure her racing heartbeat matched his, Madison took in great gulps of air as she wrapped her arms around Jeremy, holding him gently yet tightly. Neither wanted to move, their bodies molded together perfectly. Like they were meant to be. Madison nearly gagged at the thought, Jeremy unknowingly doing the same; and before they knew it, they were laughing together as they slowly untangled themselves.

"Well, that was fun," Madison laughed easily, willing the strength to return to her legs and her heart to slow.

Jeremy laughed, slowly pushing himself away from Madison, his movements unsteady.

"Now what do we do?"

"Whatever you want!" Jeremy replied helplessly, throwing his head back and gulping air with a broad smile. "Whatever you want!"

"How about erring on the side of caution," Madison said quietly as Jeremy gazed at her, "and have a coffee?"

"That, my dear," Jeremy declared, "is an excellent idea!"

And reaching for her hand, Jeremy tugged Madison away from the wall and back into the kitchen.

Sitting comfortably in the lobby of the Inn, enjoying the fire blazing in the stone fireplace next to him, Frank Stillman sat with his legs crossed, his eyes wandering aimlessly around the large room, a coffee mug balanced on his leg. Beside him sat the woman posing as his wife, a woman he detested but whose presence was necessary to keep up appearances. When their flight had been waylaid due to the storm, he'd been livid. His plans, once they'd reached their destination, were exact and well timed. This delay only screwed up what he'd considered his perfectly timed and well-laid-out plan. And to make matters worse, now he was stuck having to share a room with "his wife"! He didn't like changes; it never bode well for anyone.

The only saving grace in the whole mess—finding himself staying at the same Inn as his intended target! Evidently, she'd been waylaid by the same storm as well. Too bad for her, good for him. He could work with this! His eyes darted to the entrance of the Inn as he heard the big door swing open, a rush of cold air filling the entryway for a moment. He frowned; it was just the innkeeper returning from wherever she'd been.

"Maybe she got a flight out," the woman next to him said quietly, her eyes also wandering around the room.

If she had, she was lucky, the woman thought. *Who'd want to be stuck in this hellhole of a place?*

"She's still here, Ellen," Frank ground out.

He didn't want to be here any more than she did. Glancing at his watch, he debated on whether or not to wait longer or to just call it a night. With no flights going in or out until possibly the next day, Frank knew at least that his target couldn't go far. But he was hoping to make sure that she was at least in the building. He glanced at Ellen, noting her frustration. God, he hated the woman. Yet they made a perfect team; they had for years. But the idea of spending time in such close quarters as their guest room . . . He took a sip of his coffee, deciding he'd wait up a while longer.

Despising the man next to her just as much as he despised her, Ellen fidgeted with the end of her cashmere sweater. It didn't matter that she and Frank had worked together for years. When it came to having to pose as a loving couple, or even a couple that remotely liked each other, she'd never quite mastered that. Ironically, no one ever seemed to pick up on their animosity for each other; she supposed that was good. Evidently, she was a better actor than she gave herself credit for.

That, or they really did resemble the average married couple.

Having never been married herself, she hoped that wasn't the case! If she ever married, it was going to be for love, not for business or financial gain! A resigned smile lifted the corners of her mouth for a fleeting moment; the likelihood of her ever marrying at this stage of her life was pretty slim. Besides being in her mid fifties, her job alone made having a life nearly impossible. When was the last time she'd stayed in her pristine apartment in downtown Manhattan for more than two nights? She couldn't remember. Before this job, she'd thought she might have some time to stay home. She glanced at Frank with mild disgust. Then the office had called; Frank needed "his" partner. Right. His partner. He just needed a woman to pose as his wife to help his cover. Did he actually need her special set of skills? No. All she had to do was sit and look pretty. Sure, she could do that but hated that she was wasting both her time and energy. Her fingers itched to wrap around Frank's neck, finding those exact points that would make him scream like a girl and tell her every secret he held inside that brain of his. Did he even know the talents that she possessed?

Doubtful, she thought. If he did, he'd never let me anywhere near him! She nearly smiled at the thought. Maybe she should tell him exactly what she was capable of; it might get her out of this job and this hellhole!

Contemplating telling Frank, Ellen was interrupted by the front door opening, accompanied by another burst of cold air. And then she was there, the target. Standing at the front desk talking to the inn-keeper, what was her name? Ethel. Typical small-town innkeeper, the woman was a serious busybody! Focusing on Ethel, knowing Frank was focused on his target, all earlier feelings about him were momentarily forgotten. Time to work and knowing she might need to keep Ethel . . . otherwise occupied later, Ellen settled back in her chair, her gaze that of boredom and restlessness. Looking at her, never would anyone suspect the well-dressed woman capable of the evil thoughts that were swirling through her mind.

CHAPTER 9

BRUSHING OFF THE snow as she climbed the steps to the Inn, Madison threw a smile and an easy wave at Jeremy as he stood at the bottom in the still-falling snow. With a broad smile of his own and a quick wave, he turned, quickly disappearing into the darkness.

What a night! she thought, pausing to compose herself.

Through the etched windows of the beautifully ornate wooden door that was the main entrance to the Inn, Madison spotted Ethel standing behind the front desk. Knowing the woman would pepper her with questions, Madison prepared herself for the barrage; and pushing open the heavy door, she stepped inside.

"What a snowstorm!" Madison declared, still brushing snow from her jacket. "Is it going to stop tonight?"

Hoping the smile she hadn't quite been able to quell would be interpreted as her just loving the weather, Madison pulled off the mittens and wool hat that Jeremy had insisted she wear. Thankful she'd let him persuade her, she shook the snow from the hat before laying it on the counter.

"Supposed to snow all night," Ethel replied, her eyes racing over Madison, taking in her flushed cheeks and the genuine smile.

She knew Madison had been out with Jeremy. And she knew about the body in the alley.

"Guess you had quite the evening out," Ethel said quietly.

Pausing, Madison studied Ethel but remained silent. Just what exactly was the woman referring to?

Clarifying her statement, Ethel rushed on, her voice almost a whisper, "We've all heard about the trouble in the alley."

Oh, that. Madison's eyes dropped, her smile fading as she nodded. It was a small town; everyone knew everyone. Most likely, the news about the body had spread like wildfire. But had anyone heard about her actions in particular? The way Ethel was studying her now, Madison didn't think so. Curiosity trumped knowledge, it seemed. Thank goodness!

"It was horrible," Madison said, her tone turning sober.

There was no reason for Ethel to know this wasn't Madison's first body. Far from it. In fact, it'd just been last week when she'd . . .

Madison pulled her attention back to the here and now, rushing on, "Jeremy said the police would want to speak to me, probably tomorrow."

There certainly wasn't any rush; with the storm, it wasn't like she was going anywhere. No one was going anywhere. Ethel just nodded.

"I'm sorry you had to witness all that," Ethel said, not entirely sure she was telling the truth.

She'd heard how calm and cool Madison had been throughout the whole ordeal, a fact Ethel was keeping to herself for the time being. From the moment Ethel had met Madison, she'd known there was something about the woman. Just what it was, Ethel didn't know yet. But she'd figure it out soon enough, of that she was sure.

"If anyone asks for you, I'll be sure to call your room," Ethel added.

"Yes, thank you," Madison replied.

Turning and leaning against the counter, she made a mental note to put her "Do Not Disturb" sign out tonight. The last thing she needed was anyone going into her room, especially law enforcement!

Listening with half an ear as Ethel continued chatting with her, Madison's gaze leisurely swept the lobby and the adjacent living room. While guests were scattered throughout the large, comfortable room, the majority seemed to be gathered near the roaring fireplace.

Definitely the place to be tonight, Madison thought with a small smile, wishing for a moment that she could join them. Oh, to do such a "normal" thing!

The idle thought hadn't left her mind before her gaze stopped on a man sitting beside the fireplace. Just as her internal threat radar went off, the man turned—his cold, dark eyes catching and holding hers. What the hell? Who was this guy? Alarm bells went off in her head as her heart began to pound, and she fought to not look away.

If she turned away too quickly, she'd look guilty; the last thing she needed was to garner any suspicion. It would be the same if she blatantly stared at him. Forcing her heartbeat to slow and swiftly pulling herself together, Madison called upon her favorite trick when she wanted to throw someone off. She gave him a dazzling smile. And was rewarded with his eyes widening before he quickly looked away . . . in embarrassment? Madison nearly laughed out loud, her ploy to unnerve him working perfectly. Whoever he was, whatever he wanted, she'd just succeeded in making him feel like he'd been hitting on her. And clearly older than she was, that idea embarrassed him. What she didn't know was that it angered him as well.

Madison's eyes slid to the woman sitting next to him, her radar still pinging. The woman was obviously with him, but in what capacity, Madison wasn't sure yet. But if the ferocious glare she was giving the man beside her was anything to go by, Madison felt certain it had nothing to do with him gawking at a much-younger woman.

Oh, to be a fly on their wall later, Madison thought, dialing down her smile a notch as she took a moment to study the woman's posture.

Stiff as a board. Hmm, no, there was definitely something more here than just the reaction of a jealous wife. Something that was making her internal threat radar ping off the charts!

Her gaze slid back to the man. No longer staring at Madison, he whispered something that clearly wasn't making the woman happy, not if her set jaw and stiff posture were anything to go by. Turning her back to the couple, Madison smiled at Ethel.

"Full house tonight because of the storm?" Madison asked.

The question was innocent enough, but Ethel knew better. She'd noticed the exchange between Madison and the couple; it'd been hard to miss it! She nodded.

"That group came in earlier, around dinnertime," Ethel said, her head nodding toward the group in the living room, including the couple.

Suddenly realizing that this was the same man who'd caught her attention earlier, Madison resisted the urge to whirl around, to study the man more carefully. Why hadn't her radar pinged earlier? Simple, because he hadn't been looking at her! The cold and calculating look he'd given her was what had set off her radar this time.

"They're part of a tour group going up north," Ethel continued quietly, "not sure how long they'll be here now with the storm."

"Interesting," Madison murmured, grabbing her hat and mittens before pushing away from the desk, resisting the urge to glance back into the living room. Instead, she turned toward the stairs. "Have a good night, Ethel," she said over her shoulder before adding, "thank you for everything!"

And bounding up the stairs, she effectively silenced whatever Ethel had been about to say.

"Young people," Ethel murmured, turning back to her own work behind the desk before shifting slightly, allowing the couple still sitting by the fire to come into view.

Madison wasn't the only one to wonder about them; she'd had a feeling about them as soon as she'd met them. And it wasn't a good feeling.

In less than twenty-four hours, more had happened in their small town than had happened in years. Interesting that it coincided with Madison's arrival. Never having believed in coincidences, Ethel made a mental note to talk to Jeremy. While many in town didn't know the full extent of what Jeremy had been doing before finally coming back to settle down, Ethel knew exactly what he'd been doing—where, when, and why. Oh, yes, she'd be talking to him on the morrow. Because whatever it was, Ethel's old bones were telling her it didn't have anything to do with the weather.

Sliding the "Do Not Disturb" sign over the door knob, Madison closed the door quietly, locking it and throwing the dead bolt.

Only then did she let out the breath she'd been holding. Replaying everything since spotting the man and woman in the living room, images of people raced through her mind—none of them matching either one. Who were they, and why were they interested in her? Could she have misread it; could they just have been curious? No, she'd been around long enough to know when someone was curious and when someone was truly interested. And he was interested. And not in a good way. Her heartbeat had long since slowed, and her mind was clear now. It was only a matter of time before she figured out why her threat radar had gone off. In the meantime, she paused, glancing at her watch, it was too early to check in with Sarah by phone. But that didn't mean she couldn't e-mail her friend. And pushing away from the door, Madison quickly readied for bed, and crawling up into the big bed, she reached for her laptop.

Making herself comfortable, she powered up her laptop, gazing wistfully around the warm and cozy room as she waited for the Internet connection. Oh, to be able to spend a few days here just for fun!

Fun? What was that? She chuckled. When was the last time she'd done nothing but just gone out and had fun? The time she'd spent tonight with Jack and Nancy reminded her of just how long it'd been since she'd simply enjoyed a nice night out. Her mind jumped to the scene in the alley. No, *fun*—it seemed—was not in her vocabulary. Seemed every time she came close, such as strolling with Jeremy tonight in the falling snow, something always happened to destroy the moment—a dead body in this case.

The dead body. The couple in the lobby. Her threat radar pinging off the charts. Madison's fingertips paused over the keyboard. Definitely too much to be coincidence, of that she was positive.

Her fingers flew across the keyboard as she outlined her day, the events in the alley, and her encounter with the couple downstairs. Mentioning Jeremy, she kept to the facts, leaving out the blistering kisses they'd shared.

No need to go there just yet, Madison told herself, her body tingling at the memory.

Smiling, she reached for her bottle of water, her throat suddenly dry.

"Pull yourself together, girl!" she admonished herself softly, wishing she could ignore the fact that instead of cooling down, her body was only heating up more at the thought of Jeremy and his mouth on hers. The man could kiss like nobody's business!

Madison burst out laughing when she realized that her fingertips had risen to trace her lips as the memories flooded her mind.

Oh my god, you're acting like a schoolgirl!

And giggling, she realized she didn't give a shit! Her lifestyle didn't allow for many moments like this; she was damn well going to enjoy them when she could!

But there was no need to mention any of *that* to Sarah, she decided, finishing her e-mail and quickly sending it off. Good thing Sarah hadn't wanted to Skype with her tonight!

Sarah wouldn't have been able to read Madison's mind, but she damn well would have been able to read her face! Yeah, talk about having your work cut out for you! How does one explain having feelings for a man you only just met? Madison had many talents, but hiding her feelings from Sarah was not one of them.

With a sigh, Madison put away the laptop, leaning back against the big pillows as she gazed around the room, letting her mind drift aimlessly. When the time came, she knew she'd tell Sarah everything about Jeremy. Best friends, Madison trusted Sarah—not only with her life on a daily basis, but with her feelings as well. But right now, regarding Jeremy—yeah, she needed a little more time to figure things out before confiding in her friend. Who knows, when all's said and done, there might not even be anything to tell Sarah. Jeremy's feelings, whatever they were, would most likely change if and when he ever found out what Madison did for a living. A wry smile split her face, imagining Jeremy telling his mother that his new girlfriend was a professional assassin. Yeah, that would definitely not be dinner conversation!

Madison's eyes widened briefly as a new, unrecognizable feeling flowed through her. Suddenly, the image of Ruth hugging her filled her mind, and she instantly knew what this new feeling hitting her between the eyes was . . . acceptance and belonging. Holy shit!

Powering up her computer Sarah nursed her third coffee of the morning, smiling as she spotted the e-mail from Madison. Noting the time the e-mail was sent, Sarah shot off a silent thanks to God. It seemed Madison was finally getting into the habit of checking the time before calling. One could hope, anyway. She glanced at the clock before going back to the e-mail, the idea of calling and waking up Madison tempting.

No, Sarah decided, *the payback from that idea wouldn't be worth it at all!* Better to just appreciate that Madison had chosen to e-mail her instead of calling her at what would have been 5:30 a.m. in Germany.

Settling down with her coffee, Sarah read Madison's e-mail carefully three times before she started scribbling notes. It was clear in the e-mail that the body in the alley and the couple at the Inn had nothing to do with the job that she was there to do; Madison was confident of that. But at the same time, the body and the couple were somehow connected to Madison. How—exactly—was the question. Sarah couldn't figure it out either—yet, anyway. But Madison's threat radar was never wrong. And like Madison, Sarah didn't believe in coincidence. Not in their line of work.

Minimizing Madison's e-mail, Sarah opened a new window, pulling up the travel schedules and current locations of her team. Locating just the man for the job, and shooting him a quick e-mail, she went back to Madison's e-mail. The last thing Madison needed was unwanted and unnecessary attention, but unfortunately, there wasn't anything Sarah could do about Madison's involvement with the body. Had the tables been turned, Sarah would have reacted the same way. No, that couldn't be helped. But she could take the pressure off of Madison having to deal with whoever this couple was. Yes, Sarah decided, outlining her idea to Madison in a short e-mail.

"Interesting about the couple." Sarah wrote. "I'm on it. In the meantime, keep focused on the job at hand. I've got the rest."

Rereading her short note, Sarah quickly added one more thing. "Is Jeremy a hunk?"

Knowing Madison would hate it, Sarah went one step further, adding a smiley face to the e-mail. And with a laugh, she punched the *send* button.

Knowing it'd be a few hours before she heard anything back from Madison, Sarah began working out her next plan. Pulling up the weather forecast for Madison's current location, she sat back, frowning. The weather pattern looked worse now than it had earlier—heavy snow predicted for the next few days. Damn! Even if there was a break in the storm, would it be enough for regular flights to resume? Crap! Never mind that she needed to get Madison out of there; she needed to get her man into that town and as soon as possible!

Well, Sarah thought, reaching for her television guide, *no one ever said she couldn't think outside the box.*

Flipping through the guide until she found the show she was looking for, Sarah smiled, returning to her computer. Where there's a will, there was a way!

Hours later, Madison replied to Sarah's e-mail, her response direct and defiant:

"Fuck you."

"I'll take that as a yes," Sarah immediately replied. Clearly Madison was bit touchy when it came to Jeremy. Hmmmm.

"Fine. Yes," came the reply moments later.

"Ha!" Sarah exclaimed out loud while also scribbling a note to question Madison more about Jeremy later.

But right now, she had more important things to worry about than Madison's social life. Although Madison liking a guy was an interesting change of pace.

CHAPTER 10

PUTTING HIS PLATE in the sink, Jeremy glanced out at the gently falling snow. At least it'd tapered off some since he'd dragged his tired ass out of bed an hour ago. He had a lot to do today, and the idea of working in heavy snow wasn't appealing. Didn't matter that he was used to doing it, didn't mean he liked it.

A loud knock followed by a burst of cold air had Jeremy smiling as he turned slowly.

"Hope you've got plenty of coffee," Jack said, brushing the snow off his jacket as he strode into the kitchen.

"Always. Long night?"

"Nan, hardly slept last night," Jack said, "it won't be long now. She always gets this way just before she goes into labor. It's like a ritual with her."

"If she's that close, what the hell you doing here?" Jeremy laughed, knowing his brother wouldn't go far from his wife.

"Because this is my ritual, to get out of the house," Jack laughed. "Besides, Mom is with her."

Nodding, Jeremy let his brother doctor his coffee and settled on a bar stool.

"And because I got a call for a job today."

"Today?" Glancing again out at the falling snow, Jeremy turned back to his brother, concern etched across his face. "Where to?"

"Whitehorse." Jack sipped his coffee with a grateful sigh. "I checked the weather, I should be able to get down and back with no trouble."

"Want company?"

He could easily put off the stuff he had to do today, like talking to the police. His nerves tingling, Jeremy didn't question the sudden need to go with his brother. The timing of this job was too coincidental; his gut told him with absolute certainty that it was somehow connected to the recent events and with Madison. How, he didn't know. But by sticking close to his brother, he was sure to find out.

Hoping his brother would offer, Jack nodded.

"What time we leaving?"

Jack glanced at his watch.

"Shit, do I at least have time to go to the bathroom?"

And make a quick phone call. He needed to let Madison know he was heading out. She'd be pissed if he just left. Jeremy paused. She'd probably be pissed, anyway, especially since she knew flying in this weather was dangerous. He didn't examine why he cared one way or the other. But he did. Shit.

"Yeah," Jack laughed, sliding off the stool. "You've got time. I'm leaving in an hour. I've checked the forecast, we've got light snow for a few hours. I've worked out the timing, we'll be back before the heavy snow comes in again. Barring any unforeseen problems, anyway."

Finishing his coffee, Jack put his mug in the sink before turning to his brother.

"Tell Madison I checked, I still can't get up to her destination. This storm is big, worse up that way."

Jeremy nodded, knowing Madison would ask. Agreeing on the meeting time Jack left, followed closely by another burst of cold air.

"What do you mean you're going to Whitehorse today?"

Sitting up in bed, Madison struggled to chase the cobwebs out of her mind. She'd slept like a log! No dreams, nothing. She didn't remember anything after closing her eyes in the wee hours of the morning. Wow! Normally a light sleeper, she couldn't remember the last time she'd had such a restful sleep. It felt great! But it was dangerous too. Her eyes swept the room, relief flowing through her at finding nothing out of place. Not that anyone would be able to enter the room without her knowing it, but just the same.

The phone ringing had been what had woken her, and grabbing the SAT phone, she immediately realized it was the guest room phone ringing. A sheepish grin dashed across her face as she answered the phone with a groggy "Hello." And now Jeremy was telling her that he was flying out?

Explaining that he was going with his brother, Jeremy outlined their projected flight plan and when he expected to be back. Okay, so it sounded cut and dried, and if Jack was flying, that meant it had to be safe. Then why did she have an uncomfortable feeling about this? Her threat radar wasn't going off; she just felt uneasy, a feeling she rarely experienced. She gazed out the window at the still-falling snow. If they considered this light, she hated to see what they'd called heavy! Assuring her again that they'd be fine, Jeremy asked her about any potential plans that she might have had for the day.

"Plans?" Madison's gaze slid to the coffeemaker, and her mouth nearly watered. "Coffee first and foremost," she declared, smiling when Jeremy laughed. "After that, I'm not sure yet."

Suggesting she take the day and relax, Jeremy knew she'd never do that—especially since he knew he wouldn't do it himself. But one thing he hoped she would do—avoid talking to the police. And would she please avoid going anywhere near the alley!

"And why would you think I'd go there?" Madison asked, her voice dripping in innocence.

"Exactly," Jeremy said with a chuckle. "As much as you might not want to hear this, you and I are a lot alike. So I'll say it again. Please stay away from the alley. At least until I get back. Deal?" He waited patiently, listening to dead air.

"Fine."

"Oh my god! I bet saying that nearly killed you!"

"You got that right!" Madison admitted. "Have a safe trip, and let me know as soon as you're back, okay?"

Did he imagine it, or did she sound concerned? He smiled into the phone. That would kill her for sure, admitting she was concerned. He nearly laughed.

Giving Madison the number for his mother and for Nancy, in case she was looking for some female companionship, Jeremy ended the call with a quick "Call you later." Hanging up the phone, Madison contemplated her next move. Coffee first! And sliding out of bed, she made a beeline for the coffee machine.

Sitting in front of the fire, nursing her third coffee, Madison's mind slowly cleared. Ticking off a list of things she wanted to accomplish, she glanced out the window before glancing back to the clock on her bedside table. The boys would be in the air now, she decided. Calculating the time she had before their return, she sipped her coffee. Knowing she had plenty of time she stretched, enjoying being lazy for a few minutes. Her life didn't allow for such luxuries, and she was going to take advantage of this! Too bad she couldn't shut her mind off for a little while—now that'd be heavenly!

But there was too much to be done. Her eyes drifted to the SAT phone, then to her laptop, before dropping to her backpack. So much for being lazy. She had work to do.

Pushing herself out of the overstuffed chair, Madison swallowed the last of her coffee before disappearing into the bathroom. Allowing herself a few minutes to enjoy the pulsating shower, the hot water helping her body wake up, her mind went over the details of the day. First and foremost, she needed to avoid running into the police. She wasn't worried about talking to them; she just wanted to wait until Jeremy was with her. These were his people—yeah, she'd wait until he was back for that conversation.

Which meant she'd have to watch herself. Especially when she went back to the alley. She knew Jeremy would be furious, but she didn't care. Well, that wasn't quite true. She did. But she also knew she needed to go back to the scene of the crime. Of course, the police would have gone over it with a fine-tooth comb by now—or so she hoped anyway. But she was looking for something they weren't: a connection to the couple she'd watched in the living room last night.

Her gut was telling her that somehow they were involved; she just wasn't sure why or how yet. And there was still the matter of her connection to them. Did that connect her to the body too? Or were they two separate things connected by accident?

Not liking that idea, Madison stepped out of the shower, quickly toweling off. Wrapping a towel around her head and slipping on her robe, Madison stepped out of the bathroom, gasping when she came face-to-face with Ethel.

"Jesus, woman! Are you trying to give me a heart attack?" *Or get yourself killed?*

Anger surged through Madison as her eyes swept the room for anything out of place. And how had she not heard the woman enter her room? Because, you fool, you were enjoying the shower. Idiot! She needed to pull her head out of the clouds and back into the game, or she was likely to end up dead! Fuck!

"I'm sorry!" Ethel quickly apologized.

If the murderous look on Madison's face was anything to go by, her idea of letting herself in probably hadn't been the smartest idea. Despite the heavy robe and the towel around her head, Ethel felt the power and anger emanating off of Madison in waves that made Ethel want to take a step back. Who the hell was this woman? Suddenly realizing that Madison stood between her and the door, Ethel's shoulders slumped in defeat. She was losing her touch; that was for damn sure! She never would have made that mistake in her younger years!

"What are you doing in here, Ethel?" Madison forced herself to speak calmly.

Growling at the woman would only make things worse. Clearly, the woman hadn't been in the room for very long; nothing appeared to have been touched, moved, or taken. Madison took a deep breath, the smell of blueberry muffins tickling her nose.

"Do I smell blueberry muffins?"

With a sheepish grin, Ethel produced a small wicker basket covered by a cloth napkin. With wide eyes, Madison watched as Ethel slid back the napkin, revealing four Texas-size muffins. Madison's mouth instantly watered, and a smile split her face.

"I love blueberry muffins!" she exclaimed.

"I was hoping you did," Ethel said, hiding her relief as she handed Madison the basket. "I thought a little something special might make being stranded here a little easier."

Dropping into the chair, balancing the basket on her legs, Madison attacked a muffin, not bothering to butter it but just breaking off a piece and popping it into her mouth. Her eyes closed as she savored the sweet taste of the still-warm muffin. Breaking off another piece and popping it into her mouth, Madison sighed in happiness. When was the last time she had freshly baked muffins? The excellent dinner last night, the muffins this morning—it was becoming abundantly clear that being stranded in the middle of nowhere definitely had its perks!

Popping another piece of muffin into her mouth, Madison invited Ethel to sit with a wave of her hand. Dropping into the opposite chair, Ethel made herself comfortable, allowing Madison the chance to finish off one muffin. It didn't take long.

"Thank you so much," Madison said finally, wiping her mouth with the edge of the cloth napkin.

Between the coffee, the shower, and now the muffin, she was quickly starting to feel more human. Placing the basket on the table, Madison sat back, eyeing Ethel with curiosity. Something was on the woman's mind—of that Madison was sure. Might as well open the door, she thought, and see what walks through.

"What's on your mind, Ethel?" she asked bluntly, not surprised to see the woman's eyes widen briefly.

"I was just wondering what you might be planning to do today, what with Jeremy gone and all."

Did everyone know Jeremy's plans? Of course, they would, it was a small town.

"I hadn't really given it much thought," Madison replied carefully.

"That's a load of crap, but okay."

It was Madison's turn to be momentarily taken aback. But then remembering who Ethel was, she shook it off, admiring the woman's gumption. Not many would say such a thing to a complete stranger.

"Was there something I was supposed to be doing?"

Two could play at this game. And it was a game Madison was very good at.

"I don't know about that," Ethel said cautiously, "but I know there's something you'd best not be doing."

"And that would be . . . ?"

"Going back to the alley," Ethel stated bluntly.

Determined not to give herself away, Madison sat motionless. Just how much did Ethel know?

"Okay, Ethel," Madison began, "spill it."

Ethel's eyes widened briefly. "Whatever are you talking about my dear?"

"Oh, and cut the innocent crap while you're at it. It doesn't suit you."

Surprising Madison, Ethel laughed out loud.

"It never did," Ethel laughed, pushing herself out of the chair.

Leaning against the window sill, she watched the lightly falling snow for a moment before turning back to Madison. Gazing at the young woman who'd only just arrived the day before, Ethel held Madison's direct gaze with her own.

"How old are you?"

Not expecting that question, Madison blinked.

"Thirty," she answered automatically.

Nodding, Ethel remained silent. Rising to face Ethel, Madison pulled the towel from her head, tossing it into the bathroom. Shaking her head, she let her hair fall where it may, her eyes never leaving Ethel's.

"Why? Is that a problem?"

"No, no," Ethel said, "I was just curious."

"What else are you curious about?"

Knowing she wasn't going to be able to stall for much longer, Ethel considered her answer.

"Come on, you show me yours, I'll show you mine."

Understanding the ultimatum, Ethel nodded. "You first."

"Jeremy asked me to keep an eye on you," Ethel began, turning back to gaze out the window. "For some reason, he thought you might be thinking about heading back to the alley."

Turning, Ethel's eyes bore into Madison with an intensity that spiked Madison's curiosity even more.

"I can't imagine why he thought you might do that. Can you?"

Madison nearly laughed. Was this woman trying to intimidate her? Good luck with that!

"No idea," Madison said and was surprised again when Ethel snapped at her.

"Cut the crap, Madison, the innocent thing doesn't work for you any more than it works for me."

This time Madison did laugh, turning back to the basket of muffins. She plucked one out, picking pieces off and popping them in her mouth. She needed to keep her hands busy, lest she reach out and shake Ethel. The woman was playing with fire, and she was going to get burned if she didn't watch herself.

"Careful, Ethel," Madison admonished softly, finishing the muffin.

Disappearing into the bathroom to wash her hands, she came back, drying her hands with a towel. She'd killed someone once with just a towel. What would Ethel think if she knew that? Her instincts told her she could trust Ethel—but just how much, she wasn't sure of that yet. And the less Ethel knew, the better too. Until she got a better feel for who the actual players were in this new and confusing game, Madison didn't want to show her hand. Not unless she absolutely had to.

"I'm just looking out for Jeremy," Ethel continued, choosing to ignore Madison's icy warning. "And he's just looking out for you."

Madison nodded, understanding. She wanted to protect Jeremy too. She just wished she knew if they were protecting each other from the same thing.

"He didn't want you going back to the alley without him." Ethel paused. "Regardless of what you might think you can do, having him with you will be smarter."

"Because this is his town."

Ethel nodded, and Madison softened a fraction.

"I understand and appreciate your concern, Ethel."

"But you're going back to the alley anyway."

"I have to."

"I can't believe we're stuck here!"

Tired of listening to Ellen whining, for the hundredth time in the last hour, Frank wished he could just kill her—if only to shut the woman up!

"Nothing we can do about the weather," Frank reminded her . . . yet again.

"I heard one of the others in the group saying that a pilot took off earlier, where was that plane going?"

"That flight was going in the opposite direction," Frank said, annoyed.

Was the woman so stupid that she thought he'd let something as vital as a plane taking off slip by him? Of course, he'd already checked it out! Thinking Frank was just being curious, the young lady working the front desk at the Inn that morning hadn't hesitated to tell him what he wanted to know.

"We're going north, the storm is worse that way."

"So we're still going?" Ellen bit down on her frustration. "Given that the target's now here, I thought that might change the plan."

Despite being in the privacy of their own room, Frank still glared at Ellen, reminding her that she needed to keep her voice down.

"Oh, don't worry, no one heard me," she retorted carelessly.

"Paper-thin walls," Frank growled. Ellen laughed, rapping her knuckles on the wall.

"These walls are solid, Frank, no one's going to hear anything."

"And how can you be so sure?"

"Because," giving Frank her first genuine smile, "you didn't hear me in the room next door last night, did you?"

Promptly rewarded with a look that would make most women cower, Ellen didn't flinch. She wasn't afraid of him.

"If you didn't hear me screaming in ecstasy last night, then I'm pretty sure no one will hear us just talking."

She nearly laughed, watching Frank bristle in anger and . . . jealousy? Doubtful. But wouldn't that just take the cake!

"You bitch!" Frank snarled, balling his fists to keep from reaching for her.

If he got his hands around her throat, he knew he'd kill her.

"You couldn't wait to satisfy yourself until the job was finished? You had to risk everything by screwing the first guy you could find?"

Anger raced across her face, distorting her beauty. It didn't matter that they hated each other; to still be called a bitch, now that made her mad! The fact that he was right, that she'd slept with the first man available—well, that was true. She wasn't going to argue about that; she didn't care about that. But no man called her a bitch, and she told him so in no uncertain terms—quickly reminding him that while she had more class in her pinky than most people, she could still swear as good as any sailor, maybe better!

Needing to distance himself from Ellen as fast as possible, Frank threw up his hands in surrender before heading for the door.

"Where are you going now?" Ellen demanded.

"I need some air." *And a break from you!* "I'm getting some coffee."

Not waiting for an answer, Frank stormed out of the room, only to come face-to-face with the guest from the next room in the hallway. Eyeing the handsome man quickly, Frank squashed the multiple comments that immediately sprang to mind. Guilt was clearly etched across the man's handsome features and tempted to confront him. Frank tossed away the idea. No sense in bringing any more attention to themselves. Ellen had done more than enough for the time being. Just the same, when the man stopped in front of the elevator, Frank chose the stairway, not trusting himself in the man's presence. If the guy so much as uttered a word about Ellen, or anything, Frank knew he'd be hard pressed not to kill the guy where he stood. No, best keep a safe distance for the time being. Pushing open the door to the stairway, Frank paused on the other side. He needed to calm down! His emotions were too close to the surface, and he needed to concentrate on the job at hand. And try to ignore the fact that the woman posing as his wife was screwing a guy younger and better-looking than he was!

Still lost in his thoughts, Frank entered the lobby, making a beeline for the coffee machine. Making himself a coffee, it was a moment before he realized someone was speaking to him. Glancing up, he spotted Ethel standing nearby, an inquisitive look on her face.

"I'm sorry, did you say something?" Frank asked, tossing Ethel a blank stare.

"Just saying 'good morning' is all," Ethel smiled easily.

She was used to people lost in their thoughts, but this guy brought a whole new meaning to being preoccupied.

"And I wanted to tell you that your group's got a late luncheon planned at the restaurant."

Frank blinked at her.

"The group you came in with?"

"The group?" Frank stammered. "Oh! The group! Yes, of course! Sorry, I was a bit preoccupied." *You think?* "What time is the luncheon?"

Glancing at his watch, Frank cursed himself every which way. He needed to pull his head out of his ass and focus! Otherwise, he was likely to get himself killed!

Rattling off a time and reminding Frank where the restaurant was, Ethel turned away. Clearly, Mr. Stillman was not a chatty man—she readily deduced when he just nodded at her, remaining silent. He was an odd man, and as such, he piqued her curiosity. Her instincts telling her there was more here than meets the eye, she returned to her office, pulling the group folder from the file cabinet. Dropping into her chair, she quickly ran through the list of names, none jumping out at her—not that she'd expected that. The group had found themselves stranded here totally by surprise. None of the group could have expected the sudden change in plans. But just the same, Ethel thought, locating the group contact's name, it wouldn't hurt to find out a bit more about the folks in the group—mainly the Stillmans. Sitting back in her chair, images of the supposed Mr. and Mrs. Stillman drifted through her mind.

"There's no way they're married," Ethel murmured.

She'd been around long enough; she could spot a staged couple a mile away. Confident in her assessment, Ethel reached for the phone.

CHAPTER 11

HAVING SEEN MORE in his lifetime than he cared to admit, Jeremy rarely found himself surprised. But watching the man approaching him now, Jeremy knew it'd be a long time before he'd be this surprised again. A smile split his face as he moved forward to greet his old friend, and the two men shook hands.

"You're the last person I ever expected to see this far north!" Jeremy laughed.

"This is the last place I ever expected to be!" His friend smiled before turning to Jack. "I appreciate you being able to pick me up."

Nodding, Jack remained silent, vowing to grill his brother later on who this stranger was. Although at the same time, Jack wasn't really surprised that the two men knew each other. Jeremy rarely went anywhere without running into someone he knew somehow—the advantages, or disadvantages, to having traveled the world.

"Mr. Jones, I presume," Jack drawled, shaking the man's hand, appreciating the firm grip.

"Just Jones."

Jack nodded, again not surprised.

"Will we be able to fly out?" Not wanting to sound worried or concerned, Jones kept his voice neutral.

It wouldn't bode well for a man of his caliber to show concern, let alone fear. And he really wasn't either. But Jeremy had been right; he'd never thought he'd find himself this far north. In fact, he couldn't remember his specific skill set ever being needed in such a location. But then again, geography rarely mattered when it came to killing someone.

"If we leave now, we won't have any trouble," Jack said, eyeing the plain black travel bag Jones carried. "Is that all you've got?"

Jones nodded.

The man knew Jeremy, so Jack wasn't about to question the man on his luggage. Or lack thereof.

"Okay then, if you'll follow me, we'll be on our way."

And falling into step beside Jeremy, Jones remained silent as they followed Jack back out into the cold, moving swiftly toward the plane sitting on the snow-covered tarmac.

"Just need to sign off, and we'll get out of here," he said, motioning Jones and Jeremy to board the plane before turning his attention to the mechanic holding a clipboard for Jack.

"I've gotta tell you, man, I'm surprised to see you here," Jeremy said as Jones buckled himself in. "You gonna tell me why?"

"Not here," Jones said quietly, nodding towards Jack as he boarded the plane, disappearing into the cockpit. "When we get there."

Jeremy nodded—oh, yeah, as soon as they landed, they'd be talking!

Double-checking to make sure their passenger was comfortable, Jeremy joined his brother in the cockpit, knowing full well he was going to be grilled the entire flight home. Great. Well, one thing was for sure: he wouldn't have to lie. He honestly didn't know what would bring Jones to such a remote place. The only thing Jeremy knew for sure, though . . . if Jones was here, someone was going to die. Jeremy paused. Or was it because someone already had?

"For the record, I still don't believe you, bro," Jack laughed as he finished his landing checklist.

Fortunately, the flight back had been uneventful, and they'd made good time, landing relatively smoothly, given the snow-covered runway. But Jack was used to landing on snow and had barely noticed, concentrating instead on their now-limited visibility.

Darkness had set in, and following the landing lights in demanded his complete attention. At least it gave Jeremy a moment's reprieve; as he'd expected, Jack had grilled him most of the way home on their mysterious passenger—and hadn't believed a single word Jeremy had said about the guy.

"Seriously, Jack!" Jeremy said, unbuckling himself and pushing himself out of the seat. "I really have no idea why he's here!"

"Would you tell me if you did?"

It was a fair question, and Jeremy paused, considering his answer. Taking too long to answer, Jack nodded.

"Yeah, just as I figured."

But he understood his brother's hesitation, knowing it came from his previous occupation. The ability to keep secrets was one of many skills that Jeremy excelled in, enabling him to protect himself as well as his family.

"It's okay," Jack conceded, following Jeremy, ignoring the "thanks a lot" look his brother tossed him.

Finding their passenger stretching in his seat, Jack just stared. Looking rested and relaxed, Jones unbuckled himself and, grabbing his bag, rose to join the men.

"Enjoy the flight?" Jack asked dryly.

Most people flying in the weather they'd just gone through would have white-knuckled it all the way. Clearly not this guy. Midway through their flight Jack, doing his mandatory passenger check, had found Jones sound asleep.

"Yeah, thanks."

And nodding to both men, Jones exited the plane, ignoring the sharp, biting wind and snow that immediately battered him. Tossing Jeremy a curious backward glance, Jack followed their passenger.

"He travels a lot," Jeremy said, following his brother.

Evidently, Jack thought, watching the man striding purposefully through the snow into the terminal. A cold chill trickled down Jack's spine, an involuntary shiver rippling through him—the feeling having absolutely nothing to do with the cold weather and everything to do with the mysterious man they'd just flown in.

Two hours later, after having gone home for an extremely hot shower and some much-needed coffee, Jeremy met back up with Jack at the restaurant. Finishing his postflight report and dashing home to check on Nancy, Jack had only just arrived himself. Two mugs of steaming hot coffee waited for them at their table, and Jeremy dropped into his usual chair, Jack sitting across from him.

"Your friend's one cool customer," Jack said quietly, skipping the usual pleasantries.

"Yeah, he's unique."

"That's putting it mildly," Jack sipped his coffee. "Do you know where he's staying?"

"At the Inn, I guess."

Jack shook his head.

"What? He's not there?"

"Nope."

"Then where's he staying?"

"I have no idea. I thought you might know."

Jeremy shook his head. "Why would I know?"

"He's your friend."

"That I didn't invite," Jeremy reminded his brother quickly. "Don't forget, big brother, I didn't even know he was the passenger until we picked him up."

"True," Jack mused, focusing on his coffee.

"What the hell?" Jeremy demanded, pulling his brother's attention back to him. "What's going on here?"

Putting down his coffee, Jack took his time answering.

"Did you see where he went after we landed?"

Jeremy shook his head.

"Me neither. When I got done with the postflight stuff, he was gone." Jack paused. "It was like he was never there. And the weirdest part, no one remembered seeing him. This town's too small, no one just disappears."

You do if you're Jones, Jeremy thought, remaining silent.

"I asked around, I even checked with Ethel, nothing. It's like the guy walked off the face of the earth." Jack studied Jeremy for a moment. "Anything you want to tell me about this guy? Anything we should know?"

"Why you asking me?" Jeremy snapped defensively. "Just because I know the guy doesn't mean I'm his keeper. Sorry, Jack, but today wasn't my day to watch the guy. So no, I can't tell you anything you don't already know."

Well, I could, he mused, *but I'm not!* Besides, what he knew about Jones didn't pertain to this situation. At least as far as he knew anyway.

Leaning back in his chair, Jeremy glanced around the quiet restaurant, knowing it'd be bustling shortly. They'd made good time flying down and back, beating the dinner hour by a little bit. Tempting smells drifted out from the kitchen, and Jeremy's mouth watered.

"Boys," Ruth's firm voice had Jeremy and Jack swinging around to watch their mother approaching. "What's going on? I couldn't hear what you were talking about, but I can tell by the looks of things that whatever it is, it isn't good. Spill it."

The look of conspiracy that shot between her boys nearly had her laughing. Evidently, they still believed they could pull a fast one over on their mother.

"You're too old to ground and too big for me to take over my knee. So I'm going to trust you to just be honest and tell me what's going on."

After a moment of guilty silence, Jack sat up straight in his chair, Jeremy following suit.

So like the boys to stick together, Ruth noticed happily. Didn't matter their ages, they'd always be there for each other.

"We flew in a guy from Whitehorse, kinda different kind of guy," Jack began.

"Yeah, different," Jeremy added, "unique."

"Unique?" Ruth asked with a raised eyebrow. "Unique how?"

"Okay, that wasn't the right word," Jeremy rushed on. Although *unique* really was the best way to describe Jones. "Just not one of our usual visitors."

"Yeah," Jack finished, "he's not your usual visitor."

"You boys are so full of shit," Ruth laughed, surprising the brothers. "I've got work to do. When you're ready to talk to me, you know where to find me. In the meantime, Jack," Ruth tapped him on the shoulder, "your wife is at home resting, don't upset her." And turning to Jeremy, "And you, Madison is at the Inn, be sure to bring her over for dinner later."

"Yes, ma'am" the boys replied in unison.

"All right then," Ruth smiled at her boys, love shining brightly in her eyes, "you boys play nice."

And with a quick hug for each, she left them to their business, disappearing into the kitchen.

"I'm going to find Madison," Jeremy said, pushing back and rising. "We good?"

Jack nodded, quickly finishing his coffee before also standing up.

"Yeah, we're good," Jack smiled, offering his hand. Shaking hands, Jack pulled his brother into a quick bear hug. "We're good."

"Go home to your wife," Jeremy said, heading for the door before pausing. "And by the way, good flying today."

With a nod, Jack watched Jeremy leave before shrugging on his own coat, leaving moments later.

So much for a productive day, Madison thought, leaving the comfort of the big bed to answer the door. She'd planned on sneaking back to the alley to see if she could find more answers to the mystery from the other night. Instead she just ended up back in bed with a book she'd found in the bookcase in the lobby. That it happened to be a book she'd been meaning to read for ages didn't ease the temptation. Hot chocolate, a good book, big comfy bed, fire burning— what could be better? She smiled, giving herself a quick once-over in the mirror before heading to the door, guessing it was either Ethel or Jeremy knocking. No one else knew where she was.

Throwing open the door, her welcoming smile turned to shock as she came face-to-face with Jones. Pulling him into the room, she quickly glanced up and down the hallway before closing the door.

"No one saw me," Jones stated bluntly.

Of course, no one would see him; no one ever saw him.

"What the hell are you doing here?" Madison hissed, instantly glad she'd stayed dressed. "And how'd you get here?"

"I'm happy to see you too," Jones said dryly, dropping into the chair by the fire.

Taking a deep, calming breath, Madison sat down opposite him.

"Hi," she said finally. "Now what the hell are you doing here?"

Her mind racing, Madison squelched the million questions that threatened to burst from her. Calm down and think! Pushing out of the chair, Madison began pacing, ignoring Jones. Knowing this pacing thing was a habit of hers, Jones remained silent, knowing Madison was working things out in her mind. They all had their ways—who was he to tell her that her way was any crazier than his?

Moments later, finished pacing, she faced Jones.

"Where's Sinbad?"

Good God, her first question was about his Great Dane? He nearly laughed. Oh, yeah, the girl was crazy. He smiled. He'd always liked her warped way of thinking.

"He's home. He wanted to come but couldn't make the trip." Jones chuckled. "And I'm glad I didn't bring him. Besides not liking the cold, the big guy never would have fit on the plane!"

Madison turned in surprise.

"You flew in?" Uh-oh.

"Yeah, just arrived a little while ago."

"From Whitehorse?"

He nodded. Oh, shit.

"Two guys fly you in?"

"Yeah, brothers."

Oh, this just kept getting better and better.

"Is there a problem?"

"I hope not," Madison murmured as she started pacing again. "Why are you here?" she said, pausing in midstride.

"Sarah called me. Said you'd had some trouble and that you might be able to use me."

Shit, if Sarah had sent Jones, then things were worse than she'd imagined. Damn, she should have gone back to the alley! She might have been able to save him the trip. Wait a sec; Jones would have already been on his way. Sarah had to have contacted him last night. Crap! She needed to talk to Sarah and soon.

"Sarah's expecting your call," Jones said, knowing her train of thought.

Glancing at the clock, Madison judged the time difference; she couldn't call Sarah for another few hours. Didn't matter she was expecting the call or not. If Madison woke up Sarah one more time for anything less than a major emergency, Jones would have another job on his hands.

"Madison," Jones's voice intruded on her thoughts.

"What?"

"Sit down."

His firm command didn't allow for argument, and Madison dropped back into her chair.

"Tell me what's happened and what's going on. I already know that why I'm here has nothing to do with the job you're up here for. I know that. Tell me about the other player, the one who set off your radar. And tell me about the alley."

Taking a deep breath, Madison told him everything that had happened since she'd arrived. Well, almost everything. She glossed over the intimate details of what had happened with Jeremy.

Closing her eyes, she described in complete detail the body in the alley, how she'd found him, Mary, everything. Then, with eyes still closed, she told Jones everything about the man in the lobby. From the first time she'd seen him from behind to boldly catching his eye in the lobby.

Remaining silent, Jones let Madison run through everything at her own speed. Questions popped into his mind, but he kept silent, not wanting to interrupt her. Madison was on a roll, and he didn't want her to forget anything or have something go into the wrong chronological order. His questions could wait.

Only when she mentioned the gun did Jones shift in his chair. So someone had seen her handle a weapon. Hope the guy was impressed—Madison's skill with a firearm was nothing short of phenomenal. Pride rippled through him, remembering the first time he'd watched her with a firearm, her natural talent immediately obvious to him. Unbeknownst to Madison, he'd helped hone her skills, later bringing her to Sarah's attention. While he couldn't take total credit for the success she'd had over the years, he allowed himself the satisfaction of knowing that he'd helped her along the way. Sometimes she'd known, sometimes not. This evidently was going to be one of those times when she'd know.

Finally finished, Madison sat quietly, knowing Jones was processing all she'd told him. Calm now, Madison rose, grabbing her bottle of water, taking a much-needed swig. Offering Jones a bottle, he accepted it, opening and drinking nearly half of it. He was just replacing the cap when they were interrupted by a hard knock on the door. Her eyes flew to Jones, widening when he remained motionless. Then again, where was the guy gonna go? Outside in the blowing snow? Not likely.

"Answer it," Jones said quietly.

Marveling at his calm demeanor, Madison crossed the room, glancing back to see Jones nod before opening the door.

"Hey, how was your . . ." Shock kicked Jeremy in the gut when he spotted Jones. "What the hell? You know this guy?" What the hell was going on here?

"What?" Madison stammered, totally caught off guard as Jeremy pushed past her.

In a daze, she quietly closed the door, turning back to the men. Thinking on her feet was a necessity in her life, but for the first time ever, she was utterly dumbfounded.

"What?" she repeated numbly.

"What are you doing here?" Jeremy demanded, ignoring Madison as he glared at Jones. "How do you know Madison?"

Damn it, Jeremy thought angrily.

He'd known there was more to Madison, but no way had he seen this coming! Jones was part of a very select group. If he knew Madison, that meant—Jeremy swung back around to face Madison—that she also was a part of that very select group! Holy shit!

Remaining silent for the moment, Jones contemplated his answer. Clearly, Jeremy and Madison knew each other, how well was the question. Jones had been so focused on Madison's story he hadn't delved further. Now he wished he had. While positive that Jeremy had no idea exactly who and what Madison was, Jones knew without a doubt that it'd been Jeremy who'd seen her handle a gun.

Interesting she hadn't referred to Jeremy by name, only referring to him as "the guy she'd had dinner with." If she'd only bothered to mention that minor detail, they could have easily avoided this embarrassing situation. Jones wondered why she hadn't felt it necessary. But then again, there was no reason for her to think the two men would know each other either. Until Jones had seen Jeremy at the airport, he'd had no idea the man was even in the area. Jones wished now that they'd had time to talk after landing. Well, he'd had more pressing matters to attend to first. At any rate, that was water under the bridge. Time to move on. Slowly pushing himself out of his chair, Jones stood with his back to the fire.

"Let's save some time here, shall we? Yes, I know you both," Jones stated quietly, his eyes moving from one to the other.

Jones hadn't gotten as far as he had in the business by telling secrets; he wasn't about to tell either one exactly how he knew them. No, he wasn't going there. If they wanted to know, they'd have to get it out of each other. Jones didn't surrender confidences; he wasn't about to start now. He squashed the smile that threatened; this was pretty funny though, he thought. It definitely was one for the books!

CHAPTER 12

TENSION RIPPLED THROUGH the room as Madison and Jeremy stared at each other, each silently daring the other to speak first.

Talk about egos, Jones thought, dropping back into his chair. Well, he thought, glancing at his watch, he had time to kill, might as well sit back and watch the show. Maybe he'd even learn something new.

Minutes passed before Madison finally gave in, tearing her defiant gaze from Jeremy as she snatched up her bottle of water. How had things gotten so messed up? And why did Jeremy know Jones? She'd suspected that there was much more to Jeremy than he let on, but she'd never seen this one coming! She wished she could call Sarah, and she unconsciously glanced at her watch.

"Do you have someplace you need to be?" Jeremy asked cautiously.

Madison shook her head. "I need to make an overseas call," she said, her eyes sliding to Jones.

I'll bet you do! Jones thought, knowing she was referring to Sarah.

Wouldn't Sarah just be tickled to know what was happening? *Not.* Jones nearly laughed. Talk about a logistics nightmare! On top of the fact that it wasn't wise for a man of his caliber and talent to be caught in between two contractors—well, one contractor, he thought, glancing at Madison, and one . . . what exactly was Jeremy these days?

"Overseas?" Jeremy asked, unable to hide the surprise in his voice.

"It's work-related," Madison said, immediately regretting her words as Jeremy's eyes widened slightly and Jones shook his head.

Shit! Well, in for a penny, in for a pound. If she'd only known to expect Jones, she could have avoided all this! Her mind started churning. The only reason the two men would know each other would be through work, which begged the question: what exactly did Jeremy do that required a man with Jones's expertise? Knowing Jones wasn't about to give up any information, Madison knew she'd have to make the first move, and that meant trusting Jeremy . . . again. She took a deep breath.

"My handler is overseas."

Her handler? Oh, Christ, this just kept getting better and better, Jeremy thought, momentarily speechless.

He'd first heard the term during his time with the RCMP, later actually working with a few as well. But he'd never had direct contact with the actual . . . holy shit! The word froze in his mind as he stared at Madison, unable to hide his shock and surprise.

"You're an assassin?" Trying to get his mind around the concept, Jeremy turned away, avoiding looking at either Jones or Madison. "An assassin?" he murmured, struggling to reconcile what he already knew about Madison with this new revelation.

His mind retraced their time together, and as the pieces came together, Jeremy turned back to Madison. "Holy shit. You're an assassin."

Madison merely nodded, not exactly sure what to say yet. She couldn't deny it, so for the moment, it was better to stay silent.

"You're beyond good with firearms," Jeremy stammered before catching himself.

Get it together, you ass! he admonished himself; it's not like she's a god. *Pretty fucking close, though,* he thought, remembering how smoothly she'd handled his gun and herself in the alley. He could just imagine the other skills she possessed.

"Yeah, well, it's not something I brag about, so let's not be alerting the media, okay?"

He was taking it awfully well, Madison thought, sliding a quick glance toward Jones, who was still sitting quietly in his chair.

"Who are you here to kill?"

Madison's eyes popped at Jeremy's blunt question. Okay, maybe he wasn't taking it as well as she'd thought. Jones just smiled, nothing like getting right to the point!

"Who?"

Understanding that Jeremy was thinking of his family, she rushed to assure him they were all safe.

"No one in town," she quickly assured him, not questioning why she was so relieved that it was the truth.

Her eyes held his as she silently implored him to believe her. Remembering how she'd been with his mother, Jack, and Nancy, Jeremy slowly nodded. No, she wasn't here to hurt his family. *Damn good thing too*, he thought, feeling fiercely protective. He hated the idea of having to possibly kill Madison. But if it came down to a choice between his family and her . . . oh, yeah, he'd kill her in a heartbeat and not think twice about it. Talk about sounding cold-blooded! He took a deep, cleansing breath, forcing himself to calm down. Get all the information before you go off half-cocked!

"I believe you," Jeremy finally said, running a shaky hand through his hair.

Nodding, Madison remained silent. She'd never intended for him to find out about her—hell, if she hadn't gotten snowed in, he never would have known! In fact, she realized, taking it one step further, if she hadn't gotten stuck here, she never would have even met him! Jack would have flown her to her destination, she would have done her job and moved on, leaving no one the wiser. But no, she had to be caught in a fucking blizzard!

"Okay," Jeremy began, interrupting her thought process, "dare I ask whom you are going after?"

"No one you know," she answered immediately.

At least I don't think you know him, she thought ruefully. But then again, who'd have thought that Jeremy would know Jones?

"Who are you here to kill?" Jeremy's blunt question aimed at Jones had Madison turning.

"Yeah, who are you here for?" she asked curiously.

Jones didn't go anywhere without a reason—especially not someplace so far off the beaten path. There was no way he was there just to check up on her. If he'd wanted to do that, he could have done it from any number of other places, places that were considerably warmer. Rising from his chair and pulling out his cell phone, Jones held it out for Jeremy and Madison to see the picture on the screen.

"This guy."

"Seriously?" Madison asked, leaning in for a closer look.

"You know the guy?" Jeremy asked, also leaning in closer.

Madison nodded. "He's staying here at the Inn," Madison said, glancing up at Jeremy. "He's been on my radar since I got here, but I don't know exactly why. I don't know him or the woman he's with, I've never seen him before in my life." She turned back to Jones, "Why are you after him?"

"Because he got on your radar," Jones said quietly. "And your radar is never wrong."

Jones had a point there. If she sensed something about the guy, there was definitely a reason.

"And," Jones continued, turning to Jeremy, "because he killed your person in the alley."

"What?" Madison and Jeremy blurted in unison.

"Are you sure?" Jeremy asked, looking at the picture again. "He doesn't look the type."

The man in the picture was neatly dressed in what was no doubt was a tailor-made suit and tie; not a hair was out of place. In the picture, the man was leaning casually against the railing on a bridge over a river. Jeremy immediately recognized the picture as having been taken in France. Unless Jeremy was mistaken, the man was standing on a bridge going over the Seine in Paris.

"Man, you have been out of it for too long!" Jones said, ignoring Madison's look of surprise. "You of all people should know that a good disguise can mean the difference between life and death, my friend."

Jeremy nodded; there no sense in denying it. Jones was right. He had been out of the game for a long time.

"This guy's one of the bad guys," Jones continued, "and while normally I wouldn't give him the time of day, the fact that he's here at the same time you are, well, that concerns me a little."

"How do you know he killed the guy in the alley?" Madison asked.

"Yeah, why do you think it was him?" Jeremy asked. "What's the connection between the two? And how'd Mary happen to be there? The dead guy wasn't a local."

Mary! Oh, God. Mary's hysterical screaming had alerted them to the body in the alley. Did that mean she was a target now too? Shit!

"We think it was a crime of opportunity more than anything," Jones began to explain.

"What?" Jeremy and Madison asked again in unison.

"The victim, we've learned, was a truck driver who was passing through," Jones continued. "We think he overheard or saw something he shouldn't have and was killed for it."

"Oh my god, the guy was nothing more than a loose end?" Madison asked in disgust. "He was an innocent?"

Jones nodded, understanding how she felt. Despite the fact that they killed people for a living, even the most professional assassin had a strict code of honor. Innocent people were never sacrificed, no matter the circumstances.

"And Mary?" Jeremy asked again, remembering the hysterical girl running at them with blood on her hands.

"From what I've been able to learn, she went looking for him," Jones paused, "after the blowout with you two."

Madison and Jeremy just stared, speechless.

"You know about that?" Madison asked, not sure if she was more embarrassed or angry at his knowing about the ridiculous scene that Mary had caused.

Jones just cocked an eyebrow at Madison.

Of course, Madison smiled ruefully; there wasn't much Jones didn't know.

"Seems this girl, Mary, knew the guy from the restaurant," Jones explained, "and called him later, setting up a time to meet." Jones paused. "Beyond that, I don't know any more."

Jeremy swore under his breath. It was no secret that Mary had been trying to find a way out of town for a long time now. Only this time, her determination to get out had led her to nearly being killed herself.

"It wasn't a well-thought-out plan, what the killer did," Jones continued. "That's why I think it was more of a spur-of-the-moment thing. There was no way the killer could have known that the guy was going to hook up with Mary, that she'd be looking for him. No, he did it on the fly. And badly."

Madison nodded. There'd been that moment when she'd checked the body that she'd had the same thought. It was a messy kill, almost like it was done in a fit of rage. There hadn't been anything professional about it. Well, it might have been done by a pro, but it definitely hadn't been professional. The killer had taken a big chance, that was for damn sure. But again, he didn't know Mary would come looking for the guy either. That fact alone probably contributed to why the kill had been so messy.

"Could the killer have just wanted to make it look messy? Make the police think that a local had rolled the guy?"

It wasn't unheard of, although she doubted that was the case here. No, it was usually something she saw more of on the islands than in the far reaches of Canada—especially during a blizzard.

"That's possible," Jones said, considering the idea for a moment. "He might have also planned to do it neatly, but Mary showing up forced him to change his plan."

That definitely wasn't unheard of. Madison recalled a handful of jobs she'd done that had required her to change her plan at the very last minute. It was part of the business. The fact that she was so good at thinking on her feet was one of the reasons she was still alive today.

"Why didn't he kill Mary?" Jeremy asked, profoundly glad that he hadn't.

Jones shook his head. "Not sure, any number of reasons. I suspect that Mary didn't get a good look at him, though, lucky for her. Safe to say, if she had, she'd be dead now too."

Unless the killer hadn't had time to kill Mary and she was still a target.

"If there was even a chance that she'd seen the killer, he would have gotten to her by now," Madison said, putting the silent thought to rest.

If the guy was as professional as they now believed, he would have found a way to finish the job quickly. Loose ends were never left loose for long.

"Just the same," Jeremy said, "I'll have the police keep an eye on her and hope that this guy is caught sooner than later." He turned to Jones, "If the police are able to nab this guy, what does that mean for you?"

"It just means he lives a little longer, I guess," Jones said, not caring one way or the other.

In this case, he was getting paid whether the job was done or not.

"If the police catch him before I set my sights on him, well, it's a lot less paperwork for me."

Madison chuckled in agreement. The paperwork after a job was such a pain in the ass!

"But," Jones continued, "nothing against your police force, but do you honestly think they'll catch him before I do?"

The guy had a point. But what Jones didn't know was that many of the local police force had backgrounds very similar to Jeremy's. They weren't your average policemen. And with pride in his voice, Jeremy told Jones a little more about them, making it clear that they knew what they were doing and that they could hold their own with very little assistance from outsiders. Nodding, Jones wondered if he knew any of them; it sounded like he might.

"They're welcome to him," Jones easily conceded. "I'm happy to hang back unless I don't have a choice."

Glad Jones was offering to be a team player, Jeremy relaxed a little. The whole thing was already complicated enough, he thought, turning to Madison. One contract killer in town was enough!

Watching Madison unconsciously twirling a lock of her long hair, Jeremy's body warmed. He still couldn't believe what she was! But at the same time, he admitted that it was also a serious turn-on.

You are so warped, he thought, remembering the feel of her in his arms. He itched to have her there again. Jesus Christ! There was a killer on the loose, and all he could think about was getting Madison naked? Shit!

"Any chance we think the victim might have told Mary what he knew or saw?" Madison asked, interrupting Jeremy's thoughts.

He surprised her, immediately shaking his head in denial.

"And you know this how?"

Jeremy gave her a lopsided grin. "You forget, I know the girl. And if there's one thing I know, she wouldn't have given the guy two minutes to say anything. It would have been all about her."

Of course, Madison thought, remembering how Mary had been in the restaurant.

"I hope you're right," Jones said. "But just the same, having her watched isn't a bad idea. Just in case."

"I'm on it," Jeremy assured him, glancing at Madison before back to Jones.

For the moment, things were settled, albeit still slightly in limbo. *Now what*, he wondered.

Silence filled the room as the three of them stared at each other.

"Okay then," Jones and Madison said in unison, laughing at themselves.

"I'll be on my way then," Jones said, gathering his coat before shaking Jeremy's hand. Dropping a light kiss on Madison's cheek, he smiled, "we'll talk more later."

Nodding, Madison followed him to the door. Turning in the doorway, Jones smiled.

"I'll send along your greetings to Sarah," he said with a chuckle, enjoying the blush that dashed across Madison's cheeks.

"You do that," she said lightly. "I'm glad to see you," she added, swallowing the lump that somehow was blocking her throat and choking her up.

While Sarah was the big sister she'd never had, Jones was the big brother she'd never had—he and Sarah's twin brother, that is. The two men made a formidable team, and they'd always been there for her. She squashed the urge to hug Jones; he'd only be embarrassed. And a man of his reputation did not like being embarrassed, no matter the situation. She settled for pushing him out the door with a "See you later," closing the door softly behind him.

Turning and leaning against the door, Madison stared at Jeremy. Well, this certainly had been an interesting afternoon! She chuckled.

"What's so funny?" Jeremy asked from his place by the fireplace.

Throwing caution to the wind, she smiled.

"Did you ever, in your wildest imagination, see this coming?" Madison asked, giving up and just laughing.

What else could she do? The cat was out of the bag. Jeremy knew what she was and why she was there. Granted, she hadn't planned on him finding out quite this way, but the damage was done. Oddly enough, Madison was relieved. At least now she wouldn't have to constantly watch herself. Around Jeremy anyway. With everyone else, yes. Especially Ethel. That woman was too sharp for her own good.

"Can't say that I did," Jeremy chuckled before quickly sobering. "I'll admit I knew there was something . . . different . . . about you, but you being a contract killer? Yeah, can't say that I saw that one coming."

Madison just nodded.

"So now what?"

Her eyes rose to his. Good question! What did she do now? What did they do now? Her stomach choosing that moment to grumble, Madison smiled.

"How about dinner for starters?"

"Dinner sounds good."

Yeah, he thought, *that sounds just fine. For now.*

CHAPTER 13

DESPITE THE STILL-FALLING snow, the restaurant was busy.

"People still need to eat," Ruth reminded Madison as she led them through to "their" table.

Careful not to take Jeremy's chair, Madison dropped into the chair next to his.

"And don't forget, this weather isn't unusual for those of us who live here."

Madison nodded, accepting the menu Ruth handed her. Ordering a beer, Jeremy didn't bother to glance at the menu. There was no need.

Just as it had been the night before, dinner was excellent, and leaning back in her chair, Madison sighed happily.

"I can't remember the last time I ate this well or this much!" She smiled as her plate was taken away, replaced with a steaming mug of coffee and the dessert menu. "I can just imagine how much weight I've gained already!"

Truly surprised by her "typical" female comment, Jeremy took in the black sweater over the black turtleneck covering her svelte body. Talk about ironic! Here was a woman capable of killing without remorse worried about gaining a few pounds! It was almost laughable. And he very nearly did until he remembered the feel of her in his arms. He felt himself growing hard, the blood pouring from his brain, flowing south in a hurry, and he moaned silently. Thank God, she was engrossed in the dessert menu and had no clue the direction of his thoughts!

Deciding on a dessert, Madison put down the menu, her eyes rising to meet Jeremy's. The heat emanating from his gaze had her catching her breath before he quickly looked away. With a knowing smile, she leaned back in her chair, gracefully crossing her legs. Feeling the pull of her gaze, Jeremy's eyes slowly came back to her, not bothering to disguise his desire this time. What was the point? They were beyond that now.

"What are you thinking?" Jeremy finally asked quietly.

Talk about a loaded question! She gave him a coy smile, knowing full well what he was referring to. But she wasn't about to make it easy for him.

"The white chocolate bread pudding looks awfully good," she said demurely.

He resisted the urge to reach out and throttle her. Two could play at this game! He hoped, anyway.

"Anything else?"

"The apple crisp looks good."

He was going to kill her. "Anything else?"

"I'll tell you later," she said hurriedly, catching Ruth in the corner of her eye approaching their table.

"Tell me now," Jeremy growled, leaning closer to Madison.

Shaking her head, Madison unconsciously sat up a bit straighter as Ruth joined them.

"Okay, later," he quickly conceded, feeling his mother's hand on his shoulder before she leaned over to kiss his cheek. "Hi, Mom," he sighed, hoping she wouldn't make him stand up.

He wasn't in the mood to show off his excitement to the gang in the restaurant. But just in case, he made the motion to push himself out of his chair, vastly relieved when Ruth told him to stay seated. Dodged a bullet there!

With a smile for both of them, Ruth dropped into the chair beside Jeremy. She'd seen how the two of them had been making eyes at each other. Ruth wasn't so old that she didn't remember that warm feeling, her eyes seeking out her husband behind the bar, tossing him a seductive smile of her own. Then remembering why she'd sat down, Ruth sobered.

"Sorry to interrupt," Ruth began, "but I wanted to ask, have you seen Mary?" Jeremy sat up straighter.

"What?"

"She didn't show up for work, and I haven't been able to reach her, she's not answering her cell," Ruth continued. "I'm a little worried."

"Has she done this before?" Madison asked.

Jeremy and Ruth nodded.

"So could it just be a case of her being a no-show?"

Ruth and Jeremy glanced at each other. It was no secret that Mary could be selfish and immature at times. And she had skipped out on work a few times without calling.

"It could be," Ruth admitted. "It's just that given the circumstances, I'm more worried this time."

"Have you talked to her folks?" Jeremy asked, picking up on Madison's train of thought.

Ruth nodded; they hadn't seen her. But that still didn't give just cause for worry. Mary had friends she could be staying with—or rather, hiding out with. It was a small town but not that small. She could be anywhere.

The sound of an air horn blowing startled Madison, and she glanced toward the entrance of the restaurant.

"Trucker's coming in," Ruth announced.

"In this weather?" Ruth and Jeremy nearly laughed at the shock and surprise on Madison's face.

"They follow the snowplows through," Ruth explained, knowing she'd have some hungry men bursting through the door shortly.

Pushing out of her chair, she glanced toward the kitchen, sure they'd heard the horns and were preparing for the onslaught.

"Work calls."

"Mom," Jeremy tugged on Ruth's sleeve, and she glanced down her son, her mind already back on work. "I'm sure Mary's fine." With a tilt of his head toward the door, he continued, "Maybe she caught a ride out of town?"

It was possible. Mary had been talking about leaving town for as long as they could remember. Maybe she'd done just that. And not telling anyone—well, Mary had never been the most considerate person. It probably wouldn't have fazed her in the least to just up and leave. Tossing a glance toward the door, Ruth smiled as she recognized the truck driver brushing snow off himself. A regular on this route, the big man was a familiar face. She turned back to Jeremy, nodding.

"It's possible," Ruth admitted, making a mental note to ask the truck driver when he'd gotten settled and had some food.

It wasn't wise approaching him before then; he'd only act like a bear, grumpy and hungry. She could wait a bit. With a smile for Madison and another quick kiss on Jeremy's cheek, Ruth headed toward the kitchen.

Ruth's interruption coupled with her concern for Mary dampened their desire only a fraction. Sipping her coffee, Madison smiled over her mug at Jeremy.

"Not even sure I want to know what that smile's all about," Jeremy said, thoughts of Mary suddenly millions of miles away.

"Oh, but I think you do," Madison's husky voice rolled over him, and he could only nod.

"Then tell me," he said leaning closer, itching to touch her. "What are you thinking?"

With a seductive smile, Madison leaned in closer to Jeremy, her hand snaking out to caress his thigh under the table.

"I'm thinking that I'm going to go with the white chocolate bread pudding."

Oh, yeah, he was going to kill her. Right after he stopped laughing, that is.

Ushering Madison quickly into his house, before he'd even closed the door behind them, he pulled her into his arms. Wrapping her arms around him, her gloved hands linked behind his back as her mouth found his. Tugging off her hat, Jeremy's gloved hands buried themselves in her hair as his mouth plundered hers, his tongue diving into her mouth to find hers. Pushing her back against the wall, he pressed his hard body against hers, reveling in the feel of her arching into him. Only when his hand slid down in search of her breast did he remember their bulky coats and gloves. With a chuckle, he pulled back slightly.

"We've got too many clothes on," Madison smiled, reading his mind.

Jeremy only nodded, going to work on the zipper of her jacket as she reached for his. Pushing their coats off, Jeremy was content to let them fall on the floor but then, taking a deep breath, knew he couldn't do that. With a sigh, he released Madison, bending over to scoop up the coats before turning and hanging them on the peg by the door.

"Old habits," he said, turning back to her with a sheepish smile.

It didn't matter that he was thirty-six years old. He could still hear his mother telling him to hang up his coat and that he hadn't been raised in a barn. Taking Madison's hat and gloves, he put them aside to dry with his own before turning back to her, a wolfish grin on his face.

"Now where were we?"

Lying side by side, naked in his king-sized bed, their fingers entwined, Madison struggled not to sigh happily while Jeremy struggled not to grin foolishly.

"Wow," he finally managed to say, squeezing her hand gently.

"I know, right?" And giving up, Madison sighed dreamily.

And they broke out laughing.

"Aren't we just the pair?"

And curling up against him, she smiled against his chest, the sound of his heart beating strongly in her ear, and closed her eyes. Feeling her breath whispering across his chest, Jeremy glanced down at her.

"Are you sleeping?"

They'd had a workout; she had a reason to be tired. He grinned.

"Nope. Just relaxing for a minute."

For a minute? His grinned blossomed into a full-blown smile.

"Relax all you like," he whispered, kissing the top of her hair as he hugged her to him.

Madison let out another sigh and then was silent.

With her curled up against him, Jeremy smiled into the darkness. Outside his bedroom, a small lamp softly illuminated the hallway just enough so he hadn't needed to turn on the bedroom light when they'd come upstairs.

You mean, when you stumbled upstairs and into the bedroom, he reminded himself, his smile growing again.

They'd been all over each other downstairs, starting in the hallway and working their way into the kitchen—their hands and mouths greedily taking and giving, demanding more, offering more. Madison's sweater came off in the hallway, Jeremy's shirt coming off as they moved into the kitchen. Her shirt following the way of his shirt as he pinned her against the counter, Jeremy's hands skimmed up and over her full breasts, wanting nothing more than to free them from the silky bra that covered them. He paused only briefly when his eyes fell upon the pink bra, admittedly taken back by the feminine color. The woman was nothing if not full of surprises. And if that wasn't a total turn-on, he didn't know what was! With gentle ease, he reached behind her, smiling when her eyes widened as her bra came undone and her breasts spilled out.

"You've done this before" she smiled against his lips, her tongue sweeping into his mouth, meeting and dancing with his.

"Practice makes perfect," he whispered. "And you deserve perfect."

Needing to feel her skin against his, he crushed her to him, the truth of his words fueling the fire she'd unknowingly set.

His hands tightened around her waist, and Madison felt herself being lifted up; and sitting on the counter, she spread her legs, bringing him closer. Her head fell back with a deep sigh as Jeremy's mouth found her breast. His tongue teased her nipple into a hard pebble, drawing a moan from Madison as she held his head to her, arching into his mouth. Heat and moisture pooled between her legs, pleasure roaring through her too-long-denied body.

When was the last time she'd felt this good? For that matter, when was the last time she'd been with a man? It didn't bear thinking about at the moment.

Her hands moved to grip the edge of the counter as her body instinctively moved against his. Her panties damp, a long-forgotten ache flowed through her—the desire and need to be touched overtaking her—and she nearly moaned in frustration.

His body tuned to hers, Jeremy's lips left her breast, kissing their way back up to her mouth before claiming her lips in a searing kiss that had them both moaning. Nestling himself between her legs, she felt his hardness and strained against it. His arms tightened around her, feeling her moving against him. The countertop was just high enough; he was just tall enough. He could easily just slip inside her . . . The exciting thought raced through his mind as his hands slid down to find the button of her pants.

"You deserve perfect," he said again into her hot mouth as her pants opened.

"I deserve a bed."

Did she just say that? Suddenly, passion was sidelined as she giggled at her bold remark. Her giggle vibrated through Jeremy, exciting him more even as he realized she was right. And a bed would certainly be more comfortable for what he had in mind! He nodded and, moving swiftly, swung her off the counter and into his arms. Surprised by his gallant actions, Madison giggled again. Never had she been swept off her feet and carried in a man's arms! This was fun!

While Madison was shorter than Jeremy, she was also a solid woman; there was nothing skimpy or light about her. Jeremy took four steps toward the stairs before, with a grunt, putting her down gently, her back against his chest. His arms went around her, his hands cupping her breasts as she leaned back into him, her head dropping against his chest.

"I tried," he smiled against her throat before dropping his hands to her waist.

"You get an A for effort," Madison laughed, praying her legs would hold her up as Jeremy urged her toward the stairs.

Thankful for the railing on both sides, Madison managed to pull herself up the stairs, pausing at the top, waiting for him to steer her in the right direction. Instead, he swung her around, wrapping his arms around her and kissing her deeply.

"Sorry, had to do that," he said nonchalantly before taking her hand and leading her to his room.

Dazed, she followed him.

Soft light from the hallway lamp illuminating his bedroom, Jeremy gently pushed Madison down onto the big bed. Dropping with a laugh, she gasped as her pants were pulled down over her hips, disappearing into the darkness, followed by her panties. Cool air hit her, exciting her more, and she wiggled into the middle of the bed, gasping when he grabbed her legs, pulling her back to him. The flat of his hand rested gently on her stomach as he leaned forward, his lips running lightly over her exposed skin. Tingling, Madison struggled to not squirm under his warm lips, her legs spreading to cradle him. His lips slowly traveled downward toward her moist opening and, blowing softly on her sensitive skin, smiled as she gasped again, arching up toward him. Taking advantage of the invitation, he kissed her gently before his tongue dipped into her, causing her to cry out in pleasure.

Clutching the quilt, her hips rose to meet his mouth, her body on fire as he worked his magic on her. Pleasure raced through her, and pushing herself up, her eyes sought him out in the dimly lit room. Nestled between her legs, his hand still resting on her stomach, his tongue delved deeper into her; and throwing back her head, she moaned. Forcing herself to look again at his head buried between her legs, the tingly feeling she'd been fighting overtook her, and this time, she threw her head back with a scream as the orgasm ripped through her. Falling back, she let the tremors ripple through her as Jeremy slowly ended his onslaught. Blowing softly once more, his warm breath soothed her before he moved away. Cool air replaced his warmth, and Madison whimpered, reaching blindly for him. With a smile, Jeremy lay down beside her, his arm resting over her stomach. Turning to him, Madison sought out his waiting mouth, tasting herself while kissing him deeply. It was wildly erotic, and she reached for him, wanting—no, needing—to bring him the same pleasure.

His jeans open, with a little help from him lifting his hips, they went the way of her jeans and panties earlier. Hmm, boxers instead of briefs—she smiled to herself before they followed his jeans. Pushing him onto his back, her hand slid softly down to fondle his hardness, her fingers gliding up and down before squeezing him gently. Sure he was going to suck up all the air in the room, Jeremy groaned as her fingers caressed him as she kissed his chest. When her tongue tickled first one then the other nipple, he jerked in her hand, praying he could keep control of himself. But if she kept this up, it was going to be close!

Madison's lips danced over his chest as she moved downward. Bracing for what he knew was coming, he still jerked, harder this time, as she took him into her velvety mouth. Her tongue and lips driving him mad with pleasure, he groaned again. Her fingers gently cradling and caressing his sac, Jeremy suddenly found himself struggling not to laugh. Of all the places to be ticklish! Reaching for her, needing her to stop before he disgraced himself, either by laughing or coming—he wasn't sure which—Jeremy struggled to grab her wrist.

"Stop, stop," he begged.

And losing the battle, he laughed.

He was still hard in her mouth; what the hell was he laughing at? Her hand stilled, and with a final swipe of her tongue up the length of him, Madison rose up. Darkness hid the questioning look she tossed him, but he knew.

"What can I say," Jeremy began with a laugh, "I'm ticklish."

"There?" This was a first!

"There." Then taking her hand gently, he guided it back to him. "But not here."

Her fingers wrapped around the length of him, and she caressed him gently for a moment.

"Thank God," she smiled into the darkness as his arms came around her, pulling her down beside him.

"You have no idea," he murmured, kissing her quickly.

Rolling away from her, he swung his legs over the edge of the bed. Lying back, Madison listened as a drawer opened and closed, followed by the sound of something ripping. Then he was beside her again, hard against her hip. Wrapping her arms around him, she pulled him on top of her, opening her legs to welcome him. Settling between her long legs, he rose up over her, and with eyes open and a wide smile, he slid into her welcoming body. A sigh of pure pleasure escaped her as he filled her, and she closed her eyes, her body moving with his. Deep inside her, Jeremy moaned. Their bodies fit perfectly; he felt like he'd come home. When she wrapped her legs around him, holding him tightly to her, he buried his face in her hair, breathing in her scent as he kissed her neck, teasing her with his tongue. Minutes passed as their bodies moved smoothly in unison— their sighs mingled with deep, then shallow and sweet kisses as they murmured words of passion and desire.

Feeling that now-familiar tingly sensation beginning to build, Madison wrapped her arms around Jeremy, pulling him closer as her hips rose up to meet his in undeniable urgency. Her body rocked against his as need overtook passion, and he thrust hard and deep inside her, wanting to give her that release he knew she needed. That he needed.

Light exploded behind her tightly closed eyes as the orgasm took her over the edge, and she cried his name, taking him with her as her body exploded around him. Her name on his lips, Jeremy willingly followed her over the edge and into the abyss they silently knew they'd never escape.

CHAPTER 14

"WHY CAN'T WE go out for dinner? Why do we have to stay in?" Ellen demanded, her eyes blazing as she glared at Frank.

"I told you, it's not safe right now," Frank repeated for the tenth time, only to be rewarded with yet another frustrated sigh as Ellen slumped in her chair.

Turning and staring sightlessly out the window, Frank squelched his desire to just throttle Ellen once and for all. The woman was seriously driving him insane! As if he didn't already have enough on his mind!

Having joined their group for luncheon earlier in the day, Frank and Ellen surprisingly enjoyed the easy conversation going around the group. Made up of freelance photographers as well as those who enjoyed photography as a hobby, all were eager to continue their trek up north. Anxious to photograph the snow-covered scenery as well as the various types of wildlife they hoped to spot, their enthusiasm was contagious, and Frank found himself relaxing, enjoying their banter. Even Ellen, who'd once dabbled in photography, chimed in from time to time. Watching her smile and laugh, Frank briefly forgot their earlier antagonism—until Ellen glanced his way, her eyes icy. Looking away, he swallowed his temper, vowing to keep it under control before he did something he'd regret. Well, do something else anyway.

He hadn't intended to kill the man in the alley! Foolishly thinking the noise in the restaurant would distract anyone from overhearing their conversation, Frank had discussed his plan with Ellen over dinner. It wasn't until it was too late that he noticed the guy at the table next to them, blatantly staring at Frank, clearly shocked. Figuring if he just ignored the guy that he'd leave them alone, Frank turned his back to the guy. Quickly changing the subject, Frank made Ellen laugh, hoping the happy sound would deter the guy at the next table. Not to be put off, the guy, a trucker who frequently passed through the town, pushed all caution aside, excusing himself from the people at his table before dropping into the empty seat next to Frank.

Without introducing himself, the trucker began peppering Frank with questions, ignoring Ellen and missing the shocked look on her face. Determined to find out what Frank was up to before he went to the police, the trucker kept his eyes locked on Frank. Amazed at the man's audacity—or foolishness, Frank couldn't decide which—he brushed off the trucker's questions with a brusque "It's none of your business" and reminded the guy that eavesdropping could be a dangerous thing. When the trucker kept at him, Frank pushed back from the table. Throwing some money on the table, he nodded at Ellen and excused himself, knowing that if he didn't leave now, he'd do something that he'd regret.

Hurrying out into the snow, Frank took great gulps of air as he struggled to calm himself. How could he have been so stupid? Sure, the guy had been foolish to eavesdrop in the first place, but Frank had been stupider to even discuss the plan in a public place! Clearly, he'd misjudged the people of this small town, having assumed they were nothing more than backwoods folks.

Coming to a stop, Frank looked around, suddenly realizing he'd taken a wrong turn somewhere. Damn! For a small town, the place had way too many side streets! Turning in a small circle, Frank nearly jumped when someone grabbed his arm. Swinging back around, Frank stared in astonishment, coming face-to-face with the trucker. Didn't this guy know when to quit? Still demanding answers, the trucker kept a firm grip on Frank's arm. Viciously shaking off the trucker's hand, Frank warned him again about minding his own business, but the trucker kept peppering him.

Though the same height, the trucker clearly outweighed Frank—if the belly hanging over his belt buckle was any indication. Briefly wondering why the guy wasn't freezing, noting his open jacket, Frank stared at the trucker in utter amazement. The guy just wasn't giving up, demanding more and more to know who this "target" was that Frank was going after.

His temper boiling, Frank glanced around and, grabbing the trucker by the arm, dragged the surprised man into the alley behind them. Thinking only that he was finally going to get the answers he was after, the trucker stumbled after Frank. A few feet into the alley, Frank swung the trucker around, and before the man could catch his balance, Frank punched the man in the gut, followed by a savage punch to the face, when the man doubled over in shock and pain. His head snapping back, the trucker stumbled backward, but not allowing his opponent a minute to regroup, Frank was on him, punching and pounding the man. Trying to block the punches, the trucker struggled to fend off Frank's assault, but when a swift kick to his knee knocked him to the ground, the man realized his stupidity. Never did the trucker consider that the man dressed neatly in a turtleneck and heavy-cabled sweater and dress pants would be able to bring him to his knees!

His eyes blurry from the continual hits to his face, the trucker struggled to grab Frank, but unable to get any purchase, he instead found himself rolling in the snow, trying to get away. Trying to protect his face, the trucker screamed when Frank smashed his already-wounded knee, the pain excruciating; and writhing in pain, the trucker whimpered, pleading for mercy but getting none.

Realizing that the trucker's screams might have been heard, Frank's tactics changed. This asshole was one more problem he didn't need, and red-hot fury coursed through Frank's veins. First forced to come to this cold and barren place after his target had repeatedly slipped through his fingers and now this idiot with his unrelenting questions! Frank's rage over took him, and he kicked and pummeled the fallen man until, tiring of the beating, Frank stomped on the fallen man's throat, effectively breaking his neck, silencing the trucker once and for all.

Taking a deep breath, Frank stared at the dead man, an evil smile sweeping across his face. The trucker didn't have to die; Frank knew that. A good ol'-fashioned beating would probably have been enough. But the trucker had been stupid, letting things go further than necessary, pushing Frank beyond the brink. Suddenly presented with an outlet for his frustrations, Frank turned the trucker into an easy target, forcing the injured man to pay with his life. All well. Glancing at his bloodied gloves, Frank tugged them off, relieved to see that they'd protected his hands from bruising. While he'd long ago quit smoking, Frank still carried a lighter, and moving away from the body, he found a place further down the alley. And with a flick of the lighter, he set the gloves on fire. Too bad too, they'd been expensive gloves.

"Steve?"

Whirling around, Frank searched for the voice calling out. Far enough down the alley, darkness hid him, but could whoever was coming see the light from the burning gloves? Stomping on them, knowing they'd been burned enough to destroy any evidence, Frank slipped further back into the shadows. Moments later, a bloodcurdling scream filled the alley, and Frank knew the body had been found—by a girl, if the pitch of the scream was anything to go by. Taking a tentative step forward, Frank squinted in the darkness, barely making out the shape of the girl. As she stepped back from the body, light from the street lamp outside the alley fell on her, and Frank instantly recognized the girl as having been their waitress at the restaurant! Shit!

Sobbing uncontrollably, Mary knelt down, searching for a pulse, screaming again when her hands came away covered in blood. At the sound of approaching footsteps, Mary leaped to her feet, stumbling toward the alley entrance, oblivious to the man silently approaching from behind her. Glancing quickly at the body, Frank drifted back into the darkness as he heard voices comforting the hysterical girl. Then the silhouette of another woman entered the alley. Frank ground his teeth in frustration. His target was standing right in front of him, and he was powerless to do anything! Fuck!

Her attention on the body, Mary's sobbing distracted Madison from sensing Frank's presence as she tucked the gun into her waistband. Having retreated further back into the alley, Frank knew he was safe from being discovered. Waiting another few minutes while the police and ambulance arrived, only when the EMTs removed the body did Frank move again, making his way carefully down the alley, disappearing deeper into the darkness.

"This is ridiculous, Frank," Ellen whined again, pulling Frank's attention back to her as she pushed herself out of her chair. "I'm going to get something to eat. You can stay here, if anyone asks about you, I'll just tell them you're nursing a headache."

Still thinking about that first night in town and killing the trucker, it took Frank a moment to clear his head.

"What?" Giving her a blank stare, he absently rubbed his temples as his thoughts came back to the present. "What were you saying?"

"So glad I have your attention," Ellen said dryly.

Not that she ever expected to—she knew he was focused on other things, the least of them being her. She wasn't blind to the fact that the job he was there to do wasn't going as planned. At all. But instead of killing one person, Frank seemed intent to leave a trail of bodies in his wake. While not bothered by Frank's passion for killing—hers was just as powerful—Ellen knew she had much-better control of her temper whereas Frank did not. There'd been no need for the trucker to die; she'd known that. But as he often did lately, Frank again lost control, letting his emotions cloud his better judgment. If it'd been up to Ellen, their target would have been eliminated long ago, and things never would have gotten this far out of hand. But Frank had a personal vendetta as well, and Ellen was there only as window dressing. It grated on her nerves, admitting that, but she was also content to let Frank dig his own grave. And if he continued on, as he was Ellen was sure, he'd do just that. And there was no way in hell she was going down with the man. With a resigned shake of her head, Ellen repeated herself, ignoring Frank's scowl.

"Fine," he finally conceded, "but the less you need to say to anyone, the better, all right?"

Ellen nodded, scooping up her coat and purse as she headed for the door. Surprising them both, she turned at the door, asking him if he'd like her to bring something back for him. Shaking his head, Frank turned back to stare out the window, closing his eyes only when he heard the door open and close softly.

Things were not going as he'd planned, and he needed to rein in his temper! In all his years, he'd never had such a difficult time killing someone! But somehow his current target did nothing but thwart his every plan! First she latches on to a local guy, then turns up at the alley, then just plain disappears from the Inn for long periods of time. Never alone she'd unknowingly been protecting herself from him. To make matters worse, Frank was almost positive that his target was aware of who he was—if their brief altercation in the lobby the other night was any indication. Shit! If she'd only been able to fly on to her destination, none of this would have happened! Fucking weather!

His original plan had been to fly up north with her, killing her silently during the flight, making it look like natural causes, that by the time the real cause of death was discovered, he'd be long gone. But the incoming storm had changed his plan completely, and he'd been forced to integrate himself further into the group he'd arrived with. Damn!

He hated being around so many people. But he grudgingly admitted, at least the group he and Ellen were with were nice, decent people, and they'd been able to blend in relatively easily. Like any group, everyone was mildly curious about the others in the group. But luckily, this group seemed content to accept the most basic of answers; no one seemed interested in delving into anyone else's life. Thank goodness for small favors! While Frank had made sure their cover was airtight, that still didn't mean it was perfect. And given all the changes that had taken place, their cover might not hold up under close scrutiny. If he and Ellen could stick close to the group, they'd be okay. It was the townspeople he needed to be careful of.

The owner of the restaurant, a naturally curious woman—Frank avoided her like the plague. And her sons, he gave them a wide berth as well. The waitress who'd found the body in the alley, Frank wasn't sure about her just yet. Would she be able to identify him? She might. He wasn't sure how much she'd noticed when they'd been at the restaurant that first night, instead, ironically being more intent on the woman who was also his target. Witnessing the scene the waitress had caused, it was abundantly clear the girl was not happy about Madison seemingly latching on to a man she considered to be hers.

He was confident now that the waitress hadn't seen him in the alley, but Frank still wasn't totally convinced she wasn't a loose end.

And then there was the innkeeper, Ethel. That woman was definitely going to be a problem if he wasn't able to get out of town soon. She knew too much about everything, and while an older woman, Frank sensed she was someone to be reckoned with. Yes, he needed to avoid her as much as possible. No matter how much he might want to kill Ethel, he knew doing that would only bring down the wrath of hell on him, no matter how discrete he was. Damn!

He never should have killed the trucker. If he'd only let the poor fool live, he'd be out now enjoying a nice meal with Ellen. And now, making matters worse, it seemed that the waitress had upped and vanished as well. And while Frank could honestly say he hadn't had anything to do with that, he still felt like all eyes were on him now. And that was a feeling he despised! In his line of work, that feeling did not bode well.

Maybe he should have gone with Ellen, act like everything's fine. No, he didn't dare venture out just yet. He'd lost track of his target—no telling where she might turn up now. No, Frank decided, it was time for a new plan. Pouring himself a cup of coffee, he dropped into the chair by the fire, watching the flames while sipping his coffee, allowing his mind to calm. His stomach grumbled. He wished he'd accepted Ellen's offer to bring him back something to eat.

"You fellas will have to settle for two rooms unless one of you doesn't mind sleeping on a sofa bed," Ethel said, eyeing the two truckers who'd just tramped snow all over her nice, clean lobby. Men, would they ever learn to wipe their feet?

"Two rooms will be fine," the taller trucker smiled, slapping his friend. "I like the guy, but after ten hours on the road, I want some alone time."

Both men laughed and waited patiently while Ethel checked them into the Inn, directing them to their rooms with an "Enjoy your stay" before watching them disappear into the stairwell. Idly wondering why they didn't take the elevator, Ethel went back to her front desk paperwork.

Pausing outside their doors, pleased the rooms were side by side, the men made plans to meet for dinner before disappearing inside. Ignoring the comfortable decor of the room, Jones immediately checked the room, out of habit, for any recording devices. Knowing his partner would be doing the same in the other room, he wasn't surprised to find the room totally clean. There was absolutely no reason for anyone to suspect them of being there. As far as anyone was concerned, they were two truckers just hunkering down for the night, nothing more and nothing less.

Glancing at his watch and calculating the time difference, Jones snatched up his phone, sending a quick text message to Sarah: "We're here."

Knowing there wouldn't be an immediate reply—not that he needed one anyway—he tossed the phone on the bed before unpacking his duffel bag. Minutes later, sliding his phone into his coat pocket, Jones gave the room another quick once-over. Satisfied everything was in order, he slung his coat over his shoulder and headed downstairs to the lobby.

Spotting his friend at the coffee station, Jones sauntered over, tossing his coat on the back of a chair before pouring himself a coffee, all the while keeping his back to the front desk.

"Seems our friend is still holed up in his room, this according to Ethel."

"Ethel?" Jones asked, sipping his coffee, his eyes drifting around the comfortable living room, taking in the blazing fire that beckoned him to come and relax beside it.

At least he had a fireplace in his room; he'd enjoy it later. Hopefully.

"The lady who checked us in," his friend replied. "She's very chatty . . . in a knowing sort of way."

Jones glanced quickly toward the front desk, Ethel was talking on the phone, scowling.

"Oh?"

"Hmm," he sipped his coffee, "she's someone to watch out for. There's more to her than meets the eye."

Jones nodded in understanding. During his first visit with Madison, he'd had a little time to discreetly observe Ethel. Making a mental note to do some background on her later, Jones finished his coffee.

"His wife, however, is out having dinner."

"No doubt at the only good restaurant in town," Jones said quietly, glancing again at Ethel.

Why was she still scowling? His spine tingled.

"Who's she talking to, do you know?"

His friend shook his head, glancing toward Ethel. "Whoever it is, she's not very happy."

"Agreed."

Tossing his Styrofoam cup in the trash, Jones reached for his coat.

"Hungry?"

"Always."

And falling into step beside Jones, the two men strolled through the lobby, giving Ethel a casual wave before venturing back out into the cold. Once outside, they paused briefly, glancing idly around.

"She's worried, they still haven't found Mary yet."

"Who's Mary?"

"The waitress that found the dead guy," Jones explained.

"Oh. I couldn't get who Ethel was talking to, but this Mary person was the topic of conversation."

Jones nodded, filling in his friend while they walked through the snow to the restaurant. By the time they reached the steps of the restaurant, his friend was completely caught up.

CHAPTER 15

WHEN WAS THE last time she'd laughed so hard? Madison couldn't remember. For that matter, when was the last time she'd played in the snow in the dark—bright light from the porch their only source of illumination? Swiftly dodging the snowball aimed at her head, she scooped up a handful of snow, throwing it before she'd fully packed it down, laughing as it fell apart before coming anywhere near Jeremy. Dropping to scoop up more snow, she yelped as a perfectly aimed snowball hit her squarely in the back of her head. Whirling around, intent on throwing her own snowball, she let out a *woof* as Jeremy tackled her. Falling into the deep snow, they laughed as the fluffy snow engulfed them. Arms and legs tangled up, they ignored the cold as warm lips found warm lips and tongues briefly danced. Passion flared only to be extinguished just as quickly when cold snow found its way past Madison's coat and down her back.

"Ahh! Cold! Cold! Cold! Get off me!" Madison laughed, pushing Jeremy away as she struggled to stand up.

Laughing, Jeremy tugged her to her feet, taking advantage of her being briefly off balance to pull her back into his arms, his lips claiming hers in a searing kiss. Gripping his arms, Madison kissed him back before wrapping her leg around his and, with a shove, pushed him back into the snow. Running for the house, she nearly dove through the door, slamming it behind her. Moments later, still laughing, Jeremy came through the door, shaking snow on to the floor.

"You'd better wipe up that snow!" Madison called from the kitchen.

"Yes, Mom!"

Happy laughter his only reply, Jeremy shrugged off his coat and, hanging it up, made sure he hadn't tracked in more snow than necessary before tugging off his boots. Cleaning up as much as he could, he left to find Madison in the kitchen making hot chocolate. Remembering her naked and in his arms just a short time ago, his body quickly warmed. He smiled his thanks when a hot mug was shoved into his cold hands, unconsciously wrapping his hands around the welcome warmth. Jesus, when had he been this happy? This relaxed? Watching Madison move around the kitchen as if it were her own, Jeremy knew he could easily get used to this! And when she turned and simply smiled at him, his heart tripped. Uh-oh.

"I figured we could get warmed up then go for dessert?" Madison asked, sipping her own hot chocolate.

"Sounds like a plan," Jeremy smiled, the hot chocolate working its magic on his cold body.

Of course, it was probably the thought of Madison in his bed that was really warming him up. He hid his smile in his mug, wondering if his idea of dessert was the same as hers. The look on her face told him it wasn't.

"Great," Madison said, "because I'm starved."

She winked at him, and his body flared.

"I know I had dessert before, but it seems all the exercise I've had recently has made me develop an appetite."

If she winked at him one more time, they'd be getting dessert all right—maybe not the kind she was thinking of, but it'd be dessert just the same! Turning away and stomping down on his lustful thoughts, Jeremy noticed the blinking light on his answering machine. His stomach growled. Could he hold off checking the message until later? No, he'd better do it now; otherwise, he was sure he'd regret it later.

Following his gaze, Madison sighed. They'd had such a wonderful evening; she didn't want it to end. But the time was fast approaching when they'd need to return to the real world. She smiled wryly into her mug. It'd been nice visiting that world of laughter and fun, and she hoped she'd be able to visit it again someday.

"Better check your messages," Madison said quietly. "It might be important."

Jeremy nodded. "Sorry," he said, pushing the button to play back the message.

Despite the background noise, Jeremy recognized the woman's voice. And apparently, someone was at the restaurant looking for him.

"Who was that?" Madison asked, coming to stand beside him. "It didn't sound like your mother."

"It wasn't, it was the Annie, one of the hostesses." He paused. "She didn't sound like she was distressed, that's a plus."

"Nope, she sounded just fine to me," Madison agreed.

Turning and taking Madison's mug, Jeremy placed them in the sink.

"Guess you're going to get that dessert after all," he smiled. "And while I'd planned that all along, I will admit, this wasn't the dessert I was hoping for."

Patting his cheek lightly as she walked past him to shrug on her coat, gloves, and boots, Madison laughed.

"I know it wasn't." She threw him a promising smile. "Later."

Oh, yeah, later for sure, he thought, following her back outside into the snow.

Shaking off the snow yet again, Madison and Jeremy searched the restaurant for whoever it was that was waiting for him.

"Do we know who it is we're looking for?" Madison asked, her eyes racing over the crowded restaurant.

It amazed her that even later in the evening, the place was still jumping.

"Not a clue," Jeremy admitted.

He'd asked Annie; she just pointed toward the bar. Every man sitting at the bar had their back to them; how was he supposed to recognize someone? Voicing his frustration, he took Madison's hand; and weaving their way through the crowd, they headed toward the bar.

Coming out of the kitchen, Ruth caught sight of Jeremy, and with a distinct whistle that had Jeremy spinning around, she met them halfway. With a quick hug and a kiss on the cheek, Jeremy greeted his mother, quickly telling her why they were there. Nodding, Ruth took Jeremy's hand, leading him toward a table in the back corner. Slowing as they approached, Jeremy studied the two men, wondering why one looked vaguely familiar. The other one, Jeremy had never seen him before. Why did they want to talk to him? Throwing a cautious glance at Madison, Jeremy was surprised to see a big smile split her face. Okay, so evidently, she knew one or both of the men. And he immediately realized it was Madison they wanted to see, not him. But why hadn't whoever they were called her room? Unless they knew she wouldn't be there. Unless they knew she'd be with him. But who would know that Madison was with him? His mother, Ethel, and maybe Jack. And none of them would ever give out that information to anyone. No, someone else knew. And that thought made Jeremy very nervous.

Turning his attention back to the two men, Jeremy found himself staring at the shorter of the two men. The guy did look vaguely familiar. But who . . . holy shit! Jeremy's eyes widened as he realized it was Jones! Underneath the baseball cap, he now wore was long, mouse-brown hair pulled back into a messy ponytail, a full mustache of the same color running down into a bushy beard. Rising and offering his hand, Jeremy shook it, taking in the flannel shirt over the black turtleneck. Worn jeans and heavy work boots completed the look. No one would ever suspect this man of being an international arms dealer, among other things. Certainly, no one would recognize this rough-looking guy as being the same man he and Jack had flown in!

"Jeremy," Jones greeted him, his voice raspy now, evidently from all the cigarettes the guy smoked—a pack sticking out of his shirt pocket and his badly stained teeth evidence of the man's habit.

Nodding, not sure what to say just yet, Jeremy returned the firm handshake. Releasing Jeremy's hand and turning to Madison, Jones smiled, his nicotine-stained teeth nearly making Jeremy groan.

"Madison."

Dropping into a chair opposite the men, Madison didn't bother to hide her broad smile as she all but ignored Jones. In their profession, one of the major keys was being able to blend into any surrounding. Standing out only brought unnecessary attention, followed usually by death—and a painful one at that. Her years in the business had helped Madison perfect her own unique skill for blending in. That and she'd also had an excellent teacher, proof of his own unique talent staring back at her from under one of the best disguises she'd ever seen him use.

Piercing emerald-blue eyes watched her unabashedly. A mop of black hair hung down over the collar of his flannel shirt, his five o'clock shadow outlining his firm jaw. When he smiled his greeting, Madison nearly laughed. His teeth were nearly as stained at Jones's were!

"I hope you plan on seeing a dentist before going back to Amy," Madison chuckled.

The man just nodded, his eyes darting to Jeremy as he took the chair next to Madison.

"You know damn well he's with me and that he's cleared," Madison rushed on, ignoring Jeremy's look of surprise.

"I do," the man said, his voice rumbling up from his chest as he nodded to Jeremy.

"And why am I not surprised that you know this guy?" Jeremy mumbled, not quite sure what to think or do.

He knew Jones, but this other guy, he'd never seen him before. Of that he was positive. But obviously, Madison knew him. And if the guy was with Jones, it was a safe bet that that meant he too was a . . . holy shit, what was going on here? Was there a convention of assassins in town that he wasn't aware of? The absurdity of it all nearly had him laughing.

Knowing Jeremy was struggling to comprehend what was going on, Madison reached over, taking his hand and squeezing it gently. Appreciating her gesture, Jeremy was pleasantly surprised when she kept her hand in his, clearly not caring who saw them or what they thought of it. Making the mistake of glancing at the taller guy, it was all Jeremy could do not to snatch his hand from hers, though. Icy-cold blue eyes caught and held his gaze, their meaning clear: "Watch your step."

Before Jeremy could respond to the man's warning look, their waitress appeared, leaving off dessert menus before hurrying away. Jeremy smiled as Madison grabbed a menu, totally ignoring the three men as she studied it. Across from Jeremy, the taller man cleared his throat, pulling Jeremy's attention back to him.

"What?" Jeremy demanded.

The man's eyes widened at Jeremy's brazen tone.

Okay, Jeremy thought, *enough is enough*. Who was this guy, her brother? He swallowed hard, hoping that wasn't the case, remembering how protective of his sisters he'd been in his younger years.

Glancing up from her menu, Madison caught the exchange between the two men.

"I'm sorry," she said, sitting up straighter. "Jeremy, this is . . ." she tossed the man a questioning glance, suddenly unsure as to how to introduce him.

"Stan," the taller man said, offering a big hand to Jeremy. Taking it, Jeremy wasn't surprised by the strong handshake. He made sure his was just as strong and was rewarded with a nod from Stan.

"And no, I'm not her brother."

He paused as Jeremy's eyes widened at his announcement.

"But I'm close enough." The warning again was crystal clear: "Watch your step."

"Ignore him," Madison chuckled, "he's harmless."

Totally ignoring the stunned glances from all three men, Madison turned her attention back to her menu. Shaking his head, Jeremy suspected quite the opposite to be true but remained silent.

No sense in testing his theory. Besides, Madison's hand was warm in his; he knew she'd protect him. And he nearly laughed at the thought.

Waving down the waitress, Madison quickly placed her order before turning her attention back to the taller man. But before she could say anything, the waitress reappeared, this time with two plates heaped high with food for the guys, before quickly disappearing again into the kitchen. Watching Stan attack his still-sizzling steak, Madison silently studied the man. Stan? That was almost as good as Rick—the name he'd used for a previous job. Well, he certainly knew how to blend in. Between his disguise and his name, no one would ever suspect him of being one of the world's most renowned assassins—which begged the question, what was he doing here? Jones, she knew. But Stan? What was going on that his presence was needed? She made a mental note to call Sarah later. It was time they had a talk.

"She's expecting your call," Stan said between mouthfuls, and Madison resisted the urge to slap him.

"You know I hate that as much as Amy does," she snapped, ignoring Stan's arrogant smile as he shrugged his shoulders. "How do you tolerate that?" she asked Jones, who just shrugged his shoulders.

The men had worked together for years; no doubt they were both used to each other's habits, annoying as they might be.

Debating on whether or not to say something, Jeremy erred on the side of caution and remained silent concentrating instead on clearing his head of all thoughts, having picked up on Stan's unique yet annoying skill. There'd be time enough later when he was alone to think about the mysterious man. But for now, a blank mind was the key, and with a skill carefully honed over many years, Jeremy completely cleared his mind.

With a raised eyebrow, Stan stared at Jeremy. There weren't many who could totally block him out, but this man did just that, and fairly easily. Oh, yeah, there was more to Jeremy than they knew about. Stan's eyes moved to Madison. Did she know? He doubted it.

Dinner and dessert finished, the four sat quietly while the waitress cleared the table, leaving them with steaming mugs of coffee and hot chocolate. It was time to talk business.

"Why are you here?" Madison bluntly asked Stan.

"I'm with him," Stan said, nodding to Jones.

"Funny, that's usually my line," Jones said dryly.

"I don't care whose line it is," Madison said, keeping her voice low. "I just want to know why you're here."

Glancing at Jones, Stan remained silent.

Madison turned back to Jones, "Okay, spill it, why are you back, and," she nodded at Stan, "why is he here?"

"We're not here to interfere with your job." Jones began, "We're here to make sure nothing gets in your way."

"Meaning the guy who killed the man in the alley," Jeremy said, deciding it was safe to join the conversation.

Jones and Stan nodded.

"What's happened that you came back?" Jeremy asked Jones.

"Actually, I never left," Jones said, quickly explaining how Stan had arrived in town, providing their cover in the form of loggers. Their fully loaded rig was in the parking lot next to the airport, alongside five other rigs belonging to other drivers also riding out the storm. One of the trucks belonged to the murdered man.

"You drove up here?" Madison gawked at Stan. The man was full of surprises!

He just smiled.

"I had some help," Stan admitted, nodding toward the bar. "The guy in the brown sheepskin actually drove us up, I just tagged along."

There was no need in telling her that Sarah had made arrangements for him to meet up with the trucker in Whitehorse. Especially as until they pulled into town, they weren't sure they'd make it because of the storm. As it was, they'd been on the road two days longer than planned.

"The guy killed in the alley was a trucker, we decided to go with that angle to see if we could flesh out the killer," Jones explained, sipping his coffee.

"I thought you were going to leave it to the police," Jeremy said. "What changed?"

"For starters, Mary upping and disappearing. We want to be sure he didn't kill her," Jones began.

"And," Stan interjected, "we got a call asking us to check it out."

"Sarah," Madison guessed.

Both men nodded.

"Your handler?" Jeremy turned to Madison. "So this guy clearly has nothing to do with why you're actually here but everything to do with you."

Madison could only nod.

"So it would seem."

"We're not sure why he's after Madison, but we think he's getting frustrated and, in doing so, is being stupid and killing anyone who he deems is getting in his way," Jones explained.

"He knows who you are," Stan stated bluntly, pleased when Madison didn't blink or flinch.

"I know who he is too, though," Madison began.

"You just know what he looks like," Jones interrupted her. "Not who he actually is."

"Clearly, he must be one of us," she said, wishing she was wrong but knowing she wasn't.

Jones and Stan nodded.

"In one form or another," Stan said. "I'm in the process of narrowing it down as to who exactly he is and who he's working for. We're going to be stuck in town for another day, anyway. I'll have it figured out by then." And taken care of as well. That was the plan anyway.

"And when the weather clears, you'll be on the next plane out of here and onto your original job," Jones added.

My original job, Madison thought, amazed she hadn't given it much thought over the last twenty-four hours. She needed to focus. And to do that, she needed to be alone. She glanced at Jeremy. But how alone did she really want to be?

"What about Mary?" Jeremy's question brought Madison's thoughts back to the present.

Oh my god, she thought. How could she have forgotten about Mary? *The same way you forgot about your original job*, she berated herself silently. *Get your act together, girl, or you'll end up dead yourself!*

That chilling thought had her reaching for Jeremy's hand again, telling herself it wasn't because she was going soft but because she liked holding his hand. She refused to believe otherwise.

Ignoring Madison and her feelings for the moment, Stan turned to Jeremy.

"We're hoping Mary just hightailed it outta here with another trucker. We're checking to be sure."

"So you do think she's still alive," Jeremy said hopefully.

The girl was a first-class pain in the ass, but he'd never wish any ill on her.

"We think so," Jones said, also ignoring Madison, having caught her reaching for Jeremy's hand. "I'm waiting to hear from a contact down in Whitehorse." He glanced at his watch. "I should know more tomorrow."

"I'm talking to her parents in the morning," Stan said, nearly laughing when Madison stared at him.

True, he wasn't known for his social skills, but he was great at getting information from people. One way or the other, he usually found out what he needed to know. It was for precisely that reason that Madison was concerned.

"Don't worry," Stan quickly assured her, knowing where her thoughts had gone, "it'll be fine."

Not bothering to remind him that she hated it when he dipped into her mind, Madison just nodded. She had to let him do his work his way. She'd expect the same courtesy. And she reminded herself, Stan wasn't quite the same man he'd been a few years ago.

Rick, as he'd been known then, had been on a job when he met Amy, later marrying her. Having been in the wrong place at the wrong time, Amy was alive only because of him. Never one to kill needlessly, Rick didn't tolerate others in their profession doing it either. The men who'd attacked Amy learned that lesson the hard way . . . with their lives. Oh, yeah, Mary's parents would be safe with . . . Stan, the name he was currently going by.

"How do you, a total stranger, plan on talking to her parents?" Jeremy asked curiously, not surprised when Stan gave him that "look" again. It really was becoming annoying.

"I'm just going to tell them I'm a friend, that I met her last time I was in town." Stan paused, considering his next words carefully, knowing Jeremy was Mary's friend. "Given her personality and history with men in this town, I think they'll be okay talking to me."

Jeremy nodded, hating to admit that Stan was right. Sadly, Mary's parents knew how their daughter was around men, especially men just passing through.

"In the meantime, you," Jones began, pulling Madison's attention back to him, "need to keep a low profile. I'm not ready to flush out the guy just yet and don't need you giving him any opportunities to get near you."

Being told what to do or not do had never sat well with Madison, and her temper flared instantly.

"I can take care of myself," she snapped, immediately realizing she sounded like a spoiled brat. "Sorry," she quickly apologized, "but I can, and you know that."

"We do," Jones said quietly. "But for right now, I need you to please do what I ask."

His quiet, steely tone had her frowning.

"What aren't you telling me?"

Expecting her question, Jones shook his head.

"You're so full of shit." Leaning toward him, she lowered her voice. "I know there's more here, and I'm asking you to tell me what it is."

"Not until I know more," Jones said. "I can't tell you what I don't know."

Leaning back in her chair, Madison stared first at Jones then at Stan. Their matching blank looks told her she wasn't going to learn anything more here tonight. There was no budging these guys, and she knew it. Crap!

"Fine," she finally gave in, "I'll go back to the hotel, lock myself in my room, and be a good girl."

"Yeah, that'll be the day," Jones snorted in laughter before turning to Jeremy. "Can she stay with you?"

"Of course," Jeremy nodded, ignoring Madison's angry glare.

"Can I please at least get some things from my room?" Madison asked, her voice dripping in sarcasm.

"Already been taken care of," Jones said, ready for her angry reaction, prepared when she viciously swore at him.

The girl could definitely swear like a truck driver! Better, in fact!

Good God, who'd been in her room? Madison's mind raced frantically. Had she left anything incriminating in plain sight? *Stop it!* she berated herself, knowing full well she hadn't. At any given time, anyone could go into her room and never suspect a thing. But it still rankled, knowing someone had gone through her personal belongings. Well, she took a deep breath, there wasn't anything she could do about it now; she'd just have to deal with it.

"Exactly," Stan said, knowing his comment would royally piss her off.

She had a marvelous temper; it was fun provoking her. Glaring at Stan, she momentarily enjoyed seeing his eyes widen at the violent and ugly thoughts that she was thinking. He'd taught her well. Maybe too well!

"Okay then," Jones said, pushing back from the table as he waved at the waitress. "We'll talk in the morning."

Clearly not open for discussion, everyone shrugged on their coats while Jones took care of the check. Glancing quickly at the bill the waitress handed him, Jones pushed some cash into her hand, telling her to keep the change. With a quick "Thank you," she rushed out back to tell Ruth about the large tip her table of four had just left her. She loved waiting on the truck drivers; they always tipped well!

With a smile for her happy waitress, Ruth poked her head out to see her son leaving with Madison and the two truck drivers. Something strange was going on; she just wished she knew what it was. Or maybe it was better she didn't.

CHAPTER 16

STARING INTO THE flames, Ellen didn't hear Ethel approach.

"Everything all right?" Ethel asked softly as she came to stand next to the woman.

Glancing around, thankful the living room was empty, Ellen tossed Ethel a sarcastic smile.

"Fine," she said, knowing Ethel knew it was a lie. Elaborating, Ellen simply said, "Men."

Nodding with a chuckle, Ethel pressed a cup of tea into Ellen's cold hands. Surprised and admittedly touched, Ellen smiled her thanks at the innkeeper.

"I'm here if you need an ear," Ethel smiled before leaving the woman alone with her thoughts and her tea.

Returning to the front desk, Ethel kept busy, occasionally tossing a glance toward the living room. When a rush of cold air ushered in the two truck drivers, Ethel greeted them with a smile. She liked these two guys; she wasn't sure why, but she did. Normally, by the time someone was checked in, she knew all about them, but these two had managed to dodge her questions. They were friendly enough, but at the same time, there was something about them that Ethel couldn't quite put her finger on. Not to mention one of them looked vaguely familiar, although Ethel couldn't place him. And that annoyed her more than anything. All well, she admitted, it wouldn't be the end of the world if she were to forget where she knew one person from. Given her age, she was amazed she hadn't forgotten more people!

Enjoying a friendly chat with the two men for a few minutes, she glanced up to see Ellen standing in front of the elevator. Wishing the woman a good night, Ethel was rewarded with a smile and a wave before Ellen disappeared into the elevator. Turning her attention back to the men, Ethel paused. Both men were staring intently at the elevator. She wondered why.

"One of the women from the group that got stranded here in the storm," Ethel said. "She and her husband," she added quickly, in case the men might be interested in the woman.

Better they know now that she was married than find out later.

But unable to resist a bit of gossip, she continued on, "Nice couple, but he's an odd duck."

"How so?" Stan lazily inquired.

Turning back to Ethel, he forced himself to appear calm and seemingly indifferent. But shit! Ellen was the last person he'd expected to find here! Her presence was not a good sign at all! And how was she tied into all this? This just kept getting better and better! What the hell was going on?

One small consolation, he knew she hadn't recognized him. Few ever did. And who was this guy, Frank, that she was clearly furious with? Stan knew it wasn't the husband; Ellen wasn't married.

"She's very social, he tends to keep to himself. Not very friendly. Always scowling," Ethel continued, wondering why she suddenly felt like she was being interrogated.

"Angry he's stuck here, most likely," Jones said, careful to keep his tone neutral.

But if anyone knew more about the guy, it'd be Ethel, and they needed to keep her talking.

"Well, that certainly was informative," Stan recalled, dropping into a chair by the fireplace in his room.

Sitting down opposite him, Jones agreed, reminding himself that one needed to be careful when one wished for something. His wish to keep Ethel talking had come true in spades, and it was almost twenty minutes before the two men were able to get away from her! But between what Ethel had told them and what she'd been thinking, the two men had come away with some new and vital information— the most important being that Frank was, indeed, the man that Ellen was "married to" and was also who she was furious with. Stan filed that information away, positive it'd be useful in the near future.

Between the new development involving Ellen, and the information they'd garnered—the two men began putting together a plan that would draw the man following Madison out into the open.

"You gonna let Madison know what we found out?" Staring idly into the fire, Stan continued turning everything over in his mind.

"Not tonight, I'm not," Jones said. "And besides, right this minute, she doesn't need to know. I will let Sarah know, though," he added, glancing at his watch.

Just once it'd be nice to be on the same time zone as the woman.

"But you don't want to tell Madison tonight?" Stan prodded.

"No, and stop being a jerk to her," Jones said. "I see what you're doing here, don't think I don't."

Stan just smiled.

"Jeremy's a good guy, Madison's safe with him, trust me on that one."

The two men had been friends and coworkers for a long time, longer than many. In their line of work, long life spans weren't the norm. They'd learned from hard-earned experience whom they could trust and who was a threat. Jones knew Jeremy was no threat and someone they could definitely trust. It was oddly comforting knowing that, especially as Jones could count on one hand the number of people he trusted explicitly. One of them was sitting across from him; one was stashed away in a house nearby; and one of them was in Germany. Okay, he amended, two of them were in the house nearby.

"Madison's safe with Jeremy," he said again.

"What's his story?" Stan asked. "I couldn't get a read on the guy. There's not many who can block me out, but he did it and did it well."

"I first met Jeremy when he was with the RCMP," Jones began, quickly adding when Stan tensed up, "he was in an elite squad that worked quietly behind the scenes," Jones continued, "if you get my meaning."

Stan visibly relaxed. Oh, yeah, he got it. While he tended to avoid any type of law enforcement, Stan had, upon occasion, worked indirectly with a few he'd actually liked. Of course, none of them had had any inclination of Stan's true identity. Things, no doubt, would have turned out quite differently had they known. Stan smiled, remembering sharing a few beers with some of them—yeah, they were good guys.

"I take it you've worked with Jeremy," Stan asked needlessly.

Jones nodded. "Indirectly, but we know each other. I trust him, he's one of the good guys." Meaning they had no reason to kill him, either now or when the job was finished.

"Good to know, especially since it's clear Madison seems to like the guy."

Stan smiled, glad he wouldn't have to go up against her. She wouldn't stand a chance against him, but that still didn't mean she wouldn't give it her best shot. Literally.

"You think?" Jones smiled. "I can't remember her ever really liking anyone before. Can you?"

Stan shook his head.

"So this is a first."

"What does Sarah think?" Knowing his twin sister, she'd be as cautious, if not more than he was. "Has she vetted him yet?"

Jones chuckled. "Nope, seems Madison hasn't given her sufficient details. Like his name."

Stan laughed, like that would ever stop Sarah.

Jones continued, "But she knows there's a man in Madison's life. I think she's giving Madison some room because you and I are here."

Stan agreed. Sarah would trust them to let her know if any action against Jeremy needed to be taken.

"So Madison's got herself a boyfriend."

Pondering that thought, Stan smiled. Madison hadn't had a lot of happiness in her life; she deserved some. Remembering how his own life had changed when Amy waltzed her way into his complicated life, sometimes making it more complicated, Stan knew he wouldn't change a thing. Speaking of, he glanced at his watch; he needed to give his wife a call.

"I hope it works out for Madison."

"Do you?" Jones asked.

Stan knew what his friend was really asking and wasn't offended. The life of an assassin was complicated, to say the least—secrecy being the primary code they had to live by. Relationships were tough enough, but throw in the fact that you kill people for a living—yeah, that tended to make things just a bit more complicated. And it didn't matter that the targets were very bad people; they still died at your hand. Stan shifted in his seat. Of course, that particular fact never bothered him. When it came to work, he was a stone-cold-hearted man. But when it came to Amy, he smiled to himself—that was a whole different story.

As for Madison, she was a top-notch assassin. If she were to choose a different life, they'd miss her, both personally and professionally. But they'd support whatever decision she made. And protect her while she eased back into society. Stan smiled ruefully, having a tough time imagining Madison living in "the real world." He couldn't see her following directions and answering to others. As far as he knew, the only one Madison had ever answered to was Sarah. Well, if Madison chose that path, she'd just have to adjust.

While Madison would face some challenges, at least Jeremy already knew who and what she was. One less hurdle for them to have to deal with. Stan glanced out the window into the darkness. If Madison and Jeremy stayed here, more than likely, Madison would be safe. If she couldn't walk off the face of the earth, then relocating to this remote place in Canada was definitely the next best thing.

Pushing himself out of his chair, Stan grabbed his coat, heading to the door.

"Yeah," Stan paused, his hand on the doorknob, "I do hope it works out for her." With ice-cold eyes, he turned back to Jones, "We need to get this guy before he gets any closer to her."

Jones nodded, remaining silent. There wasn't anything more to say. Both men knew what had to be done.

"Déjà vu," Madison murmured, kissing Jeremy softly as she curled up beside him, happy to be back in his big bed.

His arm tightened around her, holding her close. Dropping a kiss on her forehead, he felt his body harden again. What was this woman doing to him? And after all that he'd learned just a short time ago, how was it that burying himself deep inside her again was the only thing on his mind? He was having a tough time reconciling the woman lying soft and warm beside him with the professional killer he knew her to be. When her fingers danced up his bare chest, skimming over his nipples, he nearly groaned. Christ, she just might kill him! He smiled into the darkness, rolling over and pinning her underneath him as he kissed her deeply, his erection hard against her belly. And that would be bad how?

Wrapping her arms around him and kissing him back, she opened her legs, inviting him closer. Rising up over her, light from the hallway falling over her face, Jeremy watched her smile grow as he slid into her warmth and wetness. Closing her eyes with a sigh, Madison wrapped her legs around Jeremy's waist as her body moved to welcome his gentle thrusts. Murmured words of sweetness mingled with sighs of pleasure filled the room as Jeremy made sweet love to Madison. When had he ever felt the need to be this tender? When had he ever wanted to be? He couldn't remember.

Their bodies moving in timeless synchronicity, Jeremy fought for control, her body beckoning him to thrust harder, deeper. Smooth, gentle thrusts became hard and demanding as his body took control, seeking release. Picking up on the change in momentum, Madison's body rose to meet his as she flung her arms out, clutching the sheets. The warm, tingling feeling in her belly caught fire; and closing her eyes, her body bowed, her guttural scream filling the room as the orgasm rolled through her. Her body tightened around him, and powerless to hold back, Jeremy followed her, groaning as he emptied himself inside her.

Dropping his forehead gently on hers, Jeremy smiled, willing himself to slide gently out of her before he collapsed on top of her. Tightening her arms and legs around him, Madison shook her head.

"Stay," she whispered, kissing his chin as he rose up over her.

"I'm too big," he said, trying to gently extract himself.

"Not anymore, you're not."

And surprising both of them Madison burst into a fit of giggles. Her raunchy sense of humor and laughter infectious, Jeremy hugged her tightly, his chest rumbling against her.

Rolling over and reaching for her, Jeremy's eyes slowly opened when his wandering hands found nothing but an empty bed. Where . . . ? Focusing his eyes, Jeremy smiled. Standing at the window with her back to him, his flannel shirt falling just below her naked bottom, Madison stared out the window. He blinked, his body warming as he watched her silently for another moment. Something outside certainly had her attention; she hadn't moved a muscle.

"Whatcha looking at?" Jeremy said, his voice low and husky from sleep.

Madison turned slightly, a smile on her face. "Morning," she greeted him before turning back to the window. "The sun's out!"

"So?"

"The sun is out!" Madison said again.

"That generally happens in the morning." Stretching, Jeremy pulled back the covers. "Come back to bed," he invited.

Catching his silky tone, Madison turned around but remained where she was. Men—was sex really all they had on their mind? Her body slowly warmed as her eyes fell on his naked chest. Well, okay, so maybe it wasn't just men. She smiled a seductive smile, pleased when Jeremy returned it with a wolfish grin of his own. Her body tingling, she surprised him by leaping on to the bed, landing on her knees beside him. Gripping her waist, Jeremy pulled her mouth to his, kissing her deeply.

He'd only just met this woman, yet she was doing all sorts of funny things to his mind and to his heart. Initially finding the bed empty, he'd squashed the unhappy feeling that had raced through him before spotting her at the window. He'd examine those feelings later. For now, he just wanted to lose himself in her again. God, he couldn't get enough of her! How many times had they made love last night? Enough times so that when they fell into an exhausted sleep, they'd slept through his alarm clock!

Pulling her over him so she straddled him, Jeremy slid his hands up under her shirt, quickly deciding that nothing had ever looked as sexy to him as her wearing his shirt did. Gently cupping her full breasts, he smiled as she closed her eyes, arching into his hands. Her head falling back, she sighed happily as she covered his hands with her own.

His cell phone buzzed from its place on the bedside table. Turning an annoyed glance at the device, Jeremy blinked, his attention snagged by the bright light streaming in the window.

"Holy shit, the sun's out!" he declared.

"You're just now realizing that?" Madison asked, momentarily distracted. "Didn't I just tell you that a minute ago?"

Jeremy tossed her a sheepish grin. "Oh, yeah," he admitted, his eyes moving back to the window for a moment.

His hands stilled as he gazed out at the snow-covered trees just outside the window. Feeling his hands begin to slide away, Madison grabbed his hands, pushing her breasts back into them. She immediately had his attention.

"Not so fast," she said as her hands molded his to her breasts. "You started this," she rubbed herself against him, "you finish it."

"Yes, ma'am," Jeremy murmured.

This time, when his hands slid away, she allowed it. Gripping her waist, he raised her up, moving her ever so slightly before sliding into her welcoming body.

"Yes, ma'am," he sighed as he slowly filled her.

"You act like you've never seen the sun before," Jeremy commented as he brewed a cup of coffee.

Doctoring it the way Madison liked, he handed it to her—or more accurately, he placed the warm mug in her hand. Her eyes never leaving the window, she thanked him, sipping the hot brew with a happy sigh.

"What's got your attention?" Jeremy asked, standing beside her with his own coffee.

"It's just so beautiful," Madison whispered.

White snow glistened in the trees, the fresh snow on the ground sparkling in the bright sunlight. A light breeze tickled the tree branches, sprinkling more snow over the already-snow-covered bushes below.

"I suppose," he said, trying to see what she saw and failing.

All he saw was lots of snow to be plowed and shoveled.

"I travel so much I rarely have time to admire any views, to enjoy the scenery around me," she said softly, her tone wistful. "I've never seen such a beautiful sight."

And surprising them both, she rested her head on his shoulder, wrapping her free arm around him as she cuddled up beside him. Wrapping his arm around her, pulling her closer, Jeremy gazed out at the winter wonderland outside his window, suddenly seeing it for the first time through Madison's eyes. He wasn't sure what was more beautiful: the fresh snow or the woman beside him.

His heart tripped, and Jeremy knew he needed to get back on solid ground. Giving her a gentle squeeze, he slowly moved away. Glancing at him briefly, Madison's eyes quickly returned to the scene outside. She couldn't seem to get enough of the beautiful view!

"I'm sure you think I'm being silly," she chuckled, but still she didn't look away.

"No, I don't," Jeremy assured her.

He understood what she was feeling; he'd had the same feeling once himself. Of course, that was years ago when he and his brothers had first arrived. It didn't take long, though, for the beautiful view to dim. Especially after it snowed for a week straight. This storm had been mild compared to some.

"But after you've plowed and shoveled it enough, you start to see it a little differently."

"I'm sure," she conceded.

"The sun was out when you flew in," Jeremy reminded her.

"It was, but that day was different." *My mind was on the job I was here to do.* "I was a little preoccupied."

And remembering that job, Madison slowly sipped her coffee. The snow had stopped; the sun was out. She'd be leaving soon. Suddenly, the beauty of the day dimmed ever so slightly.

Unaware of where her thoughts had taken her, Jeremy finished his coffee, putting the mug in the sink.

"Speaking of plowing, I've gotta go out and do some," Jeremy said, ticking off in his mind the places he was responsible for plowing. "Want to come?"

Finally turning away from the window, Madison glanced at the clock, figuring the time change. She needed to talk to Sarah. She needed the SAT phone. She needed to go back to her hotel room. She needed to touch base with Jones and Stan. She needed . . .

"Sure," she said, putting her mug next to his in the sink, "I'd love to!"

CHAPTER 17

"THANK GOD, THE snow's finally stopped!" Frank said.

"Where are you going?" Ellen said, coming out of the bathroom to find Frank pulling on his parka.

"I need to get out and get some air," Frank answered, snatching up his gloves and hat. "I won't be gone long."

And before Ellen could reply, he left the room.

"Whatever," Ellen mumbled, crossing to the window.

The glistening sun made her squint as her eyes adjusted to the brightness. Outside her window, the town looked like a winter wonderland, the houses and buildings covered in a fresh blanket of snow, smoke curling out of the chimneys. Their pace brisk, people made their way along the snow-covered sidewalks. Every vehicle she saw was either an SUV or a pickup, many with plows on the front as they drove slowly through town.

Charming, was the first thought that came to Ellen's mind, and she turned quickly away from the window.

She hated charming. She hated this town. She wanted to get out of the cold and away from the snow and back to someplace warm with lots of green grass. She paused. Would they be able to fly out now? She frowned; she couldn't be that lucky. Besides, Frank still had a job to do. She hoped his needing to get out for fresh air meant that he was working on a new plan. And one that would work. Never had a job she'd been on taken so long or had so many complications. Granted, they couldn't control the weather, but despite that, it seemed like every time Frank turned around, the target was eluding him. If he didn't finish the job, and soon, Ellen was going to take matters into her own hands and do it herself. She certainly was qualified. And she considered for a moment, being a woman might be to her advantage. She could certainly get closer to the target than Frank could. Pouring herself a coffee, Ellen pondered this new idea.

From his vantage point just inside the airport, Frank watched as Jack moved around his plane. Was he inspecting it? Did that mean he was preparing to fly out? And if so, where? And who was he taking? When Jack climbed into the plane, Frank pushed away from the wall he'd been leaning against, wandering over to what posed as a ticket counter for the small airport.

Minutes later, having learned enough from the friendly ticket agent to formulate a new plan, Frank prepared to head back to the Inn, anxious to work on the details. A burst of cold air behind him had him turning, pausing as Jack walked in.

"How's it looking, Jack?" the ticket agent asked, handing Jack a clipboard when the man reached the counter.

"Not great, I'm afraid," Jack replied, filling out the clipboard before handing it back.

Looking up, Jack spotted Frank standing nearby.

"Mr. Stillman, isn't it?"

Momentarily caught off balance by the man's greeting, Frank quickly recovered, stepping forward with an outstretched hand. Not bothering to remove his glove, Jack shook hands with the man.

"I would imagine you're wondering when you might be flying out of here," Jack said, knowing he'd guessed correctly when Frank nodded.

"I was hoping when I saw you by the plane that it meant we might be able to continue on with our trip," Frank admitted, his hopeful tone forced.

Glancing back out the window toward his plane, Jack shook his head.

"We won't be going anywhere just yet, I'm afraid," he said, turning back to Frank. "This storm isn't quite over, it's just taking a break. But," he continued, "should something change I'll let your tour guide know right away."

Relief washed over Frank as he realized Jack recognized him only as being a part of the stranded group.

You're in the middle of nowhere, stop being paranoid. No one's going to recognize you here. Your cover's intact, Frank quickly reminded himself as he glanced out the window at the plane sitting in the sunshine.

"Looks pretty good out there now," Frank commented, "you sure the storm's not over?"

The ticket agent chuckled.

"What? The sun's shining, it's beautiful out there!" Frank's sharp tone silenced the ticket agent, and immediately realizing his mistake, Frank quickly apologized. He really needed to work on his temper!

"Jack's better than any weatherman when it comes to knowing if a storm is gone or just taking a break," the ticket agent explained confidently, tossing a quick smile at Jack. "He's never wrong when it comes to the weather."

Her firm tone dared Frank to argue with her.

"Sorry," Frank apologized quickly, knowing he needed to back down this time. "I didn't mean to imply that you didn't know what you were talking about."

"No problem," Jack said.

He was used to being questioned about his weather knowledge by those who didn't know him. Fishing his truck keys out of his coat pocket, Jack looked at Frank.

"Can I offer you a lift back to the Inn?"

"No, but thanks, anyway," Frank answered with a shake of his head. "I want to enjoy the sunshine while I can."

And get away from you, he thought wryly. He didn't like being this close to one of the people he'd been intent on avoiding.

"Okay then." And with a wave, Jack pushed open the door leading to the parking lot, another gust of cold air ushering him out.

"Okay then," Frank murmured.

And ignoring the curious glance from the ticket agent, he turned, going out the opposite exit door.

"Tourists," she mumbled.

Climbing the steps to the restaurant, Madison pulled her hat off, letting her long hair fall around her in waves. Holding the door open for her, Jeremy resisted the desire to run his hands through her sweet-smelling, soft hair.

Pull yourself together! he admonished himself silently. And tossing her a wolfish grin, he reminded himself that there'd be time enough for that later.

"What?" Madison asked, catching the grin.

"Nothing," Jeremy answered quickly, ushering her into the restaurant.

Pausing inside to let their eyes adjust after being out in the bright sunshine, Jeremy spotted Jack sitting at their table.

"This way," he said needlessly, and weaving between the tables, Madison and Jeremy joined Jack.

Having only had dinner there, Madison studied the luncheon menu carefully, knowing full well that whatever she chose would be excellent. Glancing up briefly when a coffee was placed in front of her, Madison smiled her thanks at the waitress before turning her attention back to the menu, oblivious to the fact that Jack and Jeremy were staring at her.

"She seems pretty engrossed," Jack chuckled.

"She is, trust me," Jeremy said. "We've been plowing, and when I told her we'd have lunch here, you would have thought I'd just told her she'd won the lottery."

"She rode with you while you plowed?" Jack asked, stunned.

"I know, right?" Jeremy chuckled. "But she loved it. Spent most of the time laughing, as a matter of fact."

"Odd girl," Jack said.

"For sure," Jeremy agreed.

"You do know I'm sitting right here, right?" Madison said from behind her menu.

The men laughed.

"You do know we're not afraid of you, right?" Jeremy countered with a laugh.

Madison put down the menu, tossing him a dazzling smile that stabbed him directly in the heart.

"You should be."

Watching and listening to the exchange, Jack looked first at Jeremy then at Madison before going back to his brother. Holy shit, his brother was falling in love! If he wasn't already there! In twenty-four hours, his brother had lost his heart! Who'd have thought? Wait till their mother heard about this one! And the rest of the family, for that matter! Jeremy had always sworn he'd never marry, claiming he preferred being the fun brother-in-law and uncle. Not that marriage was on Jeremy's mind now, but Jack decided, looking around for his mother, Jeremy was definitely in the love phase. Jack smiled, remembering when he and Nancy had first met and fallen in love. Jeremy had given him so much shit. Yeah, well, Jeremy was about to learn that payback's a bitch. Jack struggled not to laugh out loud.

Oh, yeah, he thought, *this is going to be good!*

"Afternoon, boys, Madison," Ruth greeted them, dropping into an empty chair. "Plowing go well?"

Jeremy nodded, trying hard to resist rubbing his hand over his heart. That look Madison had given him shook him to the core.

"Are you okay, Jeremy?" Motherly concern filled her voice as she gazed at her son.

"I'm fine," Jeremy assured his mother quickly.

The look his mother tossed him told him she didn't believe him at all. Of course not, why would she? Didn't the woman have the power to know when her kids were lying? He'd never been able to pull one over her; why would now be any different.

"Really," he added with a smile, "I'm fine."

Nodding and letting it go, Ruth smiled at Madison, "I hear you rode with Jeremy while he plowed us out today."

Madison nodded, smiling.

"Enjoy it, did you?"

"I know it sounds crazy, but yes, I did!" Madison's smile grew as she glanced at Jeremy then at Jack. "Your sons think I'm odd."

"Well, you are, dear." Ruth laughed as Madison's mouth fell open in surprise. "That's what we like about you," she continued easily, resting her hand on Madison's.

Squeezing gently, Ruth smiled at the woman who'd unknowingly snagged her wayward son's heart. She only hoped Madison wouldn't break that heart.

Speechless, Madison was grateful when the waitress picked that moment to ask them if they were ready to order. Placing her order, Madison nearly sighed in relief when, after the waitress left, Jack changed the subject, bringing up his visit to the airport. Trying not to seem too interested, she listened as Jack mentioned running into Frank Stillman.

"Stillman?" Ruth said. "Oh, yes, he and his wife are with that group that was stranded by the storm."

Not surprised that his mother knew their names, Jeremy tossed Madison a guarded glance.

"They're very anxious to be on their way," Ruth added.

The men nodded, each for totally different reasons.

"But you say it'll be a while yet before that happens, Jack?"

"Storm's coming back, I suspect it'll hit before dark."

Four sets of eyes turned toward the windows, blinking at the still-bright sunlight that streamed through.

"Really?" Madison couldn't help but ask.

She hadn't seen a cloud in the sky when they'd been plowing, not even the wispy ones that Jack had pointed out when she'd first arrived. All eyes turned to her.

"I'm sorry, that was stupid. Of course, you know. It's just that it's so sunny now."

"If he says it's coming back, it is," Ruth smiled, pushing herself out of her chair. "My son, the walking barometer. When it comes to predicting the weather, I can't tell you the last time he was wrong."

"Wait, are you saying I've been wrong about other things?" Jack said in mock surprise.

Dropping a kiss on her oldest son's head, Ruth squeezed Jeremy's shoulder gently.

"That's exactly what I'm saying. Enjoy your lunch, gang," and with a laugh, Ruth headed toward the kitchen.

"I love your mother," Madison couldn't help laughing.

"So do we," the boys said in unison.

Moments later, their food arriving, all talk of Frank Stillman and his presence at the airport was momentarily forgotten.

Finishing his coffee, Jack pushed back from the table. It didn't matter that the sun was still shining; the snow would be back soon enough. And he had lots to do before it hit.

"How's Nancy doing?" Madison asked as Jack threw down some money on the table. "She must be counting down the days."

Jack nodded with a smile. "That she is. We've got an excellent midwife, should Nancy get stuck at home." Tossing a quick glance toward the door, Jack smiled. "But I'm thinking the storm should be long past by the time she's gotta go, so things should be fine."

"And it's not like she doesn't have this birthing thing down to a science," Jeremy added with a smile.

"For sure," Jack agreed, "for sure." Pausing, he glanced at Jeremy and Madison. "What are your plans for later?"

"Haven't gotten that far yet," Jeremy admitted, glancing at Madison. "I've still got some more plowing to do, but beyond that, I don't know."

Although I know what I'd like to be doing, he thought as his body warmed.

Catching the "look" Jeremy had aimed toward Madison, Jack had a good idea where his brother's thoughts had gone.

"I'm sure," Jack said, unable to resist teasing his brother.

And he just laughed when Jeremy tossed him that "fuck you" look.

"I'll catch up with you later." And with a nod to Madison, Jack left.

"He's nervous about Nancy going into labor," Madison stated bluntly.

"Absolutely, he is," Jeremy agreed, pushing back his chair and rising. "But he's got it covered. None of his kids were born when they should have been, so he's used to that. He'll be fine." And he knew it to be true. "Ready to go?"

"Don't you need to pay?" Madison asked, pulling on her jacket. Jeremy shook his head. "Jack paid."

When he saw the question in Madison's eyes, he smiled. "Don't worry, I'll pay him back later."

"Uh-uh," Madison smiled, following Jeremy out onto the deck of the restaurant.

Pulling her sunglasses on, she gazed up at the blue sky.

"You're sure it's going to snow again?"

Jeremy nodded, pulling her down the steps. At the bottom, he turned her around so she was facing the restaurant again. Then stepping behind her, he gently cupped her face, tipping her head upward. She gasped, spotting the gray clouds gathering in the distance.

"Oh!"

"Yeah, oh."

And grabbing her hand, they headed back to his truck. Taking a few steps, Madison pulled Jeremy to a halt as she swung back around. Her neck tingled; she was being watched. Behind her sunglasses, her eyes darted about; it only took her a moment to spot him. Leaning against the far corner of the restaurant, Stillman's eyes met hers for a moment. The anger and violence in his eyes pierced through her, leaving her momentarily chilled. Then, whirling around, he quickly disappeared out of sight. Shit!

"Did you see . . . ?"

"Yeah, I did," Jeremy said, pulling her to the truck. "Get in."

Her mind whirling, Madison let Jeremy push her into the truck. Suddenly, the bright afternoon turned very dark as her mind kicked into survival mode. For whatever reason, this man was after her! And it was fast becoming clear: kill or be killed. She much preferred the kill option.

Tossing Madison his cell phone, she automatically dialed Jones's number as Jeremy drove toward the Inn before making a left hand turn down one street, a right hand turn a few streets later. Four more turns and Madison realized they were pulling into his driveway.

Smart move on his part, Madison thought, *not returning to the Inn and not taking a direct route home.* The garage door open when he pulled the truck into the driveway, Jeremy steered it inside, hitting the button and closing the door behind them before shutting off the engine.

So much for plowing, he thought idly, making a mental note to call Jack. He and the others would finish it up. Jeremy blinked. What was he doing thinking about plowing at a time like this? Shaking his head, he climbed out of the truck.

"Jones is on his way," Madison said quietly as Jeremy let them into the house, turning off the alarm as they entered. "You have an alarm?"

Why hadn't she noticed it before?

Because, she reminded herself, *you were distracted by other . . . things*. She shook her head. *Get your head back into the game!* she admonished herself angrily. She was letting emotions get in her way, and because of that, she was missing things. Enough of that!

Shrugging out of her coat, Madison turned to face Jeremy. Catching his breath, Jeremy found himself looking into blue eyes as bright as diamonds and just as cold. All business now, Madison stared at him, daring him to speak. Not sure what to say, Jeremy just stood there. This was the woman he'd faced off against just two days ago. The woman who'd handled his gun like it was an extension of her own hand. The woman who killed for a living. He swallowed hard. Stillman was going to die a painful death. The realization hit him as he unconsciously took a step back.

Leaving Jeremy to process it all, Madison dashed up the stairs, disappearing into the bedroom. She didn't have time to explain; now was the time for action. Returning moments later, the SAT phone in her hand, Madison found Jeremy standing in the kitchen, leaning against the counter. Wishing she could comfort him, explain to him what she was doing, she knew she couldn't. Not now anyway. Hopefully later. Hopefully. With a tilt of her head, she motioned she'd be in the living room. Nodding, he stayed where he was. Part of him wanted to listen in on the call, the other part of him not sure he was ready for that just yet.

He thought he'd left this part of his life behind. Yet here it was—and in his living room, no less. Shit.

Outside the snow was beginning to fall again in earnest.

CHAPTER 18

SARAH ANSWERED ON the third ring. Skipping the pleasantries, Madison got right to the point, quickly outlining the latest developments, ending with her having just spotted Stillman watching her.

"Who is this guy, and why's he after me?" Madison demanded angrily. Taking a deep breath, she apologized, "Sorry, I'm just frustrated."

"I understand completely," Sarah said from her living room in Kassel, Germany. "And I wish I could tell you why, but I haven't figured it out just yet. But I can tell you, it has nothing to do with the job you're there to do."

Rolling her eyes, Madison dropped into a chair, draping her legs over the arm.

"That's a relief, I guess."

"I'll have more answers for you inside the next twenty-four hours," Sarah assured her friend. "In the meantime, stay out of his way, okay?"

"I'll try. But if he gets in my way, well, I can't promise anything," Madison said, glancing back toward the kitchen.

His back to her, Jeremy was staring out the kitchen window. Good. She knew they'd be talking later. The time for secrets had past, especially since Jeremy was involved now—whether she wanted him to be or not.

"Thank you for sending Jones," Madison said quietly.

"I thought he might be able to help, and I didn't want you alone with no backup." That was Sarah, always looking out for her operatives. "You're family first."

Madison blinked. "You read me that far away?" Like her twin brother, Sarah had a gift.

"Hell, no," Sarah chuckled, "I just know you."

Madison smiled into the phone.

"Okay," Sarah continued, "moving forward, what has Jones said about this latest development?"

"I haven't talked to him yet, he and Stan should be here shortly."

"Stan? Who the hell is Stan?"

"Your brother."

"Oh, of course, I should have known."

Where Jones went, her brother usually wasn't far away. And vice versa. They made a formidable team, those two.

"That man really has got to start coming up with more creative names. Stan? That's almost as bad as Rick!"

While the women laughed together, they also silently acknowledged that in their business, the simpler the name, the less likely one would be remembered. The man was nothing if not a pro.

"Well, let me know their take on all this," Sarah said, jotting down her brother's latest cover name.

"You don't already know?" Madison asked. "Haven't you already talked to Jones?" Hadn't he said he was going to contact Sarah?

"I did," Sarah admitted, "but he only glossed over what was going on."

Guessing what and who Sarah was referring to, Madison groaned.

"He told you about Jeremy."

"Oh, yeah," Sarah chuckled. "And I have to say, I was more than a little surprised to learn that Jones knew your Jeremy."

"He's not 'my' Jeremy. He's not 'my' anything."

"Yeah, whatever," Sarah smiled into the phone. "Jones vouched for him, and that's all I care about right now."

That being said, though—Sarah thought, flipping open a folder she had in front of her—*I'll be keeping a close eye on this relationship, that's for damn sure!*

Pulling a photograph from the file, Sarah studied it for a moment. Jeremy definitely was a handsome man.

"You're staying at his place for the time being, is that right?" Sarah asked a moment later, sliding the photo back into the folder.

"Yes," Madison answered grudgingly.

She wasn't sure what bothered her more—the fact that she had to hide or that Sarah thought she and Jeremy were an item.

Snap out of it! she told herself fiercely. This was business, not personal. Or was it? Sitting up straight, Madison glanced back toward Jeremy before pushing out of the chair.

"I just had a thought," she blurted into the phone.

"I thought I felt the earth shake," Sarah chuckled before quickly sobering. "What is it?"

"Could this be personal? Could this guy be after me for a personal reason?" Sarah leaned back, considering Madison's idea. It was possible.

"Let me work on that angle, and I'll get back to you," Sarah said, her mind racing. "Tell Jones what you're thinking." Sarah paused. "And tell Jeremy. He's involved, whether you want him to be or not."

Madison agreed, not entirely sure whether Sarah meant personally or professionally. The lines between the two were quickly becoming blurred as it was.

"I will. Jones should be along anytime now," Madison said, glancing at the clock on the wall.

Agreeing on a time when they'd talk again, they ended the call. Staring down at the phone in her hand, Madison looked up to see Jeremy standing in the doorway.

"Everything okay?"

A million questions going through his mind, Jeremy opted for the simplest and hoped Madison would open up to him.

"Not yet," Madison answered honestly. "We need to talk."

Releasing the breath he hadn't realized he'd been holding, Jeremy nodded. This was a start. Taking her hand and squeezing it gently, he smiled. Tugging her toward the couch, a loud knocking at the door stopped them.

"That should be Jones," Madison said with a sheepish grin, pulling her hand from his to go answer the door.

Glancing at the couch, Jeremy couldn't decide whether Jones's timing was excellent or totally crappy. He decided it was totally crappy.

Pacing around her living room, Sarah's mind whirled. The idea that this Stillman guy could have a personal vendetta against Madison rolled through her mind, more and more becoming a strong possibility. Yes, it was still feasible that someone could have taken a contract out on Madison, but it was also highly unlikely. Madison took jobs that required her to travel almost constantly as well as to some of the most remote places in the world. Remembering a recent job that had Madison in San Francisco one week then in New Zealand the next, only to be back in Boston a few days later, Sarah made sure Madison wasn't in one place longer than necessary. And because of Madison's specific skill set, Sarah never let her return to the same area for a year or more. No, it was highly unlikely that someone from any of Madison's previous jobs were involved now. Dead people didn't take out contracts.

No, more and more, this was looking like it was personal. But how, who, and why?

Meticulous when planning the jobs, managing Madison's schedule carefully, Sarah kept her from being anywhere long enough to develop any kind of personal relationship. And up till now, Madison had never shown any inclination to do so either. Or course, Sarah knew Madison wasn't celibate—far from it. She was a beautiful, healthy woman who didn't lack for male attention. But years of experience had also taught her to pick and choose wisely when she was in the mood for male companionship. Despite all that, for reasons she never discussed, Madison still tended to shy away from relationships. Sarah blamed Madison's parents for that.

Going back to the file, Sarah quickly reviewed Jones's notes on the situation so far, especially those referring to Mary—apparently a waitress infatuated with Jeremy. Evidently, the girl was furious over Madison stealing Jeremy's attention away from herself. Sarah quickly crossed Mary off the potential people list. Despite the fact that no one could presently account for Mary's whereabouts, Sarah already knew Mary wasn't capable of pulling off such a thing. The young girl was a waitress; she still lived with her parents. There was no way Mary could afford to put a hit out on Madison. Or anyone for that matter.

But to cover all the bases, Stan was still going to talk to Mary's parents. At this point, the more information they could garner, the better. The biggest clues could come from the smallest pieces of information.

Parents. Sarah's mind shifted back to Madison's own parents. She'd never met them, knowing only what Madison had told her about them. Despite how close she and Madison were, there were still some topics that were off-limits—Madison's parents and her true relationship with them being one of those topics. Fair enough, though, Sarah smiled; they'd never talked about her own parents either.

Maybe someday.

Would it make a difference to Madison if she knew that Sarah's parents had no clue that their twin son and daughter were highly sought-out assassins? That their own mother was more interested in the goings on at their country club than she was with her children's lives? Would Madison open up then? Sarah paused, trying to remember when she'd last spoken to her mother. It'd been months anyway. Longer since she'd last seen them.

Believing that their daughter was a financial genius living overseas and working with financial institutions throughout Europe, they also believed that their son worked for some major conglomerate and that he traveled worldwide to fix companies in trouble.

If they only knew, Sarah thought ruefully.

For the most part, it was a good thing that their parents didn't pay closer attention to their children's lives. This way, at least Sarah and her brother didn't have to come up with silly excuses as to why they kept missing holidays and family reunions.

Coming back to the matter at hand, Sarah quickly scribbled herself a note. She needed to contact her brother. If there was a personal connection here, and it was very much looking that way, it only made sense that it somehow involved Madison's parents. When it came to family, you couldn't get much more personal than that.

Knowing Madison wouldn't give up information about her parents easily, Sarah considered other avenues in which she could learn what she needed to know. For the moment, the less she had to involve Madison, the better. It didn't matter that Madison would be thoroughly pissed off at her friend for going behind her back, but what else was Sarah going to do? And besides, Sarah told herself, she wasn't meddling. This was business. A matter of life and death. Screw how Madison would feel; keeping her alive was all Sarah cared about doing at this point. She was sure Jeremy and the others would agree.

And if there was a connection between this Stillman guy, Madison, and her parents, then what? Well then, the guy would die. Simple as that.

"Slow down!" Sarah said out loud, giving herself a mental shaking.

Until she had all the information, she wasn't making any final decisions. And dying was pretty final in her book. No, first she needed to gather all the information she could on Madison's parents—and do it as quickly and quietly as possible. To protect her friend and nab Stillman, neither could know what Sarah had planned.

A shiver raced down Sarah's back. Never before had anyone targeted any of her own people on a personal level; this was a first. And very disturbing. If Stillman was connected, Sarah hoped it was only to Madison and that he wasn't a threat to her entire team. She shook her head; in the end it wouldn't matter either way anyway. The man was most definitely going to die. And very painfully.

Wandering over to her balcony door, Sarah gazed out over the city she'd come to love and consider home. She hoped she wouldn't have to move again anytime soon. But knowing at anytime she might be called upon again to kill someone herself, chances were pretty good she'd eventually be looking for a new place to call home. There were some restrictions when it came to renting an apartment in her building. She was pretty sure being a professional assassin, and an active one at that, was probably one of them. Go figure.

There was no sense in jumping the gun, Sarah reminded herself. The priority right now was finding out who Stillman really was. Because she was damn sure that wasn't his real name. Once she knew that, she'd be able to connect the dots to Madison's parents. If there were any to be connected—something told Sarah there was. Turning away from the window, Sarah readied herself to tackle the work she had ahead of her. First things first, though. Coffee. And lots of it!

Standing in the shadows near the wood-burning stove, Stan had a clear view out a window facing the driveway and the road. If any cars approached, he'd see them. The snow was falling hard now; he doubted anyone would dare approach by foot. But then again, Stan had seen people do stupider things. And he was fairly certain Stillman wasn't that stupid. That and they couldn't be that lucky. Of course, if the man had a personal vendetta against Madison, then who knew what the fool might do. No, Stan decided, Stillman wouldn't approach by foot. If they'd learned nothing else about the guy, they'd learned that he didn't like the snow. No, it'd be by car—or an SUV, in this case. Leaning comfortably against the wall, he settled in for the duration, happy not to be part of the conversation—or rather, the argument going on between Jeremy and Madison. Glancing quickly at Jones, he knew his partner felt the same.

Jeremy wanted Madison to stay at his house, where he could keep her safe. Having been on her own most of her life, the idea of someone taking care of her went against everything she was and felt. And she told Jeremy so in no uncertain terms. Stan had forgotten how well the girl could swear, turning toward the window to hide his smile.

Not about to hide from Stillman, Madison also knew she couldn't just find him and kill him. No matter how much she wanted to. No, she needed to know why he was after her. And if he was working with someone else. She suspected the woman clearly posing as his wife.

"You're sure they're not really married? They fight like they could be," Jones said with a wry smile.

"No, I'm sure," Madison said confidently, pleasing Jones.

He already knew they weren't married but was glad Madison had figured it out as well. At least this way they knew there'd be no grieving widow left behind.

"Too bad we can't just let them kill each other," Madison said with a chuckle.

That would certainly make things easier for everyone! And think of the paperwork they could avoid!

"Yeah," Stan interjected, "when have we ever been that lucky?"

"You were," Jones reminded him, "remember the Jennings guy who went off the balcony at the hands of his wife?"

Stan smiled, easily remembering the bastard who'd just been begging to be killed. Ready to do the job, instead the bastard's wife took care of it for him. In a fit of rage, she'd pushed her abusive husband off their balcony with him landing on a large rock and dying instantly. It was all done nice and neatly—more or less anyway.

"Oh, yeah," Stan nodded, "yeah, dodged a bullet there."

Holy shit, Jeremy thought, listening to them talk so easily about people killing each other.

"There's nothing easy about it."

Nearly jumping, Jeremy turned to find Stan staring hard at him. Fighting the urge to shudder under the man's hard gaze, Jeremy remained still.

"There's absolutely nothing easy about it," Stan repeated. "It's just what we do." Silence. "And you'd do well to remember that," he concluded, turning back again to the window.

"So what am I supposed to do then?" Madison asked, pulling Jeremy's attention back to her and away from Stan.

She needed to keep those two away from each other. And wasn't surprised when she caught Stan nodding slowly. God, she hated how he did that!

"I say you stay here," Jeremy ventured again before rushing to add, "No one would be stupid enough to try and attack you here."

"And you know that how?" Madison demanded.

"I have to agree with Jeremy," Jones added quietly, earning a vicious stare from Madison.

He nearly laughed; the girl had guts!

"When did you go over to his side?" Madison glared at Jones before turning back to Jeremy, realization dawning on her. "You guys have worked together before!" And just groaned when they nodded. "Duh!" she exclaimed, clenching her fists in frustration.

Jones had admitted to knowing Jeremy when the three of them had met in her room at the Inn. Why hadn't she paid closer attention to that? Why hadn't she asked questions? Because it wasn't important at the time. Well, it was fucking important now!

"Where and when? Spill it!"

Struggling not to laugh at her demand, Stan wished he had a bowl of popcorn; this was going to be a good show. And he knew when Jones snorted that his partner was thinking the same thing.

"I don't think so," Jones countered firmly. "It was a long time ago, and it has absolutely no bearing on this job here and now."

"We're in this business together," she ventured slowly. "Don't you think sharing information might be a little helpful here?"

"No," Jones said, his tone daring Madison to argue.

Agreeing with Jones, Jeremy just nodded but wisely remained silent. Rattling off a sentence filled with foul words, Madison only succeeded in making the men smile. She, truly, could swear better than any truck driver!

CHAPTER 19

PACING BACK AND forth, Frank Stillman paused long enough to gaze out at the falling snow. Damn, but he hated the snow! He started pacing again.

"You're going to wear a hole in the carpet if you keep that up."

Stopping, he glared at Ellen before resuming his pacing. He was in a mood, for sure, Ellen realized, knowing he'd talk to her when he was good and ready. In the meantime, she hoped she had the patience to wait him out. She doubted it, glancing at her watch. She'd been invited to join another couple for dinner, and she was looking forward to it. If only because it got her away from Frank. Of course, he'd been invited too, but she'd made excuses for him. The frame of mind he was in now—he wasn't going to be good company. To put it mildly.

"What are you doing?" Surprised to hear him speak, Ellen turned away from the closet where she'd been going through her wardrobe, limited as it was.

"I'm looking for something to wear to dinner," she answered, turning back to the closet. The job they were here to do wasn't supposed to have taken this long; she was running out of clothes! And the idea of wearing the same outfit again didn't appeal to her in the least. She wasn't the only one in this boat, she reminded herself; the rest of the people in their group were experiencing the same problems. Funny how that small thought made her feel a bit better, and pulling some clothes out, she tossed them on the bed. She glanced at her watch; she had plenty of time.

"What?" Frank asked, staring blankly at Ellen. "Dinner?"

Giving the man a droll look, Ellen moved around him, disappearing into the bathroom, closing the door behind her.

"I'm meeting the Wilsons for dinner," she said loudly, hoping her voice covered the sound of her locking the door. "You were invited, but I made excuses."

Staring at her reflection in the mirror, she still winced when he pounded on the door.

"Why did you do that?" Frank demanded, pounding again on the door. "I need you here!"

Ignoring him, Ellen proceeded to touch up her makeup. After running a brush through her hair, she rummaged through her cosmetics bag, relief flowing through her when her fingers brushed against the small revolver she'd safely tucked into a secret compartment. If Frank didn't pull himself together, she was going to kill him herself! The man was going nuts over this job, and it was showing.

In all the years they'd worked together, she'd never seen him so worked up over a job. No, there was more to this job than he'd told her. The basic information he'd given her originally, she thought it was enough. Clearly, she had been wrong. But he wasn't about to fill her in now, not in the frame of mind he was in! With a final caress of the gun, Ellen closed up the bag, and checking herself again, she braced herself for Frank's anger.

Opening the door slowly, Ellen paused, surprised to find Frank changing his clothes.

"I'm going with you," he announced, glancing briefly at Ellen before pulling a cable-knit sweater over his head. "A good meal and good company is just what I need."

And it'd force him to take his mind off the job for a few minutes. He needed to stop and rethink his plan, get a new perspective on things. A good meal would go a long way toward that goal. And he grudgingly admitted to himself, he did like the Wilsons. But most importantly, he'd quickly decided, hiding in plain sight right about now might be a good thing. He knew Madison and her watchdog of a boyfriend were looking for him. Seeing him in public with others, they wouldn't dare confront him. Would they? No. He wouldn't, so he was fairly confident they wouldn't either. Why do anything that would bring unwanted attention to them?

Shaking her head, Ellen continued dressing for dinner. And men complained about how fast women changed their minds? No woman could hold a candle to this man! Never had Ellen known a man who could change his mind and his attitude so quickly! It was actually a bit scary.

Still arguing over where she was going to be staying, Madison was relieved when Jeremy's phone rang. They'd been talking, arguing, debating, and arguing again for the better part of the last hour as to where the safest place was for Madison. Interjecting only when absolutely necessary, Stan and Jones had remained silent for much of the discussion, each enjoying watching Madison and Jeremy go at it, but each for different reasons. Amazed they hadn't come to blows, Stan admired Madison's ability to control herself. He was pretty sure he would have pounded the guy into the floor long before now. But then again, he wasn't Madison. And he sure as hell wasn't sleeping with Jeremy. He smiled, turning back to gaze out the window again.

Jones knew Jeremy's background, knew what the guy was capable of. And was impressed as well that the two hadn't started pounding on the other. Jones watched and listened quietly while Jeremy defended his reasons for keeping Madison at his house, all of them spot-on. And Jones equally enjoyed watching Madison try and blast every one of Jeremy's reasons to hell but finding herself unable to. Instead, she'd nearly gone nose-to-nose with the guy, stating very clearly that that she was perfectly capable of taking care of herself and had been doing a fine job of it for years now. They were fun to watch, Jones admitted, trying not to smile. But everyone welcomed the break when the phone rang, though. Disappearing into the kitchen to take the call, Jeremy took a deep breath, thankful for the interruption. He needed the time to regroup!

As soon as Jeremy left the room, Madison rounded on Stan and Jones.

"Thanks for your support," she growled, dropping onto the couch in frustration.

Weary of the arguing, Madison just wanted time to think, and to do that, she was going to need to be alone. Alone, alone, in her hotel room—not here alone. She nearly ground her teeth in frustration. She knew the guys were looking out for her safety; she understood that. But never one to rely on anyone for anything, Madison just couldn't wrap her mind around the idea of someone protecting her. She prided herself in always facing everything head-on; she'd never hidden from anything. And she wasn't about to start now. But how to make the guys understand that? She wished Sarah was here; she'd understand Madison's need to be on her own. Sarah would agree with the others that Madison needed protecting, but she'd understand Madison's side too. Dropping her head into her hands, Madison closed her eyes. What the hell was she going to do?

"You won't believe this one," Jeremy said from the doorway minutes later.

Everyone's head turned in his direction.

"Stillman is having dinner at the restaurant!"

"What?" Not sure she heard right, Madison repeated her question, "What?"

"Yeah, Stillman and his so-called wife are having dinner with another couple right now!"

Running his hand through his hair in frustration, Jeremy looked first to Jones before turning to Stan, finally letting his gaze fall back on Madison, who still wore a surprised look on her tired face.

"That was my mom. Jack spotted them and asked her to call me."

"Well, the guy's got balls, that's for sure," Stan said, turning away from the window.

At least they knew where the guy was; he didn't need to keep a vigil at the window any longer.

"Hiding in plain sight," Jones said, nodding. "He knows you won't try anything with people around."

"Bastard!" Madison rose smoothly from the couch. "But at least we know where he is for the time being," she conceded. Having resigned herself to staying at Jeremy's, she added, "At least now I can get back to the hotel to grab my things without being seen."

Three sets of startled eyes turned on her. and she gave them all a lopsided grin. "Shut up, yes, I give up." She tossed a sheepish grin at Jeremy, "I'll stay here. But I want my things."

Jeremy could only nod. While he got what he wanted, he was still surprised she'd given in to him. And he wondered if he should be worried.

"But it kills me that we can't do anything, but yet he goes out for a nice dinner!"

"You can't do anything."

All eyes turned at Stan's quiet statement.

"That doesn't mean I can't."

For the first time in an hour, Madison smiled. She knew exactly what Stan was capable of doing—Jones too, for that matter.

"What do you have in mind?" she asked, her voice dangerously quiet.

Having everyone's attention, Stan began to outline the plan that he'd literally just come up with. But hey, sometimes those plans were the best.

"Wait a second," Jeremy interrupted before Stan had barely started speaking. "I'm not sure I want to hear this. Or that I should even be a part of it."

Understanding and agreeing, Madison turned back to Stan. "Hold that thought," she said.

Rising from the couch, she tugged on Jeremy's arm, pulling him into the kitchen. Once out of earshot, she turned to Jeremy.

"I'm really sorry to have gotten you involved in any of this."

Surprised by her admission Jeremy remained silent.

"But you're right, whatever Stan's plan is, you probably shouldn't be a part of it."

Jeremy nodded. *Plausible deniability.* He knew the term well.

"I want to help you, protect you," Jeremy said, running his hands up and down her arms, wishing he could pull her into his arms and keep her there. "I know Jones, what he's capable of. The fact that Stan's with Jones, I can only imagine what they can pull off together." Jeremy sighed heavily. "I also need to protect my family."

Madison nodded, her respect for him growing by the moment. The man knew his priorities. She had no right dragging him into her dark and dangerous world. She hated that he was involved as much as he was already!

"Knowing what you know now, do you still want me to stay here?"

"Yes."

His immediate and forceful reply warmed her. He chuckled.

"Despite everything, yes, I still think the smartest thing would be for you to stay here with me."

"Okay," Madison smiled. "I will stay. Now, how about this," she began, "while Stan's telling us his plan, why don't you go back to your plowing. I'll have the guys drive me over to the Inn, and yes," she continued quickly, as Jeremy's look darkened, "I'll have them wait while I collect my things, okay?"

"Okay," he conceded.

At least she wouldn't be alone. Pulling her into his arms, he kissed her hard and fast before releasing her and stepping away.

"You have my cell, you'd better call if you need anything. Hell," he smiled, "you'd better call anyway."

Nodding, Madison smiled, her lips still tingling from the quick kiss.

Hearing the back door close, Stan and Jones remained silent when Madison returned alone. Explaining what Jeremy was doing, both men nodded in agreement. The guy was caught in a tough spot. Jeremy was doing the right thing by distancing himself from them. And of course, they'd stay with Madison while she collected her things from the Inn.

"Now," Madison said, anxious to get on with things, "what's the plan?"

"The plan is to take you back to the Inn for your stuff." Stan's droll reply earned him an angry glare from Madison, which he totally ignored.

"Ha-ha," she snapped. "Tell me, what are you going to do?"

"He just told you," Jones said, rising from his chair.

Following the men as they headed toward the door, Madison fumed. Why wouldn't they tell her their plan?

"Because," Stan stopped suddenly, causing Madison to come up short to avoid walking into his back; turning around, he nearly went nose-to-nose with her, "you know how I work. How we work. I'm not about to tell you what you don't need to know."

What? How dare he?

"This is my job!" Anger flowed through her.

"No, it's not," Stan snapped, effectively silencing Madison. "Your job isn't here, it's someplace else. This has nothing to do that job, and you know it. No, this is something totally different."

Madison opened her mouth, but grabbing her arms and giving her a good, hard shake, Stan silenced her.

"Listen," he explained quietly, "someone is after you, and we don't know why. It's our job to protect you. Our job, not yours. You of all people should know that."

Damn it if she didn't, and with a sullen nod, Madison conceded the battle.

"We good?" Jones asked, eyeing Madison, satisfied when she nodded silently.

He knew she didn't like it—hell, they'd all feel the same way if the shoe was on the other foot. And she'd be the first one telling them what Stan had just told her.

Shrugging on their coats, Stan and Madison left Jones to work out his part of the plan, and venturing back out into the falling snow, they piled into Stan's vehicle, heading back to the Inn in silence.

Brushing off the snow, Jeremy dashed into the restaurant, tossing a quick smile at the hostess before making a beeline for the bar. Spotting her son weaving his way around the tables toward her, Ruth poured him a coffee, handing it to him as he reached the bar.

Wrapping his hands around the hot mug, he smiled his thanks before drinking.

"Still bad outside?" Ruth asked.

"Bad enough," Jeremy replied, immediately feeling rejuvenated by the hot brew. His mom made the best coffee in town, not that he was biased or anything. "Seems before I finish a driveway, it's covered again." He tossed her a wry smile. "So basically, you know, same ol' same ol'."

Ruth chuckled, nodding. This storm was bad, but it wasn't the worst they'd ever seen. Not by a long shot. Glancing at his watch, Jeremy glanced back toward the entrance.

"The others will be in shortly," he said, referring to the team of men he plowed with.

Between the nine of them, they managed to keep the side streets and driveways relatively clear. Ruth nodded, the heads-up unnecessary. Knowing the boys as she did, she knew they'd be wandering in in shifts. Someone always stayed out plowing; it was the only way they could keep up.

The hot coffee working its magic, Jeremy glanced idly around the busy restaurant, his eyes lingering on one customer before skipping on. Turning back to his mother, he sighed happily when she placed a heaping plate of hot food in front of him.

"Oh, I love you," he murmured, picking up his fork and attacking the food.

Smiling, Ruth disappeared back into the kitchen. She needed to let the cooks know they had more hungry people on the way.

Happily full, Jeremy turned his attention back to the restaurant patrons as he sipped his fresh mug of coffee.

"Where's Madison?" his mother asked, reaching for Jeremy's empty plate. "She realized how boring plowing is?" she asked with a chuckle.

"She's at the Inn," he said quietly, "picking up a few things."

"Oh?"

And in that one word, Ruth asked a million questions. Knowing his mother was dying to pepper him with questions, Jeremy was admittedly surprised by her hesitation. That wasn't like her, and he wondered if he should be worried. Probably.

"Yes, Mother, she's coming to my place."

Her raised eyebrows made him laugh, and suddenly, he felt like a teenager trying to pull a fast one over on his mother.

"Come on, Mom! I'm over twenty-one!"

"That's debatable!" Sliding onto the bar stool next to his brother, Jack nodded a greeting to his mother before turning to his brother. "What have you done now?"

Laughing, the brothers shook hands.

"I haven't done anything." He paused, his smile growing. "Yet."

"I'm sure," Jack laughed, accepting the mug of coffee his mother quickly produced. Taking a sip, he sighed. Nothing better than his mother's coffee. "Where's Madison?"

"What, can't I go out without her now?"

Both Jack and Ruth laughed.

"Given that you two seem to have been attached at the hip lately, ah, no."

Punching his brother in the arm, Jeremy laughed, unable to deny his brother's accurate observation.

"Okay, if you must know, she's picking up some of her things at the Inn."

"She's going to stay with your brother," Ruth pointed out in case Jack missed it—which, of course, he hadn't. "Good thing I like her so much," Ruth added with a smile before stepping away to greet another customer.

Jeremy leaned toward his brother.

"We thought it might be safer for her at my place."

"Wise idea," Jack said, glancing idly around the still crowded room. "Good to know where everyone is."

Knowing he was referring to Stillman, Jeremy nodded.

"The guy's cocky, I'll give him that."

"Doing his best to act natural and failing miserably," Jeremy said quietly, turning his back to the room. "Have you seen the way he's sitting? Stiff as a rod. The woman, she's doing fine, but he's a wreck."

Jack nodded, also turning his back to the room.

Nancy and her cravings—animal crackers; she had to have ani-mal crackers! Despite the storm, Jack knew he had no choice but to indulge his wife. He was too young to die at the hands of very pregnant woman whose only request—okay, demand—had been for him to buy her a large box of animal crackers. Or lots of the small boxes—either would work, she'd informed him. Assuring her hus-band she was fine alone, she helped him on with his coat before ushering him out the door into the falling snow. Good thing they lived only a few streets away from the store. And the restaurant, he thought, trudging through the snow, knowing that walking would be faster. Nancy wasn't the only one with cravings. Must be sym-pathy pains, Jack decided, as he suddenly had a craving for one of his mom's homemade desserts. With an added spring to his step, he altered his course slightly, heading toward the restaurant.

A grin on his face, Jack climbed the steps to the restaurant, pausing just inside to text Nancy so she wouldn't be worried. His grin grew as she immediately replied that he'd best be bringing her a dessert too. *Oh, but don't forget the animal crackers.* Chuckling, he took a step into the restaurant before coming up short. Sitting at a round table in the middle of the busy restaurant was Stillman and his so-called wife.

"Jack?"

Turning to find his mother standing beside him, Jack was momentarily distracted, his mind racing. All thoughts of dessert fled as he gripped his mother's arm, her eyes widening in surprise.

"Call Jeremy, would you please?"

And telling his mother exactly what to say, knowing she'd repeat it word for word, Jack debated his next move. His appetite suddenly gone, he contemplated leaving, but it was too late. Stillman had seen him. Knowing there was no way he could ignore the man now, Jack did the next best thing and tossed Stillman his biggest and broadest smile, throwing the man a friendly wave as an added gesture. His plan worked. Stillman's eyes widened as he automatically raised his hand, returning Jack's greeting with his own stiff and hesitant wave.

Knowing he'd thrown Stillman off balance for the moment, Jack's appetite immediately returned, and making his way to the bar, he gave the waitress his dessert order. Turning around to face the crowded room, Jack contemplated approaching Stillman but wasn't sure how. Seconds later, his answer came when the tour guide waved Jack over.

Okay, he thought, *this could work.*

And weaving his way through the room, Jack shook hands with the man in greeting. Declining the guide's offer to join them, explaining he had to get home, Jack chatted easily with the group while waiting for his desserts. While Stillman and his "wife" said nothing, the others had many questions, mostly about the weather and their constantly changing time schedule. With the exception of the Stillmans, it was a nice group, and Jack wished he could sit and talk more with them. But when the waitress pressed two to-go boxes into his hand, Jack knew he needed to be going. With a smile and assurances that he'd let the group know as soon as the weather cleared enough for them to fly out, Jack took his leave of the group. Making his way toward the door, Jack was sure he felt Stillman's eyes boring holes into his back.

Outside in the snow, Jack took a deep breath, glad to be away from the man. Shaking off the feeling of dread that washed over him, Jack turned toward the store. If he forgot the animal crackers, none of this would matter anyway. His wife would have already killed him.

CHAPTER 20

ONCE NANCY WAS settled with her animal crackers and dessert, Jack returned to the restaurant. Relieved to see Jeremy's truck outside, it only took a minute to spot his brother in the crowded restaurant. And sliding on to the barstool next to Jeremy, Jack quietly and quickly told his brother about his earlier encounter with Stillman.

Chancing a quick glance over his shoulder, Jeremy saw Stillman leaning toward his "wife," whispering something in her ear. While he couldn't hear what was said, from the ugly look she tossed at Stillman, she clearly wasn't happy. Seconds later, pushing back from the table, Stillman rose—all but pulling his wife from her chair, ignoring her unhappy frown. Jeremy wondered if the others in their party noticed it. They'd be blind not to.

Nodding politely to each person at their table, Stillman finally turned toward the door, his wife reluctantly following him. Pulling out his cell phone, Jeremy quickly texted Madison. Then he texted Jones.

"I promise to play nice." Came the almost-immediate reply from Madison.

Chuckling, Jeremy read Jones's reply that quickly followed:

"I'll make sure she stays out of trouble."

"Everyone's in the loop," Jeremy said, turning back to Jack. "Thanks for calling me, bro."

Nodding, Jack finished his coffee before sliding off the barstool.

"Keep me posted," he said, pulling on his jacket.

Jeremy nodded. And with a nod to his mother, Jack headed for the door.

"One of these days, you'll have to tell me what's going on," Ruth said, topping off Jack's coffee.

"One of these days, I hope I know what's going on," Jeremy muttered into his coffee mug.

* * *

Poking his head out the door of Madison's room, Stan quickly scanned the hallway, relieved to find it was empty. Closing the door, he turned back to Madison, watching her stuff clothes and other items into her duffel bag. He nearly laughed when she stopped and, with hands on her hips, just stared around the room. Women. He could be packed and on the move in a matter of minutes. But women, well, that was a different story. Wisely keeping his mouth shut as Madison disappeared into the bathroom, quickly returning with a small toiletries bag, Stan made a mental note to e-mail his wife. Speaking of taking forever to pack!

Grabbing up her bag and backpack, Madison swung around to Stan.

"Got everything?" he asked, noticing an empty bag sitting on the luggage rack and some clothes folded beside it. Following his gaze, Madison nodded.

"I'm not leaving for good, I'm coming back," she stated firmly. "And in the meantime, if anyone comes in, they'll think I'm still here. Which is exactly what I want them to think."

Stan nodded, liking her thinking.

"Not that I expect anyone, but just in case."

Not wanting a repeat performance of finding Ethel, or anyone, in her room, Madison had informed the woman—nicely but firmly—that if she required any housekeeping services she'd ask for them. Otherwise, there was no reason for anyone to be in her room. Not that that would stop Stillman, though. But she'd taken precautions there too.

"Okay then," Stan said before cracking open the door again.

Finding the hallway still empty, he motioned for Madison to follow him, and together they slipped out of the room and quietly into the stairwell. Not expecting to run into anyone, Stan was still relieved when they made it to lobby level without meeting up with anyone. Poking his head out the stairwell door, he spotted Ethel at the front desk. No problem. Motioning for Madison to hang back, he pushed open the door, casually greeting Ethel as he headed toward the living room and the coffee machine. As he hoped, Ethel followed him, and pouring himself a coffee, he idly struck up a conversation with the innkeeper, keeping her attention focused on him and not the lobby. Moments later, glancing over Ethel's head, Stan saw Madison emerge from the stairwell before quickly disappearing out the front door. The burst of cold air that followed had Ethel turning. Momentarily surprised to find no one there, she quickly turned back to Stan with a questioning look, his own look of innocence immediately making her suspicious.

"What are you up to?" she murmured, her eyes narrowing.

"Me? Nothing. I just came down for a coffee."

And pigs can fly, Ethel thought, watching Stan with slanted eyes as he prepared his coffee to go.

Popping on a lid, he smiled and, with a nod, stepped around her. Then with a "See ya" and a quick wave, Stan disappeared out into the cold.

Something's going on, Ethel thought as she wandered back to the desk.

Minutes later, another burst of cold air had Ethel looking up to see Frank Stillman practically dragging Ellen inside. Angry at being caught manhandling her, Frank only nodded a curt greeting to Ethel. Ellen managed an embarrassed smile before they disappeared into the waiting elevator.

Oh, yes, Ethel thought with a frown, *something was most definitely going on.*

Nearly pushing Ellen into their room, Frank glanced quickly up and down the hallway, relieved to find it still empty before he followed Ellen into the room.

"What the hell is wrong with you?" Ellen hissed, calling on all her willpower not to kill the man where he stood. "Don't you ever manhandle me again, do you hear me?"

Her eyes blazing, she clenched her fists. Ignoring her threat, Frank moved quickly to the balcony door, swiftly drawing the heavy curtain. No sense in taking any chances that someone might be watching them, snowstorm or not.

"Shut up, Ellen," Frank growled as he began pacing around the room. "I need to think!"

"About what?"

"About what?" Whirling on her, Frank glared at the woman like she was from another planet. "Weren't you paying attention tonight?" Her drool stare added fuel to his already burning temper. "Do you think it was coincidence that the pilot and his brother were at the restaurant tonight?"

Now it was Ellen's turn to glare at Frank like *he* was from another planet.

"Actually, yes."

"What?" Frank exploded, quickly taking a deep breath to calm himself. "What?" he said again, this time a bit quieter.

Seriously, Ellen thought, was the man that stupid? His anger was clearly affecting his ability to think straight. He needed to calm down, and telling him so, Ellen patiently reminded him that the brothers did live here and their mother did own the restaurant after all. Where else were they supposed to go?

Frank's temper flashed briefly; he hated to admit it, but Ellen was right. Damn it! He was missing too many small details and needed to get his temper under control before he made another mistake! Thankful for the bottle of brandy he'd purchased earlier, Frank poured himself a glass and, not bothering to offer any to Ellen, drank it down. The smooth, warm liquid instantly soothed him, and taking a deep breath, he forced himself to relax. Ignoring the snub, Ellen waited until he moved away before she helped herself, needing the drink as much as he did but, she was sure, for totally different reasons. Silence filled the room as Frank turned to stare into the fire while Ellen stared at his back.

It would be so easy to kill him, she thought with a smirk. A knife between the shoulder blades, and it'd be done. If it weren't for the damn snowstorm and being stuck in this godforsaken place, she might have done it. But she had no clear way to escape, and it was that thought alone that kept her standing where she was. Glancing idly around the room, Ellen pondered her next move. She wouldn't kill Frank, not yet anyway. But she had to do something.

Still staring into the fire, Frank was oblivious to where Ellen's thoughts were going, his own on Madison. While he'd originally intended to kill Madison elsewhere, here was beginning to look better and better. The snowstorm might work in his favor; he'd be able to dump her body easier. All he needed was a deep snowbank. He'd watched the plow trucks move through the town. If he timed it right, he could kill her, toss her in the snowbank, cover her with some snow, and then let the plow bury her beneath more snow. They wouldn't find her until spring. For the first time in many hours, Frank smiled.

Watching him visibly relax, Ellen knew his temper had quieted, that maybe now she could talk to him.

"Would you like another brandy?" she tentatively asked, reaching for the bottle on the desk.

When he nodded, she let out the breath she hadn't realized she'd been holding. Still staring into the fire, Frank held out his glass for her to fill, nodding his thanks before raising the glass to this lips. The idea of poisoning the man rushed through Ellen's mind, replacing the knife in the back idea. Make it look like a natural death—she could leave town easily then. Shaking her head, Ellen swallowed the evil laugh that threatened to erupt from her. Dropping into a chair, she crossed her legs gracefully. If only Frank knew how easy it'd be for her to kill him where he stood, he'd never turn his back on her again!

Sitting on the edge of the bed, Frank turned on the television, effectively interrupting Ellen's thoughts on ways to kill the man. Glancing at the TV, she wasn't surprised to find him watching the weather channel; he wanted to get out of this hell hole as much as she did.

"I hope the snow keeps coming," he said quietly, his words making Ellen gape at him in shock.

Okay, the man had gone off his rocker! Maybe she should kill him just to put him out of his misery?

"I beg your pardon?" was all she managed, struggling not to choke on her brandy. "As it is, this snow won't melt until August!"

With an evil smile, Frank finally looked at Ellen.

"Exactly."

From his vantage point around the corner, Stan watched Frank Stillman practically drag his wife up the steps to the Inn. So intent on getting inside, Stillman hadn't bothered to even glance around; if he had, Stan was sure the man would have spotted him. Not that it mattered—Stillman would never recognize him. But Stan recognized him. Filing away that information for later, he stayed where he was until the couple disappeared into the Inn and Stan was alone again outside.

It was only by sheer luck that Stan had left the Inn before Stillman returned, and he was more than thankful that Madison hadn't seen the man. While Madison was normally levelheaded, Stan knew this business with Stillman was getting under her skin. While it wasn't unheard of, it was rare to be the target, and this was a first for Madison.

"It's the not knowing why that's the problem!" Madison had blurted out earlier while packing.

Stan had remained silent, but he understood. He'd been in the business long enough and had been the target more than a few times himself. It was unnerving, to say the least. The only advice he had for Madison was to keep focused, keep moving forward. Don't ever look back. Trust your instincts.

Knowing which room was Stillman's, Stan waited until he saw the light come on in room. Good, he knew for sure where the guy was now. And with a grim smile, he watched as Stillman pulled the curtains closed, confirming Stan's suspicion that Stillman knew he was a target himself now. Pushing away from the building, Stan made his way around the corner, climbing into the pickup truck waiting for him. The warm cab felt good after the wind and the cold, and Stan smiled his thanks to Madison as she sat behind the driver's seat.

Knowing he wasn't going to tell her anything, Madison put the truck in gear, turning it toward Jeremy's house.

"Stillman knows he's a target," Stan announced without preamble when they'd all gathered in Jeremy's living room. "The look on his face when he pulled the curtains—oh, yeah, he knows."

"He did look pissed," Jones added from his spot by the wood-burning stove.

"You saw him?" Jeremy asked, surprised. When he'd returned from plowing, he'd found Jones napping on the couch. "When?"

"Earlier."

"Right," Jeremy said, realizing that was about as much as he was going to get out of Jones. And he reminded himself that he should consider himself lucky he even got that much out of the guy. He turned to Madison, "Did you see him too?"

Jeremy was relieved when she shook her head. He was more tuned in to Madison now; he could tell when she was avoiding him or lying. Neither was evident now.

"So now what?"

"Now we wait," Stan said, glancing at his watch.

"For . . . ?" Jeremy prodded before being interrupted by Stan's cell phone ringing.

"This," Stan said, answering his phone. "Right on time," he said with a smile.

"I aim to please," Sarah said from the comfort of her apartment in Kassel, Germany. "Is everyone there with you?"

"Yes," Stan said, his eyes drifting around the room. Putting his phone on speaker phone, he placed it on the coffee table so everyone could listen in. "Including Jeremy."

"Okay," Sarah said, understanding. Well, Jeremy being there would make the call just that much shorter then. No problem. "Well, here's what I can tell you so far . . ."

Hanging up minutes later, the only sound in the room was from the wood-burning stove—each lost in their own thoughts. Leaning against the wall, his arms crossed, Stan let this new information swirl around in his mind until it found its place. Lying back on the couch, his eyes closed, Jones also digested the new information.

Trying to process what he'd just learned, Jeremy disappeared into the kitchen, returning with three bottles of beer and a glass of Bailey's. Nodding his thanks but remaining silent, Stan accepted a bottle. Not opening his eyes, Jones held his arm out, smiling when Jeremy pressed a bottle into his hand. A hesitant smile on her face, Madison took the glass of Bailey's, tapping it lightly against Jeremy's own bottle before taking a sip. Closing her eyes, she let the smooth liquid slid down her suddenly dry throat. Wanting to chug his beer, Jeremy fought off the urge, forcing himself to put down the bottle after a few swallows. Now was not the time to get drunk—no matter how much he might want to. No, he needed to keep his head clear. They'd just been handed some vital information. Now it was just a matter of what to do with it. Jeremy glanced around the room. Judging by their relaxed positions, no one would ever suspect that minds were churning; ideas being discarded as fast as they were formed. Each thinking something different, one factor remained the same:

Ellen was no longer the enemy.

Ellen was now an asset.

CHAPTER 21

DRIVING SLOWLY THROUGH the quiet, snowbound town, Stan gripped the steering wheel—anger and frustration flowing through him.

"You grip that wheel any tighter, and you're going to snap it."

Thinking the man had been dozing, Stan tossed Jones a quick sidelong glance before concentrating again on the snowy road.

"I was," Jones said, confirming Stan's thoughts. "Your anger is coming off you like waves, man, you've gotta tone it down."

"Yeah, well I'm fucking pissed. You might have noticed."

"I did."

Pushing himself up in the seat, Jones glanced idly out the window. A world traveler, he'd never experienced this much snow in such a short period of time. Of course, this was his first trip to the far reaches of Canada. And despite how beautiful it was here, he hoped it would be his last. But he admitted to himself, while the snow was a royal pain in the ass, it certainly added to the beauty of the area. Stan snorted, and Jones chuckled, knowing his partner had been privy to his thoughts. Tough shit, if Stan didn't like his thoughts, then keep the hell out of his mind. Now Stan laughed out loud.

"Quit thinking such corny thoughts, and maybe I will."

Grateful that his friend had broken through his foul mood, easing the tension that had been building inside him, Stan relaxed his grip on the wheel. Flexing his stiff fingers he frowned. Guess he had been gripping the wheel a bit hard.

"You think?"

Two could play at that game, and Jones tossed Stan a knowing smile.

"Fuck you."

"Evening, boys," Ethel greeted them from her spot behind the front desk as a burst of cold air announced their arrival.

Glancing quickly at the wall clock, she opened her mouth to chide them on the lateness of the hour, but Stan beat her to it when he quickly apologized for coming in so late. Ethel smiled. There was something about Stan that she liked. She had no idea why; she just did.

"Anything exciting happening?" Jones asked, purposely keeping his tone nonchalant, brushing the snow off his coat and hat before peeling both off.

She shook her head, guessing there was more to the question. She glanced at Stan. Yes, she liked him, but her eyes moved back to Jones; this man she wasn't so sure of. There was something about him that put her on edge, a feeling she despised. She shook her head again.

"It's been a nice, quiet evening," she said calmly, holding Jones's steely gaze.

No one could say she couldn't hold her own. Ethel's eyes narrowed when Jones just smiled and Stan chuckled.

"What?" Fighting the urge to step back, Ethel forced herself to remain still when Jones stepped up to the desk.

"It's okay, Ethel," Jones said quietly, gently patting her folded hands resting on the counter. "I'm one of the good guys. You don't have anything to worry about." Ethel just snorted.

"Well, that's the biggest crock of shit I've ever heard!" she burst out laughing, surprising Jones.

And before Jones could react, she'd grasped his hands in hers, squeezing them.

"But thank you."

Pulling away, she took a step backward.

"Now, I've got work to do, so you boys need to let me get to it."

Jones's mouth nearly fell open. Was she dismissing them? Them? What the hell? Who did this woman think she was?

"Come on," Stan laughed, patting his friend on the shoulder. "We've just been sent to our rooms."

Pulling Jones away, Stan steered him toward the elevator. Still surprised by the woman's spunk, Jones allowed himself to be led away.

"At least we got dinner first," he mumbled as they disappeared into the elevator, Ethel's spunky laughter following them.

Tossing his key on the bureau, Stan made a beeline for his laptop, stopping only to turn on the coffeemaker. Flipping on the gas fireplace, he dropped into the overstuffed chair, propping his feet up on the matching ottoman. Balancing his computer on his lap, Stan leaned back, closing his eyes while he waited for it to power up, his thoughts churning again.

Sure, he'd recognized Stillman, but he hadn't put the pieces together yet as to why. Now he knew—he'd worked with the guy! Shit!

Of course, Stillman had been using another name back then, and Stan racked his brain trying to remember what he'd gone by. It'd been a good seven years before. In that time, Stan had met and come into contact with so many people—and had killed more than a few of them.

He'd nearly choked when Sarah told him the news while at the same time not totally surprised either. With the exception of Jones, Stan generally worked alone, but that didn't mean he didn't come into contact with others in the profession. He chuckled, remembering back when he'd first met Amy at the hotel she worked at. Her concern about others in his "profession" having been at her hotel had prompted him to assure her that it wasn't like they had conventions or anything.

But from time to time, they did cross paths—as they had when he'd met and rescued Amy from two of them. Of course, those guys were dead now. And from the looks of it, this was going to be another one of those times. And with the same result: Stillman was going to die. The question was how. And by whose hand? It seemed there was a line forming.

A click from the coffeemaker let Stan know it was ready, and sitting the laptop on the ottoman, he brewed himself a coffee, glancing at the clock as he did so. It wouldn't matter, decaf or regular; when he was ready to sleep, he would. No, the coffee wouldn't keep him up; the hectic thoughts going through his mind would do that just fine.

Sitting down with his coffee, Stan plugged a flash drive into the laptop, and making himself comfortable in front of the fire, he went through his heavily encrypted files until he found the one he was looking for. As he thought, it had been seven years ago. Going over notes that only he would understand, Stan quickly refreshed his memory of the job and then of the man. While Stan was a master of disguises, Stillman, it seemed, was not—choosing instead to alter his appearance by using different types of glasses and then dying his hair color, occasionally changing his hairstyle. But posing most often as a businessman, he didn't need to go to great lengths to alter his appearance. Rarely did anyone remember a boring businessman.

The job had been in Chicago; a major bank in the city was laundering money for a foreign country. The president of the bank, the bank manager, and two tellers—as well as the foreign minister of the country in question—had been implicated when the scheme began falling apart. Seemed the bank president's son and the foreign minister's son caused quite the scene at a pool hall in downtown Chicago. Drinking, bragging, and losing nearly every game of pool, they drew a bit more attention to themselves than either parent wanted. Both sons were well known for their expensive tastes in women, cars, and drugs. They frequently flashed money and, once, flashed themselves—which ultimately landed them in jail for a few hours for indecent exposure. As any concerned parent would do, they reprimanded the boys, threatening them with severe consequences if they didn't tone down their actions.

But as any spoiled rich kid seemed to do, both ignored the warnings. Continuing to frequent the pool hall, conveniently located in one of the more dangerous parts of the city, it wasn't until the foreign minister's son was "accidently" killed with a pool stick that the message became clear. Seemed the son had accused another player of cheating. The exchange became heated, then violent, ending with the son having a pool stick rammed up his ass. His death was slow and immensely painful.

In shock over his friend's death, the bank president's son fled the scene, only to crash his car a few blocks away when his brakes failed. Slamming into a condemned, empty building, the car exploded, killing the son instantly and obliterating any clues as to whether it was an accident or intentional.

Stillman, or Ralph Edwards, as he'd been known then, had planned each death carefully; but not having the skills to pull it off, he'd been forced to bring in a hired gun—or assassin, as the case may be. While it hadn't been the neatest work done by the man known only as Seth, the job was completed, and Seth was paid. The two men never met, all their dealings done through a third party.

An anonymous phone call to the FDIC and The Federal Banking Commission had the other major players in the scheme arrested by lunchtime the following day. Reading about it while on his flight to Ontario, Seth tucked the file containing Edwards's picture into his briefcase, snapping it closed, considering the job finished. He never thought he'd end up revisiting it years later.

Finishing his coffee, Stan contemplated his next move. It was clear that Stillman had no idea that Madison was surrounded by a team of highly skilled assassins. But it was also abundantly clear that Stillman had developed some new skills of his own—if the beating and killing of the truck driver in the alley was anything to go by. But a man consumed by rage was capable of doing anything. What had Madison done to warrant this man's anger? He hoped Sarah could dig up more answers. In the meantime, knowing who he was up against now, at least Stan had a better idea as to how to proceed. First thing—he needed to talk to Jones. If he'd worked with Stillman, it was a good bet that Jones knew of the man as well. Had they possibly worked together in the past too?

This six degrees of separation was getting a bit too close, Stan thought, snatching up his room key and leaving his room.

"You what?" Not believing her ears, Madison glared at Jeremy as he moved around the kitchen. Ever since Sarah's call, she'd known something was on his mind, but she'd never expected this!

"I arrested Frank Stillman, or Lester Harrington, as he was called back then. In Vancouver. When I was with the RCMPs."

Even he was having a hard time believing it. But Sarah's earlier intel had confirmed it. He knew the man. But worse yet, he'd just blurted out that he'd been with the RCMPs! Not the way he'd hoped Madison would find out. Crap!

RCMP? Madison nearly choked. Jeremy had been in law enforcement? A shiver danced down her spine, and she wondered why she wasn't running in the opposite direction. Because, she realized, she could trust him. She felt it in her bones; Jeremy was no threat to her. Also, she reminded herself, if there was any danger, Stan and Jones would never have let Jeremy get this close to her. If only they knew just how close the two were now! Had Jeremy ever planned on telling her about his past? She filed the question away, knowing they'd be talking more about that later. Oh, yeah, they'd be talking later!

But right now, she had to focus on Stillman.

"On what charges?" And why the fuck wasn't he still behind bars?

"Believe it or not, it was a bar fight."

"Oh."

"Yeah, oh. He beat the shit out of a guy using a pool stick of all things. The guy lived, but he was beat up really badly. When we were dragging Harrington—oh, I mean, Stillman—out of the bar, he kept yelling that the guy was lucky he hadn't rammed the stick up the guy's ass. And that he'd seen what that could do to a man." Jeremy paused with a shudder. "Christ, that's gotta be painful!"

Shaking her head, Madison couldn't stop the shudder that passed through her either. Despite having been in the business for as long as she had been, she still found certain methods repulsive. She wondered if she knew who'd done it. She thought she did. Ick.

"Stillman didn't even spend the night in jail before he was sprung," Jeremy continued, remembering how surprised they'd been at how fast the paperwork had gone through for the guy.

It became abundantly clear when the man was not only released quickly but was also whisked out of the country equally as fast that he either knew someone very important or he himself was very important. Jeremy had suspected the later. And now he knew he was right.

"What?" Madison asked, seeing Jeremy's frown.

"The whole thing was just bizarre. It didn't make sense. What businessman goes to a pool hall? And alone, so it wasn't like he was hanging out with the boys or anything. He didn't fit in; he wasn't a player. There was no reason for him to even be there."

"Were you first on the scene?"

"No, I was backup." He was always backup, brought in only as a last resort. "They must have thought they'd need me," he said quietly, still frowning.

Something was missing. What had made the other RCMPs think his specific skill set would be needed?

"When I got there, they had Stillman subdued. All I did was deliver him to the station and see that he was booked. The others stayed behind, questioning witnesses and taking care of the injured guy until the ambulance arrived."

"I don't know the arrest procedures in Canada. Nothing happened while you were taking him in?"

"No, the guy sat quietly in the car," Jeremy remembered. "He was polite and courteous, just a regular businessman."

"You keep referring to him as a businessman, why do you say that?"

"He was wearing a nice jacket, shirt, and tie with pressed pants. And he had an overcoat."

"Pressed pants? You remember pressed pants?" Seriously? That was impressive.

"How often do you see pressed pants? And at a pool hall? You remember things that stick out, that don't belong."

Madison nodded in understanding, impressed that Jeremy had picked up on something so mundane. She paused, her eyes widening briefly. Jeremy noticed things . . .

"You're a profiler," she blurted out before quickly apologizing. "I mean . . ."

With a small smile, Jeremy nodded, confirming her suspicions.

"Well, this all explains a few things," she continued, "like why you tossed me your gun so easily that first night."

Had he known that first night? At the time, he'd thought himself every kind of stupid, tossing Madison his gun when Mary had come stumbling out of the alley. Looking back, he realized that subconsciously, he must have known Madison could handle herself. Rarely had his instincts been wrong. Evidently, he hadn't lost the gift since leaving the RCMPs. He wasn't sure how he felt about that.

"Maybe," he admitted carefully, not ready to talk about that yet. That would definitely be a subject for later. "Anyway," he continued, steering the conversation back to Stillman, "I booked him, he was in a cell for a while, and suddenly, he was freed. Before you could blink an eye, he was gone. Beyond thinking the guy knew people in high places, we didn't dwell on it, there were other bad guys out there to catch." Jeremy paused. "And up until today, I hadn't given the guy another thought."

But now, the events of that night at the pool hall came back as clearly as if they'd happened yesterday.

"Christ, how did I not recognize him here?"

Because his focus was elsewhere. But just same, it rankled. He should have recognized the man. Or at least thought the guy looked familiar!

"I need to talk to Jones."

"Jesus, it seems like everyone's had contact with Stillman at one point or another," Madison said, frustration lacing her voice. "Everyone but me. So why am I the one he's after?"

Not totally sure himself, Jeremy did have a few thoughts on the subject, though. But he wanted to wait until they were all together again before he voiced his thoughts. Glancing at his watch, he realized that wouldn't be until tomorrow now. Okay, so he could sit on it for a night; it wasn't like Stillman was going anywhere anyway. Not this time.

"The pieces are coming together, we'll get this figured out," Jeremy said with confidence.

"I hope you're right," Madison said with a huff. "I need answers! I don't know if I can wait until morning!"

Understanding, Jeremy pulled Madison into his arms, smiling at her look of surprise.

"What are you doing?"

"Killing time," he whispered, his lips tracing her throat. "Might as well do something to keep ourselves occupied," he pulled back, his eyes warm and full of desire. "Was there something else you'd rather be doing?"

Cupping his face between her hands, Madison kissed him deeply, warmth flowing through her.

"I can't think of anything at the moment."

"Seems we've all come into contact with this asshole before," Jones said after listening to Stan. "I've dealt with him twice."

"You've met him?"

Jones's droll look answered Stan's question.

"Yeah, sorry, what was I thinking?"

"That's just it, you didn't think."

Not liking his hard response, Stan started to say something, but holding up his hand, Jones stopped him.

"None of us are thinking, and that's the problem. We've all gotta stop and take a step back. But most importantly, we've gotta figure out how he knows Madison and why he's after her. We," he waved his hand, "know him professionally. But Madison, she has no recollection of the guy, and if anyone's going to remember someone, it's going to be her. So we have to assume it's something personal."

Stan nodded; Jones's thinking was sound. As usual.

"It's too late to talk more tonight," he concluded. "We'll leave Madison alone tonight. It's not like Stillman's going anywhere, anyway."

"I'm sure she's racking her brain right now, trying to figure out a connection between her and Stillman," Jones said with confidence.

Madison was racking her brain all right; when had she ever felt this good? Never, she decided as she stretched, amazed she wasn't purring. Her eyes closed she reached out, running her fingers through Jeremy's thick hair as he kissed her stomach, his warm breath teasing and exciting her. One thing she knew—stress sex was phenomenal! She smiled before suddenly gasping, as Jeremy's tongue teased her belly button before he slowly began kissing his way down. His hand gently parting her legs, he let his tongue tease her into spreading her legs wider before kissing and sucking that warm and magical place he considered to be heaven. Wet and welcoming, his tongue dove into her as his hands cupped her bottom, lifting her and bringing her closer. Gripping the sheets, Madison screamed as his tongue darted in and out of her, arching her body up and into his welcoming mouth. Her toes began tingling, and she knew she was on the edge. His tongue dipped deeper, and with a flick, he had her screaming his name as he sent her over the edge. Gripping her bottom, he drank in her orgasm before slowing sliding away.

Gasping for breath, Madison was helpless to move as he blew softly on her sensitive skin, his warm breath replacing his hot mouth. Kissing the inside of her thigh, Jeremy slowly edged his way up her body, licking and kissing her salty skin until he was lying between her legs, his lips against her throat, tracing her racing pulse. Feeling his erection, Madison attempted to rise up, wanting him inside her, but her shaky legs had other ideas, and she was powerless to move. She giggled, before groaning in pleasure as his tongue darted in her ear the same time he plunged into her wetness. Of its own accord, her body rose up to meet his deep thrusts as she wrapped her arms around him, her mouth finding his in a hot, demanding kiss.

God, he couldn't get enough of her! Still deep inside her, Jeremy rolled them over, pulling her on top of him. Tucking her knees up, Madison found newfound energy; and before her arms gave out, she rose up above him, her breasts teasing his chest. His hands gripped her waist, gently controlling her movements, wanting to last as long as he could inside her. When she leaned ever so slowly forward, her breasts over his face, he knew he wasn't long for this world as his tongue darted out to tease her offered nipple. Wanting more, he suckled her breast, his hand moving to caress the one breast while he pleasured the other. She moaned, heat and moisture pooling around his hardness as another orgasm rolled through her. Tightening around him, she took him with her—her name a gasp as he flung his head back—and his body pushed up into hers.

The sound of their heavy breathing filled the dark room.

"Fuck," Madison sighed before starting to giggle.

Jeremy smiled in the darkness. Yeah, that pretty much covered it.

"Fuck!" She giggled again.

"You definitely have a way with words," Jeremy chuckled.

"Fuck."

And giving in to a fit of giggles, Madison draped an arm over Jeremy's chest as she curled up against him.

"Fuck. Wanna do it again?"

Laughing out loud, Jeremy wrapped his arm around her, holding her tightly against him. If only he could! He kissed the top of her head.

"Give me a minute."

CHAPTER 22

POURING HIMSELF A large coffee, Jeremy stared out the kitchen window, his eyes skimming the tree line running along his back-yard. The snow was still falling, but it was definitely lightening up. Finally. Enjoying his coffee, a big smile split his face as he watched two elk emerge from the woods. The animals beginning to move around again was a sure sign that the snow was tapering off at least. Beyond the tree line, deeper into the forest, Jeremy knew there to be a clearing where a small herd tended to bed down during the heaviest part of the winter. He'd come across the clearing a few winters back while out snowshoeing with his brothers, never forgetting the feeling of awe he'd experienced as he gazed at the magnificent animals while they rested.

Seemingly not threatened by his presence, two females still kept a watchful eye on him while the others ignored him completely. His rifle slung over his shoulder, Jeremy wasn't hunting, carrying the firearm for protection only. He knew he'd never know for sure, but just the same, Jeremy let himself believe that the elk had sensed that he wasn't a threat to them. Sharing that open space with such beautiful and amazing animals, Jeremy had felt a calm settle over him that he'd never experienced before. It was a feeling he'd only ever experience again when he was in the presence of the elk herd.

Jeremy sipped his coffee, welcoming the familiar feeling as it washed over him. Watching the females skirt along the tree line, never quite venturing out into the open space, he didn't have to wait long before their heads rose suddenly, turning back toward the trees. Waiting for it, Jeremy wasn't disappointed. The bull elk was bugling, announcing his presence, and perhaps calling for the females to return to the safety of the woods and the herd. Hoping the male would show himself, Jeremy released the breath he hadn't realized he'd been holding when the females turned, swiftly trotting back into the woods. It wasn't to be this time. Too bad, he'd been hoping to catch sight of the male, hoping it was the same one he'd seen last winter with a herd of females.

While the males and females tended to split up during the winter, occasionally, a male was sighted with the females. This particular male stood out due to one side of his antlers not having fully grown out. At first Jeremy had thought them to be broken, but a closer look with the help of a high-powered telephoto lens had shown it wasn't broken but a birth defect. Yet the male had still managed to find himself a small herd; Jeremy never questioned why he found that reassuring.

Bull elk shed their antlers in March, and while on a hiking trip later that month, again with his brothers, Jeremy had come across the stunted antlers. Photographing them, he'd left them where he'd found them, not sure why but knowing he should. And he wondered, had the bull shed the defect, or would his new antlers be the same? Jeremy still didn't know the answer.

Finishing his coffee, Jeremy finally turned away from the window, knowing he'd seen the last of the elk for that day. He smiled to himself. He hadn't realized just how much he'd needed this time of peace and quiet. Watching the elk, he'd been able to forget for a moment that someone out there was trying to kill the woman who was currently sleeping in his bed, warm and naked under the heavy covers. A woman who unknowingly was stealing her way into his heart.

Jeremy smiled a wolfish grin. God, wouldn't that just piss her off! Knowing that no matter how tough she was, she still was a woman—warm, beautiful, and independent as hell. Talk about a turn-on! And he was falling fast for her. Okay, he admitted, he'd already fallen for her. Had it been the night he'd met her at the restaurant? No, he'd liked her then, but he hadn't felt anything other than basic curiosity. No, he admitted ruefully, it was when they'd found Mary in the alley that he'd begun falling for her. When had he ever met a woman as strong as he was? Stronger even. He couldn't remember.

Of course, if one was going to be an assassin, it was probably a prerequisite that you be strong and independent. Did one fill out an application for such a job? Jeremy chuckled, imagining a line at the unemployment office.

Fill out an employment application, being sure to list previous employment and experience. And can we contact your previous employers? Probably not. Does plausible deniability mean anything to you?

And do you have references? None that are alive, does that count? Jeremy laughed out loud now.

Yeah, he could pick 'em, all right.

The sound of a truck pulling into his driveway had Jeremy turning. Heading toward the door, he met Stan and Jones as they came up the front steps. Opening the door for them, the men greeted him with a grunt as they shook off the snow, peeling off their coats, hats, and boots. Then following Jeremy back into the kitchen, they made a beeline for the coffeemaker. Leaning against the counter, Jeremy watched the men pad around the kitchen in their heavy wool socks, and he laughed. Here were Madison's references, such as they were.

"What are you laughing at?" Jones nearly chugged down his coffee.

"You think our socks are funny?" Stan grunted, ignoring Jones.

He was used to how his friend drank his coffee. He didn't understand it, but he was used to it. Looking at his stocking feet then at Jeremy, then back to his socks, where he wiggled his toes, Jones chuckled.

"Shut up, at least they match."

Standing there in his slippers, Jeremy remained silent for a moment. Then unable to contain himself, he burst out laughing. He was in the company of two very powerful and dangerous men . . . wearing wool socks and standing in his kitchen drinking coffee.

Ironic didn't begin to cover it, and Jeremy laughed harder. Glancing at his own thick socks, Stan tossed Jones an amused glance before he too began to laugh, the sound rumbling up from his chest. Joining in, Jones continued wiggling his socks, making the men laugh harder. Weren't they just the toughest bunch of guys in the neighborhood! And their laughter rang out even louder.

"What the hell's going on here?"

Standing in the doorway wrapped in Jeremy's flannel bathrobe, Madison stared at the men. She didn't attempt to hide the surprise on her face.

"Who are you guys, and what have you done with my friends?"

Waking up slowly, Madison stretched, reaching for Jeremy. Her eyes opened slowly, and she found herself alone in the big bed. Disappointment shot through her before the realization of having the bed to herself hit her. The *entire big* bed. A smile curved her lips as she snuggled back down under the blankets. Jeremy's loss if he wanted to leave her alone in the great, big bed, all by herself. Despite being naked, her body warmed at the thought of Jeremy. She drifted back to sleep, the smile still on her face.

The sound of male laughter prodded her awake. What the hell? Rolling over, she stared at the ceiling, blinking as she got her bearings. The laughter continued, urging her up and out of bed. Snatching Jeremy's flannel robe from the closet, she wrapped herself in it, smiling as it swallowed her up. Pulling on a pair of flannel socks, she padded silently down the stairs, turning toward the kitchen and the sound of laughter.

Leaning against the doorway, Madison watched in wonder as the three men just stood there laughing. At what she had no idea. But she realized that this was probably the most "normal" moment she'd ever witnessed with Stan and Jones. *Normal* wasn't a part of her life, and she was thankful she could still recognize it for what it was. A smile split her face as she stepped into the kitchen, wondering out loud who these people were and what had happened to her friends?

Three sets of eyes turned, following her as she strolled into the kitchen, pushing them out of the way as she snatched a mug for her coffee. Still chuckling, the men moved aside for her.

"Don't let this go to your heads," Madison began quietly as she made her coffee, careful not to look at any of them, "but hearing you laugh was a nice way to start the day."

Silence filled the room, and glancing at each man, it was Madison's turn to laugh. The look of embarrassment on their faces was priceless!

Yeah, such big, brave men, she thought, taking a welcoming sip of her coffee.

Don't worry," she said over her mug, "your secret's safe with me." The coffee tasted heavenly! "No one would ever believe me anyway."

"Amy would," Stan chuckled again, thinking how his wife would have enjoyed this moment.

Madison nodded; he was right. Her eyes moved to Jones. Was there anyone who'd believe this man of mystery had a sense of humor? She hoped so, although she didn't know for sure. Her eyes drifted to Jeremy. Now, this man was truly lucky. He had a big family, and there was no doubt that they knew he had a sense of humor. She'd witnessed it herself. Sipping her coffee, content in the moment, she wiggled her toes in the big woolen socks. And wondered why all three men started laughing again. What was so funny?

Finishing her coffee, Madison put her mug in the sink. And turning to kiss Jeremy sweetly on the cheek, she announced she was going to take a shower. Waltzing out of the room, knowing three sets of eyes were on her, for three different reasons, she struggled not to laugh.

Putting his own mug in the sink, Jeremy turned to find Jones and Stan glaring at him.

"What?" Forcing himself to quiet his thoughts, he kept his expression innocent.

"Something you want to tell us?" Stan said quietly.

"Nope," and pushing past the two men, Jeremy followed Madison upstairs.

"When this is over, we're going to have to talk to Madison," Stan said, watching Jeremy disappear up the stairs.

"Maybe."

Putting his own mug in the sink, marveling at the feeling of doing something so "mundane," Jones turned his thoughts back to the job at hand.

"Right now we've got more important things to worry about."

"Agreed," Stan said as they wandered into the living room.

Pulling out his cell phone and dropping on to the couch, he pressed a button, waiting as the call was connected. Leaning against the wall, Jones only needed to turn his head to have a clear view of the front yard and driveway. The benefit of the snow—no one would be able to approach the house without leaving tracks. No, any approach would be from the front. Because Jones knew firsthand, Stillman hated the snow.

Time to get back to work.

Reconvening a short time later, Jones and Stan endeavored to ignore Madison's still-wet hair and her glowing skin, along with the knowledge that she'd spent the night in Jeremy's bed. For Christ's sake, she was over twenty-one! The thought still didn't make it any easier for the two men who considered Madison family.

"Stillman hasn't left his room," Stan announced, quickly bringing them up to speed. "Ethel's been at the front desk all morning, and the cameras on the emergency exits haven't shown anyone leaving the building."

"He could manipulate those cameras," Madison said, pushing away the awkward feeling she was experiencing. Stan and Jones had never seen her with a man before and she knew they were trying not to be over-protective of her. Madison struggled not to smile at the sentimental thought. "Something like that isn't going to stop him."

"How do you know?" Jeremy asked.

"Because it wouldn't stop me," Madison answered bluntly.

"Of course. Sorry." He needed to remember the type of people he was dealing with here! "So what's today's plan?" he asked, glancing at Stan and Jones.

When the men remained silent, Jeremy turned back to Madison.

"Do you have a plan?"

Shaking her head, Madison remained silent.

"Are you not telling me because of who I am or because you really don't have a plan?"

Jeremy hoped it was because of who he was. God, he hoped it was because of that!

"Who you are is a benefit, not a detriment," Stan said firmly, pulling Jeremy's attention back to him. "We need all the information we can get, and we need to use any resources available to us." The others nodded. "You're more useful than you give yourself credit for, Jeremy."

Not wanting to question why, Jeremy was relieved to hear that.

"How's it feel to be on the 'bad guys' team?" Stan asked before quickly adding, "Although I guess it's not really the first time."

"Oh?" Madison turned on Jeremy before he could process Stan's remark. "Something you want to share?" While not accusing him, her tone had turned hard, her eyes questioning.

"While indirectly, Jeremy and I have worked together before. You knew that," Jones said quietly.

Madison blinked. Of course! How could she have forgotten her surprise at finding out that the two men knew each other! And reminded herself, yet again, that she needed to get her shit together! Too many small details were slipping through the cracks!

Jeremy just nodded, remembering those cases. And the first time he'd actually met Jones face-to-face. And he smiled, also remembering the worst hangover he'd ever had that next day. Jeremy's only consolation—he knew Jones wasn't feeling that good either. He chuckled at the memory. Jones chuckled too, also remembering that night and the next morning. His respect for Jeremy had risen that night; the man could definitely hold his own at the bar!

Already aware of Jeremy's talents in the field, over more boiler makers than Jones cared to remember, the two men went on to form a bond built on respect, trust, and distance. And up until now, they hadn't seen each other since. While Jones rarely believed in it, he knew with the utmost certainty that their meeting again now—after all this time—really was purely by coincidence. And one Jones was thankful for. Besides Jeremy's specific skill set, he was equally well known and well liked throughout town—a huge benefit to them. Being associated with Jeremy allowed them to move about freely in town without raising any unnecessary suspicions.

Determined to get back on her game, Madison took a deep breath, focusing.

"Okay, so it seems you're all connected, one way or another," Madison needlessly pointed out.

Everyone nodded.

"For good or bad," she added, referring to their connections to Stillman. "You guys dealt with Stillman on business, but I haven't. At least not that I can remember. So what's my connection, and why is he after me?"

It was the same question they'd been asking themselves over and over, and still no one had a reasonable explanation. That was going to have to change and soon. Madison needed information; she needed to form a new plan. Doing nothing went against everything she was! Feeling helpless was the worst, and determined not to feel that way, she knew she needed to act! She couldn't wait for intel from Sarah. She couldn't wait for someone else in the town to be killed. It was time to go on the offensive. No more hiding.

"He needs to see me out and about," she announced.

And she wasn't surprised when Jeremy immediately objected.

"What if he takes a shot at you in public?"

All eyes turned to Jeremy.

"Clearly, the man isn't thinking straight, killing the guy in the alley is proof of that. The only thing we know for sure is that this is somehow personal to him. You being out in public is likely to set off his rage even more. He knows you're not afraid of him—hell, he probably knows that you could kill him yourself. And that makes him even crazier, more dangerous. He's going to do something stupid, and that's when you'll get him. But at the same time, whatever he does could hurt innocent people." Jeremy paused, his gaze going around the room. "I can't let that happen."

Silence filled the room. Jeremy was right. Enough innocent people had been hurt; they couldn't let that happen again.

"What do you propose?" Jones asked, breaking the silence.

"That we have housekeeping check their room first. Find out if they really are in there. If not, then we'll know. Unless there's a "Do Not Disturb" sign on their door, housekeeping has every reason to knock and/or enter."

"And if a sign is on the door?" Stan asked.

Jeremy smiled. "Haven't you ever heard of a lovely little thing called a fire alarm?"

"They're in the room," the housekeeper reported to Ethel. "I knocked, and Mrs. Stillman let me into the room. Mr. Stillman was sitting at the desk working. He never even looked up. I took out the trash, made the bed, you know, the usual things."

Ethel nodded, satisfied the housekeeper had done her job thoroughly.

"Did Mrs. Stillman speak to you? Did she make eye contact with you?" Ethel asked, trying not to sound like she was interrogating the girl.

The housekeeper shook her head. "She sat in a chair by the fire and flipped through a magazine." The housekeeper paused.

Ethel immediately picked up on it.

"What?" she demanded, before asking again in a softer voice. "What is it?"

"Just that they never spoke to each other the entire time I was in there. Not once. They barely even acknowledged one another, in fact. I thought that rather odd."

Ethel nodded; she would have thought the same. There was a companionable silence, and then there was downright ignoring each other. This sounded very much like the later. And that alone was something important.

Gossip, for good or bad, was a mainstay of housekeeping, and the girls swapped stories about their guests on a daily basis. And given that these guests had been stranded here now for a few days, there were plenty of stories to swap. Cleaning the same rooms daily, it didn't take the girls long to pick up on the guests likes and dislikes— which ladies wanted extra towels and which men couldn't seem to hit the toilet, no matter the distance. Laughter could often be heard over the sounds of the washers and dryers running when the girls started comparing and telling stories.

But not all stories were humorous. The story about the Stillmans being one. Having knocked on their door earlier that morning, clearly announcing herself, the housekeeper was just beginning to let herself in when she was told to "get the hell out of here!"

Stepping back quickly, pulling the door closed, the frightened housekeeper dashed downstairs in search of Ethel. A five-year veteran in the housekeeping department, the housekeeper had dealt with every kind of guest out there. Or so she'd thought. The evil and menace that she'd heard in Mr. Stillman's voice when he yelled at her had shaken her to the core. Now she was afraid to return to their room.

Not about to let her girls be intimidated or frightened, Ethel immediately called the room, ready to tell Mr. Stillman just what she thought of his actions when Mrs. Stillman had answered quietly. Clamping down on her temper, Ethel politely asked if everything was all right and would they be requiring any housekeeping services that day.

Glaring at Frank while she kept the receiver tight to her ear, Ellen quickly and quietly apologized to Ethel for "her husband's" rude outburst. And that yes, everything was fine, and yes, she would like the room serviced. Hanging up moments later, Ellen turned to Frank.

"The housekeeper is coming back, you need to straighten out!"

Glaring at her, Frank wisely kept quiet. He'd realized his error as soon as the housekeeper had backed out of the room earlier. He really needed to get his temper under control! Remaining silent, he nodded, turning back to his paperwork spread out on the desk.

When the housekeeper returned moments later, announcing herself as she knocked, Ellen quickly let her into the room with an apologetic smile. Then going back to her chair by the fire, Ellen proceeded to ignore the housekeeper as she performed her duties, not even bothering to look up when the housekeeper quietly wished them a good day before leaving the room. Closing the door quietly behind her, the housekeeper all but dashed back to the front desk, relieved to be out of the room.

Returning to the Inn, Jones stopped at the front desk to "chat" with Ethel while Stan went directly up to his room. Not questioning why she did it, Ethel quickly told Jones about the housekeeper's experience with the Stillmans'.

So the Stillmans not only ignored the housekeeper, but they were ignoring each other. Intrigued by that information, Jones thanked Ethel and, with a smile, took his coffee and headed to his own room. Knocking lightly on Stan's door as he passed by, he didn't have long to wait until Stan joined him. Going over what Ethel had told him, both men agreed: they needed to get Ellen alone. Preferably away from the Inn.

"Maybe not," Jones said, pondering a thought. "If we can get her into another room without being seen, that might be enough."

"How do you figure that?"

Gazing out the window at the gently falling snow, Stan briefly wondered if the snow would ever really totally stop.

"Whose room would she go to?" Jones stared at him. "Not mine!"

The idea of having another woman in his room who wasn't his wife and/or someone old enough to be his mother bothered Stan, and he nearly laughed. It wasn't long ago when the opposite would have been the case. Any woman, anytime. But that had all changed when he'd met Amy. Who knew?

Jones just laughed at Stan's outburst. Need Stan to kill someone? Absolutely. No question. But have a woman come to his room, and the guy choked! What the hell was happening to the man who had been known to have ice water running through his veins?

"Nothing!" Stan quickly assured him.

He still had what it took to take a life. No question. No problem. But he admitted, on the subject of women, things had definitely changed. And he was good with that. Fuck anyone who thought differently. Jones nodded, not needing the reassurance but glad to have it. He'd said it before—they were all human. Things changed. He and

Stan had been working together for a long time, longer than most in their business—especially given that the life expectancy wasn't that great in their profession. The idea of breaking in a new partner wasn't terribly appealing.

"You're stuck me with me, man. Get used to it."

Jones smiled, happy to do so.

CHAPTER 23

"I'M GOING OUT," Ellen announced, smirking at the blank stare from Frank.

"What?"

"I said I'm going out. I'm tired of being cooped up in this room, I'm going out."

Careful not to say much more, Ellen pulled on her coat.

"I don't think that's a good idea," Frank said, rising from his chair, glancing out the window.

"I don't honestly care what you think."

Frank turned and glared at her.

"You haven't done anything but rant and rave all morning. You scared the poor housekeeper to death, you fool! For someone who's supposed to blend in, you're doing a bang-up job of doing just the opposite!"

Resisting the urge to poke him in the chest with her finger, Ellen pulled on her gloves instead.

"If you don't come up with a plan soon, I will."

And turning, she left the room, the door closing with a quiet *click* behind her.

Standing in the middle of the room, Frank swallowed his angry reply. Clenching his fists, he turned back to the window. Anger flowed through him as he admitted that Ellen was right. Damn it, he had to find a way to control his temper! He needed to focus and concentrate on his target! But instead, his anger kept getting in the way, not letting him think rationally. He needed to fix that problem. He needed to kill Madison.

While Madison was walking around freely, he was forced to watch his every step, staying in his room as much as possible now. He paused. But she wasn't walking around. He hadn't seen her in over a day. Not in the restaurant, not in the Inn. Where was she? He stepped closer to the window, wondering if he could see Ellen as she left the Inn. But his view was obstructed by the roof jutting out over the entrance of the Inn. Turning back, he dropped into his chair in front of the fire. Staring into the flames, he let his mind wander. A deadly calm rolled through him as he imagined Madison's dead body lying in the snowbank.

Stepping out of the elevator and into the quiet lobby, Ellen glanced both ways before turning toward the living room. Finding it empty, she turned around, gasping in surprise when she came up against a hard body. Putting a finger over his lips, motioning her to remain silent, he took her arm gently, steering her into the stairwell and up the stairs. Good God, she hoped he wasn't going to make her walk up four flights of stairs! Glancing back at him, she was relieved when he shook his head.

Stopping on the second floor, he checked the hallway, relieved to find it empty. Pulling Ellen behind him, he stopped at the first door, all but pushing her into the empty room. Pausing long enough to hang the "Do Not Disturb" sign on the door before closing it, he turned back to face her. She didn't appear to be frightened or angry. But he knew her well enough to know that looks could be deceiving.

"This had better be good," Ellen said bluntly, unbuttoning her coat but not removing it.

She glanced around the room, not terribly surprised at not seeing any luggage, or anything that hinted he was staying in this particular room. Turning back to him, her gaze was more curious than anything. He didn't frighten her, not in the least, and she stared boldly at the tall man. Funny, she didn't remember his hair being so blond. And he hadn't had a beard the last time she saw him.

But his eyes were still the same, and she had to force herself not to look away. Black as ink, she knew she'd never forget those dark, deadly eyes—eyes that she'd stared deeply into moments before she'd found herself twisted around, with a knife to her throat. Thinking she was on death's door, she knew she'd go to her grave remembering those eyes.

Ellen's eyes traveled downward, immediately noticing that his hands were stuffed into the pockets of his heavy coat. Did he still have that knife? A shiver of anticipation raced through her as she took a deep breath. If he'd wanted her dead, she'd be dead already. He wasn't picky about where he killed. Her eyes moved slowly back to his.

Remaining silent, he pulled a cell phone from his pocket, watching Ellen visibly relax when she saw it. He knew she was expecting the knife. He wished he'd brought it with him. But this job required another type of weapon. And it was a weapon he was prepared to use. Pressing a button, he held the phone to his ear before passing it to Ellen. Her eyes still holding his, she took the phone, cringing when she heard a voice she'd hoped never to hear again. Her eyes dropped as she listened to the raspy voice telling her what she needed to do—when, where, and how. And did she have a problem with that?

"No," Ellen mumbled before repeating it more clearly. Then, taking a deep breath, Ellen straightened. "I expect my usual payment plus expenses for this," she added boldly.

She might be at their beck and call, but that didn't mean she did it for free. Her terms accepted, Ellen asked the necessary questions; and being told how she'd receive the rest of the information needed for the job, Ellen ended the call.

"Looks like we're working together again," she said with a smirk as she returned the phone to him.

He nodded. His finger tugging at his turtleneck, he glared at her. Catching sight of the white patch covering where his Adam's apple would be, she shrugged her shoulders.

"I can't promise, but I'll try not to hurt you this time."

His eyes rolling told her he didn't believe her. Well, that was fine with her; she wasn't so sure she believed herself either. Their eyes met and held. She knew what to expect and wouldn't be caught by surprise again. If he got in her way, she'd do more than remove his Adam's apple this time. She'd kill him.

Not if he killed her first. And not for the first time did he wonder again why he hadn't when he'd had the chance. He tugged on his turtleneck. One thing was for damn sure—payback was going to be a bitch.

Pocketing the phone, he nodded toward the door. Catching his meaning, Ellen buttoned her coat, and as he had earlier, she glanced both ways to be sure the hallway was clear before darting into the hallway and then into the stairwell. Once in the softly lit stairwell, she paused to collect herself before continuing down the stairs. Glancing once behind her, she wasn't surprised to find herself alone. Her silent friend was gone, his work, for the moment, finished. Releasing the breath she hadn't realized she'd been holding, Ellen pushed the door open and entered the lobby, tossing a small smile at Ethel before exiting the Inn. Standing at the top of the steps, she took a deep breath, the cold air stinging her lungs and making her eyes water.

Shoving her gloved hands deeply into her pockets and ducking her head, she stepped into the lightly falling snow. Her thoughts churning, she strolled aimlessly down the snow-covered street, keeping tightly to the side to avoid being hit by passing trucks as they moved slowly past her. Behind her dark sunglasses, her eyes were hard as she replayed the phone call in her mind. Seemed she wasn't the only one who wanted Frank Stillman dead. She wondered what he'd think if he knew that the cat had just become the mouse.

"Nice job!" Madison said with a smile.

"Thank you," Sarah said, leaning back in her chair, fighting to reach for a cigarette.

It was one thing to smoke while talking to Madison on the phone, but she couldn't do it when they were using Skype. While Sarah guessed that Madison knew she was smoking again, she didn't need to hear about it. They had more important matters to deal with than her smoking.

"Ellen didn't sound too surprised when I gave her the instructions."

"She wasn't," Madison said. "Stan said the relief going around in her mind was coming off of her in waves, it was all he could to stay quiet."

"I'm still impressed with his quick-change act," Sarah admitted.

Her brother was a master of disguises, but rarely did he have to change them on a moment's notice.

"I'm glad you enjoyed the show," Stan said, coming out of the bathroom with a towel wrapped around his waist, another in his hand as he toweled off his wet hair.

"For God's sake, put something on!" Both women yelled, covering their eyes.

Laughing, Stan grabbed some clothes before disappearing back into the bathroom. Chuckling from his chair in the corner, Jones steered the conversation back to the business at hand.

"When was the last time you'd talked to Ellen?" he asked Sarah.

"Three years, I think," Sarah replied from the comfort of her couch in her apartment in Germany. "She did a few jobs for me. She always got results, but I didn't like her methods, so we parted company.

After that, she literally became a gun for hire; nothing was off-limits to her."

Jones and Madison nodded in understanding. When it came to taking on jobs, Sarah was very specific about what she would take on and what she wouldn't. She might kill people for a living, but she still had her standards. It was one of the reasons she and her people were so highly sought out.

"She and . . ." Sarah stumbled, ". . . *Stan* had a rough run in while in Italy. It was separate contracts, but the targets were business partners, so the two of them were forced to work together. While we know Stan prefers to work alone, Ellen didn't care whom she worked for or with, but that didn't mean she was going to play nice. After the targets were taken out, she turned on Stan. To make a long, nasty story short, she ended up stabbing him in the throat before he stopped her."

Sarah paused, remembering in horror the blood pouring from her brother's throat, amazed he'd still be able to hold a knife to Ellen's bared throat.

"Why he didn't kill her when he had the chance, I'll never know."

Unconsciously rubbing her own throat, Madison listened in amazement to yet another story involving the twins. While Madison knew them well, she was frequently reminded that she did not know everything. She wasn't sure she wanted to know either.

"Ellen got away, thinking she'd left . . ." she paused again, ". . . *Stan* severely maimed, if not dead. I tracked her down, and after a . . ." Sarah's eyes danced away from the screen before coming back, dark and hard, "we'll say, a lengthy and painful discussion, we parted company. For good, I thought."

"Until she turned up here," Madison said, her respect for Sarah and her own specific set of skills having just gone up yet another notch.

Sarah nodded.

"Did you know she was working with Stillman?"

Sarah shook her head.

"I kept tabs on her. I didn't want her turning up on any of our jobs. But about a month ago, she dropped off the grid. I was in the process of trying to find out if maybe she'd been killed or something when I realized she was there." Anger laced her next words. "Knowing she was working with Stillman, indirectly or not, shit, I almost flew there just to kill her myself!"

"Well, it appears she's with him as part of his cover, she doesn't seem to be actively involved," Jones interjected. "I think if she was actually helping him, things would be different."

No one needed him to clarify that statement. The number of people *not* dead was all the clarification they needed.

"How'd you know she'd listen to you when you gave her the instructions about Stillman?" Madison asked.

"We didn't," Stan answered, coming out of the bathroom.

His dark hair slicked back, he hadn't finished his transformation back to his current identity, and he pulled a flannel shirt from the closet.

"It was a chance we had to take."

"She didn't seem surprised to see you alive," Madison said, watching Stan go about getting himself back into character.

She'd always admired how fast he could change personalities and disguises; it was one thing she'd never totally mastered. Other than changing hairstyles and colors, she wasn't able to do much more in the area of disguises. Another reason Sarah moved her around to vastly different places. Less chance she'd be recognized.

"She wasn't," Jones said as Stan disappeared back into the bathroom. "They ran into each other last year in Zurich. At a dinner party, of all places."

Madison nearly laughed at that one. She knew how much Stan hated such events. They all did. Spending any lengthy periods of time in public places always made them a bit antsy.

Standing in the bathroom, staring blankly in the mirror, Stan remembered back to that night in Zurich. It was the first time in his life he'd felt true fear.

It'd been months since he and Amy had had any quality time to spend together, and he wanted to treat her to something special. Contacting her father, he made arrangements for a small family reunion in Zurich. Hoping to surprise Amy, he wasn't surprised when he'd arrived home to find her packed and ready to go.

"Seriously, you didn't think I'd find out?" she'd asked innocently.

"Clearly, I was mistaken," he'd laughed, knowing Amy had, no doubt, found out from Sarah.

The two had become closer than sisters and brought a new meaning to "partners in crime." It was all he could do to bring her a surprise bouquet of flowers without Sarah telling her first.

But he'd still managed to pull off part of the surprise. Amy hadn't expected to see her father. Oh, and the five-star hotel he'd booked for them, that had been a nice surprise too. Catching the green-eyed envy look from the desk clerk, Amy wondered if the desk clerk recognized her husband. Assuring her later that he'd never stayed in this particular hotel before, Amy still wasn't convinced.

"You forget what I do for a living," Amy reminded him later as they dressed for dinner. "Working in the hotel business as long as I have, you remember people."

"No," he'd replied with a smile, framing her face gently in his hands as he dropped a quick kiss on her inviting lips. "You remember people."

And deepening the kiss, he chased away her doubts.

Meeting them in the lobby, her father had apologized, telling them that their dinner plans had unfortunately changed. He'd found out last minute that he had to make an appearance at a dinner party for a visiting dignitary. Only because he was able to secure them all an invite had he agreed to go.

Knowing her husband wasn't fond of such events, Amy had told her father that they'd pass on the dinner and meet up with him later. Expecting that, Amy had been surprised when her father had produced a list of guests who'd be attending. Handing it to her husband, he assured them both that he'd gone over the entire list; everyone was cleared.

"Well, husband," Amy smiled, "it's up to you."

While he hadn't recognized any names on the list, that didn't mean there weren't any threats. But knowing Amy's father wouldn't intentionally put his daughter in harm's way . . . again, anyway, he agreed to go. Only later would he regret that decision.

Discretion being the name of the game in her father's world, the other reason he agreed to attend was because the dinner party would be held in a lush apartment in the midst of the busy city. The visiting dignitary had specifically requested Amy's father attend and, in doing so, knew it could not be in a public restaurant.

Scoping out the building before entering, her father and husband only entered when they'd thoroughly checked the location of every emergency exit. Neither man took anything for granted. In their world, one could never take enough precautions. Secure in their knowledge of the building, the three of them went through the discrete yet thorough security at the door.

He spotted Ellen immediately. Secure in the knowledge that she'd never recognize him, he idly wrapped a protective arm around Amy. Glancing up, Amy was startled to see the anger in his eyes, and following his gaze, she saw the handsome woman standing a few feet away. Her arm looped through that of a man dressed in a tuxedo, her smile didn't reach her eyes as she gazed up at her companion as he talked with another couple. He was all but ignoring her while she appeared to be enjoying herself. It only took a moment for Amy to realize that the woman's jaw was locked tight. Her husband, on the other hand, had instantly recognized that look.

Shit, he thought angrily, *she's here on a fucking job!*

Searching for Amy's father, he spotted him by the bar, and nearly dragging Amy behind him, he made his way through the crowd.

"We have to leave," he whispered into his father-in-law's ear.

Not questioning his son-in-law, he put down his untouched drink and, turning to their host, made quick apologies, sighting an emergency at work. Not waiting for a reply, the three of them made their way toward the door. They hadn't gotten far when a scream split the air and the room fell silent.

Whirling around, pushing Amy behind him, he found himself a few feet away from Ellen. His eyes narrowed as he spotted the shiny gun in her hand. Pointed at the head of the man she'd been smiling at moments before, her icy eyes raced around the room, widening briefly when she spotted the man staring blatantly at her.

Brave son of a bitch. Stupid, but brave, she thought angrily, deciding to shoot him afterward, just because she could.

Pulling the now-cowering and whimpering man backward, she moved steadily toward the exit. Taking her eyes off the crowd for a moment, she wove her way through a group of people crouched down in fear between her and the exit.

That was all the time he needed.

Screaming in pain, Ellen let go of her target, staring in shock at the knife protruding from her right arm, just above her elbow. She could feel her fingers weakening, and she struggled not to lose her grip on the gun. She gasped in shock, instantly recognizing the knife, remembering the feel of it against her throat. How could that be? Her eyes flew frantically around the room before coming to land on the last man she ever thought she'd see again—alive, anyway. How had she not recognized him moments before when their eyes had met? Because she hadn't been looking for him! Damn! Her eyes dropped to his throat, searching for a bandage. His turtleneck covered his Adam's apple, but she was sure it was him!

Her hand was going numb, and before her fingers became paralyzed, she struggled to raise the gun, aiming it directly at him. Pushing the people on both sides of him to the floor, he dove on top of Amy, covering her body with his as two bullets sped past them, embedding themselves in the wall behind them.

Jumping up, he raced toward Ellen as she turned on her target. At point-blank range, she shot him cleanly between the eyes before lunging through the exit, dropping the gun as she fled. Knowing she had precious seconds before she'd be caught, she paused and, taking a deep breath, pulled the knife from her arm. Blood spurted out as she clamped her hand over the injury, the knife forgotten as it clattered to the floor. Pulling the lightweight shawl from her shoulders, she attempted to staunch the bleeding as she glanced around the darkened room. Pulling her scattered thoughts together, she raced across the room, remembering her exit strategy. Within seconds, she was gone.

Slowly pushing open the door, he moved cautiously into the room, already knowing Ellen was gone. Spotting his knife, he quickly grabbed it, rubbing the blood off on the leg of his pants before sliding it back into its hiding place. Glancing around the room, he guessed the direction that she had disappeared in, but he didn't follow her. This wasn't his job. He was an innocent bystander this time. And now was not the time to get involved. He didn't care why she'd killed the guy; it wasn't his business to care. She was doing a job. But one thing was for certain: she knew he was still alive. And that they'd meet again.

The room was a cluster of confusion when he finally made his way back to Amy's side. Running his hands over her face and body, reassuring himself again that she was okay, he finally took a breath of relief. Never had he been afraid before, but when the bullets were flying past Amy, he knew true fear for the very first time. Grabbing her hand, he pulled her toward the door. They needed to get out of there; he couldn't risk being questioned. Catching her father's eye, Amy tugged on his sleeve, pulling her husband toward another entrance. A hand on his arm stopped them, and turning, they came face-to-face with a military policeman. Shit! Knowing he couldn't get away without causing further trouble, he forced himself to relax and, wrapping his arm around Amy, waited for the questions. A hand on the officer's arm stopped him as his superior whispered something into the officer's ear. Turning back to the couple, the officer quickly told them they were free to go. Before he'd even finished the sentence, the two of them were out the door.

CHAPTER 24

"SERIOUSLY? THE WOMAN posing as Stillman's wife is working with us now?"

Not bothering to hide his shock, Jeremy stared at Madison. She just nodded, knowing the whole thing sounded insane. She felt the same way and said as much.

"You trust her?"

Madison shook her head.

"I don't, no. Not in the least." Madison's gaze swept the room. "None of us trust her. But we can count on her to do the job. There's money involved, and she gets her revenge—oh, yeah, she'll do it."

Her words did nothing to reassure him, but he remained silent.

Tired from plowing snow and worrying about Madison, Jeremy had been headed to the hotel when his mother had called him. Making a detour, he pulled into the parking lot of the restaurant. He hadn't even shut off the engine when one of the waiters ran out with a large box. Recognizing the restaurant's logo on the takeout box, Jeremy opened the passenger side door, grabbing the box as the waiter slid it onto the front seat. Before Jeremy could speak, the waiter gave him a smart wave before dashing back into the restaurant. What the . . . ? His phone buzzed, and pulling it from his pocket, Jeremy read the text message. Evidently. he was now a delivery boy, he thought, reading the instructions on what to do with the food. Whatever. Backing out, he continued his ride to the Inn.

Now, despite the enticing aroma, Jeremy found himself not hungry. When he'd arrived, Madison had nearly attacked him, grabbing the box of food before he was even inside the room. With a blink of an eye, they were all busy eating. But Jeremy was too wired to eat. Every time he turned around, someone new was getting involved, and he didn't like it. There were too many players, and the lines between the good guys and the bad guys were becoming very blurry. It made him very nervous.

"Explain to me again why this woman is involved? Why do you need her?" Jeremy turned to Stan, unaware of the man's earlier transition. "I thought you had a plan, that you had this covered."

Momentarily distracted by the delicious burger he was inhaling, Stan glared at Jeremy before swallowing his food.

"I do have a plan, and she's part of it."

"And?"

"And what?"

"And what's her part?" Really? Was Stan purposely trying to keep him in the dark? And if so, why?

"No, I'm not trying to keep you in the dark."

Madison shot Stan a disapproving glare as Jeremy blinked in surprise. Ignoring Madison, Stan focused on Jeremy.

"You yourself said it, you have friends and family to look out for. The less you know, the better." Stan paused, taking another bite of his burger. "Don't worry, when you need to know something, you will. Trust me on that one."

Jeremy just stared at Stan.

"What?"

"That's it?"

Stan nodded.

"You don't have anything else to say?"

"Pass the fries?"

Balling his fists, Jeremy stared at Stan before whirling on Madison. This whole thing was beyond his realm of expertise. He was a team player; he always had been. But this was a different kind of team and one he was suddenly unsure of. He glanced at Jones before coming back to Madison. Meeting his confused glance with her sympathetic one, Jeremy's anger flared. Knowing he was likely to say something he'd later regret, he grabbed up his coat and turned toward the door.

"Jeremy," Madison began, grabbing his arm.

"Let him go," Stan said firmly. "It's okay."

Jeremy paused at the door, tossing Stan an angry glance.

"He needs to work this out his way."

Turning back to Jeremy, Madison released her grip on his arm, but her eyes were wide, questioning. Cupping her cheek, Jeremy kissed Madison lightly, and with a nod to Jones, he left.

Madison whirled back around to face Stan, her eyes bright with frustration and budding anger.

"What do you have to say for yourself now?" she demanded.

"Pass the fries?"

What the fuck was going on? Jeremy wondered, riding the elevator down to the lobby. His mind racing, he stepped off the elevator, nearly walking right into Ellen.

"Excuse me," she said politely, barely looking at him as she stepped around him and into the elevator.

Too surprised to reply, Jeremy just nodded, watching the doors slide shut. What the fuck was going on?

"Are you okay, Jeremy?" Ethel's voice pulled him from his thoughts, and he turned around.

Standing behind the desk, Ethel had watched the short exchange, a million questions going through her mind.

"Tough day?"

"You have no idea."

And with a nod, Jeremy left the Inn, leaving behind a burst of cold air. Watching Jeremy disappear down the steps, Ethel glanced back at the elevator. What the hell was going on in her Inn?

"Thanks for meeting me," Jeremy said with relief.

"No problem," Jack said, "I'm glad you called. I needed a break anyway."

"Nancy driving you crazy?" Jeremy smiled at the thought of Nancy bossing around Jack the way she always did just before she delivered. It was almost like a ritual.

"No more than usual," Jack smiled.

They both knew he wouldn't have it any other way, and clinking their glasses, they drank their beer in companionable silence.

"So what's going on?" Jack asked moments later.

Jeremy wished he could tell his brother everything; but knew he couldn't. Not and have it make any sense anyway. Plus, there was no way he'd put his family in harm's way. This new twist with Stillman's so-called wife had thrown him for a loop. and he was still trying to wrap his mind around it. But there was one thing he could definitely talk to Jack about . . .

"Madison's driving me nuts."

Jack leaned back with a laugh.

"What? You find that funny?"

"Hysterically so, brother, hysterically so!"

Not sure he liked this, Jeremy frowned.

"Oh, relax," Jack laughed, "I think it's great!"

"That a woman is driving me nuts? And how is that great?"

"Because it's about goddamn time a woman got under your skin! Welcome to the club!"

And clinking their glasses again, Jack drank deeply while Jeremy sipped his own beer, still not sure if this was a good thing or a bad thing. Knowing his brother was even more confused now, Jack couldn't decide whether to laugh harder or feel bad for his self-proclaimed bachelor of a brother. He went for the middle ground, laughing while he punched Jeremy in the arm.

"Madison's cool," Jack said finally, "and she's right up your alley. When was the last time you met a woman who could keep up with you? And maybe even give you a run for your money?"

Before Jeremy could answer, Jack silenced him.

"Never, that's when. Admit it. Never. Sure, you've brought home lots of nice girls," he finished his beer, waving to the waitress for another one, "but that's all they were, nice girls. No pizazz. And they kept your attention for, what, a week at the most?"

Still not able to get a word in edgewise, Jeremy finished his own beer, nodding to the waitress when she brought Jack's.

"And when have you ever let them stay at your house? Shit! I can't remember you ever having a woman at your house beyond maybe a night."

And sometimes not even that long! Sitting back in his chair, Jack gave his brother a big, broad smile.

"I'm happy for you, man, this is great."

"But you don't know what she's doing to me," Jeremy began before his brother interrupted him.

"I don't need to. The very idea that she's getting you all twisted up is all I need to know!"

Resisting the temptation to punch his brother, Jeremy opted for drinking his beer. Jack was right, of course—something Jeremy loathed to admit. But really, had he ever known a woman like Madison? No, never. And he wasn't likely to meet another woman like her again either. A lopsided grin split his face. One assassin in the family was enough! In the family? His grin disappeared as he realized he was thinking long-term. Oh, shit, he really was in deep! Leaning back in his chair, he drank his beer, contemplating a future with a woman of Madison's caliber.

He'd traveled enough when working for the RCMPs; his family was used to him missing holidays. And they'd understood that he wasn't able to talk much about his work. But Madison, she truly was another story. Sure, he didn't know much about how she worked, but he knew Jones and that Jones was likely to pop up anywhere, anytime, and with no advance warning. Did Madison live and work like that too? He suspected she did. Could he deal with that? Did he want to?

The answer was plain and simple. Yes and yes.

"You look deep in thought, son, what's going on in that crazy mind of yours?"

Blinking, Jeremy realized his mother was standing next to him, a concerned look on her face. Jack chuckled, earning him a questioning glance from their mother.

"He's trying to figure out how to handle Madison," Jack happily and willingly informed Ruth, earning a "Thanks a lot" glare from Jeremy and an unwanted look of sympathy from their mother. When she dropped into the chair next to him, Jeremy knew he was doomed. His brother would pay for this later, he decided. Dearly.

"If it matters, I like her," Ruth said with a knowing smile.

It was never easy to talk to your mother about a girl. It didn't matter the age; girls were girls and mothers were mothers. Ruth nearly laughed out loud when Jeremy's eyes dropped and his face reddened.

"Thanks," Jeremy mumbled, wishing the ground would just open up and swallow him.

Before the end of the day, his brothers and sisters would all know about Madison—if they didn't already. He could hear his phone ringing already.

"You going to answer that?" Jack said, wondering why Jeremy was ignoring his phone.

"Crap!" Jeremy muttered, pulling his phone from his pocket. He really needed to get his act together! "Hello?"

The voice on the other end instantly warmed his heart.

"I'm headed back to the house, do you need anything?" Madison's innocent and boringly normal question was all it took to clear Jeremy's mind.

"I'm at the restaurant, come on over here." His eyes danced over his mother as she nodded vigorously, a smile splitting her face. "My mom wants to see you."

Jeremy knew instantly that the sudden silence on the other end had nothing to do with current events but everything to do with his mother wanting to see her.

"We can meet at home if you'd rather," he hurriedly added.

The silence lengthened, and he wondered if she was still on the other end.

"No, no," Madison finally said, "the restaurant is fine." She paused. "Can I get dessert?"

Jeremy chuckled. It seemed the idea of food always won out. He filed that knowledge away, sure he'd need it again in the future.

"And you'll be there to protect me, right?"

Her question, again so normal and natural, had him smiling. "Always."

Ending the call, Jeremy slid the phone back into his pocket. Picking up his beer, he leaned back in his chair, a smug look on his face.

"You happy now?"

"Yes," his mother and Jack answered together.

Hanging up the phone, Madison turned to Jones and Stan. Not saying a word, both men quickly averted their eyes.

"Shut up," she laughed.

When neither man spoke, she ignored them, knowing full well they knew she was nervous. Why shouldn't she be nervous? When had she ever had to deal with someone's mother? Sure, she liked Ruth very much, but so far they hadn't really spent any quality time together. So there hadn't been time for any . . . personal conversation. It appeared that time was about to come to an end. She swallowed hard. Christ, she really was nervous!

I'm a professional killer, I've faced worse than this! I can handle Ruth!

"Yeah, you keep right on thinking that, girl," Stan laughed, patting Madison on the back as he reached for his coat. "Good luck with that one."

And with a nod to Jones and Madison, he disappeared out the door. Glancing desperately at Jones, she suppressed the urge to slap the man when he just smiled knowingly at her.

"What am I going to do?" Madison whispered frantically, her nerves getting the better of her as she collapsed in the chair, still warm from Stan. "What do I say?"

Who is this woman sitting across from me? Jones wondered in amazement. He'd known her through dangerous and difficult times and never had he seen her so nervous before! Wow, this was a first! He wanted to laugh but knew Madison was likely to literally kill him if he did that, which made him want to laugh even harder. Instead, he shifted in his chair.

"I wish I could help you, kid," Jones said sympathetically. "But this is unknown territory for me too."

Madison nodded. As far as she knew, Jones had never had a long-term relationship with anyone. A couple of weeks was the longest she was aware of. Glancing at her watch, Madison considered calling Sarah, frowning when she realized it was probably too late to call now. And it wasn't like it was an emergency or anything.

"I dunno," Jones interrupted her thoughts, "this might not be an emergency, but it's still pretty important."

Pushing out of his chair, he grabbed his phone, handing it to Madison.

"Call her, she'll see the number and think it's me."

Knowing Sarah always answered Jones's call, Madison stood up, taking the phone. Before Jones could react, Madison surprised him, engulfing him in a bear hug. Gently wrapping his arms around the woman he'd always considered a little sister, Jones swallowed the unfamiliar emotions that threatened to choke him.

"Just make the call," he said, pushing her away.

Knowing she'd embarrassed him, Madison nodded, blinking away the sudden wetness that stung her eyes. What the hell was happening to her? She'd never been emotional, and she sure as hell never cried! She hadn't cried since . . . she couldn't remember. She wasn't even sure she'd cried when her parents were murdered.

But the tears were threatening now. What the hell? Wiping her eyes with the heel of her hand, she took a deep breath, forcing herself to calm down. She couldn't afford to have emotions like this; emotions led to mistakes. And mistakes led to death. And she wasn't about to let anyone die because of her. She pressed a button and, with a deep breath, waited for the call to be connected.

As expected, Sarah answered the phone. What Madison didn't expect was Sarah immediately assuming the worst when she heard Madison's voice and not Jones'. What had happened? Who was dead? Rushing to assure Sarah that everyone was fine, Madison rushed on, quickly apologizing for calling at such a late hour—especially since this was more of a personal call than work-related.

A personal call? Sarah's relief immediately turned to amazement when Madison confessed her reason for calling and that she needed . . . girl advice. Okay, this was a first! For a moment, Sarah wondered whom she was really talking to and what had happened to Madison. Girl advice? Making herself comfy on the couch, Sarah reached for a cigarette. There was no way she was delving into Madison's personal life without a cigarette. Maybe even two!

Lying back on the couch, her feet propped up on her glass top coffee table, Sarah listened patiently as Madison poured out her frustrations and anxieties regarding Jeremy—something Madison hadn't intended on doing. She'd only meant to ask for a bit of advice as to how to proceed with Jeremy's mother. Like any other job, Madison just wanted to work out where to start and then figure the direction she should go in from there. But once she started talking about Jeremy, it all just poured out, and she was powerless to stop it.

Sarah knew something had been brewing with Jeremy. While no one had specifically said anything, they hadn't denied anything either. It didn't take a genius to figure this one out. But what Sarah hadn't been able to figure out was the extent of their involvement. Now, listening to Madison, Sarah realized, she and Jeremy were pretty involved.

On the business end of things, Sarah wasn't happy. But on the personal end, she was positively thrilled that Madison had met someone special. She'd always known it would happen. No matter how much Madison tried to avoid it or deny it, she wasn't the type of woman to live her life entirely alone. And if what Madison was telling her about Jeremy was true, he sounded like just the right man for her in every sense of the word. Leaning forward, Sarah grabbed a pen, scribbling down some notes on the pad of paper she always kept handy.

Madison could talk about the guy all she wanted; that wasn't going to stop Sarah from still having Jeremy thoroughly checked out.

Finishing her notes, Sarah sat back, laughing out loud when Madison finally got to the real reason for calling. Seemed like Madison—a woman who killed people for a living, who wasn't afraid of anything, a woman who handled a firearm better than most men—was nervous about spending time with Jeremy's mother! Sarah couldn't stop laughing, the irony of it all too much for her. Who knew a regular woman—*a mother*, no less—would be Sarah's kryptonite?

Sarah laughed even harder when Madison went on to confess that Stan and Jones weren't any help either, instead giving her a hard time about Jeremy. Having never been teased while growing up, this was something Madison definitely had no experience with! Her first reaction had been to kill both men, but she resisted when she realized they were doing it because they cared about her. And because they could. Talk about acting like *normal* guys!

Finally having gotten it all out of her system, Madison took a deep breath, even managing to laugh a little at the ridiculousness of the situation. Sarah agreed wholeheartedly and quickly assured Madison that she'd be fine with Jeremy's mother and to just be herself.

Be herself? Who exactly was she? The answer came quickly and harshly: simply put—she was a professional assassin. And a damn good one. A frustrated sigh slipped from Madison. It was a safe bet that Ruth would not be too impressed—or pleased, for that matter—should she ever find out what Madison did for a living. Of course, it was just a hunch, but Madison felt pretty confident in her thinking. It would, however, make for interesting conversation around the dinner table when the family was together for the holidays. It definitely brought a new meaning to "How was your day, dear?" Giving up, Madison laughed, Sarah joining in. The whole thing was just too absurd!

Having taken a quick shower while Madison made her call, Jones cracked open the bathroom door. The sound of Madison's pure and happy laughter was music to his ears; it was a sound he so rarely heard. Glad in his decision to let her use his phone, he was equally proud of himself for having been right. Madison just needed some girl time with Sarah. Plain and simple. Mentally patting himself on the back, Jones closed the door; he'd give the girls a few more minutes. Finishing getting dressed, his mind quickly returned to work. Suddenly, he stopped, a smile splitting his face as he imagined his updated résumé: world renowned arms dealer, Special Operations operative, and now romance expert.

Yeah, he thought with a chuckle, if his romance advice didn't work, at least he could tell her how to kill the guy.

With a relieved smile, Sarah ended the call with Madison. Tossing the phone on the coffee table, Sarah leaned back, lighting another cigarette. Inhaling deeply, she exhaled, blowing out three smoke rings. Closing her eyes for a moment, she allowed herself the freedom of feeling relaxed and carefree. Girl talk did that. They needed to do that more often, she decided. Over coffee. In the same place and not separated by an ocean.

Wouldn't that be heavenly, Sarah thought. *Wouldn't that be . . . normal!*

Her eyes fell on the file lying next to her phone. Normal was going to have to wait, though. She had work to do. Snatching the file, she flipped it open, a picture of Frank Stillman falling out. Picking it up, Sarah studied it closely, finally seeing the resemblance. How had she missed it before? Because she hadn't been looking for it. No one had.

"Damn, if we don't have our connection," she murmured, taking another long drag from her cigarette.

Reading over the file one more time, she tossed it back on the table before reaching for another, thicker file. Flipping it open, and for what seemed like the millionth time, she studied the pictures of Madison's parents. A sad sigh escaped Sarah.

"Shit."

Glancing at her watch, Sarah gauged that enough time had passed since her conversation with Madison. Picking up her phone again, Sarah pressed a button and waited as the call went through.

"Didn't expect to hear from you so soon. Look, if it's about Madison using my phone . . ." Jones began before Sarah interrupted him.

"I know who Stillman is and why he's after Madison."

"Oh?"

"Madison killed his brother."

"Okay. She does that, it's her job."

"Stillman's brother killed Madison's parents."

"Oh, shit."

CHAPTER 25

A MAJOR RULE for an assassin's survival—never develop a personal connection with your target. The ideal job being the basic get in get-out scenario. A file with a photograph is received, the information is carefully studied, and a plan is formed. With a contingency plan safely in place, the job is executed with minimal mess and attention. Payment is received, and the parties involved go their separate ways, having never met. Nice and clean.

If only it was always that easy.

The man who killed Madison's parents had been nothing more than a two-bit thief. But while attempting to rob their home, the thief was confronted by Madison's parents; and in an act of desperation and stupidity brought on by an alcohol-ravaged mind, the thief needlessly shot and killed them both.

Alerted by a sophisticated alarm system, the police arrived in time to catch the thief as he tried to escape down the fire escape. Still in an alcohol-induced state, the thief readily confessed, and the police considered the case closed.

Transported to the courthouse for his arraignment, and where Madison would confront her parents' murderer for the first time, security was lax. Preparing to escort the thief into the courthouse, a silent yet deadly bullet between the eyes cut down the thief before he'd even cleared the back seat of the police car. Crouched down with guns drawn, the police instantly prepared to defend themselves while they waited for backup to arrive.

Minutes felt like hours as the officers waited, but no further shots were fired, either by the police or the mysterious shooter. Only when backup, followed by the ambulance, arrived did the officers turn back to their now-dead prisoner. The single clean shot to the head screamed professional kill. But why? The guy was a nobody! Hell, up till now, he'd never hurt or killed anyone. And the unfortunate victims, while wealthy, weren't powerful enough to warrant a hit being put out on the guy. So what made him important enough to be killed like this? Clearly, he'd pissed off someone.

Reaching Madison by phone, the district attorney regretfully informed Madison that her parent's killer had been shot down himself before reaching the courthouse. And because he had to follow protocol, he asked her if she had any idea who would have wanted him dead.

"Besides me?" Madison had remarked dryly.

Besides her. But the DA already knew she had an airtight alibi. It was the first thing he'd checked before contacting her.

While unhappy that she hadn't been able to face her parents' killer in court, Madison was relieved to have it all over with, telling the DA that she just wanted to put the whole thing behind her and begin to move forward—to heal. Understanding, the DA wished her well and, hanging up the phone, wondered at the nagging feeling that he hadn't seen or heard the last of her. Adding the file to a pile of unsolved cases, the DA knew there was still more to this story. But for now, he had more important and pressing cases to deal with.

In her hotel room on the Upper West Side, Madison packed her bag, anxious to head back to Chicago. Gazing longingly at the sniper's rifle lying cleaned and broken down in its gun case, she experienced a moment of regret, knowing she couldn't take the rifle with her. It had handled well, better than some she'd used. At least, she could keep the scope, she smiled ruefully, patting the secret compartment in her carry-on where the scope was safely hidden. Most likely, she didn't need to hide it, but why chance it. If airport security found a scope, they'd only want to know where the rest of the gun was. Yeah, better to keep it hidden.

Glancing at her watch, she quickly finished packing before slipping quietly out of the room and into the stairway a few feet away. Her sneakered feet were silent as she jogged down the stairs, her carry-on in one hand, and the rifle case in the other. Reaching the ground floor, she listened for a moment before continuing down one more flight. Again pausing to listen and look around, Madison slipped quietly into the maintenance room, purposely left unlocked for her. Sliding the rifle case into its designated hiding place, she made sure she left behind no prints or evidence that she'd been there before leaving the room as quietly as she'd entered.

Settling into her first class seat, Madison accepted the flight attendant's offer for a glass of champagne. Watching as the plane taxied down the runway, she sipped her champagne as her mind drifted back over the events of the last few hours. While her parents might not have been the best, they hadn't deserved to die the way they did.

Pulling the trigger and watching the thief die, Madison said goodbye to her parents the only way she knew how. Through revenge.

How could my jackass brother be so stupid? Frank Stillman asked himself yet again.

And for the millionth time, he still had no answer. Except that alcohol had clearly played a big part. His brother had never been able to hold his liquor, and when he fell on hard times, he lost himself in the bottle even more so.

Why hadn't he called? Frank asked himself yet again.

He would have helped his little brother in a heartbeat! Which was probably why he hadn't called. Frank was a successful man; his little brother was not. And he couldn't stand that he was nothing next to his older brother. They'd been close as kids, only growing apart when Frank realized his direction in life and, without a backward glance, had gone in that direction. Unbeknownst to Frank, his little brother had idolized him, and watching Frank leave, he saw all his own dreams go down the toilet. That night, while Frank was on a bus speeding toward his new life, his little brother was in a bar getting totally shitfaced.

While Frank wasn't totally surprised to learn his little brother had been shot and killed, the method in which he was killed was another matter altogether. And it was one that worried Frank immensely. What had his brother done to warrant dying in such a manner? In his neatly pressed suit and matching tie, Frank waltzed into the police station demanding answers, identifying himself as the lawyer for the thief's family. And while the guy had admittedly killed two innocent people, the manner in which he was later killed should be cause for concern. No one questioned Frank's demand for an explanation and an investigation—an investigation more for his own protection than for finding answers about his brother's killer. Frank hadn't been in touch with his little brother for years; had the kid gotten messed up with the mob? If so, Frank needed to know so he could protect himself. The last thing he needed was death by association!

Not wanting to waste the manpower or get tied up in a legal investigation, the police officer who'd been on the scene simply told Frank all he could about the shooting. It wasn't like there was lots to tell. One minute the guy was alive; the next he had a clean bullet hole between his eyes. No, they hadn't heard a gunshot, and no other gunshots had been fired. Just the one, clean shot. No, they hadn't spotted anyone on the surrounding rooftops. Although the officer did admit that by the time backup had arrived, the shooter was no doubt long gone.

While there was no need to question the officer's story, Frank still had his doubts. One shot to the head? Definitely done by a professional. Frank knew only a handful of people who could make that shot.

Was the shooter hired, or did the shooter have personal ties to his little brother?

Most likely the later, Frank decided.

And until Frank knew otherwise, he was going with that theory. His brother was a lowlife, not worth the time and planning for an execution like that. If the mob wanted his little brother dead, they would have just shot him and tossed him in the drink. No, this was something else altogether different. Shaking the officer's hand, Frank left the station, returning to his hotel, determined to find the shooter if it was the last thing he did. He owed his little brother that much.

Staring blankly out the window, Frank sipped his drink. It'd taken him longer than he'd planned to track down his brother's killer. At first it'd been his top priority. But as time went by and the trail went cold, not that there'd ever been much of one to start with anyway, Frank's priorities changed, and finding his brother's killer became less important.

Until a chance meeting in an upscale restaurant in Times Square a few years later brought it all back to the forefront.

Waiting in the bar for a business associate, Frank's attention was piqued when, by chance, he overheard two men discussing a story that'd been in the news over the last few days. Seemed a man had been killed by a single, clean shot between the eyes. No sound, no signs of the shooter, no evidence—just one very neatly killed man. While maintaining that the general public was not in any danger, behind closed doors the police admittedly were baffled. But general consensus had it that the man killed must have been targeted. The method in which he'd been killed was far too neat to be a random shooting.

Sipping his drink, Frank considered this new information. Could this be the same person who'd killed his brother? It certainly seemed so. Admittedly, while Frank hadn't thought about his brother in a while, that didn't mean he'd forgotten his promise to get his brother's killer. And now it seemed he was one step closer to finding that person.

Every assassin had their specialty. This particular kill, the way in which it was executed, there was only a handful who did that well. And Frank didn't believe in coincidences. Pleased he had a fresh direction now, he slowly began forming a new plan.

Finishing his drink, Frank grabbed his coat. It was time to change the rules of the game again. He was done being kept prisoner in his hotel room while Madison went wherever she pleased. No, he needed to take control of the situation again. The way the weather kept changing, the chances of Madison getting out of town sooner were growing. He had to move now or chance losing her again for who knew how many more years.

Having his own contacts, with the new information Frank had on his brother's suspected killer, it didn't take him long to narrow down the list of people with that specific skill set. Needing to be cautious, careful not to raise any red flags, Frank put out discrete feelers; and within a few months, he not only had Madison's name but where he could possibly find her. The fact that she was a world-renowned assassin didn't worry him; he had the element of surprise on his side.

Or so he thought.

Shrugging on his coat, Frank stepped out onto the deck lining the outside of the Inn—which, despite having been shoveled earlier, was again covered with a light coating of snow. While preferring to stay inside as much as possible, the need to avoid the lobby now was more important. Leaning against the firm wooden railing, Frank paused to gaze out over the snow-covered town, watching a few pedestrians as they trudged through the snow—no doubt headed toward the restaurant. His stomach rumbled as the tantalizing smell of beef reached him. Pulling his coat tightly around him, he glanced left then right before turning toward the snow-covered stairs leading down to the street.

Grabbing the railing to keep from falling, Frank cursed Madison yet again. Sure, he'd finally been able to track her down . . . to this godforsaken place! Would it have killed her to take a job on some exotic island? No, she had to come to the far reaches of nowhere! If that wasn't reason alone to kill her, he didn't know what was!

Well, at least he had her now. And he could finally avenge his brother's death.

CHAPTER 26

HER NERVES DANCING, Madison trudged through the snow toward the restaurant. In the short walk, she'd nearly turned back at least a half a dozen times already.

Holy shit, she thought with a smirk; in all her years, she'd never been so nervous! Who knew someone as . . . *normal* . . . as someone's mother could bring Madison to her knees in fear? A burst of hysterical laugher escaped her as she clamped down on her nerves. This was ridiculous! And besides, it wasn't like she was meeting Ruth for the first time; they'd already talked quite a few times. And those conversations had all gone just fine. Hadn't they? Yes, of course, they had! Reassured that she had nothing to worry about, Madison smiled, pushing on through the falling snow.

The sound of a man cursing caught her attention, and Madison instinctively ducked into the nearest doorway. Straining to hear, she held her breath, remaining perfectly still. Moments later, she was rewarded with hearing him curse again and immediately recognized Stillman's voice. Gauging his whereabouts, she carefully peeked around before ducking quickly back into the doorway when she spotted him trudging out from a side street across the way from her. Judging by the tone of his voice and the snow covering his pant legs, he clearly hadn't been on a shoveled path of any kind. Glancing in the direction from whence he came, she quickly deduced that he'd left the Inn using the back exit, the snow on his pants most likely from having used the Inn's outside stairway. She'd considered that route herself, but because it hadn't been shoveled, she'd skipped it, using the main entrance instead. Clearly trying to avoid being seen, Stillman had used the back exit. And he wasn't happy about it.

Wasn't he just being bold, she thought as she watched him push through the snow. What had happened to bring him out in the open? Whatever the reason, it didn't bode well for her. Watching as he reached the shoveled section of the sidewalk, he paused, brushing off the snow still covering his pant legs. At least he wasn't cursing as loud now; that was something.

With a frustrated growl, Stillman finished brushing the snow from his pants before looking both ways. Watching from her hiding place, Madison quickly ducked back when Stillman glanced in her direction before—satisfied no one was paying him any attention— he headed in the direction of the restaurant. Releasing the breath she'd been holding, she counted to twenty before peeking around. Of course, he wasn't looking for her, so he wasn't expecting to see her. A wry smile split her face; what would he do if she just strolled up beside him? Even going so far as to loop her arm through his? Madison had to force herself not to move, the urge to do just that nearly overwhelming. Talk about catching your adversary by surprise! She couldn't surprise him much more than that!

Taking a deep, cleansing breath, her eyes followed him. It was safe to assume that he was armed. She was. So there was no reason to suspect that he wasn't. And with his propensity for losing his temper and acting rashly, surprising him might not be the best idea. Not that she couldn't easily kill him where he stood. She just didn't want to do anything in plain sight. Especially when she had to see Ruth afterward. Yeah, that'd take some explaining.

"Excuse me, but I just killed a guy in the street, can we talk after I clean up?" Yeah, she was pretty sure Ruth would probably frown on that. Go figure.

But that didn't mean Madison couldn't put a little fear into Stillman. Watching him as he casually strolled toward the restaurant, she waited patiently for him to reach the bottom step of the entrance. Then sprinting away from her hiding spot, she raced down the snowy sidewalk, taking the steps to the restaurant two at a time before landing next to Stillman as he reached the top step and was pulling open the door.

"Hold the door!" she called out breathlessly, pasting a smile on her face.

Shocked to find his target standing right next to him, Stillman froze.

"Close your mouth, you look foolish."

Snapping his mouth, shut he glared at the woman, unable to believe her audacity and, he admitted, her bravery. She had guts. Acting on her earlier idea, Madison looped her arm through his, pulling off her gloves. It was all Stillman could do not to gape at her. This certainly brought a new meaning to "Keep your friends close and your enemies closer." What the hell was she up to?

"Good evening," Stillman finally managed, his smile as fake as his name. "Meeting your friends for dinner, I presume?"

Nodding, Madison threw him a dazzling smile that, despite all his angry intentions, still managed to throw him even further off balance.

"I am," she smiled, looking around the crowded restaurant, her arm still loosely wrapped in his. "I'd invite you to join us, but I see your wife and the rest of your group," she nodded in the direction of a large table, and following her gaze, Stillman spotted Ellen sitting with their group.

The look of shock on Ellen's face pulled Frank from his stupor, and pulling his arm from Madison, he snarled at her.

"Watch yourself, bitch."

His ice-cold words washed harmlessly over Madison; she'd expected some kind of backlash, no matter how lame. If this was the best he could come up with, then she'd clearly succeeded in throwing him off.

My work here is done, she thought with a smirk as she stepped away from Stillman, having spotted Jeremy out of the corner of her eye. Careful not to take her attention completely away from Stillman just yet, she frustrated him even further when he attempted to push her away but was unable to throw her off balance. Prepared for just that reaction, Madison had both feet firmly planted and her weight positioned just so; there was no way he was going to move her.

Growling, he threw her a savage glare before winding his way through the crowded restaurant, dropping into a chair next to Ellen. Careful not to look at Madison again, he focused on Ellen, resisting the violent urge to slap her when she placed a questioning hand on his arm. The urge to pull the gun he had tucked into his pocket and aim it at Madison was nearly overwhelming. Knowing he'd never make it out of the restaurant alive if he did so was the only reason he was able to resist the urge. But the idea was still tempting! Swallowing hard, he reached for a menu, and throwing it up in his face, he finally was able to block Madison's smiling face from view. God, he hated that woman!

Only when Stillman's menu blocked his view did Madison relax. Well, that went well, she thought with a sly smile as she made her way through the crowd to Jeremy's table. Rising to meet her, Jeremy kissed her cheek softly before pulling out a chair for her. Having witnessed her entrance with Stillman, Jeremy was still trying to make sense of what had just happened. Just when he thought he was beginning to understand her, she went and did something as crazy as showing up on the arm of her enemy!

"Someday you'll have to explain this all to me," Jeremy whispered in her ear as she dropped gracefully into her chair.

Tossing him a mischievous smile, Madison nodded, reaching for a menu. Suddenly, she was starving! She nearly laughed. If nothing else, her encounter with Stillman had definitely taken her mind off of having to talk to Ruth! Quickly deciding, Madison gave her order to the waitress before leaning comfortably back in her chair, sipping her coffee that had appeared just as she was sitting down. Grateful that Jack had also just returned and was now talking to Jeremy, Madison took the time to review all that had just transpired.

Her spur-of-the-moment decision to surprise Stillman had been a dangerous one. No doubt Stan and Jones would be bullshit when they found out. But they'd understand her motive and why she took the chance. Despite Stillman's temper, Madison had been confident that he wouldn't hurt her in the restaurant. Not if he wanted to get out alive. The man was crazy, but he wasn't stupid. By waiting until he was just entering the restaurant, she'd eliminated the chance of him doing anything violent, a smart move on her part. For that reason alone, she wasn't worried about Stan and Jones's reaction. They would have done the same. This was their way; sometimes chances had to be taken to acquire better intel. And in the few short minutes she'd been with Stillman, she'd learned a lot.

She still didn't know what Stillman's motive was to kill her, but she was confident now that whatever it was, it was laced with desperation—which also told her it was personal. The look of utter shock she'd seen in his dark eyes when she'd caught him outside, if it hadn't been so scary, it'd have been funny. For a moment, she was sure his eyes were going to pop out of their sockets! Unlike him, Madison was a master at hiding her feelings, feigning innocence and cheerfulness when she greeted him. And referring to Ellen as his wife, she continued to keep him off balance. While that could have been dangerous in itself, she'd also succeeded in making him question how much she actually knew about him—which in turn gave him a false sense of security and confidence.

Casting a casual glance around the crowded restaurant, her eyes bounced off of Stillman and Ellen as they sat with their heads close together. Ellen was now the wild card. It was always dangerous playing both sides; Madison hoped Ellen could pull it off. So far, it looked good, if the concern on Ellen's face as she gazed at Stillman was anything to go by. Stillman appeared to be much calmer now, even chatting easily with the others at the table. From her seat across the room, Madison was admittedly relieved to see that his eyes no longer held the anger she'd seen in them earlier. Good.

"Here's your food."

Smiling her thanks, Madison immediately sat up straighter when Ruth placed the plate in front of her. Glancing quickly at Jeremy, her eyes narrowed at his amused gaze.

You could have warned me!

When his smile grew, Madison silently fumed as she attacked her food. It was all Jeremy could do not to laugh.

"I was hoping we might have some time to talk," Ruth began hesitantly.

She'd seen the look Madison had given Jeremy and knew she'd surprised Madison. It really hadn't been intentional; their waitress was busy so Ruth had just stepped in to help. That it just happened to be for Madison's table—well, okay, so that had given Ruth the in she'd been looking for. She knew Madison was nervous about talking to her; she was just as nervous herself! Jeremy had never been this serious about a woman before. and while Ruth was suffering from the usual motherly concerns, she also knew there was more to Madison than meets the eye. And she didn't want Jeremy hurt.

Ruth had liked Madison from the beginning. But at the same time, she'd recognized that Madison was unlike any woman Jeremy had ever "brought home." While she couldn't put her finger on just what was different, her mother's intuition had never been wrong before. While Ruth had long since accepted that she'd never know everything that Jeremy had done during his time with the RCMP, she always knew he was one of the "good guys."

Ruth wasn't so sure about Madison.

She knew Madison wasn't a bad guy, per se. But there was something dangerous and very mysterious about the woman, no matter how normal she tried to act. And then there was the way she'd handled herself in the alley when they'd found the body. Instinctively, Ruth knew Madison wasn't regular law enforcement; a conversation with Ethel had only confirmed that. Ethel's history was very colorful in itself; no one knew her whole story either. So who better to discuss her concerns with than another woman who could relate better than anyone else?

The look on Ethel's face when Ruth boldly asked what she knew about Madison had been priceless. Ethel was the town gossip; everyone knew that. But what they didn't all know was that the older woman also had some incredible connections. A select few knew about them, Ruth being lucky enough to be in that group. And it was only because of Ruth's other children that Ethel had opened up to her. While seemingly having normal lives and jobs, most of Ruth's children had anything but.

Knowing that Ethel would have already done her homework on Madison, Ruth was disappointed when the other woman wasn't able to shed much light on the subject. But Ethel was quick to assure Ruth that Madison was someone they could trust.

What Ruth didn't know was that while Ethel had easily been able to find out information about Madison, she also knew it was nothing more than an elaborate cover story. The only true piece of information was that Madison was, indeed, her real name—her real first name, anyway. But as to the rest of it, everything that Ethel had read all screamed cover story. So what was the point in telling Ruth anything more? Better to be disappointed than not know the entire truth. This was definitely one of those times when less was definitely more!

Pulling herself together, Madison smiled and nodded, relieved to have a mouthful of food so she didn't actually have to speak yet. Motioning for Ruth to join them, she took another bite of food, giving herself a bit more time to compose herself. Dropping into the chair next to Madison, Ruth smiled, knowing exactly what Madison was up to. No matter what or who she might be, Madison was no different than any other woman who was being confronted by her lover's mother. Ruth nearly laughed out loud at the absurdity of it all. But knowing that would annoy Madison, she stifled her laughter quickly.

"Go easy on her, Mom," Jeremy chuckled, enjoying watching Madison squirm.

If only his mom knew whom she was dealing with. Yeah, wouldn't his mom just love knowing that she'd made a professional killer nervous! Well, really, was there anything scarier than a protective mother? He laughed then, earning himself another nasty glare from Madison. He was so going to pay later! But right now, she had more important things to worry about . . . like trying to answer the questions she guessed would be coming from Ruth. While Madison knew her cover story was perfect, she also knew there wasn't anything personal in it either. Or at least not enough to satisfy a woman like Ruth. Making a mental note to tell Sarah about this, Madison put down her silverware, and turning to Ruth, she pasted what she hoped was a confident smile on her face.

"Relax, dear," Ruth chuckled, patting Madison's arm, the gesture amazingly reassuring. "I'm not going to bite."

Nodding, Madison still found herself at a loss for words. Talk about being out of her element! Having had a less-than-warm relationship with her own mother, Madison wasn't sure how to react to Ruth. She'd liked the woman from the beginning, but now there seemed to be a more personal connection, and this was new territory for Madison. She wasn't sure how she felt about it.

"I know," Madison finally managed to murmur, wanting to shoot herself when she felt her face warming.

Damn if the woman wasn't making her blush! What the hell? Wishing she'd ordered something stronger, Madison reached for her coffee cup as she silently berated herself, *Pull yourself together! You're acting like an idiot! For God's sake, you kill people for a living! And you're worried about someone's mother?*

But it wasn't just someone's mother. It was Jeremy's mother. Fuck.

"I'm sorry," Madison grudgingly admitted. "You're not catching me at my best."

That was certainly putting it mildly! But it was a good start.

"I know, dear," Ruth smiled. "I'm a mother, it's what we do."

Madison could only smile weakly. Realizing that the best course of action might be to just jump in with both feet, she took a deep breath.

"What did you want to talk about?"

And opening the door to any and all questions Ruth might have, Madison cradled her coffee mug, thankful to have something to hold on to. A quick glance at Jeremy, a goofy smile on his face, told her he'd be no help. Yes, the coffee mug would have to do. She took another deep breath and waited.

CHAPTER 27

A SUDDEN HUSH fell over the restaurant, causing Madison to glance around nervously. What, was everyone waiting to hear what Ruth wanted to ask her? It took only an instant though, for Madison to realize that no, this was something altogether different.

Everyone's attention was suddenly focused on activity coming from the entrance of the restaurant. Along with some others, Jeremy stood up to get a better view of the commotion, his mouth falling open in surprise. Feeling cold air, Madison started to stand up, only to find Jeremy's hand on her shoulder, pushing her back down. Glancing angrily at him, she paused as their eyes met briefly. Keeping his hand firmly on her shoulder, he shook his head, relieved when she didn't fight him.

Honoring Jeremy's silent request that she stay in her chair, Madison tried to see between the people standing around her but couldn't see what, or who, was causing the commotion. And then she heard Ruth gasp.

"Mary!"

Mary? Pushing Jeremy's hand off her shoulder, Madison rose slowly so as to not draw too much attention to herself. While everyone else's eyes were on Mary, Madison sought out Frank Stillman; and for a moment, she wasn't sure who was more surprised at Mary's sudden return. Standing with the others at his table, Frank's bulging eyes answered Madison's silent question, and a smug smile dashed across her face. It was official; Frank was clearly more shocked. Now the question was, just exactly why?

Her hand lying gently on Frank's arm, Ellen could feel the tension flowing through him and wondered at it. Who was the woman at the entrance, and why was Frank reacting in such a way? Everyone at their table was standing. Ellen knew if she tried to force Frank to sit down, she'd only bring them unwanted attention. Instead she flexed her hand on his arm and wasn't surprised when, with a violent shake of his arm, he shook off her hand. But following the lead of the others at their table, they remained standing, Ellen the only one aware of Frank's rigid posture as he stood beside her. Rage all but emanated off of him, and when his head turned ever so slowly, his eyes drifting around the crowded restaurant, Ellen's curiosity rose another notch.

He's looking for me! Madison realized, watching Frank's head turn in her direction. Before he could spot her, she blended seamlessly into the crowd of people standing around her. Without taking his eyes off of Mary, Jeremy moved with Madison, his body adding to the shield of people. Frank spotted Jeremy easily but, if Madison was with him, Frank couldn't see her. With a frown, Frank turned his attention back to Mary.

Only when Frank turned away did Jeremy move ever so slightly, signaling the all clear to Madison. Standing behind him, Madison tucked her hand into his back pocket, the intimate yet comfortable gesture surprising them both. Wanting nothing more than to wrap his arms around her and to protect her, Jeremy knew he could do neither. He smiled to himself. Yeah, Madison would punch his lights out if he ever even tried such a thing.

Suddenly realizing that Mary was pushing through the crowd, seemingly headed right for him, Jeremy took an unconscious step backward, bumping into Madison. Focused solely on Jeremy, his name on her lips, Mary wove her way through the crowd toward him. The relief she'd felt when she'd spotted him in the restaurant had been unimaginable. She needed his arms around her, needed him to comfort her! He couldn't turn her away now! Oblivious to the crowd, Mary made her way to Jeremy, only to find Ruth blocking her path, effectively stopping her in her tracks.

"Mary! We're so happy to see you!" Ruth exclaimed, wrapping Mary in her arms before stepping back, holding Mary at arm's length. "Are you all right? Let me look at you! Where have you been? Are you hurt?"

Swinging Mary around, keeping her back to Jeremy, Ruth wrapped the girl in her arms again. Taking advantage of the distraction, Jeremy drifted back into the crowd, pulling Madison with him. Knowing Frank would be following Mary's movements, Jeremy knew it wouldn't be long before he spotted Madison. Damn! So much for the small advantage they'd had. Keeping Madison close to him, they made their way through the crowd, heading toward the back exit.

Mary loved Ruth, the woman had been like a second mother to her. But right now, Mary was focused only on Jeremy; it was his arms she wanted around her, not Ruth's! Trying not to struggle, Mary tried to move out of Ruth's protective hold, but the furthest she could go was arm's length. Realizing she was stuck, Mary gave herself up to Ruth's scrutiny, reminding herself that she should be thankful that Ruth cared so much. And with that thought, the tears Mary had been holding in began rolling down her cheeks.

"Oh, dear! Come with me, we'll get you a hot chocolate and get you warmed up!" Ruth exclaimed, wrapping an arm around Mary. "Jack!" Ruth glanced back over her shoulder toward her oldest son, "Call the sheriff. If he's not already on his way, get him over here!"

Not waiting for Jack's response, Ruth took charge and, announcing that the show was over, guided Mary through the crowd, ushering the sobbing girl back to her office.

"What was that all about?" Ellen demanded to know as everyone at their table returned to their seats.

"I think that was the girl that went missing a few days ago," their tour guide speculated. "I heard something about her disappearing right after that guy got killed in the alley."

Going back to his dinner, Frank ignored the questioning look Ellen tossed him. Feeling Ellen's eyes burning into him, Frank refused to be drawn in, instead concentrating on his food. He'd deal with Ellen later. Now was not the place, not if either one of them wanted to leave alive.

The man was blatantly ignoring her! Silently seething, Ellen forced her anger down, taking a deep, calming breath. Of course, Frank didn't have to acknowledge he knew anything about Mary or the man in the alley, but he didn't have to ignore her completely either! Along with being furious over his treatment of her, she was also embarrassed. And she wasn't sure which feeling made her angrier. But one thing was for sure: she was going to thoroughly enjoy killing Frank!

"I'm just glad she's back and seems to be okay," the tour guide said, finishing his dinner and sitting back in his chair.

His gaze drifted around the table, oblivious to the animosity between Ellen and Frank.

"Dessert and coffee, anyone?"

Closing the door quietly behind her, Ruth ushered Mary to a chair next to her desk. Pulling her office chair around and dropping into it, Ruth took Mary's cold hands into her own warm ones, pulling Mary's tearful gaze to her own questioning one.

"I'm so happy you're back, Mary," Ruth began softly, squeezing Mary's hands gently.

A soft knock at the door interrupted her.

"Come."

Entering silently, the bartender placed a steaming mug of hot chocolate on the desk next to Ruth before, with a nod to both of them, quickly retreating from the room, closing the door quietly behind him. Releasing Mary's hands, Ruth took the mug and, wrapping Mary's hands around its heat, sat back while Mary took one sip, then another, of the hot chocolate. Her sobs now hiccup, Mary tossed Ruth a grateful smile.

"There's more than hot chocolate in this," Mary smiled into the mug as she took another sip.

"Of course, there is," Ruth smiled.

It was her special recipe, guaranteed to warm up even the coldest of bodies—unless you were dead, of course. She was pretty sure even her concoction couldn't bring back the dead, although she thought Jack might disagree with that.

Remembering a few years earlier when Jack had been stranded in the mountains, he'd been on the verge of dying from hyperthermia when they'd found him. Jack later swore that it was his mother's special hot chocolate that had saved his life when they brought him out of the mountains.

Well, clearly, it was working this time. Mary's face wasn't as pale, and her tears had stopped. And her hands weren't shaking as much. Yes, the hot chocolate was doing its thing, as Ruth had hoped it would. Good, because she wanted some answers and preferably now and not later. Not one to pussyfoot around, Ruth got right to the point.

"Where have you been?" Ruth demanded quietly.

Knowing Ruth's propensity for being direct, Mary wasn't surprised by the question. She wasn't ready either.

"Is Jeremy here?" she asked, momentarily avoiding Ruth's question.

"No," and before Mary could ask, Ruth added firmly yet gently, "and he won't be coming."

Clearly, wherever Mary had been, her time away hadn't changed her feelings for Jeremy. Deciding to leave that topic alone for the moment, Ruth repeated her earlier question. Taking another sip of her hot chocolate, Mary knew she'd have to answer the question, either to Ruth or to the sheriff. Or both. She might as well start with the easier of the two.

"I've been in Whitehorse," Mary admitted.

Sitting back in her chair, Ruth just stared at the girl. How could that be? They'd alerted the authorities in Whitehorse!

"I've got a good friend there," Mary continued. "She let me crash at her place."

Well, that explained why Mary hadn't been spotted anywhere. She'd kept out of sight. But why? Had she been hiding from more than the authorities? Remaining silent, Ruth gazed at Mary. What had happened that the girl had been so frightened that she'd felt she had to run away? No, despite knowing Mary's feelings for Jeremy, Ruth knew that this time, one had nothing to do with the other. No, something else had happened. But what?

"Go on," Ruth urged Mary quietly, determined to let the girl tell her story at her own pace.

She was less likely to leave things out if she wasn't pushed, prodded, or rushed—hopefully, anyway.

"Steve was going to take me away from here," Mary began softly, taking another sip of the hot chocolate, its warmth giving her strength.

"Steve?"

"The guy who was killed in the alley," Mary whispered, closing her eyes.

Nodding, Ruth took a deep breath.

"I sorta lost it after Jeremy's rejection," Mary continued, not able to look at Ruth.

You think? Ruth thought, remembering that scene clearly.

Later, when Mary was calmer and things had settled down, Ruth was determined to talk to her and set her straight—once and for all—about Jeremy. But for now, Ruth wanted to hear the rest of Mary's story.

"Go on," Ruth urged.

"I'd known Steve for a while, we'd chat online sometimes, and I knew him from passing through here. When he told me he was driving through to Whitehorse, I didn't think twice and just asked him to take me with him."

Reminding him of the daughter he didn't know because of his own ugly divorce, Steve instantly took pity on Mary after witnessing the scene between her and Jeremy. Expecting to have to beg, or at least grovel, relief didn't begin to describe how Mary felt when Steve readily agreed. Not questioning the fact that he didn't ask for any explanation, Mary just focused on getting out of town and as fast as she could.

"When I met him at his truck, Steve told me he had to meet some guy first, that they had some business to discuss. But after that, we'd be on our way." Swallowing hard, Mary continued, "He told me to wait at his truck and that he'd be back shortly . . ." A tear slid down her cheek. Oh, how she wished she'd done what he asked! "That was the last time I saw him alive."

"Did he say who he was meeting?" Ruth asked.

Mary shook her head.

"He never said the guy's name, just that they had to talk privately."

Finishing her hot chocolate, Mary put the mug on the desk before clasping her hands together.

"I thought he was blowing me off, so I followed him."

Ruth sighed. The girl had serious trust issues.

"I saw him go into the alley, I heard him talking to another man. Then they were fighting . . ."

Brushing away the tears that were streaming down her cheeks now, Mary took a deep breath.

"Whoever the other guy was, he was beating the shit out of Steve."

Raising an eyebrow, Ruth remained silent.

"I could tell, it sounded horrible. And then there was silence."

Closing her eyes, Mary fought off the images of Steve's body when she'd stumbled across him.

"I called out to him, but he didn't answer. And I didn't hear the other guy. So I went looking for Steve." Mary paused. "I know it was stupid of me to go into the alley, but I wasn't thinking." Clearly not.

"Oh, Mary," Ruth sighed sadly. No one should have to witness what she'd witnessed.

"He was dead when I found him," Mary said, wringing her hands as she remembered the sight of Steve's blood on them.

Only when Ruth took her hands, entwining their fingers, was Mary able to stop.

"And you never saw anyone else?" Ruth knew the sheriff would be asking the same questions, but if she could make it easier for Mary, well, Ruth was determined to do just that.

Mary shook her head.

"I don't remember seeing anyone. But my mind just sorta shut off when I found Steve."

"I'm sure," Ruth said in understanding.

"The next thing I remember was Jeremy being there."

And they were back to Jeremy again. Not wanting the conversation turning back to Jeremy, Ruth was relieved when the sheriff chose that time to arrive, knocking softly before entering the room. Rising to greet him, Ruth ushered him into the office before slipping out to prepare another hot chocolate for Mary—and perhaps something for herself as well; she definitely could use something stronger!

Turning toward the bar, Ruth shot off a quick text to Jeremy and was relieved when her phone rang seconds later. Standing just outside the kitchen, her gaze drifting around the busy restaurant, Ruth relayed everything Mary had just told her to Jeremy. Only when Jeremy asked if the group at table 10 were still there did Ruth pause, glancing toward the table in question. Yes, they were still there; it looked like they were settling the bill now. Why, was there a problem? Explaining that he was just curious, Jeremy ended the conversation with a "Thanks, Mom. Love you. Talk later."

And the connection was broken before Ruth could reply. Snapping her phone shut, she shoved it back into her pocket, heading toward the bar. Kids. Always in a rush.

Not giving Madison a choice in the matter, Jeremy ushered Madison out of the restaurant and, practically shoving her into his truck, drove directly to his house. Thankful but admittedly a bit curious that Madison hadn't argued with him, he remained silent until his truck was in the garage and they were safely in his house. Only then did he turn to her.

"Thanks for not arguing," he said, turning on the coffeemaker and reaching for the bottle of Bailey's.

Knowing he was referring to her willingness to let him call the shots, for the moment anyway, she just nodded. Accepting the doctored mug of coffee, she perched on the kitchen stool while he prepared his own coffee.

"Don't let this go to your head," Madison smiled over her coffee mug, "but you made the right call, bringing me here."

Jeremy's eyes bulged, and when his mouth fell open, Madison laughed at his exaggerated expression.

"Like I said, don't let it go to your head."

"I won't," Jeremy laughed, sitting next to her. "But do you mind if I just sit and enjoy the moment? I've no idea when I might ever feel this way again! This is a pretty historic moment, don't you think?"

Shaking her head and laughing, Madison leaned into him, giving him a playful push. Sharing her laughter, Jeremy wrapped an arm around her, pulling her close again. Feeling her relax against him, he sipped his coffee, wanting to enjoy the peaceful moment for as long as they could. He knew it would be a short-lived moment.

"I rescued you twice tonight," he said proudly minutes later.

"You rescued me? How do you figure that?"

"No, no, I rescued you twice."

"And again, I ask, how do you figure that?"

While she didn't consider herself having been rescued in the first place, she'd give it to him that he did get her away from Stillman quickly after Mary's sudden reappearance. What else was he thinking of? She itched to slap the smug look off Jeremy's face as he gazed at her, his eyes twinkling.

"Why, I saved you from having the dreaded talk with my mother!"

Okay, she had to admit it; he had her there.

"Oh, yeah, that. I guess you did rescue me twice," she smiled as she leaned over, kissing him sweetly on the cheek. "My hero!"

Could it get any better than this? Jeremy thought, pulling her back and kissing her deeply. Right this very moment, he didn't think so.

CHAPTER 28

LEANING AGAINST THE railing outside his room, a cigar clamped between his teeth, Jones stared out at the lightly falling snow. He couldn't wait to finish this job and go someplace warm! Okay, he'd settle for a place where it just wasn't snowing! Leave it to Madison to accept a job in the middle of nowhere with the worst weather! He smiled. But that was exactly why she had accepted it. She lived for this kind of weather.

Hell, she'd done some of her best work in the worst weather, he thought wryly, remembering some of her weather-related jobs.

A job in New Orleans had put Madison in the middle of Hurricane Katrina as she went after a serial killer preying on women trying to survive the horrific storm. When his body turned up on the flooded banks of Lake Pontchartrain, it was a toss-up as to whether he died from a bullet between the eyes or snake bite. Interestingly enough, the authorities were just happy the serial killer had been stopped. The how and why, well, did they really need to know?

Another job had Madison dodging an EF4 tornado in the Midwest, her target later found draped in a tree. Despite the telltale bullet hole between the eyes, it was never clearly determined what killed the target first—the weather or the bullet. Jones suspected it was the bullet; Mother Nature just helped making sure the body was later found by authorities.

Jones smiled to himself. Madison always seemed to find a way to make the weather conditions work in her favor; this job was no different. One thing was for sure—Madison and Mother Nature made a formable team.

Yeah, Jones thought, turning as Stan joined him, lighting his own cigar, *if there was bad weather, Madison was there.* She would have made an awesome storm chaser. But instead, she preferred chasing bad people. While not a profession that most parents would be proud of, Jones, for one, was very proud and pleased that Madison was a part of his team.

"I'm not taking another job unless it's in the Bahamas," Stan stated as he puffed on his cigar.

Jones knew his partner felt the same about the cold and snowy weather.

"That and it's about time you took Amy on a nice, long vacation."

"Yeah, there's that too," Stan smiled, thinking of his wife. "Although she's nutty like Madison, she loves the cold weather." He gazed out at the falling snow. "She would have loved this."

Silence fell over them as they enjoyed their cigars, each lost in their own thoughts.

"It seems the players have changed yet again," Stan said quietly moments later.

Nodding, Jones ground out his cigar.

"So it would seem."

"Another change in plan?"

"Quite possibly."

"What I wouldn't give for a nice clean get-in, get-out job."

"Evidently, that would be too easy," Jones smiled ruefully. "Sarah's your sister, don't you have any pull?"

Stan laughed. Yeah, like he'd ever had any pull where his twin sister was concerned, especially when it came to the jobs they were hired to do.

Finishing their cigars in silence, they returned to Stan's room. No need to take any chances that someone might overhear them. Closing and securing the sliding door behind him, Stan ensured their privacy by pulling closed the heavy curtain, effectively blocking anyone from seeing inside the room. Pouring them each a cognac, they remained silent for a few moments, each mulling over his own thoughts.

"That's the thing about all this, though," Jones began, piecing things together. "Madison's original job would have been a get-in, get-out job. She's supposed to be miles up in the mountains, not stuck here. The weather and Stillman are the only reasons this has gotten so fucked up."

Stan nodded.

"And Sarah sent me only because Stillman got on Madison's radar."

"And her radar is seldom wrong," Stan said, correctly finishing Jones's thought. "And I'm here only as backup for you."

Normally the other way around, Stan was happy to help out. The two men had long since been a formidable team; it didn't matter who was point on the job.

"And now we know Stillman is after Madison to avenge the death of his brother," Jones continued.

Sipping his cognac, he stared into the fire, mulling over those new details. Knowing it was useless to rush his friend, Stan sipped his own cognac, appreciating its smooth taste.

"Madison still doesn't know that part yet, though."

"What?" Sitting up straight, Stan stared at Jones. "What do mean she doesn't know? We know. So it only follows that she does too."

"You would think," Jones nodded. "But with everything that happened tonight, I didn't have a chance to tell Madison. So she's still in the dark about his motives."

Oh, this was just getting better and better, Stan thought, tossing back the last of his cognac.

"And Jeremy doesn't know," Stan quickly concluded.

"That would be correct."

While Jeremy had called Jones earlier, alerting them of Mary's sudden reappearance and sharing his plan to take Madison back to his place, they hadn't had time to talk about anything else—not that Jones wanted to tell Jeremy, anyway. No, the news needed to come from him. Or Stan. Madison would be bullshit if it came from Jeremy, wondering why he would have been told before her. And rightfully so. Jones would have felt the same.

"Any chance Sarah might have already told her?" Stan asked, already guessing the answer.

Jones shook his head. Sarah wanted Madison to hear the news in person, not over the phone. Especially from someone hundreds of miles away. Stan wasn't surprised and knew Sarah had been right in her decision. Some news had to be delivered in person.

As if on cue, both men glanced at the clock sitting on the bedside table. Madison was a night owl by nature; she'd probably still be awake. If she hadn't gone to Jeremy's, they would have just gone to her room with this new information. But she wasn't at the Inn.

Just then, a gust of wind pummeled the sliding door. Hearing it howl, the men stared at each other. Did Madison really need to know tonight? What difference was a few more hours going to make? It wasn't like anyone was going anywhere tonight anyway, not with the wind blowing like it was. And not to mention the snow that continued to fall, no matter how lightly.

Stillman and Ellen were in their room; Ethel had confirmed that earlier. And courtesy of a few small, strategically placed weather resistant cameras, if anyone tried to use the outside stairway, Jones would know about it immediately.

Jeremy's mother, as well as the police, were keeping a close on Mary. They weren't about to let the girl out of their sight again anytime soon. So all the players were currently accounted for.

"Okay then," Jones decided, "we'll tell her in the morning."

"Right," Stan smiled, "as soon as she's had her coffee, we'll tell her."

Untangling himself from her, Jeremy eased away from Madison's warm, naked body. Slipping out of bed, he pulled on his sweats before heading to the kitchen to make coffee, making a quick stop in the bathroom first to relieve himself and brush his teeth. He hated having coffee before brushing his teeth! Okay, truth be told, he hated doing anything before brushing his teeth. Smiling into the bathroom mirror, memories of his brothers and sisters lined up in the bathroom brushing their teeth drifted through his mind. Funny, the things he remembered. And making a mental note to touch base with everyone, he rinsed his mouth and headed for the kitchen, feeling a little bit more human.

The smell of freshly brewed coffee tickled her nose. Her eyes still closed, Madison rolled over, gravitating toward the heavenly smell. Struggling to open her eyes she blinked, trying to focus on the mug of coffee that was drifting in front of her. Reaching an arm out, she tried to grab it, only to have it move out of her reach. She growled, rubbing her eyes. Her vision a bit clearer, she stared at Jeremy as he held the mug just out of her reach.

"I've killed people for less," she growled, pushing herself up into a sitting position, pulling the sheet up to cover her bare breasts. "You should know that. And be afraid. Be very afraid."

Ignoring his laughter, she held out her hand while holding the sheet with the other hand.

"I find it difficult to be afraid, knowing you're naked under there," Jeremy stated, his eyes darkening.

"Exactly. By distracting you, I've gained the advantage."

Jeremy paused, again remembering what and who she was. Seeing the worried look in his face, she nearly laughed.

"Oh, stop it! Just give me the goddamn coffee!"

"And then what?" Jeremy asked cautiously as he handed her the mug.

Taking a sip, she sighed happily before gazing up at him.

"And then get your ass back into bed!"

"Yes, ma'am!"

Stripping out of his clothes, he slid back into bed, careful not to bump her arm. The last thing he needed was hot coffee spilled on him. Or her killing him for spilling her coffee. It was a tough call which might be worse.

Lying on his side, an arm propping up his head, Jeremy watched Madison quietly. Concentrating on her coffee, she closed her eyes, enjoying the strong brew. But she could feel his eyes on her as her skin warmed. Finally not able to stand it, she turned to him.

"Quit staring at me!" she snapped, trying to sound gruff but knowing she sounded breathless instead.

"I like looking at you."

His quiet words warmed her, and she turned away in embarrassment. Surprised at her reddening face, Jeremy paused. He hadn't thought a simple compliment would embarrass her, not this incredibly strong and fierce woman. His gaze lazily moved over her body. Still covered by the sheet, he knew what treasures were hidden beneath it. And he knew there were many more treasures to seek out. Jeremy smiled to himself, he couldn't wait to start finding them!

But first he'd let her finish her coffee. And rolling over on to his back, he closed his eyes. He could wait. It wasn't often he had time to lie around in bed; a few more moments of precious shut-eye didn't bother him at all!

He came awake with a start, the feel of a warm hand stroking him and warmer lips kissing his neck. Wrapping his arm around her, he pulled her closer, turning his head to capture her lips in a lazy kiss. She tasted of coffee, and he deepened the kiss as she continued stroking him. Pushing the sheet away from her, he rolled her onto her back, reaching for her breast, caressing her lightly, gently. Sighing into his mouth, she arched into his hand as he grew harder in hers. Leaving her lips, he feathered kisses down her throat before moving upward, his tongue dipping into her ear. He smiled as she groaned. His lips tugged on her earlobe before he slid back down, pausing long enough to kiss her deeply before moving lower. Capturing the breast he'd been caressing, his tongue teased her nipple before he moved to do the same to the other one. Groaning in pleasure, unable to concentrate on what she'd been doing, she released him, her fingers threading through his hair, holding him to her breast. Oh, what he was doing to her!

His mouth still working its magic on her breast, his hand slid gently down her stomach, tickling and teasing as she opened for him. Dipping one then another finger into her wetness, he grew harder against her as her body bucked under his hand. Throwing her arms wide, she gripped the sheets as her body danced in time to the music his fingers were playing.

And here she'd been hoping to surprise him, to do all the things to him that he did to her! So much for best intentions. She laughed out loud.

Good God! What was she laughing about now? Leaving her breast, his mouth moved lower, and he smiled against her stomach when her laughter came to a sudden stop. His fingers slid slowly away only to be immediately replaced by his mouth and tongue before she could protest. Gasping in surprise as his tongue dove deep, she nearly ripped the sheet off the bed as he gripped her bottom, bringing her up to meet him. She definitely wasn't laughing now! Oh, no, just the opposite! As her hips rose up to meet his mouth, she screamed as the orgasm ripped through her.

And my work here is done. That'll teach her to laugh, Jeremy thought with a mischievous smile as he slowly moved away from her. Feeling her trembling, he slowly moved back up her glistening body as he cradled her against him.

"Like that?" he murmured as he tucked her head under his chin.

Curling up against him, she nodded against his chest as tremors still rolled through her. And unable to control herself, Madison giggled.

"What are you giggling at now?"

Her laughter was starting to give him a complex!

"Nothing. Everything," she purred against him. "I'm just happy."

He glanced down at her. Could it really be that simple? And why the hell was it so important to him? He hugged her tightly to him.

"I'm glad you're happy," he whispered.

When his only answer was silence, he glanced down at her, surprised to find her sound asleep. *Guess she was still sleepy*, he thought, amazed at how fast she'd dropped off, while leaving him still very aroused. Debating on whether or not to wake her, Jeremy lay there with her in his arms. He was as hard as a rock, but at the same time, he couldn't remember being so relaxed and comfortable. The realization that this woman had crept further into his heart than he'd realized was a bit daunting.

But that still didn't mean she was going to get off that easily. Oh, no. He counted to a hundred before carefully rolling her over onto her back. Still asleep, she murmured softly when he gently spread her legs as he rose up over her. Watching her face, he positioned himself at her opening. And brushing a kiss across her slightly parted lips, he slid into her. Still warm and wet, her body welcomed him as she moaned in pleasure, her eyes slowly opening to find him smiling over her.

"My turn to be happy," he whispered as he kissed her deeply, his tongue delving into her mouth to dance with hers.

"My turn to make you happy," Madison sighed as she wrapped her legs around his waist as he plunged into her welcoming body.

Fully awake now, she swiftly took charge, shifting her weight and easily rolling him over so she could straddle him while still holding him deep inside her. His hands dropped to her waist, and smiling down at him, she began to move. Throwing her head back with a moan as his hands rose to cup her breasts, their bodies moved together in sync. Leaning back ever so slightly, she grabbed his legs as heat flowed through her, and she felt the familiar tremors beginning. Closing her eyes, she let the pleasure overtake her, and when Jeremy's hand moved to where their bodies were joined, slipping one finger into her moist heat, she screamed as she went over the edge. Her name on his lips, Jeremy followed willingly.

Regaining the use of his legs, not caring that he wore a goofy smile on his face, Jeremy made his way back to the kitchen, returning shortly thereafter with a fresh coffee for Madison.

"Remember what happened the last time you brought me coffee," Madison said with a mischievous smile, taking the mug from Jeremy.

This time, she didn't cover herself, letting the sheet pool around her waist. Jeremy's mouth watered, but he controlled himself—or tried to.

"Yeah," he said, quickly turning away. "So you have your coffee, I'm going to take a shower."

A very cold shower. Jesus, what was this woman doing to him? With her laughter following him, he disappeared into the bathroom.

Making herself comfortable, Madison pulled the sheet up and around her, sipping her coffee. Jesus, what was this man doing to her? Gazing at the closed door, she heard the shower turn on. It didn't take much to imagine the soapy water flowing down Jeremy's hard body, making her own body tingle.

Stop it, she told herself, *stop it!*

She had a job to do; she had to focus on that and not on this man who'd somehow managed to slip beyond all her defenses and into her heart. When had that happened? She wasn't sure. Shit, for all she knew, it'd happened the first night she'd met him at the restaurant. What the hell?

Leaning her head back against the headboard, she closed her eyes. Her lifestyle didn't allow her to have long-lasting relationships.

Admit it, though, she told herself, *you've never met anyone you wanted to have a long-lasting relationship with either.*

Could she make this work? Did she want to? Right this very instant, yes. Despite everything going on around her, she was happy, relaxed, and content. When had she ever been all three at once? *With a man anyway*, she thought, remembering some of the fun exploits she'd shared with Sarah and her brother. But they were family. This was different.

Maybe she should talk to Stan. He'd met his wife under extenuating circumstances, and they made it work. Yes, she decided, opening her eyes as she heard the shower turn off, she'd talk to Stan. She just hoped he wouldn't laugh too hard at her. Of course, she could kill him if he did. But Sarah probably wouldn't appreciate that; for sure, Amy wouldn't. Jones most likely wouldn't be happy either. Shit.

Finishing her coffee before Jeremy came out of the bathroom, she climbed out of bed, her sore body bringing a smile to her face. It was a good sore, one she could definitely live with! Grabbing her robe, she pulled it on, not wanting to face Jeremy naked again. Okay, that wasn't quite true. She did want to be naked with him again. Just not right now. She really needed to concentrate on work!

When Jeremy emerged from the steamy bathroom, a towel wrapped around his hips, her mouth watered. Shit. Silence fell over the room as they stared at each other. Had they known they were nearly thinking identical thoughts, they might have laughed. Instead, they just stared, the silence growing heavier. What felt like minutes, but was in reality only seconds later, Jeremy's eyes dropped as he moved to his closet.

"Shower's free," he said needlessly, turning his back to her as he searched for a shirt.

"Thanks," she murmured.

Finishing her coffee, she placed the mug on the bedside table before disappearing into the bathroom, closing the door softly behind her.

Only when he heard the door close did Jeremy turn around. What the hell was happening to him? He couldn't decide if he should laugh or moan in frustration. One thing he knew, though, the shirt he wanted wasn't in his closet; it was in a drawer! So why the hell was he in the closet? *Because, you fool, you're hiding from her.* Oh, for God's sake! He did laugh then, realizing he was acting like a love-struck teenager! Pulling the shirt he wanted from the drawer along with a clean pair of jeans, he dressed quickly, wanting to be out of the room before Madison finished with her shower. Images of her body covered in soap as water flowed over her were more than enticing, and grabbing Madison's empty coffee mug, Jeremy all but dashed out of the room.

Leaning against the railing on his back deck, Jeremy sipped his coffee, his breath mingling with the steam drifting up from the hot brew. Having spotted the elk tracks moments after stepping on to the deck, his eyes roamed along the tree line behind his house. Judging by the falling snow, the tracks were fairly fresh, and he contemplated donning his snowshoes to investigate but quickly changed his mind. Jones and Stan would be along soon. Jeremy loved snowshoeing, and when time allowed, he'd been known to disappear for hours into the woods. He didn't have time for that today. Too bad. He wondered if Madison had ever been snowshoeing and found the idea of taking her out appealing. Normally, he preferred going alone, but the idea of having her with him warmed him. He shook his head; what the hell was he thinking?

Finishing his coffee, he turned to head back inside when he heard a snort from somewhere behind him. Freezing in place, he counted to ten before ever so slowly turning back around to face the woods. His breath caught as his eyes fell on the elk standing just on the edge of the tree line.

"Oh my god," he whispered, his breath escaping into the cold air.

Standing majestically in the gently falling snow, the bull elk raised his nose up, snorting again. Frozen in place, Jeremy gazed at the magnificent animal standing proudly in all his glory. Then, without warning, the elk swung his head around, looking directly at Jeremy. A smile split his face as Jeremy caught sight of the stunted antlers on one side.

"Glad to see you, my old friend," Jeremy whispered.

Slowly so as to not spook the animal, Jeremy raised his mug in a salute.

Sensing that Jeremy posed no threat, the bull elk stared at him for another moment before raising his head again, letting out a call that cut straight through to Jeremy's soul. Powerless to move, Jeremy watched as a female slipped out from the trees, approaching the male. Standing side by side for a moment, the bull swung his head, his antlers cutting gracefully through the snow, before snorting again. The female, her ears darting back and forth, remained beside him.

"Introducing me to the Mrs., are you?" Jeremy said quietly, no longer worried about frightening off the animal.

When the bull dropped his head in what seemingly appeared to be a nod, Jeremy chuckled. Then swinging his head again, the bull gazed upon Jeremy once more. With a final snort, he turned, swiftly disappearing back into the woods, the female following him.

Amazed at how silently they'd appeared and disappeared, a sense of contentment rolled through Jeremy, and he took a deep breath, still staring off into the trees. Not hearing anything beyond the sound of the falling snow, Jeremy marveled again at the mysteries and complexities of nature. In a world where only the strong survived, a bull elk with a stunted set of antlers still proved powerful, still proved to be majestic, and still proved to be a survivor.

Jeremy's thoughts drifted back to Madison. To the differences between their lives. Turning around, he caught Madison watching him from the kitchen window. He smiled at her. And at that moment, he knew they'd be okay, that they'd find a way to make it work. And pushing away from the railing, he went back inside.

In the distance, an elk bugled—the sound one of strength, power, and confidence.

CHAPTER 29

WATCHING JEREMY FROM the warmth of the kitchen, Madison sipped her coffee, lost in thought. She'd seen the bull elk and the female and had been in total awe of them. But she was more taken by Jeremy's reaction to the animals. It was like he knew them, like they were old friends. She'd heard stories about people who lived in the wilderness and their sometimes-mysterious relationships with wild animals. She smiled, remembering the movie *Dances with Wolves*. Kevin Costner's character and his relationship with a lone wolf had fascinated her while the movie had entertained her. Blinking, her eyes met Jeremy's as he gazed at her through the window. Evidently, life really did imitate art—or, in this case, the other way around.

A rush of cold air hitting her chased away any remaining sleepy cobwebs as Jeremy came back inside, stomping his feet just inside the door.

"Morning again," Jeremy smiled, shrugging off his coat.

And he was caught totally by surprise when Madison launched herself at him, kissing him deeply, pushing herself away before he had time to wrap his arms around her. He stood there blinking, the taste of her coffee on his lips. Again, his body warmed. If she kept this up, they'd never get out of the house!

And that was bad how?

"Morning again," Madison said before clearing her throat. "Morning," she repeated more clearly.

Turning back to the coffee machine, she silently prepared a fresh mug of coffee for him, doctoring it just the way he liked it. When had she noticed how he took his coffee? Handing him the hot mug, she leaned back against the counter and just stared at the man. What the hell was happening here? When had she become Suzie Homemaker?

"Thank you," he said quietly, letting the coffee cool for a moment before raising it to his lips.

It was just the way he liked it. Nodding, she remained silent; her mind rattled as she struggled to put things into the proper perspective. She'd worked lots of jobs with men before; never had any of them affected her like Jeremy. It scared her. And warmed her too.

You're so screwed. And turning, she wandered into the living room, dropping onto the couch in front of the wood-burning stove. Drinking his coffee, Jeremy gave her a few seconds before he followed her. Sensing her confusion, he dropped into his favorite chair across from the couch; they needed a little space. Refusing to meet his eyes, Madison gazed out the window.

She was beautiful, sitting there with her legs gracefully crossed, wearing a heavy, black cable-knit sweater and a white turtleneck. Flannel lined jeans and heavy socks completed the outfit. Her long, dark hair was in its usual long braid and was draped over her shoulder. He wondered if Madison knew she played with the end of the braid when she was thinking, as she was doing now. He guessed now was probably not the time to point out that fact. She was, after all, a professional assassin. She'd probably killed people for less. He paused. When had it become so easy for him to accept who and what she was? And with so much ease that he could joke about it? Oh, shit.

You're so screwed.

Having a tough time fighting her feelings for him, Madison glanced quickly at Jeremy before her eyes darted away again. Did he have to sit there staring at her? As if he knew what she was feeling? She paused. Did he? Could he? She turned back to him, and their eyes finally met and held.

What the hell, she thought; they might as well get it out in the open now, before it got any worse.

"I like you a lot," she admitted ruefully. "I didn't want to, but I do."

"I'm falling in love with you." Oh, yeah, it just got worse. "I didn't want to, but I am."

Knowing he totally caught her off guard, Jeremy sat back quietly. He was just as surprised himself. But all well, the damage was done; there wasn't much he could do about it now. Except hope that she wouldn't up and leave him. Or kill him. Either one would be bad. When Madison remained silent, Jeremy shifted in his chair, wishing she'd say or do something.

"Sorry," he finally said, "I really didn't mean to blurt it out quite like that."

He was falling in love with her? Her? She killed people for a living! She traveled the world; she was never in one place for any length of time. She killed people for a living! And now, apparently, for the first time ever in her life, she was rendered totally speechless! Thank goodness, Stan and Jones weren't here to witness this! They'd never let her live it down! Suddenly, she sat up straight. Stan and Jones! Crap! They were on their way over!

"What is it?" Jeremy asked. "What's the matter?"

Looking a bit frantic, Madison pushed herself up off the couch.

"Stan and Jones are on their way over."

"Oh, shit."

"Yeah, oh, shit."

"What do we do?" Jumping up, a guilty look plastered on his face, Jeremy looked around as if expecting Stan and Jones to walk around the corner.

"You're asking me?"

"They're your friends!"

"Yeah, but it's not like they're my parents or anything!"

Suddenly realizing how ridiculous they sounded, they both burst out laughing.

"Well, this is different," Jones said as he and Stan stood in the doorway watching the two of them laughing uncontrollably. He glanced at Stan. "Have you ever seen such a thing?"

"Can't say that I have," he replied. "Who's that, and where's Madison?"

Realizing they had an audience, Madison and Jeremy struggled to stop laughing, turning to stare at Jones and Stan.

"And could they look any guiltier?"

"I don't think so," Jones said with a knowing smile.

Jeremy cleared his throat, while Madison attempted to squelch her laughter. But it was tough!

"How'd you guys get in?" she demanded, still not able to hide her smile. She turned to Jeremy, "How'd they get in? I didn't hear them knock!"

"We didn't knock," Jones said with a shrug.

Madison turned on Jeremy, "You left the door unlocked?"

Surprised by her accusation, Jeremy started to explain, but Jones beat him to it.

"Key," Jones simply said, holding it up to show Madison.

"Alarm code," Stan said, tapping his temple with his finger.

"Oh," Madison said quietly before turning back to Jeremy, "sorry."

Jeremy just nodded. He'd have reacted the same way.

"How long have you been standing there?" she asked, turning back to the men.

She prayed it hadn't been long. If it had been, that meant she was slipping. And a person in her line of work, slipping meant dying a whole lot faster. She shuddered at the thought, suddenly not wanting to question why.

Death was a way of life in their business; there was no getting around that grisly fact. Madison just chose to not dwell on the subject; truth be known, there wasn't anything she could do that would change the fact, anyway.

She didn't have a death wish, but suddenly, Madison realized she did have a reason to live. She stared at Jeremy as she tried to swallow the lump in her throat. Oh, shit! Did she love him too?

"We just got here," Jones said, interrupting Madison's thoughts as he sat on the couch. "Just in time to catch two fools laughing hysterically." He glanced at his phone. "I think I got a video," he glanced at Stan, "I should post this on Facebook, don't you think?"

"Absolutely," Stan said, trying not to chuckle.

But the look of stark fear on Madison's face was beyond priceless! And Jeremy, well, if he didn't shut his mouth soon, he was going to catch flies.

"Shut up! You did not!" Madison yelled, trying to grab Jones's phone, but he was faster, sliding the phone into his pocket and out of her reach. She turned to Stan, "He did not!"

Shrugging his shoulders, Stan wandered into the room, taking up point by the window, giving him a view of the front yard.

"I'm so going to smack you both!" Madison growled, turning back to Jeremy. "This is your fault!"

"Mine? When did this become my fault?" not prepared for her attack, Jeremy stared at her.

"If you hadn't told me . . ." Jeremy slapped his hand over her mouth, effectively silencing her.

She glared at him but stayed silent when he removed his hand. She really needed to get herself under control; she was acting like a silly schoolgirl! But damn it, she'd been thrown a curve she wasn't prepared for!

"Excuse me," she growled before dashing out of the room, desperately needing some space.

Seconds later, they heard footsteps retreating up the stairs.

Silence filled the room as the men stared after Madison. Without a word, Jeremy grabbed his coffee cup and quickly left the room. Hearing the coffee machine brewing, Stan and Jones knew him to be in the kitchen, evidently having decided not to follow Madison. Probably a wise idea.

"What just happened here?" Stan asked in wonder.

He'd never seen Madison this way before. It concerned him more than he wanted to admit. Pulling out his phone again, Jones shrugged his shoulders.

"I'm not entirely sure," Jones replied, swiftly typing a message into his phone.

Knowing he was texting Sarah, Stan glanced out the window. They had too much work to do for Madison to be going on a roller coaster ride with her emotions. And who knew she even had emotions!

"I've never seen Madison this way," Stan softly admitted.

"Me neither," Jones agreed.

"This could be bad."

"Very bad."

"What's our next move then?"

In their line of work, it wasn't unusual for plans to change on the spur of the moment. Granted, they tried their damnedest to avoid that, but it happened more often than not. Heaven forbid, anything go smoothly. That would certainly make things dull. Stan smiled to himself—*dull*, now there was a novel concept.

Jones's phone pinged, and glancing at it, he nodded. Sliding the phone back into his pocket, he stood up.

"Our next move is to get some coffee."

Nodding, Stan turned toward the kitchen, only to be stopped by Jones's hand on his chest.

"And to keep an eye on Jeremy. Most likely, he's having a time of it too."

Stan nodded but couldn't help rolling his eyes. They were assassins, not relationship counselors!

"I know," Jones agreed, his own thoughts mirroring Stan's.

"We don't get paid enough for this shit," Stan mumbled, following Jones into the kitchen.

"I dare you to ask for a raise."

"Fuck you."

"I should have known you'd call," Madison grumbled into the phone, not surprised when her phone had vibrated or at the name on the caller ID.

Normally, Madison looked forward to Sarah's calls; the woman changed her caller ID more than most changed their underwear. On any given day, Sarah changed her ID five or six times, depending on what was happening. But today Madison didn't find Sarah's caller ID humorous at all.

"Dr. Ruth? You couldn't come up with something better than that? The woman's a sex therapist, for God's sake!"

"So your sex life isn't the problem?"

Madison nearly ground her teeth in annoyance.

"Then what is the problem? Maybe you need Dr. Phil?"

"I'm going to fucking kill you," Madison growled, hating that Sarah was hitting so close to home.

"Get in line."

Sarah's icy tone stopped Madison in her tracks, making her sit up and remember who she was talking to—and remembering the number of times someone had actually tried to kill Sarah.

"I'm sorry," Madison quickly apologized, physically sitting up straighter in her chair.

Needing a moment to think, she'd made a beeline for upstairs, ending up in the bedroom of all places. Sure, just hide in the room where the reason she needed to think was all around her that much more!

You're so screwed, Madison thought, closing her eyes in frustration.

"Who called you?" she finally asked.

"Jones texted me," Sarah replied, her voice softer. "But I knew before he called."

Not surprised, Madison didn't question Sarah and her ability to know things. She just did, and that's all there was to it.

"If it weren't for the damn weather, I'd already be on my way, you know that, don't you?"

"Yes," Madison said and was shocked to hear the tremor in her voice.

Oh my god, I am not going to cry! Wiping her hand across her eyes, Madison swallowed the tears that threatened.

"What the hell is happening to me?" she blurted. "This is ridiculous! I've gotta stop this emotional shit!" But she knew it was easier said than done.

"It's okay," Sarah said gently, wishing she could be there to comfort Madison and cursing the weather every which way. "I know you hate admitting you care. But trust me, it really does get easier."

When Madison's parents had been murdered, Sarah had been there to comfort Madison, saying much of the same thing. Knowing Sarah was right, yet again, Madison took a deep, cleansing breath.

And then told Sarah everything about Jeremy, about their budding relationship, how he made her happy, how they laughed, everything. And ended with telling Sarah about Jeremy's declaration that he was falling in love with her and that maybe she loved him too!

Sarah listened patiently as Madison poured out her heart in a rare show of emotion and vulnerability. Sarah wasn't totally surprised. It was bound to happen eventually. Madison was a beautiful woman, a desirable woman. The fact that she'd managed to keep other men at arm's length for this long only proved that Madison was also very cautious and even more careful with her heart. She'd had short relationships; she'd had men in her life. But none of them had meant anything to her, and she'd left them behind without a second glance.

What was interesting to Sarah now was that Madison had only just met Jeremy, but already they had a connection stronger than any Madison had ever had before with anyone. No doubt the extenuating circumstances under which they'd met only enhanced that connection. Yes, it was all very interesting.

Moments later, coming to end of what she hoped wasn't an epic drama, Madison sighed. And admitted she did feel remarkably better.

"So there it is," Madison said in conclusion.

"Madison," Sarah chuckled, "you are so totally screwed, my friend."

"I was afraid you'd say that," Madison confessed with a small smile. "Yeah, I'm doomed."

Downstairs, Stan and Jones cornered Jeremy in the kitchen. Expecting nothing less, he appreciated them giving him a couple of minutes to sort things out first. Jeremy knew admitting his feelings to Madison would surprise her; he just hadn't realized how much. And was that a good thing or a bad thing? Granted, they hadn't known each other very long, but he trusted his gut; he always had. And so far, it had worked out pretty well for him. He just prayed that his luck would hold out this time.

But one look at their stoic faces had Jeremy convinced that his luck had just run out. Shit.

Determined to play it easy, Jeremy offered the men coffee. Accepting it, silence filled the room as the men went about doctoring their coffee. Leaning against the counter, Jeremy waited. If Stan and Jones wanted to know something, they were going to have to ask; he wasn't about to volunteer any information. Not yet anyway. And not about this. This was personal. He'd tell them anything they wanted to know about Stillman; that was business. But he and Madison, that was a totally different subject altogether.

"Personal or not, we need to know."

"What?" Jeremy turned in surprise at Stan's blunt statement. "How'd you know . . . ?"

"Because the bastard has a very annoying gift," Madison said from the doorway.

All eyes turned to watch as she waltzed into the room. Stopping in front of Jeremy, she gave him a dazzling smile before pulling his head down for a quick, searing kiss.

"And he knows I live to piss him off every chance I get," she whispered as she pulled back slowly. Turning to face Stan and Jones, she smiled saucily at the stunned look on their faces. "Lighten up, boys!" She smiled, linking her arm through Jeremy's. "He and I are a thing, and you're just going to have to deal with it."

She gazed up at Jeremy and nearly burst out laughing. He looked as stunned as the others. Good! She wasn't going to be the only one whose emotions were on a fucking roller coaster! She was going to take all of them with her on this ride!

Slowly pushing away from Jeremy, she leaned against the kitchen counter, turning her attention on Jones.

"Sarah said you have information for me? Let's have it."

And with that statement, they were back to work, Jones thought with great relief.

"That I do," Jones began, his gaze encompassing all of them. "Buckle up, everyone, I got the latest intel from Sarah. And you're not gonna believe this one!"

CHAPTER 30

"I KILLED STILLMAN'S brother?" Well, wasn't this just an interesting turn of events! "Are you sure?"

Jones nodded. He'd been just as surprised as she was to learn these new facts. But knowing Sarah was very thorough, he didn't doubt the information and knew Madison's question was rhetorical. The intel was good.

"And just when was I supposed to have done this?" Madison asked, giving Jones that "because, you know, I've killed so many people" look. "Can you be a little more specific?"

Jones swallowed. Here's where it was going to get complicated—as if it wasn't already complicated enough!

"Evidently, while he was in police custody and was being taken to the courthouse . . ." Jones began.

And watching Madison's eyes widen, he immediately knew she remembered the job and knew exactly who Jones was describing. Holy shit!

"Well, this certainly explains a few things then, doesn't it," Madison said nonchalantly when Jones finished sharing this new information.

Well, at least, now they knew. And now she could focus on developing a new strategy.

Good then, she thought, taking a deep breath.

And catching Jeremy's perplexed look, she turned to him, "What?"

"You find out you killed his brother, and all you can say is, 'this explains a few things'?"

What the hell? His mind whirled as Jeremy struggled with this new knowledge.

"You killed his brother!"

How would he feel if one of his siblings was killed? He'd want justice, to be sure. Revenge wouldn't hurt either.

Understanding Jeremy's gut reaction, Madison considered her next words carefully. This was the moment she'd been dreading—when Jeremy truly realized just what she did for a living. Her eyes slowly rose to his. Would he run swift and fast in the other direction now? Could she blame him? But this was what she did. And it wasn't something she was going to apologize for—not now, not ever. And he needed to understand that. She took a deep breath.

"I know what you're thinking," she began softly.

"I sincerely doubt it," he snapped, interrupting her. "How could you?"

She killed for a living; he knew that. But now the truth of it was in his face. There was no more pushing the knowledge away. He had to face it . . . and figure out what to do with it. As he turned away, her words stopped him.

"You're thinking that if one of your brothers or sisters were killed, that you'd want revenge. Justice, at the very least. I get that. And in that respect, you're thinking Stillman has a valid reason for wanting me dead."

Her cold words cut through him. When she put it like that . . . Jeremy didn't want her dead, though! Just the opposite! He turned back to her.

"I know that feeling too, of wanting revenge."

He cocked an eyebrow at her. *Really?*

She glared at him but swallowed her anger at his doubting her. "Yes, really."

"And you know this how?" the words were out before he could stop himself.

"Because my parents were murdered, that's how."

Before Jeremy could react, Madison nailed home her point.

"And we now know Stillman's brother was the one who killed them."

Silence filled the room.

"I can't help the fact that they're one in the same. But I killed him because I was hired to. The fact that I got some revenge out of the deal was nothing more than a well-deserved bonus."

Jeremy was speechless. His eyes jumped from Madison, to Stan, to Jones, before coming back to Madison. He gave her credit; she didn't back down from his stare, holding his gaze with bright, clear eyes. Jeremy didn't doubt for a minute that her conscience was clear. He swallowed hard, not quite sure what to think or how to feel about that.

"I'm sorry to drop this on you like that," Madison finally said, knowing Jeremy was having a difficult time processing it all.

Sadness flowed through her. If they'd never met, if they hadn't become involved, Jeremy never would have been the wiser. There wouldn't have been a need. Instead, he was knee-deep in the middle of this mess that she'd unknowingly caused.

"I was just doing my job," she said quietly. "And this is a consequence of that job."

Could it really be that simple? She certainly made it seem so. But it wasn't, not to him. As she'd said, she was just doing her job; Jeremy understood that. And he hated that he did. But now her job had brought trouble to his town. And possibly to his family. He needed time to think this one through. And he hoped he could.

"I need some air," and turning, Jeremy left the room.

Moments later, they heard the back door open and close.

"Well, that went well," Stan said from his place beside the window.

"Shut up," Madison and Jones said in unison.

The cold air working its magic, Jeremy's mind cleared, allowing him to work through some details of his own. It didn't take him long to come to his own conclusions and he quickly rushed back inside to tell the others.

Gathered around the coffee table in the living room, their heads together, they all looked up as Jeremy burst into the room.

"We've got Stillman's real name!" Jeremy exclaimed, stopping to pull off his hat and gloves.

Ignoring Stan and Jones, Jeremy focused on Madison. Confident in his thinking he quickly rushed on. "It's right in front of us!" Everyone stared at him. "Follow me here, you start with getting a contract to kill someone," he paused for dramatic effect, nearly laughing at himself. He sounded like he was discussing the weather or something! "You must get the name of the target, right?" Suddenly realizing where Jeremy was going with this, Madison nodded slowly.

"Stillman is an alias," Stan interjected, earning an "I know that!" look from Jeremy.

Stan smiled; he was beginning to like this guy!

"But who's to say the name of the guy who . . ." Jeremy paused, his eyes softening as they touched on Madison, "who killed your parents . . . was an alias?"

"Most likely, it wasn't," Madison mused with a smile. "He wasn't that smart, if I remember correctly."

Her smile grew and glancing at Stan and Jones, Madison immediately knew they were on the same page.

"Most likely, he was going by his real name."

She rose gracefully, and gently cupping Jeremy's still-cold face, Madison pulled his head down, kissing him lightly.

"Good thinking there, Sherlock!"

"You'll be part of the team before you know it," Jones smiled.

"Whether you like it or not," Stan added as Jeremy smiled grimly.

While admittedly, he still hadn't gotten his head wrapped around all this, knowing he'd contributed a little made Jeremy feel a bit better.

"You helped a lot," Stan said quietly, ignoring the embarrassment on Jeremy's face.

While they would have eventually come to the same conclusion, the fact that Jeremy had done so—and so quickly—was a telling sign. Stan was impressed. And very pleased. He knew a team member when he saw one. He was relieved Jeremy was that team player now. It would help later.

"You realize this nearly changes things altogether," Madison said.

"What, the guy isn't going to die?" Stan and Jones asked in surprise.

"Oh, no," Madison gave them an evil smile. "Stillman's going to die. And painfully so."

Both men nodded in agreement while Jeremy struggled to keep his mouth from falling open. Should he even be listening to this conversation? Holy shit, what was happening here?

"Relax, Jeremy," Jones assured him, "it's okay. You're not an accomplice to anything here, we're just talking. Casual conversation."

"Casual?" Jeremy let out a sarcastic laugh. "Right."

"It's not like we're plotting his death or anything," Stan said with a devilish smile.

Jeremy stared at him.

"Trust me, you'll know when we are."

That was precisely what worried him.

"If you guys don't need me, I've got work to do," Jeremy said hurriedly, suddenly needing to quickly distance himself from the group.

Before he heard things, he'd be better off not hearing—for now, anyway.

Rising from her seat, Madison followed him out, staying silent while he pulled on his jacket, hat, and his boots and gloves. Knowing he was going out to plow, she agreed with his decision; given what he'd just learned, she understood his need to do something completely normal. She knew his life had just been totally turned upside down and that he was having a tough time digesting all he'd just learned. She could only imagine the thoughts rambling through that mind of his right now.

"I'm sorry for everything that you've just had dumped on you. I can't even imagine what you must be thinking," Madison said with a deep sigh. "I'll bet you're wishing you'd never laid eyes on me now," she said, trying to interject a little humor and failing miserably.

Standing up straight, Jeremy stared into her eyes that sparkled like sapphires and shook his head. Gathering her into his arms, he buried his face in her hair.

"You couldn't be more wrong," he whispered, his warm breath tickling her ear. "But we do need to talk alone."

She nodded against him.

"When I get back, okay?"

Again she nodded, stepping back from him.

"You know," she began, "you really did impress the guys back there." She paused. "I was really proud of you," she whispered, feeling her face grow warm.

On one hand, Jeremy was doing all he could to keep what was happening at arm's length, but he'd just proven that he wasn't afraid to step up to the plate when necessary either. Her heart warmed, knowing she could trust him. She could count on one hand the number of people she trusted.

"Thanks," he murmured. "They would have figured it out, I'm sure."

"Absolutely," Madison agreed, she wasn't about to sugarcoat it. "But you got there first."

"I never was one for standing in line when I could get somewhere first," Jeremy said with a smile.

And pulling her to him, he kissed her hard and swiftly. When she opened her eyes, he was gone. With a happy smile, Madison returned to the living room.

"Don't you just look happy," Stan said with a grin.

"Shut up," Madison laughed, not bothering to deny it, before quickly sobering. "We've got work to do."

And she had a plan in mind.

CHAPTER 31

RETURNING A FEW hours later, Jeremy found Madison curled up on the couch, sound asleep. Tired himself from all the plowing he'd just done, the idea of joining her was more than enticing, and he started peeling off his clothes. He'd just pulled off his jeans when Madison mumbled softly and, rolling over, promptly fell off the couch, landing hard on the floor.

"What the . . . ?" she groaned, opening her eyes and finding herself on the floor.

And where was the laughter coming from? Slowly rolling over, Madison spotted Jeremy standing a few feet away in his long underwear and thermal shirt. And he was laughing at her!

"How long have you been standing there?" she demanded, pushing herself up and into a sitting position.

"Long enough," Jeremy laughed, offering a hand and pulling her to her feet. "I found you asleep and was just about to join you when you hit the floor."

And laughing harder, he pulled her down beside him on the couch, wrapping an arm around her. When she tucked her legs up underneath her and all but snuggled up next to him, Jeremy nearly sighed in happiness.

It didn't get any better than this, he thought, closing his eyes, holding her close.

They sat in silence for a few minutes, Madison slowly waking up and Jeremy slowly falling asleep. Debating on whether to let him drift off or wake him up, Madison opted for the latter, hating to but knowing they needed to talk. Leaning back a fraction and glancing at his face, she paused. His eyes were closed, his breathing regular. He was sound asleep. And would be snoring any minute now, judging by the way his head was leaning back against the couch. That was reason enough to wake him up, she thought with a smile. But knowing he'd been working, she decided to give him a reprieve, just this once.

When he started snoring like a banshee a few minutes later, Madison knew his reprieve was over, and gently nudging him in the ribs, she slowly woke him up. Moments later, sitting up straight, Jeremy surprised her by being nearly wide awake. Unlike herself, evidently, he woke up easily and, to her surprise, ready to go. Not her—waking up was one thing she did very slowly! She smiled.

"Feeling better?" Madison couldn't resist asking, amazed at how alert he seemed to be.

He nodded.

"That's all I needed, just a couple of minutes to recharge," he said, pushing himself up off the couch before disappearing into the kitchen.

Returning a moment later, he handed Madison a bottle of water while he drank from an orange juice container. Choosing to ignore the "guy thing," Madison sipped her water.

"When did the guys leave?" Jeremy asked, dropping back down beside her.

"Not too long after you left, actually."

Sipping her water, she watched him out of the corner of her eye.

"We made a few plans," she said softly.

When Jeremy just nodded, Madison sensed that he really didn't want to know much more. And for now, as far as she was concerned, he really didn't need to know, anyway. She was content to leave it alone for now.

Jeremy didn't need to know that Jones was contacting Sarah, that they were working their way backward in hopes of finding out

Stillman's real name, and that Stan was going to contact Ellen, her part in this whole thing also changing. Knowing this was a personal vendetta against Madison and not an actual contract, Ellen might opt out. Just another reason they always had a backup plan—a few of them, in fact. It was a necessity in their line of work. Not having a backup plan was a surefire way to end a career that much faster.

"Today's been a day of surprises, I don't mind saying," Jeremy said a few minutes later.

Madison could only nod, not sure whether Jeremy was ready to talk or not. Letting him take the lead, she remained silent.

"So you were hired to kill Stillman's brother." It wasn't a question.

"Yes."

"So it wasn't a revenge killing."

"No, I told you that already. When I was hired, I had no clue who he was. I only found out later, while I was planning out the job."

"It's hard swallowing all this," Jeremy admitted. "Only because of my dealings with Jones did I know about . . . you . . . Well, not you specifically, but . . ."

"I get it," Madison said with a smile.

"Yeah, well, anyway, trying to reconcile what you do with knowing you the way I do," Jeremy paused, looking down at her, "it's hard to put the two together."

Understanding, Madison just nodded.

"You aren't going to kill me in my sleep, are you?"

The question was out before he could stop it, and Jeremy threw a sheepish grin at Madison and was relieved when she smiled up at him.

"If I kill you in your sleep, it'll only be because the sex was that good."

Laughing, she pushed herself up off the couch and headed for the kitchen.

"Gotcha worried now, do I?" she laughed, tossing him a quick glance before disappearing into the kitchen.

Worried wasn't quite how he'd describe it; he thought with a wolfish grin, before he quickly followed her into the kitchen. Finding Madison making hot chocolate, he stood in the doorway, watching her. Nothing screamed domestic like making hot chocolate. When she pressed a hot mug into his hands, he smiled, knowing she'd kill him where he stood if he said that out loud. And that was not how he planned on dying! Especially when there was a nice, big, comfy bed upstairs! At that very moment, he couldn't think of a better way to go! And taking a sip of the hot chocolate, Jeremy forced his body to calm down. There'd be time enough for that later. Not dying, of course. No, he had no intentions of that happening anytime soon. But that didn't mean they couldn't spend the rest of their lives practicing!

Suddenly realizing he was thinking about the future, he quickly sobered, gazing at Madison over his steaming mug. Holy shit! He'd just jumped from thinking he was in love with her to living happily ever after with her! *Slow down, man!*

Taking another sip, he did have to admit—she made a killer mug of hot chocolate. And he was right back where he started. Shit.

Watching him, Madison knew the questions would be coming, and she hoped she was ready for them. She'd never been in this position before; she'd never had to explain herself to anyone. She hoped she could do it. Sliding onto a kitchen stool, she crossed her legs gracefully, balancing her mug on her knee as she gazed at him. Waiting. It didn't take long.

"Have you been doing this all your life?" Jeremy finally asked, and Madison caught the hesitation in his voice.

"Doing what?" she asked.

She needed him to actually say it. He had to say the words. He knew it too. He was just having a tough time getting the words out. He needed to treat this delicately, if that was at all possible. But he had to try.

"Have you been . . ." he paused, searching for the right words, "a professional assassin long?"

There, it was out. Sure, he'd referred to her that way when he'd first found out about her. But now . . . now it was different.

"Yes, most of my life." Her eyes dropped for a moment. Taking a deep breath, her eyes came back to his. "I am a professional assassin," before quickly adding, "and a damn good one."

Was it his imagination, or did he hear pride in her voice?

"And being what I am, there's a very important fact you need to know and understand."

His raised eyebrows urged her to continue.

"I am not—and I repeat, not—a coldblooded killer."

Okay, Jeremy thought, he hadn't been expecting that! And found himself intrigued as he waited for her to explain.

"Stillman is a coldblooded killer," Madison stated bluntly. "I am not."

Sliding off the stool, Madison faced Jeremy, glad, at least, that she'd gotten that out. She'd never considered herself a coldblooded killer, never. She was cold, yes. Methodical, yes. Deliberate, very much so. Calculating and efficient, yes! Those were all skills necessary to keep her alive! But she also had a heart, and a big one. She'd never killed needlessly. Ever. Sure, the thought might have crossed her mind; she'd be lying if she said otherwise. But she'd never acted on it. And she knew she never would.

Jeremy's face remained expressionless as he listened to Madison as she explained herself as best she could. He knew she was saying things she'd never said to anyone before. He heard her words, knew they were sincere. But at the same time, he found himself feeling as if she'd slapped him across the face with the reality of her life and what she did. For a moment, he didn't recognize the woman standing proudly in front of him. How had he managed to ignore all this before?

Because he'd met and fallen in love with a woman who'd been stranded here by a snowstorm. A smart, highly skilled woman who, he knew from the beginning, had a colorful background that rivaled his own. A woman he could talk to, who was as close to his equal as any woman he'd ever met. It was easy to gloss over her true profession; he hadn't needed to examine it that closely. Until now.

She truly was a hired gun! Holy shit. And if it hadn't been for the snowstorm, she would have just flown up into the mountains, done what she was supposed to do, and then disappear again. He never would have met her, never would have known her. Never would have laughed with her. And he never would have felt her soft body next

301

to his, to know what it was like to be buried inside her warmth. To hold her close, her body draped over his. And he wouldn't have ever known she was nothing more than a hired gun. But she was more than a hired gun. Much more. And he knew it. He smiled.

Not wanting to look away, Madison held Jeremy's questioning gaze with her determined one. Would he accept her, accept what she was? She didn't expect him to understand her—not right away, anyway. But she prayed he'd accept her. And if he didn't? She idly thought about the overnight bag upstairs. She could be out the door within minutes and never look back. It wouldn't be the first time she'd made such a quick exit. But it would be the first one that hurt.

She didn't want to leave. Her breath caught as the realization hit her. She wanted to stay. Here. With Jeremy. Good Lord, what had happened to her? She'd fallen in love! Fuck!

When Jeremy smiled at her, Madison's heart skipped a beat. Now she just needed to know if it was a good smile or a doomed smile. Her head tilted to the side as she considered his smile, watching it grow. It didn't look like a doomed smile; in fact, he almost looked . . . happy! Moving swiftly, Jeremy surprised Madison, grabbing her and pulling her to him. Wrapping her in his arms, he kissed her deeply—the love he felt for her flowing through him and into her.

Losing herself in the kiss, Madison clung to Jeremy. Okay, so it had been a good smile!

"Wow, it's true that makeup sex is the best!" Madison said from under the covers, her bare leg draped over Jeremy's bare leg.

"Honey, that wasn't makeup sex."

"What?"

"That was 'I know what you do and I like it' sex!"

And with a laugh, Jeremy pulled Madison under him.

"And since you didn't recognized it the first time, I guess I'm just going to have to show you again!"

"Guess you'll have to do that!" Madison said, opening her legs and welcoming him back into her warm body. "It might take a few times for me to get it, though. You good with that?"

Jeremy sighed deeply as he plunged into her. Wrapping her legs around him as her body rose to meet his, Madison giggled.

"Guess you are."

The events of the last few days rolling around in his mind, Jeremy shoveled the snow from his walkway. Sure he could have dragged out his snow blower, but he needed the physical exertion brought on by shoveling. Considering the fact that he'd gotten very little sleep last night—no thanks to Madison, he thought with a smile—he was amazed he could even lift the shovel! He laughed out loud. What a night it'd been.

In between making love, she'd told him more about her life; and in turn, he'd told her more about his. Glossing over the classified work he'd done with the RCMPs, he'd told Madison about his years spent chasing the "bad guys," as his mother liked to put it. Of course, he'd never been able to tell his mother—or his family—that while he mostly focused on blue-collar crimes, he'd spent a fair amount of time tracking major terrorists as well.

Jeremy smiled. It was nice being able to share that detail with Madison, though. She understood and accepted it. But what she hadn't accepted was the fact that he couldn't tell her how he'd met Jones. Of course, it'd been on a job; but when, where, and how, Jeremy was sworn to absolute secrecy. No matter what. And valuing his life, he wasn't about to tell. Not even Madison.

She'd rolled over in a huff before thinking she might be able to torture the information out of him. And rolling back over she immediately went to work with her hands and mouth.

Jeremy stopped shoveling, laughing out loud at the memory. And how it'd backfired on her. When he'd finished with her, she had barely even known her own name! Of course, he wasn't much better off himself. His laughter grew louder.

"What are you laughing at, you fool?"

Turning, Jeremy spotted Madison standing in the doorway, wrapped in his robe. Her long hair hung loosely around her, and remembering its sleek and soft texture as he ran his hands through it, his body began to warm. Deciding he'd shoveled enough, he planted the shovel in the snow and headed for the door.

Backing away to allow him entrance, Madison planted a quick, warm kiss full of promise on his wet and cold cheek. That simple action had Jeremy pausing, and he stared, unblinking, at Madison. And suddenly, with that one simple action, he knew: he loved her.

Thankful she'd gotten dressed, Jeremy leaned against the kitchen counter; while Madison sat eating her breakfast—he glanced at the clock—at nearly one in the afternoon. Yeah, she definitely wasn't a morning person. He wondered how her job affected her sleep schedule.

"I do my work in the afternoons."

Madison chuckled at the look of surprise on Jeremy's face. He hadn't realized he'd spoken out loud.

"Really?" He nearly slapped himself at the stupidity of the question.

Her "duh" look on her face told him she'd nearly done the same.

"Actually," she admitted moments later, "I rarely sleep when I'm working. Not until the job is finished."

He nodded, admitting he worked the same when on various jobs. Silence filled the room as they gazed at each other. They had so much in common, yet they were so very different. She killed people for a living. He'd killed a few himself. She was paid to do it. His country thanked him for doing it.

"Seems weird to be discussing our . . . careers . . . like normal people," Jeremy said.

"I'm sorry, are you implying we're *not* normal people?" Madison laughed.

"Not in the least!"

"Thank God!" Madison rose, putting her plate in the sink before hip bumping Jeremy. "Because I'd hate to be normal! It's so overrated, don't you think?"

Oh, yeah, he loved her.

"I was thinking . . ." Standing next to Jeremy, gazing out the window, Madison wondered if she'd ever see the elk again. She hoped so. She glanced at Jeremy; he was staring at the kitchen wall.

"What?" he mumbled, suddenly seeming preoccupied.

"That maybe we should just run away with each other."

That had his head snapping around, his eyes bulging.

"What?"

"That'll teach you to not pay attention." Madison smacked him on the arm.

The words had slipped out before she could stop herself, and she wasn't about to repeat them. That would mean she'd actually had the thought. And she hadn't. That was her story, and she was sticking to it!

"Sorry," Jeremy said quickly, turning around.

"What were you thinking?"

"I was thinking that you were seriously focused on something else."

"What?"

Jeremy's sheepish grin had her slapping him again. "What?"

"You really want to know?"

"Yes!" She did! She sucked in her breath. Didn't she?

"I was thinking that I really need to paint the kitchen walls."

Madison stared at him. Was he serious? With everything that was going on, he was thinking about painting? She swung around to stare at the kitchen wall. She tilted her head to the side. Then turning back around, she smiled.

"It could use a little sprucing up, I guess," Madison admitted. "Are you thinking the same color or something new?"

Oh, yeah, he seriously loved her!

CHAPTER 32

THE SNOW WAS finally beginning to lighten up, the sky slowly clearing. In the distance, rays of sunshine burst through the clouds, a welcome sign that the storm was nearing the end of its reign over the town.

Relieved more than he cared to admit, Jones turned back to face the others. Once again settled in Jeremy's living room, he knew they'd all had enough of the snow. Well, except maybe Jeremy. No doubt he was used to it, living through it every winter.

Huddled on the couch with Madison, Jeremy casually draped his arm over her shoulders while Madison read through the paperwork containing information on the job involving Stillman's brother. Having handed her the folder as soon as he'd walked through the door, Jones let his gaze rest on Madison for a moment while she read it before his eyes moved to Stan. Neither man could remember Madison ever being this comfortable around any man before, especially when they were around. Fighting his concern that she was losing her focus, Jones turned away, not wanting the others to see his frustration.

Stan didn't need to see it; he could feel the waves of frustration rolling off of Jones. It didn't take a clairvoyant to know Jones was worried. He was as well. But as long as Madison was reading the paperwork, Stan was going to stay out of her mind. She didn't need any more distractions.

Minutes later, when her eyes rose, he let out the breath he hadn't realized he'd been holding. Her steely, cold eyes caught and held his, and Stan instantly knew that not only was she completely focused but that she was ready to put their plan in action. Relief flowed through him, and mentally pulling Jones's attention back to him, Stan nodded to his partner. It was going to be all right.

Tucking the paperwork back into its folder, Madison handed it to Jeremy, having already committed it to memory. While much of what she'd just read she'd already known, Sarah had been able to provide some new and, as always, interesting information.

Flipping open the folder, Jeremy took his time reading, not wanting to miss any detail, no matter how small. Here was another window into Madison's world. If he was ever going to totally understand and come to grips with who and what she was, it was imperative that he look carefully and thoroughly through that window now.

Jeremy already knew from Madison that Sarah contacted her with jobs that needed to be done. Madison was given the information she needed and was then left her to her own devices to plan and execute the job the way she saw fit. Madison never knew who the client was, only the target.

Well, that certainly brought a new meaning to confidentiality, Jeremy thought, his eyes narrowing as he continued reading the file. In this case, it was clearly evident why not knowing the client was a good thing, and his eyes rose to Madison's. She just nodded.

Rarely did Madison ever have the need to question who the client was; rarely did she care. Sarah took care of all the details; that was her job. And Sarah protected the client's identity as well as Madison's. It was better all-around that way. But in this particular case, even without divulging the client's actual name, Madison had a pretty good idea who it was who'd hired her to kill Stillman's brother—or at least the organization. And while she normally didn't accept jobs with ties to organized crime, sometimes when the mob called . . . well, you answered.

Finishing his reading, Jeremy tossed the folder onto the coffee table as he put the pieces of what he'd just read all together in his mind. He pushed himself off the couch, needing to walk and talk off what he'd just learned. While working with the RCMPs, talking out complicated cases with his team had been imperative. It was just as imperative for him here and now as well. His gaze encompassed the group before settling back on the folder.

"Okay, let's talk this through," Stan announced, ignoring the glare Jeremy tossed him.

The snow stopping and Stillman's ever-increasing anger and frustration were causing their window of time to become that much more limited. They needed to finalize their plan and put it in action. And soon. There was no time to waste now.

"What do we know so far . . ."

According to the file, Stillman's brother had been heavily involved with the mob. But his drinking problem proved his downfall when, having had too much to drink, the man had opened his mouth to an undercover agent resulting in the death of a legitimately innocent young woman.

"Legitimately?" Jeremy asked. Was there such a thing where the mob was concerned?

Evidently. According to the file, the young woman—while related to a major mob figure—had long ago separated and distanced herself from the family and had been living a nice, quiet life away from all of them. The young woman's mistake had been to come back to visit another relative. Finding herself seriously in the wrong place at the wrong time, she'd been caught in the middle of a firestorm. The young woman, along with her relative, was killed.

Unfortunately, it wasn't an uncommon occurrence, Jeremy admitted, having dealt with similar scenarios himself with the RCMPs. Like they had, the agents got whom they were after; but because Stillman's brother couldn't handle his liquor, two innocent people had also died.

And it only got worse from there for Stillman's brother. It seemed the innocent young woman was also the daughter of the godfather's right-hand man. One did not live long after screwing one of your own, especially someone that important.

"Hmmm. So it was a revenge killing," Jeremy pondered briefly. "Just not yours."

"You could put it that way. I sorta killed two birds with one stone," Madison said with an evil smile, "or rather, one bullet."

"Now that we know the why exactly, we need to decide on the how," Stan said, glancing at Jones and Madison. "I don't know about you two, but I've got a good idea."

Madison had an idea of her own and was surprised when Stan nodded at her. Good grief, couldn't he stay out of her mind just once?

"No," Stan said before continuing, "because I like your idea better."

All eyes on her, Madison quickly pulled her thoughts together before outlining her plan. The first thing, she wasn't going to tell Stillman what she knew; it wouldn't matter anyway. She was sure he'd never listen to her—not at this stage of the game anyway. The man was on a one-way track; the only thing that was going to stop him now was his own death.

Good thing that could be arranged.

Finally! The snow was winding down! They'd finally be getting out of this godforsaken place! Frank thought as he watched the weather channel. He'd had enough of this town and its people. He needed to get out of here! Right after he killed Madison.

Looking up when Ellen walked in, Frank told her about the pending forecast and his hopes of them being able to leave soon. Relief filled Ellen; she too was ready to get out of town! The first thing she was going to do when she returned home was to book a trip to the warmest and sunniest place on the face of the earth. If she never saw snow again, it'd be too soon.

"Wonderful!" Ellen exclaimed and was rewarded with a smirk from Frank.

He knew she wanted to be out of there as much as he did, if not for different reasons. Putting down the magazines she'd brought up from the front desk, she turned back to the door.

"Where are you going?" Frank demanded. "We have plans to make!"

Freezing in place, Ellen counted to ten before slowly turning around.

"I'm going to see if I can find the tour guide. I'm sure he's seen the weather too, maybe he can tell us exactly when we'll be leaving."

She glared at Frank, wishing she could just kill him here and now. The feeling was becoming harder to ignore.

"I would think the more details you have, the better you can work out your plan." She paused, struggling to keep the disdain out of her voice and knowing that she was failing miserably. "But I could be wrong."

Longing to slap the smug look off her face, Frank clenched his fists. Damn, if she wasn't right! Damn, he needed to pull himself together!

"Of course, you're right," he acknowledged as gracefully as he was able.

Knowing what that cost him, Ellen just nodded; and before he could say anything else, she left the room. Spinning around to the window, Frank took great gulps of air. The relief that he felt knowing they'd be leaving soon was nearly overwhelming. But he had more important things to concentrate on now.

He had what he thought was a perfect plan to kill Madison—one that would point the finger at someone other than himself as well. While he wasn't sure how she'd figured it out, Frank suspected that Madison knew she was a target. But he still had the advantage; she didn't know why, and she didn't know what he was capable of doing. Well, she might know that—especially if she suspected that he'd been the one to kill the man in the alley. He shook off that worry; it wouldn't matter in the scheme of things. He glanced out the window; it was still snowing lightly. Once he knew what the group's departure plan was, he'd be able to put his own plan into action.

Filling her coffee mug, Ellen moved over to stand beside the fireplace. One thing she'd noticed during their stay there, the fire had been burning cheerfully every day. They burned real wood in the living room. None of that gas fireplace stuff here, Ethel had said proudly.

"Relaxing, isn't it?" Coming to stand beside her, the tall man gazed into the fire.

"Yes, very," Ellen said, surprised to admit that she meant it.

The blazing fireplace really was cheerful. Oh, yeah, she'd been here too long! She turned to the man.

"I understand the group will be leaving the day after tomorrow," she said casually, sipping her coffee.

"I'd heard the same," the man answered, enjoying his own coffee as his gaze drifted over the others congregating in the room. "I know everyone will be relieved."

"Some more than others, as I'm sure you can imagine," Ellen smiled into her coffee mug.

The man nodded.

"Will you be going out on the same day?"

The man shook his head.

Wishing she could ask him his plans, she knew he'd never tell her. And it was probably wise she didn't know.

"Well, I'm ready to go, that's for sure. All I have to do is close my suitcase, and I'm ready!"

"Good to know," the man said, finishing his coffee, and with a final nod and a wish for her to have a nice evening, the man strolled away.

Gazing into the fire for a moment, Ellen remembered something she'd meant to ask the man. Turning, she searched the room for him, but he was gone. Damn.

"Looking for your husband?" the tour guide asked as he joined Ellen beside the fireplace.

Trying to look contrite, Ellen smiled and nodded, keeping the fact that Frank Stillman was the last man on earth she'd ever be looking for to herself.

"I thought I saw him coming in, but I guess not," Ellen said, putting her coffee mug down. And with a bright smile, she quickly excused herself.

Her mind racing, Ellen waited for the elevator, not in the mood to take the stairs. When she heard her name called, she turned and nearly groaned when she saw Ethel motioning for her to come to the desk.

"I have something for you," Ethel said quietly, handing Ellen an envelope.

"What is it?" Ellen asked, automatically reaching for the envelope.

Turning it over, she frowned. Other than the Inn's name in bold print in the upper-left-hand corner, the envelope was blank.

"How should I know?" Ethel answered innocently.

With a raised eyebrow, Ellen gazed at Ethel, sure that the woman knew exactly what was in the envelope. No doubt she knew who it was from too.

"Thank you," Ellen said as she turned away back to the elevator.

"We'll be sorry to see you leave," Ethel said to her back.

Yeah, sure, you are, Ellen thought as she stepped into the elevator.

Returning to her room, Ellen found Frank pulling on his coat, wrapping his scarf around his neck. Ignoring her as he stuffed his wallet into his pocket, she watched as he patted his jacket, clearly making sure he had everything he needed. She wondered what was in his other pocket and suspected it was a gun.

"Where are you going?" she asked, forcing herself to keep her tone neutral.

If he suspected anything, then the game was up. Turning around to face her, his icy glare sent shock waves of fear through her, and for the first time, Ellen found herself truly afraid of the man. Up until now, she'd known she could handle him. But now, something was different. She couldn't put her finger on it, but something had definitely changed. Crossing the room, she poured herself a brandy, taking a long sip of the warm liquid, enjoying the feel of it sliding down her suddenly dry throat.

"I'm going to check out our escape route," he said, picking up his gloves and hat. "I want to be sure everything's in place." He smiled at her, making Ellen that much more nervous.

Something wasn't right. What had happened in the short time she'd been downstairs? She forced herself not to look frantically around the room . . . For what, she wasn't sure. Instead, she just nodded as Frank moved past her before pausing at the door. Turning, he smiled at Ellen, and it was all she could do not to shiver—the look of evil on his face nearly her undoing.

"Don't worry, everything's going to work out beautifully," he assured her with a silky voice.

And with a soft click of the door, he was gone, leaving Ellen with a very bad feeling.

Downing the rest of her brandy, Ellen looked around the room, wishing she could put her finger on why she felt such a sense of dread. Assuring herself that there was no way Frank could have found out about her plot to kill him, she pulled the envelope out of her pocket, reading it quickly. As she'd expected, it simply stated where to meet and at what time. Only then would she receive her next set of instructions. Glancing at the clock on the bedside table, Ellen gauged how much time she had left; and pouring herself another brandy, she sipped it as she began packing. By the end of the day, Frank Stillman would be dead and she'd be headed home. And then on to someplace warm! God, she needed a vacation!

Smiling at Frank as he exited the elevator, Ethel moved to intercept him at the front door.

"Your group will be leaving soon, Mr. Stillman," Ethel said, "we'll be sad to see you leave us."

Not wanting to waste time with the woman, Frank squashed the urge to push past her, instead forcing himself to stop and speak to the annoying woman. He stuffed his hands in his pockets, his right hand coming to rest against the small pistol he had deep in his pocket. The feel of the gun in his hand calmed him, and he smiled at Ethel. He might not be able to ignore the woman, but that didn't mean he had to be polite. He'd had enough of that, and throwing caution to the wind, he turned on her.

"Nice sentiment, but I know you can't wait to see us go," he said with a sneer and wasn't surprised when Ethel's eyes widened. "And I can't wait to be gone. Excuse me."

And moving past her, he disappeared out the door. Watching him pause outside to pull up his coat collar before tugging his hat further down on his head, Ethel rushed back to the desk as soon as

Frank disappeared from sight. She didn't know what, but something was very wrong.

"Thanks, Ethel," Jeremy said, ending the call.

Punching another button, he listened as the call went through.

"He's on the move," Jeremy said before hanging up.

Placing one more call with the same message, he turned to Madison as she leaned against the kitchen counter.

"Evidently, time's up," she said casually, and Jeremy nodded.

He knew he should be surprised at Madison's calm demeanor; but at the same time, it was oddly comforting too. If she wasn't worried, then there was no reason he should be. But he was. Glancing at his watch, he figured how much time before they needed to leave his house. They had a little time.

"Madison," he began carefully, trying to find the right words so he wouldn't sound stupid, "what happens after today?" Okay, that didn't sound too stupid.

"What do you mean what happens?" she asked, glancing up from her computer.

Another benefit of hanging out with a retired RCMP—a seriously protected Internet, something she was immensely thankful for. For the last hour, she'd been able to review information that Sarah had sent regarding Stillman and his brother. Despite having Stillman's real name now, she still referred to him as his alias. It helped her keep the jobs separate. But it was a relief, having the pieces finally all come together. Too bad, for Stillman anyway, that it wouldn't make any difference in the end.

"What happens when this is all over?" Jeremy asked quietly.

Using the time it took to shut down her computer, Madison considered his question. Funny, she hadn't actually thought about the job she'd originally been hired for, the job that had brought her here in the first place. She blinked. And Sarah hadn't sent her any new updates on it either. It was very possible that since the storm, the objective might have changed. She knew the team she was to have met up with had been evacuated; she didn't know if her target was one of them, though.

"I honestly don't know," Madison finally answered.

"Do you think you could stay here awhile longer?"

God, he hated that his heart was racing! That he was so nervous about her answer. Gazing at the man she'd lost her heart to, Madison realized too late that Jeremy had forgotten that she actually still had a job to do—that this mess with Stillman had nothing to do with her original reason for being there. Pushing away from her computer, she took his hands, staring sadly at their entwined fingers as she carefully considered her answer.

"I . . . ah . . ." she gazed up at him with bright eyes, "I can't stay." She squeezed his hands gently before stepping away from him, suddenly needing the space. "I still have a job I have to do."

Her last words were spoken so softly Jeremy almost missed them.

"A job?" His eyes widened. Shit! How could he have forgotten? "Oh, yeah," he mumbled, turning away as he rushed to collect his thoughts.

Leaning against the counter, Madison remained quiet. What could she say? Taking a deep breath, Jeremy turned back to her, wishing just once he knew what was going through that complicated mind of hers.

"Right, your job."

Madison just nodded. He knew what and who she was. And he realized now that it was going to take him much longer than he'd thought to fully come to terms with her chosen way of life.

"If it's okay with you, can we just focus on the here and now?" Madison asked with a hesitant smile. "And then talk about what comes next afterward?"

He nodded. He just hoped there would be time to talk afterward.

"I do love you," he said, amazed at how calm his voice was. He tossed a goofy smile at her. "I just thought you might like to know that."

Unable to stop herself, Madison giggled.

"I'm pretty sure I love you too," she said, surprised when her heart soared at the idea of her loving someone—no, not someone, Jeremy.

"You're pretty sure?" Sounding insulted, he frowned at her. "You're pretty sure?"

"Well, you know, this is a tough thing, this love stuff. It takes some getting used to. And you're not the easiest guy to love, you know." She couldn't stop smiling.

"Me? Not easy to love? What's not to love?" He pounded on his chest. "I'm super easy to love! Just ask my mom!"

Rolling her eyes, Madison laughed.

"Yeah, like she's objective!" It was Jeremy's turn to laugh, especially because she was right.

"Okay, let's see, I know!" He slapped the counter, "Ask Ethel, she loves me!"

"Yeah, let's ask Ethel, the woman with her own deep well of secrets, like I could believe her!"

"How'd you know about Ethel?" Jeremy asked in surprise. Only a select few knew about Ethel's colorful background.

"Oh, please, you didn't know she used to be an operative?"

Madison nearly laughed as Jeremy shook his head in wonder.

"Well, one thing's clear," he gave her a questioning look. "I've got way better intel and connections than you do!"

He shrugged. "I've been outta the game for a while."

"You think?" she laughed now. "Maybe you should consider getting back into it?" Madison froze as her words sank in.

Their eyes met and held. Did she dare ask? It was either now or never.

"Would you consider that?" she whispered.

Would he? He hadn't thought about it. He hadn't needed to. And shrugging his shoulders, he let the idea ramble around in his mind for a moment. His mother wouldn't be too happy about it; he knew that. He thought about his brothers and sisters and how he'd been enjoying his nice, quiet life—until Madison flew in, that is.

"I don't honestly know," Jeremy finally answered truthfully. "It's not something I can just say yes or no to. You know that."

Madison nodded; she did know that. But that hadn't stopped her from hoping he'd say yes.

The phone ringing put a quick end to their conversation.

"But just the same," Jeremy smiled, reaching for his phone, "call Ethel, she'll tell you she loves me!"

Madison's laughter in his ears, he didn't immediately recognized the voice on the other end of the phone.

CHAPTER 33

"DAMN," JONES MUMBLED as he gazed at Ellen's lifeless body.

Crumbled on the floor, her bulging eyes and bloated face told him all he needed to know. She'd been poisoned. And it'd been powerful stuff.

"Good heavens!" Ethel exclaimed, spotting the body before Jones could block her view.

She'd seen her fair share of death in her lifetime; seeing another dead person didn't shock her. Not expecting to find a dead person, now that had surprised her.

Alerting Stan and Jones that Stillman had left the Inn alone, Ethel had remained at the front desk, ready to waylay the man should he return unexpectedly. Hurrying to Ellen's room, the men instantly became concerned when there was no answer. Rushing downstairs, Stan returned quickly with Ethel and the master key.

Opening the door and announcing herself out of habit and propriety, Ethel let the men in, but not before spotting Ellen's body on the floor. Pulling Ethel into the room, Stan stayed at the door, leaving it open just a crack, allowing him to keep watch. Needing to be sure Ellen was dead, Jones checked for a pulse, shaking his head when he found none. Her body warm to the touch, he knew she hadn't been dead long. And he quickly deduced how she'd been poisoned when he spotted the empty glass on the floor beside her, having rolled out of her lifeless fingers when she'd collapsed. Wanting to inspect the glass, Jones knew he couldn't compromise the crime scene. And that's what it was now.

"Ethel," Jones began, but she was already two steps ahead of him, having pulled out her cell phone and dialing 911.

"We need to be moving along," Stan said quietly while Ethel relayed the details over the phone.

It would only be a matter of minutes before the police would arrive, and they couldn't afford to be anywhere near the crime scene. In total agreement, Jones moved carefully away from the body; and with a nod to Ethel, the two men left, quickly returning to Stan's room.

While Jones called Jeremy, Stan packed up his belongings. Ellen's untimely death had moved up their timetable considerably now. Churning out new scenarios as he packed, Stan knew removing Ellen from their plan wouldn't take much doing. Always prepared with a plan B, he didn't even consider Ellen's death a blip on the radar—although he was surprised that a woman of her caliber had allowed herself to be poisoned. Talk about underestimating your opponent. Well, she'd paid the price dearly. At least he wouldn't have to worry about running into her again; the next time might not have worked out as well.

Ending his call, Jones waited as Stan checked the room to be sure he hadn't forgotten anything. And with a final glance around the room, closing the door quietly, the men slipped out, moments later leaving the Inn through a side entrance.

Sitting with his traveling companions in the restaurant, Frank turned as two police officers came in. He'd been expecting them and was prepared to act shocked and surprised when they told him of his "wife's" death. Forcing himself to remain calm, Frank watched wide-eyed as the officers ignored him completely, approaching another table nearby. Without incident, the officers pulled a man from his chair, quickly and efficiently handcuffing him before leading him out of the restaurant. The entire altercation took less than a five minutes.

"For a small town in the middle of nowhere, they sure do have a lot of excitement," one of the others at his table commented before they all returned to their food.

Not sure if he was relieved or disappointed, Frank turned his attention back to the group. Plans were in the making for them to leave town the following day; he needed to pay attention to the details.

"Oh, yeah, you should have seen his face," Stan said, pulling the mustache off his face with a grimace as he shrugged out of his policeman's jacket. "He was sure we were there for him."

Accepting the coffee from Madison, Stan took a sip of the warm brew before continuing.

"He's going to try and say she committed suicide."

"Seriously?" Jeremy burst out. "Does he think we're that stupid?"

"Evidently, he does," Stan said.

"Just because we're in the middle of nowhere doesn't mean we don't have skilled police officers!"

In fact, some of them had worked with him; those guys were more than qualified to safely police their small community.

"It's to our advantage that he's thinking this way, though, it's what will slip him up in the end." Which, if Stan had his way, would be very soon.

"Did you get anything else from him?" Madison asked.

Stan shook his head.

"I didn't want to take too much time and chance him paying me any unnecessary attention. The curveball he's about to be thrown will be more than enough to draw him out, I think."

Everyone agreed; they couldn't afford to make Stillman suspicious now. Turning to Jeremy, Stan smiled.

"Thank Ethel for her idea, it worked great."

"I will," Jeremy said, knowing Ethel would be pleased to hear it.

"It was quick thinking on her part, that's for sure," Madison said in admiration.

Clearly, the woman hadn't lost her touch or her skills.

Madison turned to Jeremy, "And thanks to your guys for not asking any questions!" Jeremy nodded, having already done so.

Not about to go against protocol, Ethel had called 911 immediately after they'd found Ellen's body. But her second call was to the chief of police, the two of them having been friends for years. Since Ellen was most definitely dead, there was no need for the ambulance to rush right over, and she asked if the chief could come alone? While the chief was still with Ethel at the Inn, Jeremy had called him, asking for his assistance in "a small matter." Having known and worked with Jeremy for years as well, the chief didn't have any trouble with playing along; in fact, he rather relished the idea. Like Jeremy, he was glad to dust off his old skills from time to time and put them to good use.

It was clear to everyone that Ellen had been murdered—poisoned. But why had Frank killed her? And why now? This rash and sudden move didn't bode well for Frank's state of mind. Eliminating his own partner? The man clearly was edging closer to the deep end; once going off of it, who knew what he'd do and who might get hurt. No, they had to stop him and soon. But it had to be done carefully. Clearly, Stillman was expecting Ellen's body to be found, him being the logical suspect. He had to have something on Ellen if he thought the suicide story was going to work. Unlike Ellen, they weren't about to underestimate Stillman. But that didn't mean they couldn't throw him off-kilter a little bit. They still had the advantage. Stillman was still focused on Madison; he didn't know about the rest of them. And they were going to make sure it stayed that way.

While Stan, now disguised as a local police officer, and the chief "arrested" their man in the restaurant—Jones, Ethel, Jeremy, and Madison were putting the finishing touches on another plan. Stan's news that Stillman was planning on using the suicide defense only made their plan that much more perfect, and they prepared to put it into action.

Glancing at his watch Frank resisted the urge to squirm in his chair. He'd been sitting with his group for over an hour while their tour guide went over in lengthy detail their travel plans. Only when Jack sat down with them did Frank tense up.

Careful not to let his eyes linger on any one person for too long, Jack went over their tentative flight plan for the next day. While everyone had enjoyed their brief stay in town, he knew they were anxious to get back to their original trip. The catch was that to make it possible for them to leave, they'd be flying out on a smaller plane, not the large one they'd arrived on. He explained that due to engine trouble, their original plane was out of service; and because of the storm. they weren't able to get the parts needed to make the necessary repairs. So it'd been decided that if the weather cooperated, they'd fly out people in groups, instead of making them wait any longer.

Agreeing with this new plan, the group talked among themselves for a few minutes, allowing Jack a moment to study the group. And Stillman. If Stillman's narrow gaze was anything to go by, the man was clearly not happy with the flight plan. Well, if he thought this was bad, wait until he heard the rest of it!

Agreeing that this was the smartest plan, the group's guide proceeded to list off who would be going on the first flight and what time they should be ready to go. Judging by the angry glare Stillman gave Jack when his name wasn't included with the first group, as Jack had expected, the man was not happy! Glancing around the group, Stillman considered asking another couple if they'd switch with him; but knowing he didn't have a good enough reason and not wanting to bring unnecessary attention to himself right now, he kept his silence. When they found out he'd suddenly become widowed, he was sure someone would offer him their seat. He could wait.

Leaning back in his chair, Stillman gazed around the room, his eyes landing on Mary as she stood beside the bar chatting with a customer. He hadn't seen her since her return and wondered if she was going to be another loose end he needed to tie up before he left. His anger at being stuck in this godforsaken town one more night was immediately redirected toward Mary as he imagined killing her with his bare hands. Realizing he was flexing his fingers, the thought of them around her throat tantalizing, he stopped himself, shoving his hands into his lap.

Pull it together, he ordered himself!

He could easily get away with saying that Ellen had killed herself, but Mary? No, too much attention was still focused on the girl right now. Even he realized, if another body showed up, no one would be going anywhere anytime soon.

Her back to the crowded restaurant, Mary's spine tingled. Slowly turning around, she glanced around the room, her eyes catching and holding Frank's. Not recognizing him, Mary just nodded and gave him a small smile before turning her attention back to her customer. Seconds later, something had her turning back to Frank again. This time he returned her smile with a nod of his head. Whatever, Mary thought, he wasn't her type anyway. She turned back again to her customer, unaware that she'd just avoided a violent death sentence.

A tap on his shoulder had Frank turning back in his seat.

"This message just came for you," the hostess said, pressing a piece of paper into Frank's hand.

Before Frank could question her, she stepped away, returning to the hostess stand at the front door. Unfolding the note, his eyes bulged as he read the request written in neat handwriting, no doubt belonging to the hostess. Glancing around the room, Frank struggled to hide his shock.

"Is everything all right, Frank?" their guide asked quietly from his seat beside Frank.

Nodding, Frank swallowed hard before giving the guide a weak smile.

"My ahh . . . my ahhh . . ." he stammered before collecting himself. "My wife wants me to bring her back a sandwich," he blurted.

With a knowing smile, the guide nodded. His own wife had had the same request earlier. Snatching up the menu, Frank was relieved when the guide turned his attention back to the group. Had the guide noticed his shaking hands? Frank didn't think so, and burying his face behind the menu, he ground his teeth.

What the hell had happened? He'd watched Ellen drink the cognac! There was no way she could be alive! He'd made damn sure of that! The amount of poison he'd poured into the cognac bottle was enough to kill a horse, for Christ's sake! There was no way she could be alive! Could she? No, he told himself, there was no way. Even if the paramedics found her in time to pump her stomach, there was no way she'd be alive—not after ingesting that much; and the type he'd used, it went to work within minutes.

A part of him had wanted to wait while the poison did its job. He wanted to see the look on Ellen's face when she realized that she was going to die by his hand. He'd begun planning her death shortly after their arrival, having decided that she not only knew too much but he really didn't have any further use for her. Her actions were making him nervous, and not trusting her any longer, he began plotting her demise. Fortunately, he always traveled prepared, making him able to put his plan into action at a moment's notice. But he still wished he'd been able to see the look on her face. But to make the plan work, he had to be elsewhere when they found her. Bitch, she thought she was so much better than he was. Well, he showed her! She wouldn't mess with him ever again.

Or so he thought. What could have happened? Could she still be alive? No, he knew she was dead! So who called the restaurant? Who knew he was there?

The innkeeper! His eyes hardened. He knew there was something about that woman. She must have sent the message. But why? The answer came quickly: to get him to leave the restaurant. But then what?

Madison! Was she in on this? Had she confided in the innkeeper? That was the only logical deduction. Knowing Madison's specific skill set, Frank knew that as soon as he stepped out of the restaurant, he was a dead man. Madison could be hiding anywhere, ready to take a shot at him. No, he wouldn't leave the restaurant—not alone, anyway. Shit!

Momentarily distracted by a group of burly men arriving at the restaurant, Frank watched as they made a beeline for the bar. Calling out greetings to the owner and other friends, they took their places at the bar.

"And there's why we can hopefully fly out tomorrow," Jack said with a smile as he waved at the guys. "They're the snowplow drivers," he quickly added, noticing the questioning looks around the table.

Excusing himself from the table, Jack joined the men, relieved for an excuse to get away from Stillman and happy to join his friends.

Going over the departure details one more time, their tour guide pushed back from the table, declaring them ready to go the next day. With smiles and relieved laughter, the others began excusing themselves from the table until Frank was left alone with only his thoughts for company. He knew he should have left with the group; they would have made the perfect cover. But then again, if Madison was as good as he'd heard she was, it wouldn't make a difference. In her line of work, the job was always done, no matter what—or who—got in the way.

Rising from his chair minutes later, Frank scowled at the hostess as she reminded him sweetly about the sandwich for his wife. His thoughts jumbled, he left the restaurant, pausing just outside with a furtive glance left and right, ignoring the five big, orange snowplow trucks lined up out front. Tugging his scarf tightly around his neck and adjusting his hat, he shoved his hands into his pockets, his fingers wrapping securely around the butt of his gun.

With renewed confidence, Stillman stepped off the porch.

CHAPTER 34

FROM HER VANTAGE point, Madison watched Stillman as he made his way carefully down the snow-covered steps of the restaurant. So far, their plan was working perfectly; Stillman had been totally caught off guard by the message supposedly from Ellen. That'll teach him to leave a job before making sure it's done. Of course, he wasn't going to have to worry about making that mistake ever again if she had her way.

Watching as Stillman glanced nervously around him, Madison knew he was looking for her. Waiting as he made his way down the steps to the snowy sidewalk, she stayed well out of sight, needing him safely away from the restaurant before she made her move.

When Stillman stepped between two parked snowplows, a voice came through Madison's earpiece, telling her to move and to move now! Sprinting from her position, she darted across the street to her next vantage point, whispering when she was situated.

"Copy that," Jones replied from his own vantage point.

Having a clear view of Stillman, Jones relayed to the others his suspicion that Stillman had a gun—or at least some kind of weapon; his hand hadn't come out of his pocket since leaving the restaurant.

"Maybe the guy's just playing with himself. He is a dick, after all," Stan remarked dryly into her earpiece.

Madison smiled; the man was most definitely a dick!

Focusing on her target as he emerged from between the snow-plows, Madison quietly relayed his current position. Then, not able to resist, she also relayed the important fact that Stillman had just now removed his hand from his pocket.

"Clearly, he's finished," Madison whispered before adding, "in more ways than one."

Poking his head out from between the massive snowplows, Stillman glanced both ways before stepping out from the safety of the big trucks. With a brisk step, he held his head high as he wove between the snowbanks to find the sidewalk on the opposite side. *He wouldn't go down easily,* he told himself as his hand dipped back into his pocket, fondling his gun.

Focusing on the snowy sidewalk, he was forced to pull his attention away from searching for Madison to watching where he stepped. The last thing he needed to do now was to slip and fall! Damn snow! He couldn't wait to get away from this godforsaken place! If he never saw snow again, it'd be too soon!

Distracted by the sounds of the big trucks starting up, Stillman turned his head toward the noise, immediately regretting his action as he lost his footing and slipped. His arms flailing, he managed to stay on his feet, only to realize he'd strained a muscle in his back in doing so.

"Goddamn it!" he growled, stopping to rub his back through his heavy coat.

There was no way he could continue walking on the sidewalk; it was too slippery. He'd have to walk in the street. But at least he would get better traction there.

"Fucking snow," he mumbled as he found a break in the snow-bank, and stepping out into the street, he glanced both ways before turning in the direction of the Inn.

The street was empty and eerily quiet, the only sound coming from the plow trucks behind him. Stillman felt like he was walking through a tunnel, dwarfed by the snowbanks on both sides.

How could people live like this? he thought as he made his way down the street.

At least, they offered a bit of cover, though. Glancing idly at the buildings, he was reassured by the fact that none of them would offer Madison a good vantage point; none of them were that high. So unless she was on the other side of the snowbank, there was no place she could hide. The odds were even. He didn't like that prospect, but he could work with it, and his eyes dropped as he stepped further into the street to avoid a pile of slush.

"Stillman." His head snapped up as he heard his name. "I'm right here."

And suddenly, Madison was in front of him. Surprise stopped him in his tracks, and he stood stock-still, blinking. Where the hell had she come from?

Well, it didn't matter, she was here now, and he was going to kill her. His hand slipped into his pocket.

"Before you do anything rash, you should know . . ." Madison began, hoping she wasn't running out of time, "your brother wasn't a personal hit."

His hand froze around the butt of his gun, and he stared at her.

"Well, yeah, he was," she continued with a satisfied smile, "but only after I'd been hired."

Stillman growled, and Madison rushed on, her voice growing louder.

"But it was the mob who hired me."

"The mob?" The words were out before Stillman could stop himself. And he realized he wasn't totally surprised.

His brother had always been an accident looking for a place to happen. Evidently, he'd found that place. But that still didn't mean he wasn't going to avenge his brother's death. It was a matter of family pride now. His hand tightened around the gun as he stared at Madison. And he frowned. Her hands hung at her sides, empty. What the hell?

"It doesn't matter," Stillman said, shaking off the feeling of uneasiness that suddenly was creeping through him, "you pulled the trigger."

"What was that you said?" Madison asked, cupping a hand to her ear.

"I said," Stillman automatically replied before the sounds of big trucks approaching registered, and he paused.

His eyes widened at the sight of a plow truck as it came roaring around the corner behind Madison, its bright-orange plow down, pushing the snow effortlessly out of the way. Seemingly ignoring the big truck as it converged on her, Madison kept her eyes on Stillman. Christ, it was a standoff! Who would flinch first? The thought raced through Stillman's mind seconds before he realized that here was his way out. The plow was going to hit Madison; the crazy bitch was standing right in its path! Well, let it hit her! He couldn't be blamed for her stupidity! His fingers relaxed their grip on his gun as he held Madison's steely gaze with one of his own.

Cheeky bastard, Madison thought as she started counting down in her mind. She could almost feel the snow hitting her from the plow behind her, and arriving at zero, she dove out of the way of the approaching truck. Landing with a thud, she rolled, watching the plow roar past her.

Shit! Stillman realized too late. Watching Madison dive between a break in the snowbank, he whirled around in search of another break near him, only to come face-to-face with a plow coming directly at him. How had he not heard it coming from behind him?

Because, he belatedly admonished himself, *you were too busy concentrating on Madison! That bitch!*

With no break in the snowbank close enough, Stillman dove to the right as the plow clipped him, instantly breaking his ribs, hip, and left leg as he was tossed into the air like a rag doll. Before he landed, the plow coming from the opposite direction caught his limp body, breaking and crushing the rest of it as he was tossed into the air again. Finally coming to land over the top of the opposite snowbank, Stillman's body shook as blood oozed from his broken parts. With great effort, he turned his head, watching as Madison approached, brushing snow from her body. Coming to stand in front of him, she stared at him. There wasn't anything that wasn't broken on the man's body; death would take him soon. But in between now and then, she could still have some fun with him.

"Don't," the single word came clearly through her earpiece, and she silently cursed herself for not having removed it first.

Joining her, Stan and Jones stood silently as Stillman glared at them, his eyes quickly dimming in intensity. His fingers clutched his gun, as his eyes dropped to his arm, staring blankly. Only when his brain slowly registered that his arm was no longer attached to his body did Stillman drag his eyes back to Madison. Before he could make a sound, Madison shook her head, and turning on her heel, she walked away.

"You knew better than to go up against her," Jones said quietly as he and Stan watched the light go out of Stillman's eyes.

Ironically, Stillman did know that—his last thought being that he probably should have heeded that advice.

CHAPTER 35

FRESHLY FALLEN SNOW blanketed the town, effectively burying all traces of violence and death that had overtaken the town in just a few short days. Glistening sun danced over the snow as a strong wind blew away the last of the clouds, ushering in a brilliant blue sky.

An undercurrent of excitement could still be felt throughout the town as people continued to talk about the idiot who'd been run over by the snowplows. What kind of fool ventured into the street when the big trucks were out doing their job? Deemed an unfortunate accident, the police had quickly closed the case, anxious to have normalcy return as quickly as possible to their small town. Everyone agreed, they'd had more than enough excitement for a while. And if this was what happened when tourists came to town, then maybe they were better off without them.

Sending the tour group off with a smile, Ethel couldn't seem to bring herself to invite them back again. Sure, it'd been fun dusting off the old skills and putting them to use again, but she thought—watching the door close behind the last of the guests—she was perfectly happy living her quiet, little life, thank you very much.

Miraculously, the plane in which the tour group had arrived on had managed to be fixed in time, thus allowing everyone . . . with the exception of two . . . to fly out together, "back to civilization," as the tour guide had joked. Ethel struggled not to push them out the door, wishing them safe travels before nearly slamming the door behind them.

Standing in the middle of the suddenly empty lobby, Ethel took a deep, cleansing breath before turning at the sound of the elevator opening behind her. Reminding herself she still had guests, she turned with a forced smile as Stan and Jones emerged from the elevator. Her smile quickly turned real. Now, these boys she was seriously going to miss! Knowing they'd never tell her where they were headed, she quickly settled their bill, and with a hug and a knowing smile for each, she sent them on their way. One guest was left in the Inn now. Reaching for the house phone to call the last guest, a burst of cold air stopped her, and glancing up, Ethel saw Jones in the doorway.

"Don't bother," he said. "She's long gone."

With a nod, Ethel hung up the phone, finding the lobby and the doorway empty when she glanced up again. For a moment, she wondered if he'd ever been there or if she'd just imagined it. She smiled; she was going to miss those guys!

A steaming mug of coffee in his hands, Jack closed his eyes in pleasure as the warm liquid flowed through him. Immediately invigorating him, he smiled.

"What's that smile for?"

Opening his eyes, his smile widened as his mother sat down opposite him. He leaned over, kissing her warm cheek.

"Nancy's home and sleeping!" With a raised eyebrow, Ruth stared at her son. "Which means she's not having any cravings, and I get a few minutes of peace and quiet!"

Ruth laughed as Jack glanced at his watch.

"But the best part, Lizzy is arriving this afternoon to help out!"

Never had Jack been as happy as when his sister had called, announcing that now that the storm had passed, she was on her way. The snowplow crew had done an exceptional job. The runways were free and clear now, and flights were returning to their normal schedules—which also meant he could fly out as well. His eyes drifted toward the door.

"Has anyone seen or heard from Jeremy?" Ruth asked quietly.

Jack shook his head, still amazed at how much things had changed in just a few short hours.

"He must know Madison's gone, don't you think?"

"You would think," he said with a shrug of his shoulders. "But then again, I didn't find out until after she was gone. And I was supposed to be the one flying her out!"

He shifted in his chair, remembering his surprise when he'd arrived at the airport earlier, ready to prep his plane for Madison's flight out. He'd always known as soon as the weather cleared that she'd be going, no matter how much he hoped she'd stay. He couldn't remember his brother ever being so taken with a woman. It was going to suck when she was gone, having to deal with his brokenhearted brother. Thank goodness for Lizzy! She was going to be helping more than just Jack and Nancy.

Finding his experienced maintenance crew just standing around when he arrived at the airport, Jack began barking orders. They had a flight to prep for, and why weren't they doing anything? Only then did the head of his team step forward, telling him about the private jet that had landed earlier that morning and, picking up a single passenger, took off again with almost no turnaround time. Walking out on to the tarmac, Jack stared up at the blue sky. It didn't take a genius to know that Madison had been on that plane. He smiled sadly as he watched some clouds drifting aimlessly, remembering the day Madison had arrived. And he wondered if Jeremy knew she was gone. Christ, he hoped so!

With a shrug of his shoulders, Jack tossed a sullen gaze at his mother. While he'd tried, Jack hadn't been able to reach Jeremy yet, so maybe his brother didn't know. No, that was exactly *why* he hadn't been able to reach Jeremy—because he did know.

Jeremy knew full well that Madison was gone. He'd woken up to find her side of the bed cold and empty. God, he hated clichés and was furious to find himself in the middle of one! But he'd known she would be gone; she'd all but told him. He couldn't be mad at her. But he was. Hell, who was he kidding? He was bullshit! After everything they'd been through, she just upped and disappeared. No, he reminded himself, she hadn't disappeared. He knew where she was. She was working. She still had a job to do, and she'd had every intention of doing it. It was what she did—who she was.

Fuck. That still didn't make any of this any easier.

Staring out the kitchen window, Jeremy sipped his coffee, trying not to remember the mornings he'd done the same thing with Madison. They'd played house well together. He couldn't help it and smiled, remembering when they'd joked about doing just that and how neither of them were good at it.

In the distance, he heard an elk bugle and closed his eyes, immense sadness stabbing him. Fuck.

He'd been at home when Stillman was killed, Madison insisting that he in no way be involved with what was going to happen. Her thoughtfulness had touched him, but he'd hated not being able to help her. But also knew she was right. Whatever happened afterward, this was his home, and life had to continue on.

He hadn't been privy to the plan for killing Stillman either, and after hearing how the man had all but been decapitated by two snowplows, he was rather glad he'd been left out of that one. And he had made a mental note never to piss off Madison, Stan, or Jones! He'd heard in detail how they'd found Stillman's body, and just imagining it had made his stomach turn. Of course, he'd immediately known who'd been driving the trucks; it didn't take a genius to figure that one out. But when questioned, Jeremy could honestly say he'd been at home, thus keeping any unnecessary attention away from him and his family. For that, he was thankful. Who knew assassins could be so considerate.

Madison had turned up on his doorstep later that afternoon, her bags packed, telling him she was leaving. He'd grabbed her, pulled her inside, had kissed her hard and deeply, then had dragged her upstairs. Okay, so he hadn't really dragged her. He smiled wryly. Really, it had been more of a race up the stairs, seeing who could get whose clothes off the fastest. He remembered it almost being a tie as he'd buried himself deeply inside her, his name on her lips as she quickly reached climax.

They made love fast and hard. Hot and sweaty and breathing hard, they shared a couple of bottles of water before attacking each other again ferociously, before finally falling into a brief, exhausted sleep. Waking up a couple of hours later, they made love softly and gently, laughing at how romantic they were being before jokingly gagging at the idea of either of them ever being romantic!

Arms and legs wrapped around each other, her head on his chest, the steady sound of his heart beating against her ear—they finally slept. He woke hours later to find her gone. It didn't matter that he'd known she was leaving. It didn't matter that she'd left a heart-wrenching letter. She was still gone.

Putting his mug in the sink, Jeremy readied himself to face his brother and his mother. Glancing at the clock, he was relieved to know that at least he'd missed the luncheon crowd and would be there before the dinner crowd arrived. But it was still going to suck, he told himself as he climbed into his truck and headed into town.

"What can I get you, Jeremy?" Mary asked softly as she placed his usual coffee in front of him.

Of all the people in the world, Mary was the last person he needed to see right this very moment, and it took all his strength and patience not to glare at her. Instead, he focused on the menu. Why, he had no idea—it wasn't like he didn't have it memorized. But he couldn't talk to Mary, not yet. Hoping she'd catch on, he was surprised when he felt her hand gently on his shoulder.

"I'm sorry about everything that happened," she said quietly, "especially for how I acted." She paused, unsure as to how to proceed, wishing Jeremy would at least glance at her. When he didn't, she squeezed his shoulder gently. "I'm just really sorry." Taking a deep breath, she turned to leave.

"Thanks, Mary."

Tossing a sad smile at Jeremy, she just nodded. At least she knew he'd heard her.

"You handled that well," Ruth said softly as she sat down next to him.

As Jack had done earlier, Jeremy leaned over and kissed her cheek.

"You taught me well," Jeremy said, leaning back in his chair, his eyes drifting around the ever-crowded restaurant. He knew he was looking for Madison. And he knew he wouldn't see her.

"I did, indeed," Ruth smiled.

And knowing she wouldn't have her son's attention for much longer, she quickly filled her son in on the latest gossip about town (not that there was much after all the excitement they'd just had!) and the fact that his sister would be arriving—she glanced at her watch—anytime now. Jeremy's eyes lit up. Lizzy would snap him out of his depression.

"You called her, didn't you," he said drolly.

"Why, of course, I did, son, I'm your mother."

And standing up, she dropped a quick kiss on Jeremy's head before heading back to the kitchen.

Jeremy just shook his head. Leave it to his mother. Thank goodness for her! Opening the newspaper that he'd grabbed on his way in, Jeremy hid behind it. None of the stories were catching his attention, but it was effective at keeping people away from him for the moment.

"Anything good?"

Still hiding behind the paper, Jeremy smiled. Now there was a voice he'd been needing to hear! Slowly sliding the paper down, his smile grew.

"Same ol' stuff," he said, rising from his chair and pulling his sister into a bear hug.

He hadn't realized how much he needed to see her until she grumbled that he was suffocating her. Of course, she was holding on to him just as tightly.

"Shut up," he mumbled, lightening his hold, "I just need to hold you for a second."

"You weren't kidding when you said he'd be emotional." Jeremy froze. "Thanks for that warning."

Jeremy felt, more than heard, Lizzy's laughter as she gave her brother one final squeeze before pushing away from him. Holding him at arm's length, Lizzy watched Jeremy's eyes move past her to fall on the woman standing directly behind her. For a moment, Lizzy didn't dare let go of her brother, worried that he might collapse. Her mother had filled her in on Madison and how they all thought Jeremy felt about her. And that she'd left. Honestly not sure how Jeremy was taking it, Ruth and Jack were sincerely worried. Watching Jeremy's reaction now, Lizzy knew without a doubt how her brother felt. But she still held on to him. Until she spotted their mother approaching. With a cry of joy, Lizzy let go of Jeremy and fell into her mother's open arms. Jeremy was momentarily forgotten as the two women hugged and cried.

"Happy family reunion," Madison said softly, her heart twisting as she watched Lizzy and Ruth hugging. Swallowing hard, she faced Jeremy, "Hi."

"Hey."

They stood facing each other. She hadn't even been gone twenty-four hours, but she felt like she'd been gone a lifetime.

"Mind if I join you?" Unable to stop herself, she tossed him a mischievous smile. "I believe you've got a chair with my name on it."

A smile split his face. Damn her!

"I do believe you are correct," Jeremy said, stepping around the table to pull out a chair for her, tipping it sideways for a moment. "This one, in fact, does have your name on it."

With a happy laugh, Madison dropped into "her" chair. She had no idea who had put her name on the chair or when; she just knew someone had. And it made her feel like she belonged. A unique feeling for her. She squashed the emotions that feeling brought on, concentrating on Jeremy instead. She'd examine those other emotions later. She'd been coping with them since leaving that morning; it wasn't likely they were going to go away anytime soon.

She had a job she needed to finish; that was her first priority. She couldn't focus on anything else until that was finished. She knew Jeremy understood that. He didn't have to like it, but he had to understand it.

As promised, Sarah had a plane waiting for Madison. After everything that had happened, Madison knew she couldn't ask Jack to fly her out; that simply wasn't going to work. Making a mental note to contact Jack and explain it to him later, Madison had boarded the plane without a backward glance. Once settled in her seat, she closed her eyes, willing herself to fall asleep before the plane took off so she wouldn't chance looking out the window. After the night she'd spent with Jeremy, she needn't have worried. Exhausted both mentally and physically, she was asleep almost before she buckled her seatbelt.

An hour later, she awoke feeling a little better; and glancing out the window, she saw they were approaching a town. Already? She blinked. They weren't in the mountains—or at least not the ones she'd expected. What was going on? Her eyes widening, she glanced toward the door leading to the cockpit. Had she been compromised? A moment of dread raced through her before she took a deep breath, telling herself to settle the fuck down! Pulling out her SAT phone, she turned it on, gazing out the window at the fast-approaching town as the phone powered up.

Minutes later, Madison leaned back in her seat with a sigh of relief. Seemed her travel plans had just changed, her original job no longer needing to be done. Thanks to Mother Nature and the deadly avalanche she'd unleashed, Madison's target was no longer a threat— his body having been found at the bottom of a ravine after being swept away by the heavy snow. Who knew Mother Nature could be so helpful? Madison chuckled.

"Hell hath no fury like a woman scorned" . . . Evidently, Mother Nature wasn't immune to that one either.

Anxious to stretch her legs and being given a thirty-minute window, Madison exited the plane. Avoiding the airport, she stayed outside, watching as luggage was stored on the plane as a tall, attractive woman crossed the tarmac. Making eye contact, the women nodded at each other before the tall woman disappeared on to the plane. Giving herself another couple of minutes, Madison returned to the plane; and taking her seat, she smiled, introducing herself to the woman now sitting opposite her.

Only when the plane was in the air and headed toward its final destination did the two women realize who the other was—both having previously been told about each other, albeit at different times and by different people. Well, what a coincidence!

Coincidence, my ass, Madison thought.

No, she knew Sarah had had a hand in this one. Maybe Stan and Jones too, she wasn't sure. But she knew only Sarah would be able to pull off a stunt like this one. Well, she just hoped it worked. There was still the off chance that Jeremy wouldn't be happy to see her again—not this soon, anyway. Taking a deep breath, Madison gazed out the window. She'd faced death; she killed people for a living. Yet never had she been as afraid in her life as she was right now.

They sat in silence, just staring at each other. From across the room, Ruth and Lizzy watched as Madison and Jeremy wordlessly battled with one another.

"If they don't do something soon, I'm going to do it for them," Lizzy said.

Chuckling, Ruth agreed. The suspense was killing them!

Unable to take it any longer, Jeremy stepped off the cliff into the unknown.

"I'm happy to see you," he said quietly.

"Same here."

"How long are you staying this time?" Now that he'd taken the first step, he jumped in with both feet. No beating around the bush. He was going to have answers.

"I thought I might stay for a while," Madison said softly, "if that's okay with you."

Not the answer he was hoping for, but he could work with it.

"What happened to the job?"

Ready for that question, Madison tossed him an easy smile.

"Change in plans. Mother Nature didn't just throw us a curve, she helped me out too."

Jeremy raised his eyebrow in question, urging her to add, "There was an avalanche."

"Oh," Jeremy said, remembering the avalanche he'd read about earlier in the day. In the northern mountains. A guy had been killed. Jeremy's eyes widened. A guy had been killed!

"Oh!" he said again, putting the pieces together.

Madison just nodded. "Yeah, job was done without me even having to be in the area," Madison said. "And the best part, there's no paperwork, and I still get paid!"

Jeremy laughed at her warped sense of humor.

"Those are definitely the best jobs to have," he laughed, also beginning to relax.

This might just work; they just might be able to make this work. But they still had hurdles they'd have to get over. He didn't know about her, but he was willing to work at it.

"So where do you go from here?" He paused, approaching the first hurdle. "Where do we go from here?"

His heart nearly stopped when Madison sat back, a huge smile splitting her face. Uh-oh. This couldn't be good.

"I was thinking Australia." Nope, this wasn't good at all! "Don't you have family there?"

Oh, yeah, this definitely was not good. This was great!

"Funny, you should ask. As a matter of fact, I do!" Jeremy smiled broadly, reaching for Madison's hands.

Laughing happily, they held hands for a moment like lovestruck teenagers before they pulled apart making gagging noises, making them laugh even harder.

Glancing over his shoulder, Jeremy found his mother and sister hovering nearby. He smiled at them.

"Check please!"

ABOUT THE AUTHOR

RETURNING WITH HER second book, Dana's love for traveling and adventure is what truly inspires her to write. Her travels having taken her from Northern Canada, to Europe as well as to Australia, she calls the Lakes Region of New Hampshire home.

From her Writer's Room, her unique sense of humor often finds a voice through her characters, both old and new, as she brings her characters to new life.

Dana balances her time writing with horseback riding and spending time with friends from around the world and nearby. She's just recently embarked on another new adventure, having just bought her first horse in over twenty years.